REDEM

ALL BECAME AGONISING white as the comet struck and announced its unwelcome arrival. Mortensen instinctively screwed his eyes shut and so couldn't see the unstoppable blast wave as it tore across the world in the wake of the strike, scalding the skies and turning the wasteland to glass.

He felt it though. A sensation he would never be allowed to forget: a corporal memory; the last feeling his flesh would ever register. The inferno rolled over him like a tidal wave of superheated vengeance, flensing skin from the muscle and sinew underneath and baptising what was left in the apocalyptic fires that followed. Thrashing in an acid bath of agony, Mortensen screamed for a death that never came…

A WARHAMMER 40,000 NOVEL

REDEMPTION CORPS

Rob Sanders

For TC, Jonah and Elliot – you know why...

A BLACK LIBRARY PUBLICATION

First published in Great Britain in 2010 by
The Black Library,
Games Workshop Ltd.,
Willow Road, Nottingham,
NG7 2WS, UK.

10 9 8 7 6 5 4 3 2 1

Cover illustration by Jon Sullivan.

A CIP record for this book is available from the British Library.

UK ISBN13: 978 1 84416 360 1
US ISBN13: 978 1 84416 361 8

See the Black Library on the internet at
www.blacklibrary.com

Find out more about Games Workshop
and the world of Warhammer 40,000 at
www.games-workshop.com

Printed and bound in the UK.

IT IS THE 41st millennium. For more than a hundred centuries the Emperor has sat immobile on the Golden Throne of Earth. He is the master of mankind by the will of the gods, and master of a million worlds by the might of his inexhaustible armies. He is a rotting carcass writhing invisibly with power from the Dark Age of Technology. He is the Carrion Lord of the Imperium for whom a thousand souls are sacrificed every day, so that he may never truly die.

YET EVEN IN his deathless state, the Emperor continues his eternal vigilance. Mighty battlefleets cross the daemon-infested miasma of the warp, the only route between distant stars, their way lit by the Astronomican, the psychic manifestation of the Emperor's will. Vast armies give battle in His name on uncounted worlds. Greatest amongst his soldiers are the Adeptus Astartes, the Space Marines, bio-engineered super-warriors. Their comrades in arms are legion: the Imperial Guard and countless Planetary Defence Forces, the ever-vigilant Inquisition and the tech-priests of the Adeptus Mechanicus to name only a few. But for all their multitudes, they are barely enough to hold off the ever-present threat from aliens, heretics, mutants – and worse.

TO BE A man in such times is to be one amongst untold billions. It is to live in the cruellest and most bloody regime imaginable. These are the tales of those times. Forget the power of technology and science, for so much has been forgotten, never to be re-learned. Forget the promise of progress and understanding, for in the grim dark future there is only war. There is no peace amongst the stars, only an eternity of carnage and slaughter, and the laughter of thirsting gods.

There were two of them. Women.

Boots. Bodices. Bodies borne of fire and atonement. Even in the murk of the maximum-security oubliette he could make out the distinctive garb of the battle-sisters. A pair of nimble little penitence engines, come to work off their own sins in the condemnation of others.

'Sisters,' Mortensen acknowledged across the filthy cell. With poetic synchronicity, coiled power lashes slipped from the sisters' slender gauntlets and began to crackle and dance on the floor like death-throe serpents. One motioned him to get up. Grunting, he kicked himself away from the soiled wall. As his nakedness passed between their joint four hundred pounds of man-hating flesh, Mortensen enjoyed their loathing. Assuming the supplicating demeanour of a good prisoner, he took a seat at the plasteel table and chair in the centre of the chamber with the light and his visitors.

A shadow momentarily enveloped the room as a dark shape dropped in through the ceiling threshold. At first Mortensen took it to be a body: perhaps one of his men. Far too elegant for a flailing corpse, the form somersaulted and landed gently in front of the table. Her heavy ribbed cape – like the wings of a gargoyle – parted to reveal livid, black armour and the dazzling reflection of a maze of polished adamantium pins inserted into her bare cranium, each pin a centimetre equidistant from the others. As she lifted her chin Mortensen found himself fixed in the steely gaze of an older woman, her eyes like the twin barrels of a storm bolter – impassive, unswerving and on target.

She took him in with the kind of fascination most people reserve for keen blades and caged reptiles: the Guardsman's physique, the schola tattoos, the erubescent scarring that danced across his muscular flesh like camouflage scalded into the skin. The florid pattern became even more intense across Mortensen's shaven head and chest, only broken up by the cruciform of numerals inked across his scalp and a short, ragged beard around a snarl that passed for a mouth.

The interest was reciprocated. It had been an impressive entrance, but at that moment Mortensen found himself admiring the jump pack the battle-sister had used to negotiate the oubliette's roof threshold and the new possibilities it offered: in a cell with the sole exit situated in the ceiling, the only way out was up.

Even before he knew what he was doing, Mortensen was on his feet. With the unreal speed and fluidity of a drinking-hole gunslinger, the woman had dipped her hand into a holster and drawn a tapered pistol. There was a brief crack of las-fire and a flash filled the room. The blast hit him square in the centre of his chest, the momentum carrying his knees over his shoulders. The battle-sister's pistol was back in its holster before Mortensen hit the ground in an untidy, unconscious heap.

Shrugging the seconds he'd just spent in oblivion from his aching skull, Mortensen grabbed the back of the chair and

pulled himself to his feet. Running fingers across his chest
he found a shallow scorch mark seared into the flesh above
the sternum. The power pack on the sister's pistol must have
been fried. Mortensen's face split into a grin.

'Let's try that again,' he sneered, his grip tightening on
the back of the chair. The battle-sister stared on in staunch
silence, nodding an order to the other two sisters to close in.
Hefting the chair above the ground, Mortensen spun on his
heel and let it go, burying it in the tumbling form of his
nearest assailant.

He turned to meet the second as she tried to rush him
from the other side. The crackling tip of her power lash
snapped around his left wrist, locking itself off. To any ordinary man, the mere touch of the weapon would feel like
wearing a set of manacles pulled from a blacksmith's fire. It
wasn't exactly a concubine's caress for Mortensen either but
his benumbed flesh gave him the seconds he needed to withstand the worst the lash had to offer. Grabbing a length of
whip with one hand he yanked the sister towards him,
swinging his right fist around to meet her. With the second
sister on the deck Mortensen uncoiled the power lash from
his wrist and brought it back to life with a click of his thumb.

The blistered sinew of his wrist smouldered and
Mortensen clenched both his fist and his teeth as the ghostly
scorch of the searing weapon finally hit nerve sensitive tissue underneath. The first sister held back, allowing her
compatriot time to shake Mortensen's jackhammer blow
from her skull; they remained together, side by side. What
they had just witnessed made them wary: his gift, his curse.

Mortensen gave them a nasty smirk. When a comet had
struck the hive-world of Gomorrah, Mortensen had been
baptised in the apocalyptic fires that had laid waste to the
planet. He had been burned from the temple to the toes and
had lost much of the feeling in what was in between.

The three of them circled each other like gladiatorial warriors, the sisters occasionally cracking their remaining lash at him in the hope he might return the compliment and provide them with an opening. When he had them where he wanted them, Mortensen granted their wish. The battle-sisters effortlessly sidestepped as Mortensen slid down on one knee and sent the tip of the spitting weapon harmlessly through the air between them. Like scorpions rearing their tails for the kill, the sisters took full advantage and thrashed their own whip towards him. But it was too late. Mortensen's weapon was already entangled itself in its intended target – the centre leg of the plasteel table. Tugging at the lash with all his strength, the table shot across the room, hamstringing the two women from behind and sending them tumbling towards the metal floor.

With the Adepta Sororitas down, Mortensen had expected the remaining battle-sister to go for her pistol again. Fading power pack or not, the weapon was still better than nothing. Sending a ripple through his power lash, he freed it from the table leg and announced his intention to fight.

Within moments the prone battle-sisters were back on their feet and forming a living, breathing barrier of righteous hatred between Mortensen and their brash leader. He gave them a brazen flash of his eyes: 'Don't know when to stay down eh? Or maybe you're getting to like it…'

They advanced, impassive and unruffled. Mortensen's smirk faded. He was being toyed with: a puritan's plaything. The battle-sisters were soaking up punishment like a barrack room punch bag, each blow taking them one step closer to the redemption they craved. Mortensen, on the other hand, had been to hell and back way before he ever reached the cell and was starting to question how much more abuse he could conceivably weather. The answer to his question came sooner than he thought.

'Stand down,' the battle-sister instructed, at which her
henchwomen went limp and peeled off to stand sentinel on
either side of the oubliette. She wanted to face him alone.
Mortensen gave a mock bow of the head, as if he and the
battle-sister were facing each other across a spire ballroom.

'Obliged to you,' he said, cracking his knuckles and moving in on her. Disconcertingly, all the battle-sister did was
saunter around the front of the table and rest her backside
on the rim.

That wasn't the only thing that was bothering Mortensen.
His fourth step hadn't felt as steady as his third and his fifth
barely carried him at all. Finding himself back on the floor
at the battle-sister's feet, Mortensen started to realise that
he was in trouble. Again. Gritting his teeth and abandoning the whip, he took the last few metres arm over arm,
before pulling himself up using the side of the table and the
sister's holster belt. His legs felt like they weren't there anymore and he began to feel the same sensation in his arms.
If he could just get his hands around her neck – but that
thought faded as his eyes came level with the battle-sister's
elegant laspistol.

'Needler,' Mortensen grunted, and fell as the palsy
reached his straining fingers.

He hit the filth-encrusted floor with less grace than he
would have imagined possible, before getting on with the
important business of internal cramping and convulsions. It
was difficult to concentrate during this period, but Mortensen
was certain that he heard the slick clunk of a pistol longslide
being cleared. This was confirmed a muscle-spasming
eternity later when a crystal casing hit the floor next to him.
The tiny transparent vial, threaded through with a violaceous
liquid, rolled this way and that in the miniature squall of his
staggered breathing. Flipping him over with the wicked tip of
one armoured boot, the battle-sister took him away from the

kaleidoscopic world of the needler chemicase and stood astride his paralysed form.

'Be gentle with me,' Mortensen jeered and managed a crooked smirk. The freshly primed needler came out and hovered once again above his chest.

'Don't worry, major,' she assured him, the cold certainty of her words cutting through his hive-world smarm. 'You won't feel a thing.'

CHAPTER ONE
Damnation Games

I

IT WAS THE same dream.

Mortensen knew it was a dream because he was home and the home he knew was long gone. Knee-deep in fine caustic ash, he was stumbling his way up a mountainous dune. His drill slacks were sweat-stained rags clinging to his brawny frame and his feet were raw in his boots. Spreading his fingers like grapnels, he punched handholds into the desiccated slip face and made a desperate scramble for the dune's shifting summit.

Gomorrah.

He drank in a scene of unrivalled bleakness. A rolling dune sea of corrosive, crescentric slag-heaps as far as the eye could see – pockmarked with industrial craters and bottomless, open-cast scars that even the insatiable ash wasteland couldn't swallow. And where this blighted landscape met a primordial sky that boiled with sickly rage, a bloated city sat, spewing further poison into the rust-scorched heavens. Haephastus Hive squatted like some industrial behemoth, its prospector shanty towns slipping between the bleached dunes like exploratory tentacles, searching for the next motherlode, the next heavy metal seam or horde of long forgotten archeotech.

Behind him, the 'Claw' poked an accusatory set of masonry pincers at the filthy heavens. Mortensen had no idea what the architectural abomination had been in its former life, but now the two towers – the shorter leaning with seeming precariousness on its grotesquely lofty counterpart – formed the two vertical chromo-wings of Gomorrah's infamous schola progenium complex. Atop the tallest, Drill Abbot Proctor would be observing his progress across the dunes; chronometer in one bony fist, magnoculars to his beady little eyes, his toothless chops mumbling an incessant stream of senile curses. Knowing his momentary pause would have sent the good abbot into an apoplexy of eyeball-popping profanity, Mortensen dragged his limbs from the strength-sapping ash: he would pay for that.

Lost in the grim spectacle of the hive he barely noticed when the spent, feeble sunlight suddenly evaporated. A deathly coolness swept across the barren waste as the cloudbank above Mortensen was enveloped in angry, black shadow. As he stared into the deepening sky the perverse eddies and twisters responsible for the dunes' seasonal migration died about him and the air grew still and lifeless.

On the horizon, just beyond the mighty hive, a colossal berg of dirty ice and rock suddenly split the sky asunder. Mortensen had never seen anything as big – not even the hive – and for a long moment the only expression his body could produce was an awe-inspired gawp. For the first time in sixteen hours, Mortensen was confident that Abbot Proctor's magnoculars were not burning into his sweaty back.

As the gargantuan object fell it writhed with white flame and trailed a firestorm of friction and combustible atmospheric gases. Cloud vaporised on contact and sheet lightning rippled out in concentric waves, as what Mortensen could only imagine was a comet breached the percolating smog layers and tumbled towards the surface. In the appalling seconds of helpless horror that followed, Mortensen found himself ghoulishly shuffling towards the vision.

Then impact.

All became agonising white as the comet struck and announced its unwelcome arrival. Mortensen instinctively screwed his eyes shut and so couldn't see the unstoppable blast wave as it tore across the world in the wake of the strike, scalding the skies and turning the wasteland to glass.

He felt it though. A sensation he would never be allowed to forget: a corporeal memory; the last feeling his flesh would ever register. The inferno rolled over him like a tidal wave of superheated vengeance, flensing skin from the muscle and sinew underneath and baptising what was left in the apocalyptic fires that followed. Thrashing in an acid bath of agony, Mortensen screamed for a death that never came…

II

ZANE MORTENSEN SAT bolt upright in the bunk, gulping feverishly at the cool air of the quarters. Dragging back the blanket he threw his legs over the side and dug the soles of his feet into the metal of the deck. *Deliverance* felt cold: the deep freeze of the empyrean creeping through the escort carrier's superstructure. With warp travel came nightmares, as every good Guardsman knew, but for Mortensen this was normal fare. That monstrous calamity waited for him behind each eyelid: for him sleep meant reliving the unliveable. Cradling his brutally shaved head in his hands he let the ghostly afterimage of the dream fade from his mind.

There was movement in the covers beside him. He watched a slender hand reach out groggily before letting soft fingers drift in mock affection across the taut muscle of one scarred shoulder. It was Vedette, one of his storm-troopers. The arrangement was largely casual, unspoken and restricted to the long months spent in transit between one warzone and the next.

The simple warmth of the action was lost on Mortensen's nerve-dead flesh, the difference between what he could see and feel making him nauseous, and he brushed her delicate fingers from his arm. She moaned softly and retracted, turning over in the bunk.

'Sir.'

The bulkhead rolled aside and the glowtubes glimmered to life. Corporal Sass stood in the entrance looking more stricken than usual. Mortensen squinted through the harsh glare. Sass took a couple of dramatic steps inside the cabin. 'Major, we have a problem.'

Mortensen gave the young hiver crabby eyes. 'I already have a problem, corpsman.' He stuffed a cigar butt between his teeth. 'You.'

The storm-trooper continued his vexed advance, to the major's dismay. Mortensen had a soft spot for the Necromundan, but he was wound tighter than a tripwire. The boy's prodigious mathematical abilities and indefatigable memory – the consequence of his mother's taste for crystal ersatz – was a bottomless pit of Tactica protocol, field stratagems and strangely useful useless information. This made Sass an invaluable asset and a perfect choice for the major's adjutant.

'You should really hear this, sir.'

Slipping on his boots, beret and a pair of starched blood stripe slacks, Mortensen crossed the cabin and pushed his bulkhead aside. To the officer's surprise he found Master Sergeant Conklin playing sentry at the door: beret crooked and resting the snub muzzle of an autopistol against the cold metal.

'What?' Mortensen rumbled as the sergeant raised his grizzled eyebrows.

'You're not gonna like this, boss.'

Bulldozer loyalty was Wendall Conklin's speciality: he was well liked amongst the men, among whom his reputation as Mortensen's top hatchet man was legend and the bark of his bolter was always welcome. Mortensen couldn't find it in himself to like the man, however. Under fire he often found himself deferring to the cold logic of his adjutant or Vedette's cool common sense, rather than the brute killer instincts of his veteran sergeant – utterly dependable though he was.

'I'm already not liking it.'

Mortensen took in the corridor with one suspicious glance and then pinned the two storm-troopers with wary eyes. 'What is it?' he put to them in single and deliberate syllables. One looked at the other in expectation. Sass twitched. Conklin flared his nostrils. 'Am I in the habit of asking rhetorical questions?' the major added with rising choler.

The master sergeant's face creased with addled irritation. He wasn't much one for long words or their meanings.

Sass raised an inquiring finger: 'Sir, would that not be a rhetorical question?'

Mortensen growled.

Sass lowered his finger and took it towards the cabin vox. 'Like I said, sir, you are going to want to hear this for yourself.'

The wall-caster erupted in a cacophony of static and garbled vox-traffic. For a few seconds the ear-splitting scramble continued with Mortensen glowering at his adjutant, his patience almost spent. Then he caught something he recognised – something all Guardsmen recognised – the nineteen megathule, air-seething crack of ragged las-fire and the screams that usually accompanied it.

Mortensen put his hand to the wall and leaned in closer with his experienced ear. Volscian-pattern. Hive produced. Unrivalled power economy and the almost indistinguishable hiss of gas-coolant that preceded each snap – both of which were peculiar to the model.

This was not good news. Volscian-pattern las-fire meant that the firefight wasn't part of some horrific, empyreal boarding action – which ironically might have been simpler. Volscian las-fire meant Volscians and *Deliverance's* payload was the 364th and 1001st Volscian Shadow Brigade companies. As Sass thumbed through the vox-channels it became apparent that the entire carrier was alive with profanity and gunfire. The whoops of trigger-happy Volscian hivers cut through the las-chatter of barrack-room battles and ambushes. Sinister threats and promises were being exchanged across the channels, which had been jammed open on all decks, accompanied by the thudding whoosh of pistols and the occasional thunder of grenades.

Fortunately such small arms posed no danger to the reinforced hull and its pressurised integrity.

'They have their weapons,' Vedette said. She was out of the bunk and pulling on a vest over her bleached, Mordian bob. 'Which means the officers are involved, also.'

Sass and the major nodded in grave agreement.

'Gang war?' Conklin offered. 'The tats and sashes – Underbloods this and Kinfolk that…'

'The Volscians are undoubtedly stratified by House and gang loyalties,' Sass interrupted with nerdish authority, 'but it seems unlikely that a force so divided – so intent on fighting each other rather than the greenskins – could have garrisoned the Kintessa Gauntlet for the past thousand years.'

Conklin shot the adjutant a sour glare.

'Come on,' Mortensen snarled, silencing the wall-hailer. 'We all know it's Fosco.' He stared at the floor for a moment, collecting his thoughts, and then looked at them each in turn.

'Sass – I'm going to need Captain Rask.'

'But all this deck's channels are jammed.'

'Get the master vox from Diederick's bunk.' The comms-officer was always fiddling with the damn thing. 'Patch into the brigadier's personal channel. If Rask's not messed up in this then you'll find him monitoring the vox-waves.'

'Brigadier Voskov's personal channel is going to be security encoded,' Sass protested.

'Something makes me think that's not going to stop you,' the major told him with a reassuring slap on the back. 'Hurry.'

As the adjutant slipped out of the cabin Mortensen turned on his sergeant. 'Weapons?'

'Hellguns, targeters and carapace are all stowed on the birds. The carrier deck officers have the hangars in lockdown.'

'How do we know that?' Mortensen asked: that kind of information certainly wasn't coming in over the vox-channels.

'Minghella was up in medical, checking on Diederick, when it broke out,' Conklin informed him. 'Bunch of hivers stormed the bay and shot up the infirmary. Diederick took two more in the chest but Rhen got him back down here. They had to go around the flight deck. Navy boys have sealed themselves in.'

'And Sergeant Minghella?' Mortensen put to Conklin. The major had the feeling he was going to need his medic.

'Nothing he won't walk away from,' the master sergeant assured him. 'He's working on Diederick now. All we have are our side arms.' Conklin flashed his autopistol at the major. The corpsmen carried side arms at all times for personal defence. The pistols were as much uniform as the blood stripes, berets, belts and tunics that made his storm-troopers the target of colourful nicknames amongst regular Guardsmen. To the Shadow Brigade they were 'Glory Boys' and 'Toy Soldiers' – but this bothered the major and his men little. They'd been called a lot worse and in turn had far worse names for their regimental counterparts: men who fought for tithes and out of fear rather than for Imperial pride.

Mortensen bridled: his squad might very well have the honour of reinstating some of that fear today. A duty he'd be far happier to perform without the involvement of Commissar Fosco.

Fosco had joined *Deliverance* at St Guise, spelling immediate doom for the tiny carrier. Brigadier Voskov already had the Volscian 364th Shadow Brigade drilled into as well-oiled a machine as any officer could come to expect from a hive-world regiment. Besides Mortensen's storm-troopers, *Deliverance* also carried the Volscian 1001st and it was the unfortunate honour of this freshly processed regiment to receive as their commissar the infamous Fritzel Fosco.

Mortensen didn't know whether it was the strange warp currents the carrier had beat up through on its arduous trek along the Kintessa Gauntlet or the fact that Fosco was a creed-obsessed psychotic who had simply spent too long in the cardinal world hellhole that was St Guise, but it had swiftly become apparent that they were all on a passage to mutiny.

From Rask the major learned that the Commissariat had moved Fosco all over the sector: he was well known as an imperious tyrant and a bane to all who served with and under him. He'd declared the armed transport *Achates* and all on board her heretic and undeserving of the Emperor's protection. He had been part of – and many claimed afterward, the cause of – the notorious Port Spiterri Revolt. The Jopall 44th Indentured; Colonel Da Costa's First Moloch Rifles, the 201st Noctan Strikes, the Tallarn 800th (formerly known as the Abu al-Din Sunfighters); the last of the Gorgone Deepers: the list went on – all regiments to whom Fosco had been attached – all regiments whose commanding officers had appealed to the Emperor when they heard that the Commissariat was moving the volatile Fosco onto his next assignment. The First Moloch was notable as the regiment that during the Blight Wars lost more Guardsmen to Commissar Fosco's battlefield executions than to the hrud infestation they were combating.

The relief of the regimental commanding officers was brief, however, as in each case a parting shot was delivered – often to the head – before Fosco and his staff were moved on to their next, ultimately doomed regiment. Fosco never saw a disciplinary committee (he was too well connected – although no one seemed to know how) but would occasionally take benediction leave amongst the lofty towers of St Guise – from where the Volscian 1001st had recently received him.

Vedette snatched up her belt and holster from where they were hanging on the bunk and tossed the major his own. Gone was the desperate fervour of the previous night's embraces. Gone was Vedette the casual lover, and in her place was Corporal Vedette the professional.

As he caught the belt he went through the perfunctory motions of checking the autopistol's clip and chambering the first round. He thumbed off the safety and grunted to himself: wouldn't be needing that.

A sudden hammering from the corridor brought all three heads up in the cabin. Conklin threw himself from the doorway and across the passage, chunky autopistol clasped in both hands and aimed at the block bulkhead. Vedette went down on one knee in the cabin doorway, leaving Mortensen the fire arc above her head.

More hammering proceeded – the metallic clatter bouncing around the corridor as yet another untidy volley of las-bolts impacted from the other side.

'Somebody wants in,' Mortensen muttered.

'It's okay,' Conklin assured them gruffly, 'I've already locked it off.'

Vedette wasn't convinced, not least by the way her master sergeant was tightly holding his own pistol on the doorway.

'Until somebody hauls a plasma or a vape gun down there,' the corporal corrected him.

'Yes,' Mortensen nodded, 'we don't want to be here when that happens. Fall back.'

The three storm-troopers backed away from the block bulkhead as an increasingly furious barrage of bolts was carelessly blasted at the pressure-sealed door. Vedette and Conklin held their weapons on the corridor in the event of a breach while the major fell into a sidle up the corridor wall to cover their backward advance in case they were cut off from the rear.

'Can I take it all routes into the block have been secured, sergeant?'

Conklin chuckled nastily. 'I hope you don't think tipping you out of your bunk was my first priority, boss.'

Mortensen nodded in silent agreement. That was Conklin: provokingly proficient.

The trio backed out of the corridor and into a small apex that formed the hub of several troop block passageways. There Mortensen found the remainder of his storm-troopers: informally known amongst the other regiments as the 'Redemption Corps'.

Diederick was a blasted and bloody mess on the floor, his ruptured gore spreading slowly out across the metal deck. Sergeant Minghella straddled the comms-officer, his head bowed and his chest heaving with the past exertion of keeping the trooper alive.

'Rhen.'

Rhen Minghella contorted his already hideous, dog-face features and wrapped his fleshy lips around a stream of ugly curses. The Corps medic pushed himself up from the deck and the body. His uniform was dishevelled and soaked through with his patient's blood and not a little of his own.

Without looking at Mortensen he wiped the deep red of his hands down on the only part of his tunic that wasn't bathed in bodily fluids.

'I regret to inform you of Specialist Diederick's untimely death, sir,' he reported dourly.

Trooper Pryce jangled nearby as he knelt to close the storm-trooper's glazed and lifeless eyes – his neck a nest of cords, chains and ribbons, each supporting some saint-adorned medallion, lucky home world charm or Imperial effigy. Pryce adored the creed and Mortensen often caught the soldier offering prayers to his God-Emperor, although the major suspected this was more out of a pleading desire to survive the horrific situations he was routinely plunged into rather than pious devotion.

Mortensen pursed his lips: he didn't have time for the indulgence of one of his medic's bad moods or lectures. 'Vedette, watch the corridor,' he ordered. The other two were being covered by Sarakota – who looked strange with a snub pistol in his hand instead of the anti-materiel length of his sniper Hellshot – and Gorskii, the Redemption Corps' Valhallan demolitions man. Or more accurately woman, but it was hard to tell through the hair of her upper lip and the flash scarring that ran down one half of her face.

The Redemption Corps were a mixed group – from schola students to veterans: the best that being born on a dozen different worlds could offer. Each brought their own natural talents to Mortensen's small, elite storm-trooper company, honed to zealous perfection in the sector's various schola progenium institutions and drawn together to damn the enemies of the Imperium.

'Conklin – what's down here? We're obviously going to need a little more than faith and thigh-huggers,' Mortensen put to the sergeant, slapping his holster.

'Orlop deck houses the sick bay–'

'Medical is overrun,' Minghella shot at them irritably.

'...midshipman's berths, some of the maintenance and ministration compartments.'

'Gather what you can. Anything useful.'

Conklin went left but Gorskii put up one long-fingered hand.

'Midshipman's berths sealed from inside,' she notified him in her Slavic drawl.

'The crew won't want any part of this,' Vedette clarified.

'No,' Mortensen added, 'this is Guard business. Pryce, go with him.'

Darting past an impassive Sarakota, Conklin and Pryce disappeared down the adjacent corridor. Appearing in their place moments later was Sass, emerging from his cabin – master vox carelessly thrown over one shoulder and headset held to one ear.

'Captain Rask for you, major,' Sass announced, not a little pleased with himself.

Mortensen took the headset and pressed the vox-bead to his grizzled chin.

'Talk to me Tyberius – tell me I'm still dreaming,' the major rumbled.

'I wish you were,' came the tinny reply.

The vox lent the voice a quality of great distance and detachment, especially as it was, bouncing around the metal walls of the block apex. There was also something

smooth and well-worn in the captain's tone, however –
something familiar and business-as-usual about his
manner.

Captain Tyberius Rask had initially joined *Deliverance* and Brigadier Voskov with the 1001st Volscian
Shadow Brigade – a company he'd personally tithed
and processed on Volscia. Despite not being a Volscian
himself, Rask soon became a rising star amongst
Voskov's tactical staff – and through his keen understanding of the hive-world mindset and an ability to
harness Volscian strength, he unleashed the 1001st's
natural talent for slaughter. It had been this success
that inevitably threw Rask and Mortensen together.

As Voskov's chief tactical officer, the captain inher-
ited responsibility for Mortensen and his 'Redemption
Corps'. Zane Mortensen was widely known as a difficult if ruthlessly effective officer – right down to his
apocalyptic survival on Gomorrah, a frankly unbelievable service record and barrack room rumours of his
supposed indestructibility. Rask should know: it was
his current duty to dispatch Mortensen and his storm-
troopers on the innumerable spearheads, infiltration
missions and special operations that had earned
Mortensen half such a reputation.

It was very much this status – as the unit's strategist
and the final voice they heard before being dropped
into some deathworld hellhole or other – that as a routine, steadied nerves and lent welcome focus and
direction to bloody, battlefield situations often bereft
of such luxuries.

'Is the ship secure?' Mortensen asked. Gunfire
exchanged on the bridge might end their journey
through the empyrean pretty definitely – one stray
shot into an essential piece of equipment like a Geller

field runebank would be enough to seal the fate of every man on board.

'The ship's fine. Look, we haven't got much time,' Rask replied.

'We have weapons fire on the barracks decks,' Mortensen informed him. 'Is the materium breached? Is it warp fever?'

'It's not immaterial exposure. It's not a mutiny: fighting is restricted to the starboard barracks decks and some forward areas. Captain Waldemar thought it prudent to seal Guard habitation off – just until the stomach goes out of the ringleaders.'

Mortensen rolled his eyes.

'Told you,' Vedette added.

'So it's the hivers?' the major put to Rask.

'It's the Volscians; affirmative.'

'Are you telling me that naval security is just going to sit watching bulkheads while the 1001st tear each other up?' Mortensen rumbled.

'Guard business. Waldemar won't order his men in until both weapons and the rebellion are put down. He won't risk the ship.'

Mortensen nodded slowly to himself.

'So who's offering the resistance?'

'Small pockets of Shadow Brigade soldiers, either too loyal or too frightened to join the action – most led by sergeants or the odd lieutenant.'

'Are you in charge up there?'

'The regimental command structure is intact: Brigadier Voskov and the senior staff are up here on the bridge. He's put the 364th on high alert, and sealed off their quarters, just in case the dissention spreads. We've already have enough Volscians shooting at each other.'

'Why do that when they can shoot at me and my men instead?' Mortensen sneered moodily.

'I don't know,' Rask countered. 'I hear you're a real hit with Gomez and the Second Platoon.'

'Talking of creed-freaks, what about Pontiff Preed?'

'Voskov sent him down to steady the 364th. Look, Zane, you have to understand: this is not a mutiny. Several Shadow Brigade officers authorised distribution of weaponry to their platoons and took hostages.'

'Hostages?'

Rask breathed hesitation back across the channel before: 'Regimental Commissar Fosco and his personal staff.'

Mortensen let the headset drop to his thigh and shook his head with venom. 'Son of a…' It was his turn to check Vedette: 'What did I tell you?'

'Look Zane – I'm sorry to do this to you – I know how you feel about the good commissar.'

Mortensen brought the headset back up. 'You really don't.'

'And I don't think that many of us up here would disagree with you my friend – but we've got a little problem called Tactica regulations. We've got to put this insurrection down: the Imperial Guard does not negotiate with insurgents. You know that. I need the rebel command structure neutralised. Only then will Waldemar send in naval security.'

'And Fosco?'

'Of course, the hostages are a consideration.'

'So that bastard can wreak more havoc. If Fosco walks out of there, it'll be all day firing squads.'

'Zane – it's either that or face one ourselves when we get to Spetzghast.'

'Me and my men – we're instruments of Imperial justice; the left hand of the God-Emperor, if you will – that I don't doubt.'

'Major, your loyalty to Emperor is beyond question,' Rask assured him with the smoothness of an expert salesman. 'That's why I'm on a vox-set to you instead of conducting pointless negotiations with the hostage-takers.'

Mortensen's bitterness had yet to find expression, however. 'So Fosco stirs up the Volscian hivers with his brutal ways. They're brutal enough and strike back. Now my men and I have to spill the blood of brother Guardsmen and clean up this mess. I don't know. You reap what you sow. Somehow, I feel this was inevitable. The Commissariat need men of character, not cruelty: they should be amongst our best, not our worst. I mean – castration; servitude in perpetuis; tongue clipping – since when have these been a soldier's punishment for anything? But I guess it saves the bother of actually having to organise the firing squads, with most of the punished choosing to swallow their side arms instead–'

'Major Mortensen: like myself – you and your men have your orders.'

Rask's flat ultimatum hung in the stale air of the apex.

Sarakota backed up a step, admitting his sergeant and Trooper Pryce. They carried between them an engineering tool crate that they unceremoniously emptied out on the metal floor beside Diederick's body. As well as the servitor tool attachments and various blessing oils, Mortensen could make out some flashlamps, a few corroded power packs, a bundle of dirty rebreathers and a plasma welding torch. The major grunted.

'Do we have a plan?' he asked Rask finally.

'You're going to love it.'

III

'THIS HAS GOT to be the worst plan I've ever heard,' Wendall Conklin announced to anyone who would listen. 'And I've heard some beauts.'

'Help me with this, will you?' Mortensen put to the master sergeant, as much to shut him up as anything.

Vedette was backing up with the plasma torch, after cutting a ragged hatch through the heavy metal decking. Lifting the solid slab of flooring clear with lungfuls of exertion, the two storm-troopers held it for the dangerous moments it took Gorskii and Minghella to get their fingers underneath the dead weight and help toss the improvised hatch aside.

Sass swept in quickly with a sparked flashlamp but was forced back by the liberated stench that rose like a physical force to meet him. It was an almost overpowering concoction of petrochemical smog and stale sewage.

Vedette's handiwork had also cut free the top section of a rusted deck drain. Covering his nose and mouth with the cuff of his uniform, the major's adjutant leaned back in with the lamp and flashed it both ways up the dribbling conduit. Satisfied, he pulled himself upright.

'Good work,' Mortensen muttered, going in for a closer look himself. Once again Sass's arithmetical gifts had been a boon. With the most basic of descriptions Captain Rask could offer from the bridge cogitators and runeprints, the storm-trooper had located the pipe running underneath the cabin allocated to Pryce and Sarakota with little more than some grumbling and measured pacing.

'We're going to need the masks,' Vedette ventured, abandoning the plasma torch.

'I'd say,' Minghella agreed, covering his mouth with his beret.

'One of them doesn't work,' Conklin informed them.

'Well, then I guess that's yours,' Mortensen returned. He looked up at Sass. 'Leads to the bilge, you say?'

The adjutant nodded: 'The bilge compartments run the length of the ship. If the data Captain Rask has given us is even half-accurate we should be able to access large areas of the lower barrack decks from down there.'

'The plasma?'

'Spent,' Vedette confirmed.

'We'd better hope for some kind of maintenance exit on the other end,' Mortensen mused miserably.

'Looks like a squeeze,' Minghella observed, his brutish features screwed up more hideously than usual.

'Yes,' the major agreed, 'and it ain't going be pleasant down there, so we'd best make it count on the other side.' Climbing into the pipe, Mortensen knelt down in the shallow pool of stagnant bilge water.

His crisp blood stripe trousers soon became sodden with muck and oil. His autopistol sat in his belt and holster, which he'd piled on the deck beside the opening. Dumping the leather harness in the stinking slime at his knees, he added a ready sparked flashlamp and a cog-hammer he'd requisitioned from the tool crate. The wicked claw that adorned one end had appealed to the major immediately as a suitable tool for both clearing obstructions in the pipe and skull-hooking potential adversaries.

'Any last words before we commit ourselves to this?' Mortensen put to the rest of the gathered Redemption Corps storm-troopers. When no one answered he added grimly: 'Any better ideas?'

More silence.

Taking this as a signal Mortensen slid the pile forwards through the chemical sludge and slapped on a bulky, rubber rebreather before lying bare chest down in the pipe with his arms forward. Using his elbows and toes he began to squirm bilgeward. He wasn't ecstatic about sitting his side arm in petrochemical slime but without room to actually draw his weapon he thought it best to have it up forward where it could still give a good account of itself in the confines of the conduit.

Claustrophobic just didn't seem to do the experience justice. Mortensen braced himself against the cold metal of the piping – flexing his shoulders and back muscles – but the drain was fairly unforgiving and appeared to respond by squeezing back. That wasn't the worst of it. The rebreathers were largely ancient and cracked and admitted much of the stomach-churning reek they were meant to circumvent. A few metres into the conduit crawl the pipe filled with the wretched echoes of both Conklin and Pryce throwing up in their masks. After a cacophony of spasms and spitting Mortensen checked with the pair, but the master sergeant simply swore and informed his CO that the smell of vomit was preferable to what they were squirming through.

The agony of an hour's crawl followed – Mortensen's splattered flashlamp revealing metre after endless metre of cramped and corroded horror as he edged it through the detritus of the duct. Acid-soaked muscles blazed along with the ghastly gulps and gasps of lungs desperate for clean air. The crawl gave Mortensen more than enough time to contemplate the job ahead.

Rask's mission was simple. Evade the inevitable obstruction of bulkheads, firefights and a barracks block in lock-down by traversing the transport's keel along one of the many bilge channels that ran the length of the vessel. Conklin had suggested working their way over to and hooking up with some of the isolated groups of loyalists scattered throughout the starboard decks but Rask had advised against it. He had told the sergeant that the pockets of resistance were largely unarmed and those that weren't were certainly low on ammunition. Most were also pinned down by much larger groups of aggressors and were more than likely injured, which would offer more of a handicap than an advantage to the Redemption Corps.

Rask's operation relied much more on mobility and infiltration. Mortensen could hardly disagree. In their current predicament his storm-troopers were hardly outfitted for a spearhead. The captain actually favoured a single, bold, unanticipated strike right at the heart of the insurrection – to 'cut the head from the angry serpent', as he put it. Rask had faith that such an action held the best chance of success – success determined as the retrieval of any remaining hostages and the unconditional surrender or destruction of rebel Shadow Brigade forces. Then, and only then, would Waldemar, *Deliverance*'s lord and captain, authorise his naval troops in to secure the barrack decks.

Acquiring the hostage takers would be another thing entirely. Rask didn't even have confirmation on their identity and location. The most likely candidates were a triumvirate of Shadow Brigade officers, two lieutenants and a captain, whose platoons had become the prime focus of Commissar Fosco's wrath.

Company Captain Obadiah Eckhardt, First Lieutenant Diezel Shanks and Lieutenant Nils Isidore had all lost men to Fosco's campaign to purify the men of the 1001st of their hiver ways and customs. Instead of immersing himself in Shadow Brigade culture and using it to unify the men – as Rask had done in tithing them – Fosco had attempted to eradicate it. He claimed that the strength of the Imperial Guard was based upon uniformity: billions of souls all pulling in the same direction, and had little time to pander to the fighting strengths of individuals, their units or their regiments.

This approach did not sit well with Mortensen – whose own inimitable style of leadership marked him out as a target for such accusations. Without Rask's silver-tongued diplomacy and tact the Redemption Corps would have long become a target for Fosco or some other bloodthirsty puritan. The schola progeniums were brimming with creed-thumping sadists like the commissar and Mortensen refused to have such men in his unit – which unfortunately made the Redemption Corps appear ever more irregular against the backdrop of the uniform billions that men like Fosco were attempting to cultivate.

Regardless of the major's feelings, the predicament demanded a rescue attempt and Eckhardt, Shanks, Isidore and their compatriots had to be neutralised. It was a storm-trooper's lot. To be better. To be above common regimental concerns and do the good work of the Emperor – wherever it took them.

At that moment the Emperor's good work took Mortensen from the crippling confines of the drain and out through a gash in the floor of the pipe, splashing him down head first in a petrochemical sinkhole.

Beneath the oily surface Mortensen heard the *thudgush* of others, freshly baptised in the bilgewater filth. The major's lamp struggled to penetrate the blackness, blinking a ghostly beam that brushed the thrashing of boots and limbs as his fellow storm-troopers fought to right themselves in their new surroundings. As the soles of his boots touched down on something reassuringly solid the major pushed for the surface and treated himself to a lungful of foetid air. Like everyone else, he retched, bucked and coughed as his throat refused to admit the rancid stench.

Tearing off his mask Mortensen tossed the useless thing away and gradually – back rising and falling like a wounded animal – acclimatised himself. One by one the others followed suit, before hawking and spitting their stomach-churning disgust into the still black waters around them.

Lamplight sheared through the inky darkness: probably the first light down there for hundreds of years. They were right in the bowels of the ship, in one of the foul bilge drains into which every drop of piss, oil, blood, sweat and everything else descended – wrenched keelward by the irresistible force of *Deliverance's* artificial gravity. The air – if it warranted such a description – was acrid and stale, hanging as it had in the compartment amongst a forest of quietly corroding pipes and the bubble of fermenting bilge-slime.

Mortensen turned his lamp on his squad. They were a sight: like septuplets yanked from a womb of filth.

'Sass?'

'Best probably to avoid the deeps: we don't really want to be swimming through this muck.'

'Agreed.'

The corpsman turned his lamp back on the conduit from which they'd fallen and the gaping hole that had admitted them. The conduit was riddled through with rust and decay and the entire bottom section from the point of their exit onwards had been eaten away by the corrosive powers of the toxins they had been crawling through.

'It's simple really,' the adjutant told them, between retching and spitting. 'We need to follow the path of this conduit until it meets the steam trunk demi-juncture. Then we'll know for sure that we're under the barracks deck.'

'And this steam juncture thing: you'll know it when you see it?'

Sass nodded.

The bilge was like another world and it was hard for Mortensen to imagine such a place existed hundreds of metres below the soles of his boots as he went about his normal regimental business. Solid blackness reigned here above the equal blackness of the perco-lating petrochemical slime. The corpsmen's flashlamps brought light to the denizens of the deep here: proba-bly the first time the bilge space had experienced light since its original dry-dock engineering, when *Deliver-ance* had been a sprightly young carrier, eager for action and a taste of the void. With millennia to develop and evolve, the bilge sections now boasted their own ecosystems.

Hydrocarbon-hungry bacteria swarmed the oily waters to a primordial sludginess, which in turn was feasted upon by tiny lice and other chitinous micro-arthropods, both flitting above and below the inky surface. Stoolies dribbled from every conceivable solid surface, including the thickets of thin rusty pipes that ran up into the darkness, like slinking flypaper, mopping up the lice and absorbing them through their fecal skin. The descendants of the original rats on board, now all but pinkish, translucent tails with a vice-like pair of jaws on one end, slithered their horrible way through the black waters. Mortensen got to wondering what fed on the highly mobile and muscular rat-tails, hoping that the disgusting food chain ended firmly there.

They were into their second hour of a jogging trudge along the shallows of the bilge lake when he had his question answered.

A fat, broken pipe ran out of the wall, its smashed end hanging over the still, glassy surface of the oil, seeping rusty effluence into the bilge. As his lamplight glanced off the horrible paleness of a form at the pipe Mortensen froze, bringing his autopistol up to meet the threat. The surprise came mostly from its size: a spindle-limbed crustacean, a myriad of twitchy legs and slender pincers, reaching, snatching and cutting at something in the pipe. It towered above them, its many limbs terminating in a clear shell that exhibited the ghastly inner workings of its body. The shell was shaped like an obscene flower, fat at the bottom, the underside of which was a mincing mouth, constantly supplied with scraps of flesh from the wicked claws that thrashed back and forth to supply it with food. The top of the shell tapered to a twisted funnel, which widened again like the end of a bugle or blunderbuss.

As the storm-troopers neared, Mortensen held up one arm indicating a full stop. The gargantuan thing seemed very invested in its activity, which upon inspection appeared to be slicing up and devouring a nest of bloody, swarming rat-tails. The major approached slowly, his pace steady and even, clambering over the pipe with deliberate movements. At one point the crustacean experimentally reached out a large pincer and plucked at the storm-trooper's boot, but Mortensen dashed the claw-tip aside with a swipe of his pistol. The creature became a wall of pincers, all retracted and ready to slice, the rest of its body still as the pipe disgorged mauled rat-tails into the shallows about it. Vedette and Gorskii primed their pistols, but Mortensen held up a free hand, before swiftly indicating with his fingers that they should cross the pipe behind him.

Minghella and Sarakota scuttled swiftly over the conduit, followed closely by the others as the creature tiptoed left and right, reacting to the new activity along the shoreline. With the squad across, Mortensen backed down the other side and retreated, boot behind boot. Within moments the hideous thing was back to tearing apart the squirming nest. A few hundred metres further on and Sass mercifully stopped them.

'I think this is it.'

'You think?' Conklin grumbled.

The adjutant was flashing his light into the gloom above; it was joined by the rest of the available beams.

'The steam trunk demi-juncture,' Sass announced.

Mortensen nodded: he didn't know exactly what he was looking at, but mostly it resembled one rusty throng of pipes and conduits running into another throng. Many of the pipes were shattered and broken so only the stubs of channels running vertically up into the ship were visible.

'Boss,' Conklin murmured: his was the only flash-lamp not on the encrusted ceiling. Mortensen followed the beam and the line of his pistol muzzle until he found the gangly legs of another hulking crustacean. This one was holding still in the shallows, the blunderbuss snout of its shell pointed at the ceiling. Its body chugged horribly until suddenly a bloodied fountain of vomit-splatter spouted skyward from the opening. Most of the regurgitated mess decorated the ceiling, but some of the muck hit its intended target, one of the broken pipe openings. As the shell heaved its last, the spidery thing crawled off into the thick waters, dipping below the surface, the trumpet end of its shell top now serving as a snorkel.

'Major,' Sass called. He'd been prancing around in the shadows, his own lamp exploring the insides of similar conduit openings above. The storm-troopers took several exhausted steps towards him and stared ceilingward. 'Unspark your lamps for a moment,' the adjutant advised.

'Is he friggin' crazy?' Conklin growled.

'Do it,' the major ordered, snapping off his own in good example.

The bilge compartment returned to its vast darkness and although there was black, open space all around him, Mortensen couldn't help but feel the claustrophobia of the creepy sensation that there were things all about him in the void. Then he saw it: the reason Sass had asked for the lamps to be shut off, the reason for their neck craning and idiot stares.

Light. Tiny pinpricks of dim light, filtering in from the vertical termination of a pipe opening above their faces. The opening was just wide enough to admit a corpsman. Gorskii uttered something in her thick

Valhallan dialect, which could have been anything, but sounded like a thanks or blessing. As always Conklin was the first to rain on their parade.

'Is that something moving?' he put to the group. He wasn't wrong – occasionally individual dots of light were momentarily eclipsed, giving the impression that something had already made its home in the pipe. The sergeant grunted and cocked his pistol. 'We'll soon sort that out.'

'Sarge, can we really risk gunfire this close to the insertion?' Vedette put evenly into the darkness. As a Mordian she'd lived on a nightworld and so the lightless environs of the bilge had been less of an ordeal for her. Of all the storm-troopers she'd slipped and stumbled the least through the hellish murk. She displayed no less deftness and precision in the correction of her superior, 'I mean – we could be right under them. Yes?'

Conklin's disappointment was obvious, even in the dark and without visual confirmation from his face: 'Probably.'

With the lamps snapped back on the storm-troopers set about making their ascent. Without the kinds of specialist equipment they habitually relied upon for the wide range of infiltration scenarios in which they were usually involved, the corpsmen had to go back to basics. Mortensen unclipped his belt and wrapped it tautly around two emaciated pipes running parallel and ceilingward. Stuffing his pistol and cog-hammer into his blood stripes he pulled hard on the belt and settled his boot, one on each rusty pipe, crushing and squelching stoolies underfoot. Sliding the belt up through the stoolie slime he clambered up the pipes, the inside edge of each boot fighting to find purchase on the corroded metal surface. Each of the

Redemption Corpsmen followed suit, struggling up behind their major, up into the gloom.

Apart from Pryce slipping and giving Conklin a faceful of stool-caked boot, the ascent went without hitch. Mortensen then used the wicked claw of his cog-hammer to smash back and forth inside the confines of the pipe, the fragile metal caving and providing the major and successive climbers with ready-made hand and foot holds. Reclaiming his belt, he climbed into the opening, up towards the beckoning barracks above.

Twenty minutes into the pipe climb Mortensen came face to face with the obstruction his sergeant had identified earlier. Requiring both hands for the climb Mortensen had ordered his men to abandon their lamps and simply scramble for the light. He could barely make out their forms with his eyes and their ghastly movements were lost on his nerve-insensitive skin, but as the illumination increased, so did his disgust. With every heave upwards more of the wretched things moved from their home, clinging to the pipe walls, and scuttled up his arm, nipping at his neck and cheeks with under-developed claws.

Their shells were soft and their pincers stubby, but they could still draw blood or take out an eyeball. His rising revulsion made him angry and Mortensen slammed his muscular back into the pipe wall, splitting open several larger specimens. This tactic proved ultimately fruitless, however as the swarm built around him and only dropped the thrashing bodies of half-crushed beasts down on his compatriots.

The strange behaviour of the spindly crustacean below, mulching up its prey and fountaining the regurgitated blood and guts up into the pipes, made more sense now that they had discovered the monster's spawnlings up there. Food for the masses. Now the little bastards had thought that Mortensen and his storm-troopers were their next serving.

Thirty metres of sickening trauma later, the major cleared the swarm, which was good for all concerned. The downside was that he'd hit fresh piping, clean and rust-free, that resisted the persuasions of his cog-hammer. Using the filth that soaked his clothing and smeared his body, he spread himself agonisingly across the diameter of the pipe, knees pushing against one side of the smooth conduit, shoulder blades against the other – his body writhing and shimmying up in between. It was the final, punishing ordeal of their nightmare negotiation of the carrier's bilge. With limbs aflame with exertion and only twelve dots of light for a target, the Redemption Corps pushed relentlessly up the pipe and back to the sanity of deck-level.

IV

As HIS FILTHY forehead touched the clean metal of what turned out to be a drain grating, Mortensen allowed himself a moment of silent relief. Looking up through the holes that had offered him those hopeful pinpricks of light, he could make out a barracks shower room. He smiled. Rask and Sass had been dead on target. His limited field of vision revealed no occupants and this was supported by the fact that the drain, which usually collected the overflow, wasn't raining water down on them.

Bracing the cog-hammer's claw against the grate it took little force to pluck off. Sliding it to one side, Mortensen clambered out of the drain, slipping and sliding momentarily on the clean shower-room floor. Taking a couple of low steps forward he scanned the length of the communal wash-room while the remainder of his team extricated themselves and drank deep the fresh air of the barracks.

Mortensen took them in, catching a glimpse of himself in a battered mirror. They all looked like hell. Their blood stripes and jackets were black and sodden and their flesh was painted with filth, unintentionally camouflaged, with only the whites of their eyes peering out from their soiled skin. Most of them, including Mortensen, still retained their berets, which seemed quaintly ridiculous bearing in mind what they had just been through. Vedette even fell to straightening hers as soon as she was out of the conduit and cleaning down the soles of her boots. Mortensen did likewise: they didn't want to betray their presence with filthy footprints.

Extracting the length of a fat silencer from his holster pouch Mortensen screwed the barrel into the muzzle of his grubby autopistol. The storm-troopers followed suit with a sense of purpose at odds with their fatigue and taking a few more lungfuls of sweet air, the squad stalked their way through the showers and out through the locker room.

Holding the autopistols in both hands for greater control and accuracy the troopers padded through between lockers and benches, scanning the walkways for Guardsmen at rest or lying in ambush. In fact, Rask couldn't have picked a better entry point: what kind of Guardsman would be pre-occupying himself with personal hygiene during a full-scale military revolt?

Out on the main corridor, the column of storm-troopers hugged the walls, making swift but deliberate progress into the starboard barracks. The ghostly echoes of distant firefights haunted the passageways and several times the soldiers had to throw themselves to the walls as Sarakota, on point, gave the signal. The sniper had exceptional hearing, giving the squad ample time to conceal themselves as ragged groups of Volscians ran across junctions, whooping like madmen and firing celebratory las-bolts off around them.

Mortensen had no intention of engaging such groups: he was not here for a messy firefight. That meant wasting rounds and killing fellow Guardsmen – an eventuality he would rather avoid until it became unavoidable. Right now he needed information more than bodies and the officers' mess afforded him opportunity to gather just that.

The bulkhead was open and he could hear voices inside. The wall-hailer was a discordant play of insanity, Guardsmen yelling and shooting their elation back and forth across the unlocked deck-channel, with little in the way of tactical information available. The actual voices inside were harsh, yet quieter, and punctuated with occasional bouts of lazy laughter.

Mortensen shot Sarakota a look; the sniper shot him back five fingers, then eight. He could count no more than five individual speakers, but it was hard to tell how many more might be present but silent. Holding his hand above one shoulder, Mortensen began to count his storm-troopers down.

There were in fact eight, but as the troopers rushed the door, Mortensen found three of them splayed out across several mess tables, blind drunk. The silencers gaped their way in through the door, the troopers entering with smooth determination: Sarakota peeling left and Vedette right.

A master sergeant – from his stripes and the staples across one mangled eye – was sitting amongst the officers' benches, legs splayed, recounting some past heroism to a gathered audience of hivers, several of whom were clutching Volscian-pattern lasrifles.

The soldiers were typical Shadow Brigade, with sloppy dress and scuffed boots, their arms and faces decorated with tattoos and studs denoting gang membership and House allegiance. They were born for urban warfare and had a natural affinity for merciless killing, but their mindset was all messed up with the complexities of hive loyalty and this didn't sit well with the Imperial Guard's mandate of a singular devotion to the God-Emperor and his representatives. Mortensen knew the patterns and the problems, hailing from a hive-world himself. It was exactly this, particularly the Volscian wearing of blood honour sashes, ornamentals and bandanas that Commissar Fosco had unwisely got into the minute he'd arrived on board *Deliverance*.

The grizzled sergeant wore such drapery over his flak jacket and had his weapon stretched across the back of his shoulders, with his arms hung over the extended stock and barrel, as the Guardsmen passed several liberated decanters of amasec around.

As Conklin held the door, the rest of the stormtroopers swept in, gabbling orders and savage warnings to the group. None of the inebriated Volscians actually got the stocks of their rifles off the deck floor and it was only the Shadow Brigade sergeant – his crooked face melting from mirth to fury – who actually made any attempt to bring his weapon to bear.

The room slowed to a stand-off: Vedette, Pryce and Gorskii thrusting their barrels into the faces of the

armed Guardsmen and Sass and Minghella securing
the seemingly unconscious men on the tables.
Sarakota had the master sergeant in his sights with
Mortensen standing defiantly at the centre of the intru-
sion, his autopistol now lowered.

As the barking subsided and the sergeant glared,
Mortensen gave him the grim ultimatum of an uncompromising stare returned and deathly words.

'I have no quarrel with you, brother,' he addressed
the hiver sergeant, 'but if you do not immediately surrender your weapon, this next breath will be your last.
Think about it.'

The sergeant's chest, the focus of Sarakota's closing
muzzle, momentarily froze. A ripple of defiance
crossed the Volscian's repulsive features, before softening, followed by the casual tossing of his lasgun onto
the table. With a slovenly grin he leaned back, placing
his hands behind his head. The remaining weapons
clattered to the deck as the Guardsmen replicated the
surrender.

Mortensen nodded at Conklin who buried the grip
of his weapon in the wall-hailer, smashing the vox to
uselessness. In turn the corpsmen swept forward,
scooping up the lasrifles, as Mortensen advanced, placing his own weapon on a nearby mess table.

'Who's in charge here?' he asked the rebel Guardsmen.

'I am,' the sergeant leered.

Mortensen spun, cog-hammer suddenly in his
hand, and swinging for the sergeant's face, tearing the
smirk from it with the tool's cruel claw. Blood sprayed
the wall behind as the sergeant was torn from his
chair and vaulted a nearby mess table, his jaw hanging
off.

The sergeant had been reaching for the hilt of a hive dirk, slipped into the leg of his boot. It seemed that the sergeant had no intention of being taken: seeing the Redemption Corps as the enforcers of Commissar Fosco's justice. That alone made Mortensen uncomfortable – but he had a job to do. Grabbing the hive dirk Mortensen skipped up a bench and onto the table. Leaping down with purpose he landed amongst the rapidly sobering Guardsmen, snatching the nearest up by his short hair and wrestling him to the wall. Mortensen tossed Minghella his hammer before restraining the young Volscian's forehead with one grimy hand. Mortensen slipped the narrow blade of the sergeant's knife into the Guardsman's mouth which was already open and full of panicked conciliations. Holding the knife in one white-knuckled fist Mortensen stretched the corner of the Volscian's mouth as far as it would go without splitting.

'Who's in charge?' Mortensen put to him dangerously.

The Guardsman's answer was immediate, if hampered by the presence of a blade in his mouth: 'You are!' This was echoed by others in the gathering. Pulling the blade from his mouth Mortensen positioned its tip carefully under the Guardsman's chin, pinning his head to the wall. With his free hand he began the disconcerting process of unbuckling the belt holding up the Volscian's fatigues. The wide-eyed Guardsman choked back a protestation as Mortensen's own eyes flared.

'I have questions. You have answers. If you don't give me the exact answers I need, like your sergeant, you will not leave this room in one piece. Do we understand each other, Guardsman?'

The Shadow Brigade soldier nodded. Mortensen mirrored the gesture.

'Where are they holding Commissar Fosco?'

The truth just fell out of him like vomit, sudden and involuntary.

It seemed that the insurgent Volscians had set up their base of mutinous operations around the Regimental Armoury, the Shooting Range and Tactical Starboard.

Mortensen wasn't finished. With one hand he unthreaded the Guardsman's belt and slapped it across one shoulder: 'And who are "they"?'

The hiver looked slightly surprised that the major didn't already know but with a little knifepoint insistence he gushed forth as he did before, memory kicking in.

'Guardsman Quoitz, Guardsman Remerez, Guardsman First Class Hecklenbrock...'

Mortensen gave a nasty chuckle and tapped the tip of his blade on the Guardsman's lips to shut him up.

'No, no, no. Guardsman: who do I have to kill to get some peace and quiet around here?'

The Guardsman stammered: 'You mean, who's in charge?'

Mortensen gave a slow nod.

The Volscian caught himself: 'You are, sir!'

Several of the storm-troopers couldn't resist a smile. Mortensen took in the room.

'New entry technique,' the major jested. 'Kick in the door and ask the Volscians a couple of difficult questions.'

'Or not so difficult,' Sass added.

'Targets!' Conklin hissed.

The storm-troopers fell into a coordinated two-step sequence of securing their prisoners and covering the door. Sass and Minghella went down behind the mess tables, whilst Gorskii and Pryce put their detainees' heads on the deck. Sarakota and Vedette swept forward, criss-crossing the mess doorway with their newly claimed lasrifles: all out of sight.

Conklin opened the door wider – not wanting the squad to be trapped inside – and lay in wait behind, crouched with autopistol ready to kneecap the first unfortunate to enter the room.

Mortensen moved his knife deftly under the Guardsman's throat and sidled the prisoner along the wall – the fatigues falling down around the Volscian's ankles – and aimed his own pistol parallel along the wall.

Heavy bootfalls filled the corridor, with some gasps and calls. A small crowd of Guardsmen thundered up the passage, met by several others coming the other way. It was hard to make out amongst the running and yelling, but someone definitely shouted 'Found 'em!'

The storm-troopers tensed, leaning into the doorway, fingers settled firmly over triggers.

'In the galley and deep storage – got some of 'em trapped…'

The throng hammered off down the corridor, mindlessly drawn to the site of the new information like a pack of dogs on a scent trail. Mortensen centred back in on his prisoner.

'Okay, we are running out of time here, so I'm going to make it easy for you. I'm going to give you names, you nod. Captain Eckhardt?'

A hesitant nod; like a considered betrayal.

'Lieutenant Shanks?'

A definite nod: nobody liked Shanks.

'Isidore?'

'Lieutenant Isidore is dead,' the Guardsman informed them.

Mortensen raised an eyebrow: dissension in the ranks, that was good.

'Who else?' he insisted. Eckhardt and Shanks couldn't possibly have mobilised this number of men alone.

'Sergeant Mako.'

Mortensen pursed his lips. He'd heard of Mako: a real bruiser and lower decks troublemaker, with plenty of pull through his gang affiliations to bring Isidore's men over to Eckhardt. He'd probably killed Isidore himself.

Mortensen threw a glance at Conklin, who checked the corridor. The major rotated one finger and the storm-troopers began their retreat, slipping one by one, weapon last, out of the officers' mess the way they had entered. Mortensen backed away from the Guardsman, allowing the Volscian a moment to collect himself. His hands moved up to his face, to check it was still there, but all he found were a few nicks where the major's blade had caught him. Then he turned his eyes down on his fallen fatigues and his regimental-issue underwear. No sashes or adornments there.

As Mortensen's filth-encrusted face left the room he gave a grin, the whites of his teeth bright against the background of his grimy features.

'See you at the court martial.'

The major grunted. A court martial if they were lucky: most would be executed for their insubordination. As the bulkhead closed Mortensen found himself back out on the main corridor. He span the bulkhead pressure wheel and handed the unfortunate

Guardsman's belt to Conklin: 'Tie it off.' The sergeant managed a wicked grin of his own before going to work on the wheel.

To Sass the major ordered, 'Get us to the Armoury.' He doubted the corpsman had ever been down there but he knew he could rely on the adjutant's almost photographic memory for such seemingly useless information as the deckplans for their own vessel.

'The most direct route, or the long way round?'

'And the long way entails?'

'Maintenance ducts and vents.'

Mortensen shook his head. The long way would undoubtedly be the stealthiest, but time was lives and if the men holding the galley were anything to go by, there was little time left. Besides, Mortensen had had enough of crawlspaces for today and he told Sass as much.

The corpsman moved several places up the silently advancing column of storm-troopers and tapped Vedette – their current pointman – on the right shoulder, prompting her to peel off right at the next junction.

As it turned out, Mortensen's decision had been a mistake and the storm-troopers' progress was slow regardless, running into group after group of gathered Shadow Brigade Guardsmen, forcing them to divert or hold fast in empty companionways and bunk-ups. The situation was rapidly tearing itself apart, with rebel soldiers now at each others' throats as well as those of the loyalists. Beatings were rife and some sections of the barracks were shot up and in a state of ruin. Dormitory Section 6 was actually aflame, with someone still having the presence of mind to have sealed it off. Either way, Mortensen and his men were forced to go around, moving like soundless chess pieces, from strategic formation to formation, corner to corner, corridor to corridor.

Vedette found a bruised and beaten Guardsman, sitting on his backside in the middle of the passage, cradling a laspistol. He looked up but barely knew where he was and the Mordian gave him a taste of her boot to seal the deal.

Rounding a hazy apex, the corporal caught a bolt in the thigh, prompting the squad to drop and assume fire positions. Mortensen hauled her back, handing her over to Minghella and allowing Sarakota to push forward. The sniper turned his head, tuning into the shots and footfalls. Satisfied he reported that the pattern of fire was random and not actually aimed at them: Vedette had just got unlucky. The medic hastily patched up the leg, field-style, with the Mordian gnashing her teeth through his inspection and rapid dressing of the wound – angry at herself more than at Minghella's attentions.

In order to avoid the savage slaughter party taking place down the shot- and smoke-choked passageway Mortensen ordered a brief diversion through the ventilation floorspace. Sass assured them that the Armoury was a few minutes scramble from their present position, which was small enough to justify one more claustrophobic experience, and the major went to work tearing up a nearby floor panel with his all-purpose cog-hammer.

While this was happening a Shadow Brigade officer ran up out of the murk at them from a different corridor. He was as surprised to see Pryce, as the storm-trooper was to see him: he'd been covering the angle and the Volscian was bare-foot, unarmed and had made little in the way of sound. He skidded to a stop on the grille floor, allowing the reality of the moment to sink in before about-facing and sprinting back up the corridor. The devout Pryce brought up his lasrifle to down the officer but Mortensen shouldered the lasgun aside, intent on conserving their ammunition. Finding one further use for the hammer he tossed it handle over head at the fleeing uniform. The heavy cog struck the Volscian down as it thumped into the back of his neck with sickening impact. The officer lurched, bouncing off the wall before tripping, rolling and coming to a full stop in an untidy heap by the other wall.

Pushing Gorskii into the hole to rotate point, Mortensen shoved Pryce to the rear.

'Assist Vedette,' he barked at the trooper: the crawl wasn't going to be kind to the Mordian's bound leg, 'and watch our backs.'

Dropping in one at a time and disappearing into the floor, Pryce pulled the panel back over behind them. It wasn't the rear they had to worry about, however. A few corners' shuffle later, Sass directing the Valhallan through the maze of ducts, Gorskii had her own heart-pounder to contend with. Still, silent and lying in wait down one of the twilight sub-ducts, the glint of a galley knife came at her. Cutting her to the bone, the blade slid across one cheek, adding yet another horrific scar to her collection, before she got to grips with the wild arm that had thrashed at her in the confined space of the duct. With her rifle slung and little use in the confines of the vent she had been leading with her autopistol. Desperate eyes came at her from the dark and before she knew it she was in a full-scale murderous tangle with a Volscian, who had one hand around the handle of the knife and the other tightly wrapped around the silencer of her side arm.

The scuffle continued with Sass abandoning his own weapon and trying to wrestle the knife out of the soldier's spasming grip. Conklin jammed the barrel of his lasgun forward over the adjutant's shoulder in an attempt to get a point-blank shot off, but Sass grunted something and pushed himself up on his knees, forcing the rifle up into the vent metal.

Another hot slice across the forearm had done it for Gorskii, however, who brutally butted the soldier full in the face, painting his cheeks with her own blood. The pistol went awry and the soft thud of a silenced round plucked at the soldier's forehead. He went suddenly limp, resting against the duct wall before sliding backwards to reveal a bullet hole and a gore-smear that followed his descent.

Sass pushed past the gushing Valhallan, who was now attempting to stifle the blood flow from her razored cheek. The adjutant checked the Guardsman for a pulse, but there was little hope: the auto round had blown the back of his head out.

'Friendly down,' Sass reported dourly, prompting Gorskii to peek from behind her bloodstained palms.

'What?' Conklin rumbled, already riled about his diverted shot.

Sass jerked a thumb down the sub-duct from which the Guardsman had attacked them.

'Galley. He's a loyalist. Why would a rebel be hiding down here with a kitchen knife?'

Sure enough the distant sound of sporadic las-fire and furious threats bounced up the sub-duct at them.

After a moment to allow the realisation to sink in Mortensen simply ordered: 'Push on.'

'Boss, don't you think we could–'

'Take point, sergeant.'

It would be easy to allow themselves to get pulled into the galley firefight, rushing to the aid of the pinned-down loyalists. Conklin clearly wanted to take it to them. Mortensen would give him his chance: where it mattered, however, down in the Tactical Bay.

With the master sergeant's boots behind it the screen at the end of the vent flew off and clattered to the Armoury floor. The insurrectionists were long gone – the sergeant had already checked – and so, as the Redemption Corps came to realise as they piled out of the duct, had the weaponry. Mortensen had hoped to bolster their own pitiful armoury, which as it stood amounted to little more than a few spent rifles and pistols packing a single clip of uniform requirement ammunition. The 1001st's stocks had been completely ransacked, by rebels or loyalists or in all likelihood, both. Captain Eckhardt had not left sentries because there was nothing left to guard.

With a little more space and room to breathe Minghella went to work on fixing Gorskii's apparently vampiric face and checking the dressing on Vedette's leg. Once again Conklin was on the door, closing it to a crack. He didn't want to draw attention but also wanted enough of a gap to spot someone approach.

'Well?' the major asked gruffly.

'Shooting Range; just out front here. Can't see anyone – but I can hear a bunch of shots, so someone's getting some practice in.'

'Bottom or top?'

'We're at the bottom of the range.'

'Sass?'

'The Armoury and the Range are part of the 1001st's Tactical Bay. If it's anything like ours, it'll be set up part gym, part CQ Tactical Training.'

Mortensen spat.

'I'll give you one guess where they'll be holed up.'

The storm-troopers didn't need guesses.

Eckhardt was no fool. He'd dragged his hostages to the one place on the ship that was designed to be difficult to breach. The Close Quarters Combat Tactical Training repro or CQ as the sergeants called it: essentially armaplas walls (to enable use of live ammunition without the danger of accidental injuries and fatalities), mocked up as a labyrinth of rooms and gauntlets for the training of close quarters combat and urban pacification techniques. The Volscian 1001st were essentially a hive-world garrison regiment and excelled at this kind of carnage. The Redemption Corps were not exactly amateurs either, but as every good Guardsman knew, it was easier to hold a strongpoint than to breach it: which was exactly the kind of logic Eckhardt was counting on.

Mortensen hovered by the door: 'Okay – this is it. I'm not going to dip it in honey for you. Sarakota, Conklin and I will take care of the sentries on the Shooting Range…'

Minghella piped up. He usually did get extra crabby just before the real butchery began and the bodies started piling up – something to do with his Departmento Medicae pledge, Mortensen supposed.

'How?'

'I have no idea,' the major told him honestly. 'But when we do, you are going to rush the CQ and start taking it room by room, section by section until we find and plug the bastards. Now is that a great plan, or what?'

'Well apart from being suicidal,' Sass mused.

'Suicidal is what we do, people. Perhaps we could concentrate on the positives.'

'They won't be expecting it,' Vedette offered, getting to her feet and hobbling for the door.

Mortensen nodded his agreement, the tone sinking back to the dour realisation that the bolts were about to start flying. 'Corporal Vedette, Sergeant Minghella: if Sergeant Conklin and I should fall, your orders are to complete the mission with whatever resources you have left at your disposal.'

Minghella glowered, an evil temper descending.

'Is that clear?' Mortensen turned and put to the Mordian.

'Crystal, sir.'

V

THE SHOOTING RANGE was a small nexus of activity.

Eckhardt had clearly left a group to hold the entrance to CQ, but inevitably the hours had dragged, the elation of their initial capture of Regimental Commissar Fosco had faded and the boredom had set in. At that point, the Shooting Range had beckoned.

The company captain's own aide, Lieutenant Phant, was currently in a contest with a silver-haired Volscian, the two of them packing lasrifles; dared and cajoled by eight other Guardsman, who were splitting their attentions between demonstrations of marksmanship, injecting combat stimms and cross-talk from the portable vox-hailer they were struggling to keep on frequency.

Two of the target clamps hanging in the arc-lanes were no longer holding plas-lite silhouettes of generic enemy forms. Instead the targets had been decorated

with the burned and blasted bodies of Piggot and
Nordhoff, two of Commissar Fosco's regimental aides.

The Volscians had been taking turns shooting at the
bodies. The contest had been running for hours and in
order to keep the bodies in one piece the hivers had
been forced to strap them into extra flak jackets and
reduce the power setting on their rifles.

As the seething bolts riddled the pair of corpses,
Phant screamed his victory, generating a whooping
response of mixed celebration and derision from his
crowd of spectators. The end of the firing range was
dark and unclear – hazy with smoke from the smouldering bodies. Only a fresh inspection of the mauled
targets would settle it and the old-timer depressed the
stud that operated the pulley system, dragging the
dead weight of the bodies with some strain, up to the
waiting contestants.

As the cadavers rocked to a halt, Phant once again
screeched his callous merriment. Several witnesses
closed in to examine the hammered flak, scorched
flesh and ruptured organs, pointing at patterns in the
marksmanship and arguing amongst themselves.

At that point Mortensen gave them a demonstration
of his own.

The major and Sergeant Conklin had made further
use of the vents to move between the Armoury and the
Gallery: going up through the roof section of one and
climbing down through the ceiling of another. During
the Volscian reload, as Phant and his competitor
exchanged taunts and mock aggression for the amusement of their gathered appreciators, the
storm-troopers had climbed down onto the back of
the target corpses at the far end of the shooting gallery.
Concealed during the resumed contest, the corpsmen

held on tight to the smouldering bodies as they had
been winched back down for inspection. Pulling
themselves up on the clamps, the two storm-troopers
aimed their silenced autopistols over the shoulders of
the shattered aides and blasted the marksmen off their
feet.

As the shock wore off, the other sentries began to
scramble for their own weapons. Conklin shot a third
through the heart and a fourth in the throat, but
Mortensen had to retreat behind Nordhoff's body
once again as the Guardsman hauling the portable vox
produced a laspistol quicker than he'd anticipated and
began simultaneously blasting and stumbling away.
His attentions were soon split between the two bodies,
causing Conklin to duck also, giving his rebel compatriots time to regroup and join in, slamming the
bodies with bolt after bolt.

A fresh pattern of fire suddenly lanced between the
two targets, originating from the darkened end of the
arc-lane. Sarakota had dropped down from a separate
ceiling vent further down the range and had been waiting in the shadows, moving slowly and close to the
floor; head down, listening intently to the clicks,
clunks and blasts of weapon use at the Volscian's end
of the shooting gallery. There he had waited for the
major to spring the trap.

Now that the real shooting had begun, the Redemption Corps' sniper was in his element. Of course,
Sarakota was much more used to the bipod bulk of his
anti-materiel Hellshot, but a Volscian lasrifle felt better
in his hands than a snub-nosed pistol.

The first two were clean headshots in close succession:
at that moment the hivers could barely comprehend that
they were under attack from a third shooter. Snapping to

automatic the sniper drummed a generous blast into the vox-operator, who was trying to juggle the demands of firing and tuning at the same time: the first blast into his equipment, the second into him.

Swinging around on the target clamp and with the weight of Nordhoff's body to counter-balance him, Mortensen's toecap found the face of a Guardsman who, under fire from Sarakota, had unwisely moved forward to take advantage of the cover. The force of the kick flung the Volscian to the floor and his weapon across the deck. Mortensen let go of the target clamp and landed amongst his enemies on the range. Using the silencer of his auto-pistol he scooped an advancing bayonet aside as a Guardsman ran at him with his las-rifle. Producing the Volscian's dirk from his belt he slashed him across the chest before dropping to the deck and slicing deep into the flesh behind his right knee. The Guardsman went down and Mortensen snatched up his bladed rifle.

A second burly Guardsman tried to rush him from behind but was plucked from his feet by Sarakota's unswerving aim. A third ran past, the piling bodies spooking his resolve, and was narrowly missed by a swipe from Mortensen's bayonet. Stepping out from behind Piggot, Conklin finished him with a fully automatic burst of silenced fire from his side arm.

The only moving Volscian left was the soldier Mortensen had floored and disarmed. The Guardsman got shakily to his feet, running this way and that, his eyes fleeting from Mortensen blocking his way to Conklin looming over him, pistol drawn. His death came from Sarakota, however, courtesy of three las-bolts that pinned him to the range wall, two in the chest and one between the eyes.

It had begun.

Storm-troopers streamed from the Armoury, tearing up towards the entrance of the CQ, Vedette hobbling close behind and barking orders. Sarakota sprinted up behind her, the pair meeting Mortensen and the master sergeant by the improvised doorway. As ordered by the Mordian, the first group had already filed in.

Closer to the CQ it became apparent to Mortensen that something was burning: the coarse stench of promethium hung in the air and a thin column of smoke was drifting out from somewhere near the centre of the armaplas maze, reaching for the bay ceiling.

'That doesn't look good,' Mortensen muttered, as much to himself, as he inserted a fresh power pack into his lasrifle. There was time for little more, however: his men had already encountered resistance.

The CQ was pure hell. From the sound of the gunfire the rebels numbered at least a platoon but it could easily be two.

Eckhardt held all the cards. He knew all the gauntlets and bolt-holes, all the dead-ends and bottlenecks, and although he couldn't have anticipated the Redemption Corps' attack – their stealth and sacrifices making for an assault that had more punch and initial momentum than it deserved – he soon bogged them down in the deadlock of room clearance, giving the captain's gathered Guardsmen time to explore their advantages.

Mortensen didn't have time for such luxuries as a stalemate. Without doubt Eckhardt would already have vox-recalled reinforcements from other areas of the Barracks to cut off the rear. The only way to end this was indeed as Rask had said, 'to cut the head from the angry serpent'. And that meant pushing the boundaries and forcing the deadlock.

Room after room fell to the storm-troopers as the combination of guts, skill and drillwork conquered weak hearts holding strongpoints. Volscians died in their scores as doorways and thoroughfares became channels of light, energy beams thrashing at each other across the closed confines of mock streets and buildings: real blood spilt on a make-believe battle-ground.

As the Redemption Corps stepped through the carnage they scooped up Shadow Brigade helmets and flak vests from the dead and dying; weapons too were hoarded as power packs ran dry, so that soon each trooper was carrying two other rifles slung as well as the lasgun held in their cramped hands.

The injuries started to mount up also, impairing mobility less than might be imagined, since progress was already unbearably slow; but Minghella couldn't get to anyone because without his additional fire-power the gauntlets wouldn't have been broken at all.

Conklin lost a couple of fingers to a gas-mask wearing, chainsword-wielding maniac who two seconds later was sitting in a mound of his own entrails: only then, after he tore off his mask did the storm-troopers realise that Sergeant Mako was dying among them. Moments later, Vedette took another bolt, in exactly the same thigh as the first, putting her arc of fire parallel to the floor for the following agonising minutes.

Pryce, miraculously, only lost an ear to a heavy bolter that the rebels had wheeled in to bolster a failing hold-point, when he should have lost his head. While the corpsman gave thanks to the Emperor, Sarakota took a stray round from the very same piece of equipment, as the thing minced up an armaplas wall he was using for cover. Gorskii and Mortensen both took shrapnel through their back armour, just to take the bolter, as the rebel Guardsmen tried to immobilise their lost field piece with grenades.

After turning the heavy weapon on the fleeing Volscians, allowing his messed-up squad time to establish a presence in the room, the major actually turned the remainder of the explosive ammunition on the adjoining wall. The ragged hole admitted his stumbling squad, with Minghella dragging both Vedette and Sarakota through. Luckily the heavy bolter round had passed clear through the sniper, but he was bleeding like a sack of wine and without kit or a spare pair of hands, the medic could do little to stop it. As a parting gift, fresh Guardsmen from the CQ hub, who were trying to push past their blasted, exiting colleagues, sent a volley of las-fire after the Redemption Corps, burying several bolts in Pryce's side and shoulder.

Even with his mathematical abilities, Sass could little know the layout of the 1001st's CQ. There were no schematics and even if there were, the Shadow Brigade sergeants probably changed it regularly. What there was, however, was a pattern. The Redemption Corps were so used to following the young Necromundan that they didn't question his instruction to follow. Even Mortensen, in the searing heat of the battle, fell into line. With the flak in his back beginning to make itself known to nerve-sensitive flesh underneath, the officer probed the wound with blunt digits, finding a glowing shard of metal and plucking it from his flesh. With a grimace he tossed it aside.

Heaving Sarakota to his feet, the major dragged him through a series of ungarrisoned doorways and corridors. Across a mock street the squad came to rest in a long, oblong room where they unburdened their wounded and checked their weapons. Sass disappeared briefly into an adjacent room before bolting back in.

'I think that the hub lies somewhere beyond that wall,' he put to the shot-up squad. Humour was in short supply. Somehow they managed it.

'You think?' Conklin challenged, spitting blood.

Mortensen checked out the wall at the end of the street, the one his adjutant was alluding to. His mind whirled. He had seconds to make a decision or he and his men were dead. Rebel Guardsmen were already working their way through Sass's evasion route.

He took in his corpsmen. If they had been an ordinary regimental squad they would have been declared combat ineffective rooms ago. Besides himself, only Minghella and Sass could walk unaided. He could only walk because he felt the white hot shards of shrapnel buried in his back – chewing up flesh and muscle with every movement – less so than Gorskii, who'd been hit in the same blast.

The wall was made up of several stories of armaplas, replete with sham windows. Windows had not been the Redemption Corps' friend up until this point. An ambush had nearly cut them in half through a street-side corridor close to the CQ entrance and a shot from an itchy-fingered sniper at a small opening three rooms in had smacked Sass's precious head into a wall. It would have taken it clean off if it hadn't have been for the face guard on the Volscian Interceptor helmet he'd donned from a fallen hiver.

Suddenly Gorskii let out a rasping gasp, before toppling forward from her position on the floor. Minghella rushed over from where he had been tending Pryce's wounds and rolled her over. She was sitting in a growing pool of blood, although it had been hard to tell with the amount of gore now splattered across the room. He rolled her back and put his ear to her mouth and chest.

'Rhen?' Vedette asked, gritting through the pain of her own injury.

'Shrapnel must have pierced the heart; perhaps a lung also,' he murmured and straddling her began to administer emergency measures.

Mortensen looked from the grim fury of Minghella to Conklin, burying his mangled fist under one arm, to Vedette, whose bright urgency cut through him. Looking back across the street he began to fancy that the shadows of renegade Volscians were gathering in the rooms they had passed through opposite.

Moments later Mortensen's fears were confirmed.

'They're coming, major,' Sarakota coughed, spitting bloody phlegm. Away from the overpowering sizzle of weaponry and screams he could hear the tap of tentative boots, as the rebels picked their way cautiously through the passages.

'Sergeant,' Mortensen announced, 'Vedette. I need every available Volscian in that street section: they're already assuming attack positions.'

Conklin clumsily grasped his bloodied weapon. 'Let them come and get it.'

'I want you to wait.'

'You want us to what?' Vedette hissed through clenched teeth.

'Let them pool; let them gather,' he told them.

'In numbers, they'll overrun us,' Conklin protested. 'Bottlenecking them is the only hope we've got: you know that.'

'No,' Sass reasoned. 'The only hope we've got is to get to Eckhardt.'

Mortensen threw his rifle to the adjutant and then, producing his autopistol, handed it to Conklin who stuffed it in his blood stripes bleakly: Mortensen was going to need both hands.

'Bring 'em down on you. It'll give me a chance. Then hold this room, as long as you can.'

Mortensen went to the doorway. It was the signal. The order had been given and the Redemption Corps began squirming through their own blood, setting up the angles and closing down the room with deadly, overlapping arcs of fire that covered all the doors and exits.

As for the major, he had his own fire arcs to contend with. Accelerating from the door in an explosive burst of speed he tried his best to offer the Guardsmen opposite little in the way of a target. They could little expect him to take such a bizarre action and were predictably slow to open fire, single shots sizzling the armaplas of the walls and floor about him.

He hit a top sprint just metres from the end of the street section, aiming for a corner where his speed would offer the best advantage. Leaping, he hit the opposite wall with the sole of one boot, bounding across the corner to the adjoining wall, where the toe of his other boot carried him a further few metres back across. Throwing up outstretched palms like grapnels, his fingertips found the fake, glassless windowsill.

Bolder Guardsmen, urged on by the lack of resistance being offered by the storm-troopers, were now heading out onto the open street section and cracking off shots at the fast-moving Mortensen. Heaving himself up to the opening, the major crawled through. Getting down the relatively serene far side of the wall was much simpler and just required letting go.

The fall was untidy and involved bouncing off the wall halfway down and striking out his left leg for a landing. Although he couldn't feel much of it, something gave in the leg upon impact and Mortensen found that his descent wasn't quite over, toppling forward and crashing into the floor.

Instinct made him grab the leg; he couldn't extend it but he couldn't tell whether it was broken or just badly sprained. There was little time for such trivialities, however, as a second later he was set upon: a rifle butt smashing his face, while a series of boots and blows rained down on his head and back. This went on for an indeterminable amount of time: whenever he brought up his face, to get a look at his attackers or mount an attack of his own, he was met with another savage staccato of fists and rifle stocks. At last the brutal assault came to an end and Mortensen could open his eyes. One still burned white, while the other could detect a slender shadow that passed across the ground in front of him.

'Bring him to me,' came the clipped, cultured tone of an officer, and before he knew it, Mortensen had been dragged and deposited in a heap in the next room: the hub, he presumed.

Ultimately it was a disappointment, little more than an open space with some benches, a table, a vox and a handful of men. House banners decorated the walls and gang symbols – the Underbloods, by the look of the scrawl that had been dashed onto all available surfaces by hivers with more paint than talent.

Mortensen couldn't tell whether his plan to flood the street section with Volscians had been successful or whether the whole revolt had been managed from this squalid little showing. He reasoned that it didn't take much to lead men to lose themselves or to uncage the savagery in men's hearts, after their treatment at the hands of Commissar Fosco and his staff. The major spat his bloodied disgust, as well as a tooth or two, at the floor: he couldn't stand weakness in those around him and the men in the room just made him want to vomit. In many ways they deserved each other and if Mortensen could have been anywhere else than between them, then he would have been: even *Deliverance*'s rancid bilge.

Through the wall the havoc had begun. The Shadow Brigade must have been at the door because Mortensen could make out the distinctive thud of autopistols amongst the combined, ragged whoosh of lasrifles: there was no need for silencers now. The two hulking sentries that Eckhardt had retained, the two that had given the major such a welcome, now wrenched him up, thick, meaty fingers clenched under each arm.

Something burned in the corner of the room and the reek of roasted flesh clung to everything. The charred remains were curled up in a foetal mercy stance, shreds of black leather lining the smouldering scene. Mortensen could only guess this to be Cadet-Commissar Bohrz, Fosco's despicable apprentice. The good commissar himself was still alive, although beaten to blackness like a rotten fruit and tied up securely on one of the benches.

He was bare to the waist and the sparse hair stringing its way across his shiny, bald pate was wet. Droplets of something Mortensen could only guess was promethium were rolling down the commissar's sour face and sagging belly. A barrel near the doorway confirmed this and supported the elbow of First Lieutenant Diezel Shanks.

Shanks gave Mortensen his dead-fish eyes. There had always been something dark and unhealthy living behind those eyes, something that had found expression in the murderous chaos of the revolt, but that would have surfaced, regardless. Eckhardt and Fosco might have driven each other to desperate measures but Shanks would have found a way to stray from the path sooner or later; in turn the extra poison he would have poured into his company captain's ears would have ensured it.

Eckhardt turned.

Obadiah Eckhardt was a spire-born: hive nobility through and through. He was young for his rank and impulsive – as the revolt had proved – but he was a charismatic leader, tall and almost romantic in his looks and language: the antithesis of Mortensen himself.

Despite the unruly demeanour of his mutinous troops, he was still dressed immaculately, his uniform and cap crisp, a rich cloak hanging from his wide shoulders and a glorious sabre hanging at his side. He still displayed the sashes, trinkets and tattoos of his fellow Volscians, but they were worn with moderation and taste. He even managed a good-natured smile.

'Major Mortensen: we missed you at your quarters,' Eckhardt began contritely. 'I'm sorry about that. We might have saved you the trip.'

'No trouble,' Mortensen rumbled back.

'Knew you'd throw your lot in with this bastard and his minions,' Eckhardt censured.

Fosco suddenly roared to life, spitting forth insults and accusations with swollen lips and a jaw that barely worked. Eckhardt closed on the commissar, bawling back his own effete abuse, the rabid exchange – without doubt one of many over the passing hours – ending with a savage back-handed slap from the captain that span the commissar's body off the bench and onto the floor.

Getting a grip on himself, Eckhardt turned back on Mortensen. 'Men like you can't think for themselves. You take solace in your orders and your duty when all the while, all you amount to is a tyrant's plaything. That's why I sent my people down there – to slit your damned throats.'

'Still breathing over here,' Mortensen goaded the officer.

A skull-cracking blow to the back of the head put Mortensen back on his knees, followed by a rhythmic pummelling that fell on him from above. As Eckhardt's bully boys administered their brutal reprimand, Fosco erupted again, prompting Shanks to step forward and bury his boots in the commissar's kidneys.

'Enough!' the captain screamed. Eckhardt was shaking, his eyes tensing and narrowing with each breath.

'You're a mindless animal, Mortensen: those cowards holed up on the bridge have sent you to make their representations...'

Mortensen's back began to throb with crude laughter. Eckhardt's face screwed up further: a mask of hatred and righteous fury.

'You think this humorous, freak?'

'Save it!' Mortensen growled through his fading mirth. 'I'm not here to negotiate with you, Eckhardt. I'm here to kill you; and as for orders and duty, I can assure you that the pleasure will be all my own.'

The hulking hiver sentries went to fall on him again with the stocks of their rifles but Eckhardt belayed them with a single, strained utterance. The captain's eyes glowed bright with odium and insanity and then suddenly there was calm and he returned to his charming self.

'Well, look at you. You do look a state. Where you've been, I can't quite imagine. Lieutenant, let's make the major a little more presentable shall we?'

Shanks extracted a pail that had been bobbing around the inside of the barrel and filled it with promethium. Stepping forward he doused Mortensen with the harsh liquid – the same treatment that Fosco had presumably received and definitely the same as Cadet Bohrz.

'Refreshing,' Mortensen informed them as the sentries lowered their weapons and took a step back. Usually the rebels would be treated to thrashing and screaming, as the chemical torment washed over burns, cuts and wounds. The major simply blinked determination back at them.

'Well, we shall be refreshing something for you, major,' Eckhardt promised darkly. 'Your memory, I hope. Gomorrah, wasn't it? Burned from top to toe, they say. They say you can't feel a thing. Let's put that to the test, shall we, freak? Shanks. Flare.'

As the first lieutenant handed Eckhardt the tube with relish, Mortensen slipped the Volscian hive dirk from his boot. Perhaps it was the genuine fear – if Mortensen fancied he felt such a thing – of burning alive (again), or the simple fact that it was probably his last opportunity to act, but the blade was out and it was hungry.

Thrusting the dirk upwards, one hand on the hilt, the other behind its small pommel, Mortensen sank the blade up into the first sentry's throat. He was preparing for the light show and had held his rifle slack by his side. The second bully boy brought up his weapon, but desperation had made the major faster, swinging the blade back around in a wide, forceful arc that sliced across the other Volscian's throat.

The moment of panic that the sentry had felt the moment before he died spread and both Eckhardt and Shanks were galvanised into action. The captain tried to fire off the flare but Mortensen was already moving, shouldering the toppling sentry into the noble and sending the pyrotechnic harmlessly at the bay ceiling.

Shanks had gone for his weapon – a plasma pistol. Stumbling over the prone form of the commissar, Mortensen fiercely sunk his fingers into the shorter man's neck and smashed his head into the wall. Grasping him by the back of his flak vest, and almost losing his knife, Mortensen toppled the senseless lieutenant head first into the barrel of promethium. He would have kicked and flailed, if it weren't for the fact that he was already unconscious and so therefore had no other choice but to drown.

The storm-trooper suddenly felt the tug of his back flesh tearing. He couldn't feel the pain, only the momentum of Eckhardt's sabre as it effortlessly sliced through the flak plate and into his skin.

Spinning forward Mortensen rolled along the wall, making a failed attempt to scoop up Shanks's plasma pistol. Eckhardt's spire blade was there also, sparking off the outside of the barrel and then carving up the wall as Mortensen twirled aside in an ugly pirouette. The Volscian captain's form was excellent, not that Mortensen knew much about such things; he was more of the school of, the blade goes in and the guts come out, swordplay. Bringing up his own pitiful blade he managed to turn aside several elegant flourishes before the captain danced the sabre across both his forearm and forehead.

Blood cascaded down over his good eye and for a moment the major was temporarily blinded, falling back into the corner and trampling the funeral pyre that was Cadet Bohrz's remains. A venomous slash across the shoulder convinced Mortensen that he couldn't defend against a blade he could not see and so dropping his own, he lurched forward, feeling for the captain's throat with eager digits.

The two soldiers fell back rolling, with the heavier Mortensen pinning Eckhardt to the ground. The sabre was too long to slip inside their homicidal embrace and so amongst the grunts and gasps, all Eckhardt could do was crack the storm-trooper in the side of the shaven head with his elaborate guard. Mortensen wasn't letting go, however. Now that he had his filthy palms around the rogue captain's throat he proceeded with pneumatic force and patience to crush the life out of the Volscian.

All but blind, Mortensen saw little of the Shadow Brigade officer's last moments: the bulging whites of his eyes and dread gape of his mouth as he felt it all, including his life, slip away. The major heard it though, in the gargle and crack of the officer's wind-pipe and the clatter of his fine sword, as it tumbled from his impoverished grip. Mission complete.

The next thing that Mortensen heard was the swollen rasp of Regimental Commissar Fosco across the floor at him: 'Well, get over here, you fool, and help me up.'

Wiping the blood from his eyes Mortensen ignored the commissar and picked up Eckhardt's elegant blade. Cleaving the razor-sharp edge through what was left of the Volscian's shattered neck, Mortensen grabbed the captain's head and hobbled across the room with it.

'Bloody savages, the lot of you,' Fosco bleated at the apparent mutilation. 'Now bring that blade over here.'

Mortensen dropped the sword and fell into a crouch, like a discus thrower, and tossed Eckhardt's horror-stricken head across the armaplas wall and down into the street section on the other side. Hovering for a moment, the major tuned into the sound of rapidly dissipating las-fire and the gathering murmuring of rebel forces, coming to terms with the grotesque reality that they were leaderless.

Snatching the vox-hailer from the set on the table Mortensen adjusted the channel. It took him a moment to raise Rask on the bridge, while Fosco watched him with rising bile, no doubt planning in detail the long reach of his vengeance on board *Deliverance* and its implementation as soon as he was free. And perhaps that was one of the reasons Mortensen hadn't freed him.

The major kept it brief on the vox: 'It's done: send in naval security and the damned medics.' Rask went to say something, probably congratulatory, but Mortensen cut him off.

Grabbing Fosco by his binds, Mortensen hauled him up and slapped him back down on the bench before collapsing beside the commissar. Leaning forward he put his head between his knees, the sickening tang of adrenaline subsiding, and slowly bled.

'Look here, major,' Fosco put to him, the imperious edge that was a constant feature of his voice barely dulled by his circumstances. 'There is much work to be done. The Emperor's justice must once again prevail on this ship. Common fighting men need to know their place and you and I are going to escort them there. Now a strong stomach will be needed and consequence employed, but most where it is most needed. Do you follow me, sir?'

Mortensen let the commissar's words hang before mumbling: 'You are talking about firing squads. Executions.'

'Well of course I'm talking about bloody firing squads, you idiot – have you smacked your head or something? The 1001st will be purged of its backward hive-world ways and seditious allegiances: there is only one true loyalty and that is to the Emperor himself. In punishing the many, we may still save the souls of the few: for the good of the Guard. Now, are you with me?'

The commissar held up his bound wrists in expectation. Mortensen's head swam with the Fosco's terrible words, the words of Eckhardt and Rask and his own.

It was done before his heart settled upon it, but settled upon the dark course of action it had. His elbow shot up, hammering Fosco's ridiculous head full force and snapping it backwards. The commissar's neck whipped back, his head settling back on his body. Gore rolled from the ragged cavity in the centre of Fosco's face. His nose was now situated somewhere inside his brain, along with several shards of skull. Mortensen sat there for a moment as the commissar tried to speak.

'For the good of the Guard,' Mortensen told him, getting to his feet and limping away, leaving Regimental Commissar Fosco to blink his haemorrhaging life away.

'Not him. Have him taken to whatever passes for an infirmary in this roach nest...'

'This isn't a simple procedure. I don't have the staff or the equipment for this. You're asking me to put this patient through a complex and unnecessary operation that will undoubtedly cause him further suffering. To attempt such an aggressive course of treatment at this late stage will almost certainly kill him. When they're this far gone, the warden usually has me·make them comfortable and let them go...'

'The canoness may still have some use for him. The choice is simple, sawbones. Fix him or share his fate...'

'No, not that one you idiot. I need something with a haemostatic clamp, something that I can diffraction fuse to the bone. Damn it! He's bleeding out again.'

'He wants to live: I'll give him that. Stats – nominal to profile. He's going to need another transfusion, though. Gets worse; guess who his rhesus match is? Luthar-Zeke Troggs, the Malfunction Junktion Maniac. Couldn't have been me or you or one of the guards? No, our boy's only match is a solitary confinement crazy with over two hundred and twenty-five confirmed kills. Well, let's get this over with. He needs plasma. Grab the ether gas-gun and a transfusion kit. Let's hope Troggs is in the giving vein…'

Krieg was awake. It hit him all at once: the rush of sensation. The nerve-shredding screams; the tang of saniseptic; light – clinical and harsh. His body felt at once leaden and feather light and he lay there for a moment, taking deep lungfuls of air with a chest he could barely feel.

Once more the silence was smashed by a fresh eruption of agony from the next gurney. Allowing his head to roll to one side, Krieg could make out the dull tiles and outdated medical equipment of a small sickbay. Behind a flapping drape a shadow puppet theatre played out a gruesome scene, with two shapes struggling with a third, projectile blood spurts slapping against the thin plastic and trickling down the inside of the curtain.

'Emperor's wounds! Hold him down,' shot a voice Krieg faintly recognised, though he struggled to place it with his drug-addled brain. 'You're as bunglefingered as you are witless.' More miserable roars followed. Something finally gave as an upsurge in the shrieking led to one of the shadows stumbling at the curtain. 'Would you look at that?'

A gore-smeared glove slipped out of the drape and deposited a wickedly serrated piece of shrapnel in a surgical basin on a nearby trolley. As the curtain opened, Krieg caught a brief glimpse of the trio beyond. The glove belonged to a lofty surgeon-type, all aquiline nose and tombstone teeth, dressed in spattered apron and thick goggles. The patient was still quivering with pain, his ribcage *heaving and the back of his blood-matted head coming to rest in the crackling folds of a plastic pillow. Equally, his face was a pulpy mess and partially obscured by the shoulders of a close-shaved orderly, but the uniform was Navy, so Krieg reasoned that it must be one of the gunners or air crew.*

This got Krieg wondering what his own face looked like. He tried to reach for a speculum on the gurney cabinet but found that his right arm was heavily bandaged and trussed to his chest, his fingers resting on his left shoulder. Struggling over onto his side he managed to grasp the mirror with his other hand and inspected the damage. A child's painting was the first thought that came to mind: a child working with only red, black and blue on its palette. Everything seemed to be working and in its place, but Krieg didn't feel like he was looking at his own features. One notable addition was a ragged scar, bifurcating its way across his cheek, lips and chin. The stitches were neat and tight and gave the impression of a zipper running across his face.

An explosion of expletives from the surgeon denoted another blunder by the orderly and deterioration in the status of the patient. There was a clink as another barbed piece of frag was deposited in the dish.

Casting bloodied eyes around the room Krieg found his cap and leather greatcoat hanging on a peg by the infirmary door, the webbing shredded and a rent where the right arm used to be. The door itself was a security bulkhead with a pedal and a scratched plas porthole. Through the porthole he spotted a stylised skull helmet he recognised immediately. The bleached bone of the helmet frontispiece bobbed in and out of view as its owner stood sentry outside the surgery, occasionally peering in through the shaded, reinforced lenses of the skull sockets.

Krieg flicked his eyes between the porthole and the frantic shadows behind the drape: now or never. He never thought to actually check his legs. They could have been broken or trussed up like his arm, but as he pulled aside the foil sheet he found to his delight that they were relatively unscathed. The gap-toothed surgeon had had little reason to molest them further and Krieg was still wearing his Commissariat braces, breeches and boots.

Pushing himself off the sheet he limped across the room, the creak of the gurney lost in the struggles behind the drape. Whilst the cocktail of tranquilisers coursing through his veins shielded him from the agony of such movement, he did feel sluggish and fragile and was acutely aware of the limitations his battered body was placing on his fanciful expectations. For a dangerous moment he almost tumbled, his frostbitten foot failing to take his full weight.

Krieg slid up against the wall and buried himself in the leather folds of his greatcoat. He didn't have to wait long. Within moments of the bone faceplate appearing at the porthole there was a hydraulic whoosh and the security bulkhead rolled open. An ebony-clad figure in Sororitas power armour rushed in, the skull helmet scouring the room, the business end of her ivory-inlaid bolter pointing squarely at Krieg's empty gurney.

With whirlwind impatience the sentry tore back the drape to reveal the orderly and surgeon up to their elbows in the Navy grunt's gore, giving Krieg just enough time to slip his free hand through the folds of his leather greatcoat and the battle-sister's bolt pistol out of her ermine-lined holster. The sister tore around to find herself staring down the barrel of her own weapon.

'Lose it,' Krieg commanded, his voice hoarse but full of determination. 'And the helm.'

The battle-sister's shoulders slackened slightly before tossing the bolter onto Krieg's gurney. Unclasping the seals, she pulled off the skull-faced helmet, allowing a platinum bob of hair to fall and shimmer back into place. Krieg nodded slowly. 'Thought it was you.'

'Do you really think this wise, cadet-commissar?' the young battle-sister asked, her full, dark lips forming a petulant pout.

'Me and my armour-piercing rounds will be the only ones asking questions here today,' Krieg returned with venom. 'Now, tell me where I can find that skeetmunger major.' He shook the pistol at her. 'We have some questions for him also.'

The sister flashed her eyes at him: 'I'm not at liberty to give you that information…' The bolt pistol crashed, sending an explosive bolt sailing past the battle-sister's ear.

'I mean it,' Krieg told her rawly.

Keeping the pistol on the sister, Krieg gave the surgeon his bloody eyes, before waggling the fingers of his trussed arm. 'You responsible for this?'

The horse-faced man nodded fearfully. 'C-C-Crayne. Incarcetorium Medical officer.'

'This is a prison?'

Crayne nodded.

'Well, Crayne, thank you. Now, I'm going to tell you what the sister and I here, already know. She'll die before she gives me that pathetic piece of information. You, on the other hand know what this can do,' Krieg said, moving the muzzle across to the medic. 'And worse, whatever it does do, you know that your bald friend here will be doing the procedure. So, without further delay, where is that malingering…'

'Solitary confinement,' Crayne blurted without hesitation, 'one of the oubliettes, I think: cell-block Gamma.'

The battle-sister's top lip curled. 'You do this and you'll never wear that cap again,' she assured him, nodding to the aquila-embossed commissar's cap hanging from the nearby hook.

Krieg ignored her and scanned the surgery thoughtfully.

'Will he make it?' the cadet-commissar asked, twitching the bolt pistol at the unfortunate Navy crewman.

Crayne shook his head slowly, clearly wondering whether or not it was the right thing to do. 'I can make him comfortable, but he won't be saved.'

'Do it, then.'

The gangling medical officer selected a tranquiliser from his utensil tray and stung the patient in the neck with the powerful sedative.

'Thank you Crayne. You'll be relieved to know that this very difficult day is almost over for you. Now, if you would be so good as to make everyone else in the room, including yourself, similarly comfortable,' Krieg entreated with the flash of a smile for the seething battle-sister, 'I'll be on my way.'

CHAPTER TWO
All Roads Lead to Terra

I

THEY CALLED IT Camp Carfax, after the slipway.

Sixty million square metres of open ground. On a densely populated world like Spetzghast, that kind of luxury was usually reserved for the mercantile houses, geno-industrialists and broker barons: Arch-Commissary Oszminog, Lord Ballantyne and his inbred hierocratical cronies. Carfax Drydock was a veritable oasis of breathing space, making your average hull-welding Spetzghastian dizzy with agoraphobic excess. Only the ancient *Wastrel*, a cyprid-encrusted haulage brig, sat suspended in dry-dock after a light collision with an asteroid.

Lieutenant Koulick Krieg had come to the Bethesda subsector capital three months ago, seconded to the retinue of the mysterious Inquisitor Aurek Herrenvolk. The 123rd Pontifical Strikes were a venerated company of Inquisitorial storm-troopers that had been provid-ing security for the Ergotia witch trials, conducted under his old master Brutus Schenker, but Herren-volk's need on Spetzghast was deemed greater and the contingent of Inquisitorial storm-troopers was hastily extracted, leaving the outranked Schenker with only his own operatives and some local high-plains muscle to conduct the trials.

Krieg had warmed to Schenker, who was hands-on in his duties and a respectably tough son of a bitch. He found his new lord and master to be a completely different animal. Whereas Schenker had a nose for corruption and a common sense, meat-grinder approach to combating the evils of heresy, Herren-volk preferred to work at a distance and rarely left the confines of his sleek Inquisitorial corvette, sta-tioned in high orbit around Spetzghast. Barrack gossip put this down to some horrific disfigurement or debilitation earned during his famous service in the Hellicon Mitigations. Krieg thought it more likely that Herrenvolk was a psyker who worked pri-marily through his recruits and operatives, as some inquisitors did – never having to get their own hands dirty. Although the lieutenant had never seen the esoteric inquisitor, the Pontificals had shared the corvette with a whole host of Herrenvolk's staid henchmen, savants and of course, the Ecclesiarchical forces that shared responsibility for the investiga-tions on Spetzghast – the Sisters of the Immaculate Flame, although the Sororitas largely restricted them-selves to the cloister decks.

As Krieg emerged from the shadow of the *Wastrel*, he caught sight of the network of razor wire compounds, the temporary lookout posts and killing grounds established in between. Carfax had become a provi-sional Ordo Hereticus internment camp, holding upward of two thousand Spetzgastian heretics and unbelievers.

Reports of an epidemic of cult-related spree killings had originally brought Inquisitor Herrenvolk to the far-flung Bethesda subsector. The killings seemed random enough. Plenty of blood was spilt amongst both the urbanites who toiled in the surface granaries, depots and warehouses, seeking respite in the bars, scud-wrestling pits and obscura dens in between – and their betters, who made unimaginable wealth trading bulk wares in the bustling emporia and exchange sectors. The slaughter often involved firearms, but not exclusively and affected both sexes in terms of victim and perpetrator ratios. Local chasteners eliminated the possibility of a drug problem, but were so deep in bodies, anything was possible. Spetzghast had hardly ground to a halt, but there were enough delays and concern to warrant higher authorities becoming involved.

Aurek Herrenvolk was a natural choice for such an assignment: a notable case at the beginning of his career involved mass ritual slaughter by berserkers belonging to Death Cults on Gasaki V. Early investigation by the inquisitor's agents had turned up little in the way of similar Chaos practice on the giant trade world.

Like any populous Imperial planet, cult activity on Spetzghast was endemic. Amongst the more colourful factions Krieg had witnessed were the 'Mezzanine'; various Wyrm Cults; Dark Technology nuts and the disturbing Rebus Sectarians.

Amongst these oddities, the Carfax Inquisitorial internment camp mainly housed sect associates of Anatoly Spurrlok's 'Doomsday Brethren' – a popular

Redemptionist personality cult, based around geno-industrialist Spurrlok and his 'finding' of the God-Emperor in the Lazareth system. The 'Brethren' had followers in all areas of Spetzghastian society, their numbers concentrated around the cooperatives and the lower freight stacks, especially the organic vaults and tower silos.

Isolated Redemptionist cults were a common phenomenon throughout the Imperium, but Herrenvolk's apprentice, Interrogator Angelescu, had found a pattern in the killings and connected it to the actions of certain more outspoken members of the Brethren. Greater credence was lent to the young interrogator's theory when he was found desiccated in a dust silo where he had been buried with his bodyguards in six kilotonnes of cereal grain. Resources were re-allocated and the Brethren cited as a prime threat.

As Krieg and his men walked the axis between the dozens of fortified compounds that made up the camp, floods of cultists abandoned their prayers and polygamous huddles and washed up silently against the barbed fences. The object of their drop-jaw reverence and dread was Krieg's latest capture: the man himself, Anatoly Spurrlok. Prognosticator of planetary cataclysm and galactic doom, Spurrlok was the spiritual leader of the 'Brethren' on Spetzghast and a one man walking personality cult.

He wasn't walking now, however, as Krieg had him lashed to an adamantium crucifix in the style of the Imperial aquila – the motorised treads of which were cutting up the slipway decking. When the cultists looked at their hallowed leader they saw a demi-god: Krieg saw a monstrous, biologically enhanced creation. His skin was like parchment, stretched well beyond its fading elasticity to accommodate more muscle and sinew than the geno-industrialist's frame could bear. The vat-grown muscle added grotesque bulk to his torso and arms and was threaded through with bulbous, designer glands to drive the extra mass. If this wasn't enough, with his spindly head and legs, the proportions of Spurrlok's body were thrown out further by the presence of unnatural muscular configurations where they shouldn't be. The cultist's body was criss-crossed with bulbous tendons, nerve clusters and the brawn needed to drive them.

With his arms painfully stretched across the span of the Imperial eagle's gleaming wings, the false prophet's skull nestled inside a carved effigy of the eagle's noble head and beak. Here a void current was passed between Spurrlok's temples, making it impossible for the heretic to pass water unaided, let alone conceive of an escape plan.

'All yours,' the lieutenant told the members of the Frateris Militia at the gate of the Narthex. All bare flesh and leather, the brothers peered out of zipper slits in their conical hoods in dumb silence. Krieg hadn't quite got used to the zealots' unsettling stares – that was if a silent and all but featureless leather hood qualified as a stare. The Inquisitorial storm-trooper had little desire to see underneath the masks, however, fearing that the features beneath might be more unsettling still. As a mark of the upmost respect and servitude to St. Valeria the Younger, the Aphonac-Stack Probists had bitten off their own tongues in order that the impurity of faithless lies not pass their lips. The fanatical Probists – like the Sisters of the Immaculate Flame they served alongside – prized truth over all things.

An austere Sister of Battle carrying a skull face-plated helmet under one arm came forward and gave Krieg's crucified prisoner an impassive glance. Her platinum fringe sparkled in the poor illumination of the slipway. The 'Narthex' was the Adepta Sororitas's base of operations in the camp, where senior heretics were tried and tested and the most dangerous cultists imprisoned in stasis tubes. It was also where the sisters slept under the watchful eye of Immolators and Exorcists and kept common Guardsmen like Krieg awake at night with their martial beauty.

'Be careful,' the lieutenant called after the battle-sister as she joined the squad of Celestians escorting the itinerant crucifix inside. 'Don't underestimate him; my men found that out the hard way.' He gestured to several stretchers being lugged into the tent-sanatorium. A chastener and a couple of Krieg's storm-troopers had been foolish enough to come within grasping distance of Spurrlok's girder arms and had paid the price. Twisting and turning in ways Krieg hadn't imagined possible, the demagogue had splintered bones and torn limbs clean out of their sockets, before smashing the men into the rockcrete of the vault floor.

Unimpressed, the sister held him in a withering gaze: 'Would you like Canoness Santhonax's personal gratitude, lieutenant?'

Krieg couldn't help the shimmer of a wounded expression that crossed his boyish features. Perhaps it was this that momentarily softened the battle-sister's stony gaze, or the stifled amusement of Krieg's own men. 'The Emperor expects, lieutenant… the Emperor expects.' Then, she was gone.

Krieg shouldn't have been surprised: the Ecclesiarchy and Inquisition worked together across the galaxy, towards common goals and identical purpose. They were very much separate organisations, however, and had their own very particular ways of working towards those goals. Tension, all to often, was the unavoidable byproduct.

Krieg collected himself. 'Sergeant Odell!'

'Sir?' the hefty officer snapped to.

'Dismiss the chasteners; they should return to their precinct. Have our men turn in. They'll need their strength. We're going back into the vaults tomorrow at dawn. The sisters should have some further intelligence for us by then.'

'Very good, sir,' Odell boomed, masking grunts of exhausted disapproval from the storm-trooper unit. 'You heard the good lieutenant. Hit the showers. You smell like a swarm of pack-rats. Dead ones, at that...'

II

THE PAVILION WAS less glamorous than the Narthex, lacking as it did the Imperial Creed paraphernalia and consecrated instruments of interrogation-art. From here Herrenvolk's Inquisitorial storm-troopers ran their operations and monitored day-to-day activity in the Ordo Hereticus internment facility. Instead of ornately armoured Celestians, the command post of the 123rd Pontifical Strikes boasted a pair of staunch Inquisitorial storm-troopers who stood sentinel while Captain-Commandant Kowalski oversaw the smooth running of the camp. Krieg went limp inside as he realised that even they were missing this evening, suggesting that Kowalski was out on his rounds – walking the base camp perimeter and springing surprise inspections on the sentries. This was the captain-commandant all over: devoted to his paranoia.

Krieg had come to dread these reports. Upon operation completion he was invariably on the verge of
physical collapse, run as he was from one side of the
underburgh to the other in the pursuit of faithless
deviants and the oxygen of any heretical purge:
information. A capable officer, if a little narrow-
minded, Kowalski fancied himself better than a
heretic's turnkey, and had of late taken to pumping
the lieutenant laboriously for every mission detail:
Krieg's mounting successes and growing reputation a
constant threat to the camp commander's own
prospects.

With Interrogator Angelescu dead and Herrenvolk
apparently elsewhere, the Ecclesiarchy was now effec-
tively running the Ordo Hereticus purgation on
Spetzghast. Canoness Diamanta Santhonax was in
command of the coordinated Ordo/Ministorum purge
and for the past few weeks Kowalski and Krieg had
taken their orders from her.

Whereas Krieg's impressive accomplishments had
long reached the ears of the battle-sister, Kowalski was
still viewed as a cog turning inside a well-oiled
machine. So the captain-commandant routinely had
Krieg turn in gratuitously extensive mission details,
firstly to find ways in which the lieutenant's achieve-
ments could be turned to reflect favourably on his own
and secondly to exhaust the junior officer further and
limit his ability to accomplish his next unnecessarily
perilous mission.

'Sir?' Krieg called in through the Pavilion entrance.
He had to make sure. If he tried to get some sleep, the
commandant would only have him roused anyway. To
his surprise, he heard low voices and ventured slowly
through the nets. Krieg recognised one of the voices

immediately: the sibilant menace of Lieutenant Cyrus Rudd of Beta Platoon.

'That's groxcrap and you know it. Krieg? Captain, that gretch-fondler's nothing a fragging won't see to—'

'I said it's out of my hands. Do you get it? Came from the top. Orders, lieutenant.'

'Rutger's well overdue; and what about the hours I put in on that Mezzanine connection? Who's taking care of my interests, eh? Krieg walks around with a stick up his backside and gets thrown a bone? How's that work?'

'What do you want me to tell you, Rudd? It's a done deal. Krieg's a political animal. In that department he excels even me. Deal with it. Look at it this way: at least we get shut.'

'There's more than one way of getting shut,' Rudd assured him.

Pushing his fingers between the folds of camo-netting, Krieg created an opening in the Pavilion entrance. There stood Rudd, running that steel comb through his greasy white hair and feasting raw pink eyes on Krieg's entrance. Kowalski's sergeants stood nearby with tin mugs of steaming recaff, soaking up the lieutenant's words with appreciation. The captain-commandant himself wasn't even looking at Rudd, his head buried in a data-slate.

Krieg strode in under Rudd's baleful gaze and offered the captain his report tablet. The sergeants stiffened, but Kowalski feigned disinterest, taking the tablet and clicking his fingers at the sentinels. The sergeants drained their mugs and left, leaving the three officers alone. As he turned, Kowalski was obviously surprised to see Rudd still in the room.

'Dismissed, lieutenant.'

Rudd hovered long enough to register his displeasure before turning to leave. He clipped Krieg's shoulder as he did.

'Screw this,' he spat at the camo-netting and sauntered out of the Pavilion.

Krieg gave the captain a questioning glance, but Kowalski just shrugged it off, throwing the lieutenant's report tablet on a table buried in maps and schematics.

'Don't worry about him. His blood's up.'

'His blood always is,' Krieg returned.

'You apprehended Spurrlok?' Kowalski asked, attempting to change the subject.

'It's all in the report, sir.'

Kowalski nodded and poured himself a mug of recaf. He didn't offer Krieg one.

'Look, I won't beat around the proverbial: orders came through today – you're being transferred from my command.'

Krieg nodded, pride preventing him from pretending that he hadn't overheard the conversation by the door. Kowalski snorted softly. 'Canoness Santhonax has requested an officer for special operations. I recommended you.'

'I very much doubt that,' Krieg said coolly.

Kowalski let the insult wash over him. 'I'm giving your platoon to Jonze.'

'He's a good man.'

'They're all good men.'

'Some better than others,' Krieg assured him, clearly thinking of Rudd.

'Krieg, I'm going to level with you,' Kowalski spilled, unusually animated. 'I don't like you, I never have. Not exactly a team player – but you get the job done and that is your saving grace. That kind of nark, inflexible attitude has earned you enough enemies around here. A bit of advice: consider it a parting gift. Keep going that way and you're going to end up on the wrong end of your own bayonet.'

'Anything else, sir?'

Kowalski shook his head slowly. He snatched a slate off the side and tossed it to Krieg, who caught it awkwardly.

'Report to her ladyship at eight hundred hours. Whatever it is, it'll be a fool's errand, you know that, don't you?'

The lieutenant stared at the floor. 'Now get the hell out of my sight.'

Krieg saluted crisply and left the Pavilion for the last time.

III

THE WARDROOM OF the *Wastrel* was hardly an appropriate venue for a briefing, being grubby, cramped and decorated with wall-to-wall hive porn, but it was private and gave a sweeping view of the internment camp.

Krieg noticed little of this, finding, as he did, the silhouette of Canoness Santhonax framed in the starboard viewing port. He found himself lost in her numbing gaze, the radiance of her obsidian armour swallowing the room like a black hole. She stepped lightly towards him, drawing back a sable hood to reveal the network of pins inserted across her shaven skull. Remembering himself, Krieg dropped to his knee and bowed his head.

'Ma'am,' he acknowledged her obediently.

'Come here, where I can see you,' she said softly, motioning the lieutenant over to the viewport. Krieg did as he was bid.

'I've been looking over your record. Fairly impressive,' she told him, staring out across the internment camp. 'Galtinore Legionnaires, 123rd Pontificals, now ordo special operations: you're quite the rising star, lieutenant.'

'I am at your disposal, your ladyship,' Krieg avowed.

'Of course you are,' Santhonax concurred confidently. 'Dedication to duty and loyalty to the cause are qualities that will always find a place in service to the Ecclesiarchy – as I'm sure Lord Herrenvolk would agree.'

Krieg nodded. The Order of the Immaculate Flame was one of the Ecclesiarchy's many militant arms, but with the Sororitas and the Ordo Hereticus working so closely, it was difficult to tell where the authority of one organisation ended and the other began.

'If I may be so bold as to ask, ma'am,' Krieg ventured, 'have the heretics divulged further indications of their intentions?'

'Very much so: we learn more by the hour of the threat these arch-recusants pose to the system. Your capture of Spurrlok would seem a major blow to their operations. I had my sisters begin interrogations last night. Unfortunately we had to undo most of his magnificent work.'

Krieg nodded: he'd heard the screams, even from his bunk.

'Like his brethren, Spurrlok demonstrated the same resilience to our methods of inquiry. I had one of the inquisitor's savants, Warratah Chandra, oversee the psychic aspects of the interrogation – but he drew a blank. Literally. It is his belief that Spurrlok's heretics are joined in mind in such a way as to share their strength and resist us.'

Krieg wasn't surprised. The heretics he'd come into contact with had largely seemed cold and emotionless; that was apart from the minority that had gone haywire in public and embarked on a slaughter spree.

'All this despite Chandra failing to find an actual honest-to-Throne wyrd among them,' the canoness said with regret. 'Angelescu's hunch was correct. There is definitely a connection between the killings, the 'Doomsday Brethren' and Spurrlok's agricultural freight charters in the Burdock Worlds. Some dark force is at work here: whether it is the damned, the witch, the filthy xenos or them all, we will discover and destroy it. I am afraid, however, that in many respects your efforts in locating Anatoly Spurrlok were in vain. As ever in our line of work, he's not the key: he's just one link in a long chain attached to the lock that binds them.'

'We shall double our efforts,' Krieg vowed.

Santhonax gave him a lofty smile: the kind older women reserve for naive, younger lovers.

'I have other work for you, lieutenant. Three weeks ago, Inquisitor Herrenvolk sent an urgent message by astropath to Field Marshal Rygotzk at Scythia. He had intended to speak with Chapter Master Argolis of the Astral Fists, but they have moved out of sector to halt the advance of the Echidna Splinter Fleet.

'The Burdock Worlds have always had problems with greenskin raiders, being so close to The Deeps, but Rygotzk believes that recent attacks across the agri-worlds might actually presage a coordinated ork incursion this time. Presently, however, it is a watching and waiting game on the rim and Herrenvolk pressed the Field Marshal to spare us some of his manpower.'

'Surely the Pontificals and the Sororitas have the outbreaks on Spetzghast covered…'

'Spetzghast is only the beginning. Inquisitor Herrenvolk has discovered a data trail of evidence implicating similar heresies on several of the outlying worlds and the fabricator moon of Illium is in open rebellion.'

Krieg was shocked. 'How could we not know?'

'Idle bureaucracy in the main. Both Algernon and Tancred's World reported cult murders to authorities on Spetzghast, but these weren't acted upon until similar outbreaks appeared on the capital. As for Illium, the Mechanicus are traditionally reticent about handling security on their own installations.'

'But they have forces of their own,' Krieg interjected.

'The fabricator moon has a standing legion of skitarii and a quarto-legio of Imperial Titans standing sentinel over the most valuable installations, on permanent loan from the Legio Invictus on Ninevah. The authorities are mostly genitors, and members of the Adeptus Biologis – the politics in this region leaning towards the organicist side of the spectrum. The local populations, however, are largely Spetzghastian immigrant labour who work the culture mills and vat labs, engineering the biological frames of servitors and cyborganic automatons. Whatever happened on that moon, it seems things got a little beyond the skitarii forces; and now, by extension, us.

'Rygotzk has released the 364th and 1001st Volscian Shadow Brigade companies from his reservist forces, under Brigadier Voskov – a capable man I'm told. Hopefully the extra muscle will help the Mechanicus skitarii forces get the populous back under control. This is where you come in.'

'Ma'am?'

'The reason that I am telling you this is that yesterday it became known to me that a small force of storm-troopers make up part of Brigadier Voskov's troop convoy under a Gomorrian major called Zane Mortensen.' The canoness laid special emphasis on the outfit's name, so much so it appeared as though she'd just swallowed some kind of arachnid.

Krieg had heard of Mortensen and his team. The major's reputation preceded him. As a Galtinore Legionnaire Krieg had arrived late to the trenchworld of Chaspia; by then the foxhole labyrinths and continental earthworks of the contested planet were ancient monuments to the billions who had perished there. The Legionnaires had barely touched down on earth that was more blood than grit before being told to pack up and return to their drop-ship. Mortensen's Redemption Corps had been brought in during the same reinforcement, but hadn't spent three days in processing, as the Galtinore Legionnaires and countless other troops and regiments had. There was no hurry to the front lines of a world that had been contested for the best part of three hundred years.

During this time Mortensen and his men had been picking their way through the booby-trapped expanse of the Knoblus tunnels. Within hours the anthracite shafts of the heavily fortified Augusta-1 Shale Plant had been blown and sealed. Defensive positions were formed and Imperial forces waited for fuel production and the great blighted war machine of the infested Fatherlanders to grind to a halt. Within the year Chaspia was back in Imperial hands, but by then Krieg was hunting wyrds with Schenker and the 123rd Pontificals in the Barraglades.

'The Redemption Corps,' the lieutenant repeated. 'Impossible missions, that kind of thing,' Krieg continued, not quite liking where this was going.

'Reckless deviants, I would say,' Santhonax retorted caustically. 'I once had the unfortunate duty of visiting Gomorrah. Even as hive-worlds go, Gomorrah was a festering sore on the underheel of the Imperium: a dominion of vice and villainy. Wiped clean by the wrath of the God-Emperor himself. On that one point, the Redemptionists and I agree. What is left of this renegade civilisation is now back here, trading their poisonous ways under the banner of salvation.'

'But, the Redemption Corps is a storm-trooper outfit.' Krieg put to her. 'The Commissariat would have reported traces of deviancy in the ranks and exercised their authority.'

'Do not underestimate the emptiness in men's hearts. It is an unquenchable vessel that consumes all it can and then looks for more: sometimes in the darkest of places. Spetzghast is tainted: Algernon, Tancred, Illium also. Heresy would breed like bacteria in a den of iniquity like Gomorrah. Breed in the men who herald from there.

'The troops under his command are similarly tainted – I am sure of it. You cannot serve with the polluted without becoming polluted yourself. And they are not the only ones. The very vessel that carries him and his men, His Beneficent Imperial Majesty's Escort Carrier *Deliverance*, experienced a mutinous overthrow mere weeks from Spetzghast. The entire 1001st Shadow Brigade – almost five hundred fighting sons of Volscia – have had to be quarantined and creed-sanctioned for re-instruction of faith. Do you really think I have the sisters to spare for such diversions? Beyond the loss of the regiment itself, of course.'

'I've heard of Mortensen,' Krieg confirmed.

'Then you know what they say about him. That he can't be killed? That he is a saviour? The fire of the Emperor burning in his veins?'

'Sounds like empty-headed propaganda to me. Gossip and egotism run amok.'

'You disappoint me, lieutenant. Your own reputation isn't sullied with such naivety,' the canoness said lightly.

Krieg recovered quickly from the sting in her slur: 'Let me put it this way. I have heard priests say similar things to troops in the heat of battle, even trade on the regard of certain officers, you know, to spur them on.'

'But this isn't in the heat of battle, lieutenant. Neither is it idle gossip. It is belief and it is dangerous. Surely you would not want to see star temples constructed from the souls of the Imperium's honest fighting men?'

Krieg shook his head.

'Surely Major Mortensen cannot be held responsible for the communication of rumours that are beyond his control?' Krieg offered.

'He can,' Santhonax snarled with conviction, 'if he is their originator. What matters here is not what Major Mortensen does – he is beyond doubt a very gallant officer – it is what he believes. For if he believes, then this is not rumour: it is cult.'

The word hung in the cool, stagnant air of the wardroom. 'Cultish practice will not be tolerated amongst the Emperor's subjects.'

'Of course.'

'The individual is nothing; the body Imperium, everything. We can't have personality cults threatening uniformity of purpose – not now, not ever. The Emperor sacrificed himself for mankind; now he requires the sacrifice of his people. The vainglorious serve themselves. It is heresy and it is dangerous. It's already spreading to other regiments and interfering with the Emperor's work. It must and will be stopped.'

Santhonax turned and recovered a data-slate and a courier package from under the wardroom table.

'You will transfer to the Redemption Corps and make regular reports on the major's actions and behaviour and submit them with your regular supply despatches. Brigadier Voskov and I shall monitor and assess Major Mortensen's fitness for command and act accordingly.'

Krieg's head swam with the sudden complexity of it all. The canoness thrust the slate and package towards him, which the lieutenant cautiously took. 'Eternal vigilance is the hallmark of a true Imperial servant,' she advised him.

'Won't the major be surprised if an Inquisitorial storm-trooper simply gatecrashes his unit?'

'You are no longer a storm-trooper,' the canoness assured him. 'You are still in the employ of the ordo but report to me. In order to oil the cogs of this transition, Lord Commissar Verhoeven has approved your entry as a cadet-commissar, effective immediately. I know that this is highly irregular but the lord commissar appreciates the gravity of the situation and is willing to overlook these irregularities in order that the transfer and your new rank pass scrutiny.

'You begin your rotation with a storm-trooper unit: and what better than the unit belonging to the infamous Major Zane Mortensen? Besides, Commissariat officers lost their lives attempting to bring rebel elements on board *Deliverance* to justice. Reinstatements onboard will be expected. As such, you are perfectly placed to make observations of Major Mortensen's command conduct. Getting close to Mortensen is all that matters. You will acquire the proof we need to make judgement on this heretic in our midst.'

Krieg was staggered. Within minutes he'd gone from frag bait to defender of the Imperial creed. Overcoming the initial thrill of promotion, he attempted to engage his brain once more. With consideration came suspicion.

'This is a deep honour, your ladyship, but I cannot help thinking, well, to put it bluntly: why me? Wouldn't an Imperial agent be a more appropriate choice?'

'Modesty, as well as integrity?' Santhonax asked, rolling her eyes. 'Because you have the appropriate experience and credentials to join the major without arousing his suspicion: allocation to a storm troop will just appear to be part of your training rotation. Because you have served under difficult men before. Because you keep your nerve and do your duty. I am sure that you will know how to act if the major is found wanting and you will carry the authority of Imperial law. Besides, the Emperor's loyal agents will be involved when the time is right,' Santhonax pledged, her words laced with venom.

She checked her holochron. 'You report to Regimental Commissar Udeskee on board the carrier *Deliverance*. Of course, the only person you actually report to now is myself. Brigadier Voskov and his command structure have transferred to the *Purgatorio* in the wake of the rebellion. Udeskee, however, is attached to the Volscian 364th and is the only other Commissariat officer on board. Your rank as cadet-commissar necessitates an initial contact. Shuttle leaves in ten minutes. Bay Sixteen.'

Krieg didn't quite know how to acknowledge such an offer and in the end settled for a crisp salute and a tight smile. 'Your ladyship.'

'Good luck, "Cadet-Commissar Krieg". And remember, the Emperor expects.'

Krieg ducked out of the wardroom and ran for the shuttle.

IV

As HE HURRIED out of the *Wastrel's* airlock it suddenly occurred to Krieg that he would need his personal belongings from his tent. Leaving the dry-docked haulage brig he bolted up the slipway, careering through the camp, dodging startled Guardsmen and precariously stacked equipment, the cadet-commissar skidded to a halt outside of his billet and parted the mesh drapes. It was only inside that he realised the danger he was in.

The shelter was neat, cool and bathed in the sodium light of a lamp-pack. The lamp-pack caught his attention immediately. It wasn't on when he left. Krieg took a deep breath and a good, long look around his quarters. He finally found the device under his bunk: wire sensitive seismic demolition charges, with a bunch of pin-primed frag grenades for good measure. If he'd tried to sit down on the berth, he'd be in pieces right now, splattered all over the hull of the *Wastrel*.

Rudd. Bastard.

He'd heard Rudd threaten a fragging in the Pavilion, in front of Kowalski, but Krieg hadn't thought the lieutenant foolish enough to convert hot words into explosive deeds. The captain-commandant wasn't wrong about Krieg, though: he did have a way with people – and not necessarily a good one.

Realising that anything in the billet could be rigged and that nothing sentimental was worth dying for, Krieg backed slowly out of the tent. In the doorway, something touched his shoulder and he turned slowly, making his hellpistol rock where he had hung it, with its holster and power pack. Bagging the supercharged weapon for practical rather than sentimental reasons, Krieg left the site of his intended murder, dashing across the dry dock deck towards Bay Sixteen before anyone else tried to kill him.

'I'm going to kill that Krieg.'

'You don't mean that.'

'I mean it.' Dekita Rosenkrantz paced up and down the squalid confines of the cell, feverishly checking the holochron on her wrist.

'That might be difficult, my child,' sniffed Pontiff Preed, adjusting his monocle. The huge priest towered over her like a natural feature – his obscene belly and the chins that sat like tyres around his throat marking him as a man who had eaten his fill and the fill of many others, in the name of the God-Emperor. 'He's probably already dead.'

'I asked him to file those damn tallies.'

'Tallies?' Preed echoed as he squinted, sizing up the door. His cracked eyeglass fell and dangled from a cord on his belt. Rosenkrantz pulled up the sleeve of her flightsuit to reveal a thirteen-digit number laser scanned into her flesh.

'Jopall Indentured,' Rosenkrantz confirmed. She grunted and rolled back the sleeve. Everything on Jopall was tallied:

the loss of an enemy life; the defence of an Imperial one. Recompense was recorded and accounted for in order that the citizens of Jopall could work off the crushing debts incurred during their unproductive childhood. The ship's commissar, or in the case of the Guard, the company commissar, was charged with the welfare of troops under his supervision and this included responsibility for itemising and filing all Jopall tallies with the proper home world authorities. 'Krieg holds all the tallies for me and my crew.'

Preed nodded with regret before cracking his robust knuckles and charging his three hundred kilos of pure bulk at the cell door. The impact was deafening and Rosenkrantz saw the wall around the door visibly quake: the door however, remained exactly where it was. Preed rubbed his hulking shoulder before ambling in disappointment to the corner of the filthy cell.

'Plate draconium; probably cruciform bolt-locked and set with inertia seals…' the priest appraised.

Rosenkrantz sagged and crumbled into a heap on the rockcrete bunk. 'Why are they doing this? They're supposed to be on our side.'

'They aren't on anyone's side, my child,' the gentle giant soothed in his most clerical voice. 'They're their own side.'

A roar that was anything but clerical shook the air and a ripple of rage cascaded down the pontiff's mammoth form. He threw himself at the cell door once again, pummelling the dull metal with his muscular fists. The mighty priest rained a thunderstorm of blows down on the pitted surface of the door, but failed to make any impression on it. With his chest heaving, the pontiff moped over to the solid bunk and rested his backside. It almost painted a comical scene, the svelte young pilot in her flight suit, resting her head against the man-mountain that was Preed.

'How long have we got?' the pontiff put to her.

Rosenkrantz hesitated: 'An hour… maybe.'

'An hour?'

'If we're not off world in an hour we won't need Deliverance to fly through space,' the pilot assured him.

Preed suddenly put up his hand to silence her and clambered awkwardly to his feet.

'What?' Rosenkrantz demanded, but the priest didn't seem to hear her. Putting a mangled ear to the floor he listened intently.

'I must stop you there, my daughter,' he said, rearing up to his full height and making the sign of the aquila. Again he cracked his knuckles and got to his feet, stretching the muscles in his fat neck like a pugilist. *'It seems that our prayers have been answered.'*

'Pontiff, what's going on?'

'The sisters – I think – or their Militiate brothers. They're moving along the cell-block. I can hear cell doors being opened.'

From their own door came the excruciating sound of metal grinding on metal: the bolt-lock. Moments passed. Preed and the pilot were suddenly privy to the sound of screams from the next cell, punctuated by the chemicular whoosh of a melta gun as the battle-sisters went about their cleanse and burn mission with impassive economy.

Rosenkrantz backed towards Preed and stumbled as her boot caught one of his huge sandals. As she turned she saw the gargantuan priest had picked up the ceramite bunk and was holding it above his head like a barbell. His arms trembled and thick rivulets of liquid effort rolled down the sides of his snarling face. *'Get behind me,'* he managed.

The cell door suddenly swung open and the pair found themselves looking up the smoking twin barrels of a multi-melta. The weapon rumbled its superheated intention to fire. With a belly-grunt of exertion Preed let the ceramite *block fly. The zealot frater beyond had barely a second to respond and all he could manage was a flash of his gauntleted palm at the priest in protest. The block smacked him into the corridor wall and crushed him with all the impunity of an unstoppable force.*

Before Rosenkrantz realised that her flesh hadn't actually been charred from her bones, the monstrous priest was out of the cell and storming the corridor. Sticking her head out of the cell door, the flight lieutenant watched him cannon-ball his way towards the cell-block bulkhead.

A number of militia members stood sentinel with chunky autoguns and flamers. They went to prime their weapons, but found the three hundred kilo blitzkrieg charging up the corridor towards them too much of a spectacle. By the time their first round had chambered Preed had smashed their shaven heads into the wall with his oncoming shoulder and stampeded them underfoot.

Keeping her head down, Rosenkrantz swept across the corridor and went for the melta operator's holstered stub gun. In a small booth a few metres down, two Incarcetorium guards carrying riot shields and convulsion mauls stood by the cell-block door controls. At first they were completely stunned by the havoc being wreaked by Preed up the corridor. As soon as they saw the pilot they glowered before activating their mauls and rushing in.

Rosenkrantz feverishly tore at the brother zealot's stub gun, unable to find the holster's safety strap. As the guards closed in she abandoned the side arm in favour of the buckled multi-melta on the floor nearby. The weapon was too heavy to carry so Rosenkrantz angled the barrels upwards with the grip and depressed the ignition stud.

The guards soon lost their bravado and came to a skidding halt just in front of the weapon's thermo-bleached muzzle. The chemicular whoosh they'd all expected didn't

*happen. Instead, the heavy weapon chugged and sparked
before emitting a gaseous growl of indigestion and growing
suddenly hot to the touch. Dropping their suppression
equipment the prison guards made a bolt for the control
booth. Rosenkrantz had only one place to go: back in the
cell. Rolling across the corridor she slammed the cell door
shut as the multi-melta's pressurised pyrum-petrol flask
went supercritical.*

The plate-draconium absorbed the worst of the blast but
the extreme heat of the detonation had warped the door off
its reinforced hinges. As it fell inwards, Rosenkrantz was
treated to a view of the glowing molten ceramite of the walls
outside. Peering out she could see that the guards had been
erased off the face of the planet and that Preed was thundering towards the cell-block bulkhead.

A lone battle-sister stood in front of the bulkhead,
swathed in striped ermine. She shook the stray tresses of her
jet-black hair from her eyes and hit the alarm button. Preed
roared as the bulkhead slammed down behind her and
increased his belting pace up the corridor. With klaxons
piercing the air and lights flashing in the ceiling the battle-
sister put her hand on the grip of her holstered pistol, but
thought better of it, drawing instead the shimmering blade
of a beautifully crafted power falchion.

Swinging the flare-clipped tip of the sword around her
with practiced fluidity she prepared to face her attacker. The
battle-sister positioned the blade for an entrail-spilling
undercut. Preed didn't stop though. He just kept coming, as
though he were going to blast straight through the security
bulkhead. Hitting her with the force of a monitor train,
Preed smashed the battle-sister into the bulkhead with the
uncompromising bulk of his corpulent belly. The priest held
her there for a moment, allowing a final gasp to escape from
her body. Her neck had been snapped and her crushed arm,

pinned to the door, let the padded hilt of the power sword topple from her fading grip. Pulling away with a bestial grunt of satisfaction, Preed allowed the sister's broken body to crumble to the ground.

As the pontiff got a grip on himself, Rosenkrantz stepped out into the cooling corridor.

'Get the corpsmen out of the cells,' he bawled up to her.

'The bulkhead?' she called back over the searing alarm.

'Probably welded shut and bricked up from the outside by now,' Preed informed her regretfully.

'Good job I blew a hole in the floor then.'

CHAPTER THREE
Truth be Told

I

ROSENKRANTZ TOOK ONE last drag on the lho-stick before crushing it into the ramp with the toe of her boot. She hugged herself against the chill of the dry-dock as it proceeded to slip unwanted fingers of frosty air in between the buckles of her flight jacket. She hit the stud on the hull vox.

'Chief, give me the payload description. At least I'll know what I'm looking for.'

There was nothing for a few moments; just the drowsy blink of the vox-bulb. 'Chief, get off your backside.'

The vox gushed static at her before giving way to Crew Chief Nauls's leatherneck drawl. 'Slate says one passenger.' In the background Rosenkrantz could hear a card game in progress.

'No vehicles or munitions?' she returned.

'I may not be the sharpest tool in the wrench locker, but I can read, skipper.'

'Okay, chief, well you see that little silver stud that says "Cockpit"?' Rosenkrantz asked with no little pedantry. 'I want you to press that and get Benedict to stir the tanks. I'm going to give our cargo another two minutes and then I'm taking off. Do you think you can manage that?'

'It would give my life the meaning I've been looking for, skip.'

Rosenkrantz flicked off the vox and sauntered around the side of the aircraft. Hovering under the fuel tanks, she was rewarded by the percolation of promethium from above. She reached up and caressed the fuselage of the aircraft. The *Vertigo* was a Spectre-class Valkyrie armoured assault carrier. She had the mean lines and rugged gracelessness of her Valkyrie and Vulture cousins and then some, but there was something reassuring about her swollen underbelly and thundering engine quad. Unlike her troop carrier cousin, however, she was designed to transport small vehicles and light ordnance. An unpracticed eye might dismiss the *Vertigo* as a Guard mule. She was this, but much more. She bristled vulgarity in the form of snub, belt-fed weaponry and rocket pods and the thrust of her aquiline cockpit section commanded the respect of a Catachan terror bird, sweeping its ungainly beak in for the kill. She was a thoroughbred of her class.

'She's beautiful.'

Rosenkrantz spun around to find that she was being watched. He stood by the ramp, the veins in his neck still pulsing from his short run to reach the aircraft. Rosenkrantz figured him for a courier: young, stormtrooper fatigues, lieutenant's stripes and a plump diplomatic pouch bearing the sinister blazonry of the Ecclesiarchy. 'I'm Krieg,' he enlightened her.

'You're late,' Rosenkrantz corrected him with a scowl. 'I expected more of one of you glory boys.'

'This is Bay sixteen?'

'You're in the right place.' Rosenkrantz motioned the officer up the ramp. 'You can stow your gear anywhere you like. There's plenty of room. You're my only consignment tonight.'

She depressed the vox-stub once again, alerting her co-pilot: 'Benedict. Fire them up. We're leaving.' She raised her eyebrows at Krieg and added into the vox, 'Finally. Ramp closing.'

At the far end of the Spectre's large belly compartment a number of the aircrew had set up a card table using munitions crates and the carrier's water cask. The players were all engrossed in their game of crazy eights: they were playing with a rolling pot and a Ballamehrian double-deck. Lho-sticks drooped from the corners of their mouths and they didn't even look up from their cards as Rosenkrantz and their guest approached.

'The crew,' Rosenkrantz stated simply. 'If you'd like to lose some money, they appear to have a card game going.'

'No thanks,' Krieg declined. 'Do you have anywhere I can get changed?' A couple of the crew grunted with amusement.

'Yes,' Rosenkrantz replied. 'Here. This is a Navy transport, lieutenant, we don't stand on ceremony...' The flight lieutenant had to stop, because as she was dressing him down, Krieg had thrown her the diplomatic pouch and proceeded to dress down himself. The spectacle of the storm-trooper unbuttoning his fatigues right in front of her drew more guffaws and the odd jeer from the aircrew.

Nauls flapped his hand at the other card players. 'You all pipe down now. Let's play some cards.' His face split into a bright grin. 'Can't you see the skipper's busy?'

Rosenkrantz turned and gave him a Thartusian salute with her finger. 'You reading this okay, chief?'

'I'm getting that loud and clear, skipper,' Nauls crowed back at her.

Rosenkrantz turned back to find Krieg almost down to his Guard-issue briefs.

Thrusting the ordo package straight back at him, she opened a nearby locker. 'You can use the side-arms store.'

'Obliged to you,' Krieg nodded, gathering his clothes and disappeared inside the tiny armoury. Rosenkrantz struck off in the other direction, mounting the bottom rung of the cockpit companionway, the crew's horse-play following her ascent.

II

THE SPECTRE SCREAMED skyward leaving the mercantile burghs and sprawling commercia of Spetzghast behind them. Soon, the encroaching twilight claimed them too, leaving Rosenkrantz to worry about the swarm of stratospheric commercial traffic streaking across the reinforced canopy of the *Vertigo*.

Vector wagons and skiffs played cat and mouse amongst fast moving cavalcades of air freighters and atmos-tankers. Whilst not comfortable, it was nothing Rosenkrantz hadn't negotiated before. There was only one moment of dread uncertainty: a decrepit passenger liner called the *Witch of Shandor* wandered into a cross current and lost several of its giant tail fins, one of which threatened to cleave the *Vertigo* in two.

Rosenkrantz had to bank sharply and cut between the ore cars of a nearby trampgalleon.

'Sorry,' Rosenkrantz called over the crew vox. 'Benedict, have that liner's signature code reported to the port admiral's office for citation.'

'Affirmative, flight lieutenant.'

The co-pilot had been human once, but now he was Benedict: a naval servitor. Truncated at the waist, the co-pilot was really one with the Spectre, his legs lost in some forgotten, horrific craft-to-craft collision and his spine a nexus of power couplings and nerve ports. 'We're leaving the commercial traffic lanes,' he informed Rosenkrantz, moments before the Spectre breached the thin, cobalt cloudbank and gave the pilot an eyeful of Spetzghast's looming sun.

As a brown dwarf, Sigma Scorpii wasn't hot enough to achieve hydrogen fusion like many stars; instead it was forced to resort to burning baser fuels at its core and casting the dismal bronze light of a dying fire across the system. Lying much closer to its sun than most inhabitable planets could afford, a Spetzghastian view of Sigma Scorpii still made for a breathtaking sight.

Upon leaving the mercantile world's cerulean skies the traffic disappeared and the relative emptiness of the ionosphere beckoned. Spetzghast's spectacular ring system drew overhead. The girdle of dust, rock and metal encircled the planet at right angles to its plane of orbit, running pole to pole, and was attended by a myriad of shepherd moons, keeping the asteroid belt in good order.

Here giants ruled.

In low orbit a flotilla of bulk cruisers kept station on an outlandish rogue trader vessel. Pregnant fluyts and sprint traders bearing the Spetzghastian mercantile seal were harried into position by system ships under the wide gunports of patrolling monitors and adamanticlads. Each vessel was accompanied by its own flock of smaller tugs and luggers: cargo lighters and freight barges.

At the epicentre of this activity was the *Exchequer*, a spindly orbital dock that was itself dominated by warships of His Beneficent Majesty. The *Stang Draak* hung like a colossal heirloom above Spetzghastian skies. As the system garrison ship and one of the Exchequer's permanent fixtures, she was a constant presence and had been for as long as anyone could remember. One of the last of her class serving in the Imperial Navy, the grand cruiser's lances stood as a deterrent to any enemy foolish enough to sweep in under them.

Despite being a frontier system, fairly distant from the hub of Imperial worlds in the Kaligari Cradle, Spetzghast had largely escaped the attention of warmongering alien races and traitor fleets. It had been at least a millennium since Arch-Admiral Coppola's Ravish Armada had passed through the system causing mass panic and centuries of following consternation. The real extent of the hive-world's problems, were limited to pirates and smugglers, run down by Navy brigs and waspish gunships.

The only other vessels in dock were the newly arrived *Purgatorio*, a Dictator-class beauty, and a pair of Firestorm-class frigates; they had been escorting a small convoy consisting of a nimble Guard carrier, two bloated supply ships and the *Ursa*, a superheavy transport.

As Rosenkrantz banked towards the flotilla, a small alarm bell rang in the cockpit. Benedict reached over and disabled it before scanning his runescreen and rapidly digesting the data it was feeding him. 'Flight lieutenant, we have a proximity warning, port-side aft.'

Rosenkrantz stared out of the canopy, but all she could see was stars.

'I've got nothing.' Her instrument panel suddenly came alive followed by an explosive force from port that violently rocked the gun-freighter. 'What the hell was that?'

In answer to her question a pair of Interceptors surged past them, rolling wing over wing and forcing her to veer to starboard. Like a pair of shepherds, the fightercraft guided the assault carrier off course.

'I'm getting a vox message,' Benedict informed her, clutching his headset. 'We are ordered to abandon our present heading. They are transmitting new coordinates.'

'Confirm and execute,' Rosenkrantz ordered, unbuckling her safety harness to get a better view out of the reverse of the canopy. Then she saw it: the oily shimmer of reflected stars. They had nearly run into a cloaked vessel: something with stealth plating or an advanced optical shielding system. 'Scan for threshold beacons, taxiway signatures...'

'Affirmative. I have a partial reading for you, flight lieutenant.'

'Proceed.'

Rosenkrantz watched the data flick up on her sensorium: *Dread Sovereign* – Inquisitorial Corvette. 'Cease datastream,' she snapped, 'and terminate the scan.'

'But flight lieutenant–'

'Do it! And give me those coordinates,' she said, strapping herself back in.

'Affirmative.'

Rosenkrantz heard footsteps on the companionway.

'Skipper.' It was Spreckels, one of the Spectre's gunners. Rosenkrantz didn't turn around.

'Spreckels, I'm a bit busy at the moment.'

'Chief's respects, skipper. He wondered if he might have a word–'

'Tell him I have no idea what beats a quartz flush in crazy eights.'

'...on a secure channel.'

'What?' Rosenkrantz peered around with a scowl. Spreckels wasn't the only one in the companionway. 'What is this, a vrekkin' town meeting?'

When Spreckels realised that there was someone behind him the colour dropped from his face and he pinned his back to the cockpit wall. Krieg stepped forwards, fully clothed this time. For less licentious reasons, Rosenkrantz wished that he wasn't.

'Commissar,' she acknowledged, taking in the gleaming black greatcoat and peaked cap. Krieg ducked in under the canopy, past a completely oblivious Benedict and spotted their Interceptor escort.

'Problems, flight lieutenant?' Krieg asked her. Rosenkrantz looked at the fighters, then back at the commissar.

'One or two.'

III

THE AIRCRAFT FOUND *Deliverance* in low orbit, nestled between the two portly transports, at the rear of the convoy. The Defiant-class carrier rode out the swells, the blade of the Voss-pattern prow cutting through the ionosphere.

As the Spectre's ramp caressed the deck Rosenkrantz's flight crew crowded the hold but parted like drapes as Krieg dropped from the companionway, cutting a black swathe through the Navy gunners in his boots, breeches, leather coat and cap.

He was met on the flight deck by a master sergeant and a grizzled captain who sported a cocky smile and a limp. Captain Rask apologised for the major's absence, explaining that *Deliverance* had just been ordered off station and that Mortensen had been called to a meeting with the Brigadier. Rask seemed likeable and tried to make regimental small talk. The lacklustre exchange barely carried them across the hangar. The surly sergeant continued to look as if he'd just swallowed a bug and eyeballed Krieg from below his crooked beret with obvious suspicion and sour hostility. His name was stencilled into his flak jacket: 'Conklin'. It might as well have read 'Maniac'. Krieg noticed that his hand never strayed far from the fat autopistol that dangled from his belt. He hoped that it was a veteran's twitch rather than a signal of open hostility at his arrival.

As they made their way around the stacked freight and super-charged fire support variants of the redoubtable Centaur chassis, Krieg noticed Rask's limp become more pronounced, attempting to keep up with his own bold strides.

'Injury?' Krieg enquired.

'Permanent,' Rask replied with a smile.

'Want to see something permanent?' the master sergeant droned, holding back with Rask and sticking two fingers up at the captain. The bionic replacements hung in a provocative 'V'. Rask beamed at the sergeant with irresistible charm. Conklin just chuckled to himself.

Krieg's modest quarters were situated on the deck above the storm-troopers' billets; his superior's were port-side aft, with the officer's quarters of the 364th. It was clear that Rask was thrilled to hand the cadet-commissar over to his assigned aide, Specialist Golliant, at the door. The captain then went about his business, leaving Conklin to strike up a filthy cigar and wait a little way down the corridor. A young Volscian Guardsman walked passed, dripping with Tactica-unapproved adornments like a bandana and a sheath of stiletto knives across his chest. Krieg went to remonstrate the hiver but caught himself: he'd only been on board a few minutes. As the Volscian passed Conklin, he hovered. The sergeant stamped his boot and hissed, 'Boo!' driving the young soldier off down the corridor.

To Krieg's relief Golliant wasn't one of Mortensen's men, he was a thoroughbred Volscian – he had the square jaw and grim, garrison world eyes of that besieged planet. Golliant was unusually broad, even for a native Volscian, his powerhouse shoulders rounding off girder-thick arms and a neck that would have been at home on a grox. He'd been a champion wrestler before PDF and subsequent Guard service intervened and had lost all but the gargled whisper of a voice to an early opponent who'd garrotted him with a length of razor wire. This wasn't an illegal move on Volscia and Golliant had fought on and won the bout. He still wore the ragged, stapled scar across his throat to prove it.

In the Shadow Brigade his monstrous biceps had found natural work wrapped around an equally monstrous heavy bolter but he was now assigned as a cadet-commissar's aide. An unusual move – but Krieg thought he could follow his superior's thinking. As a representative of the Commissariat amongst mean, hive-world trash like the Volscians, Krieg would need someone to watch his back on the battlefield and just about anywhere else for that matter. The commissar clearly trusted in Golliant's simple loyalty and had even more faith in the nightmare wrestler's ability to dissuade any but the most foolish of gangers from interfering with the cadet-commissar's business.

'Commissar Udeskee will see you now, sir,' Golliant rasped and opened the door. Krieg mumbled thanks and ducked inside.

Udeskee's quarters were a marked difference to the spartan simplicity of his tent back at Camp Carfax. Early Farranbourgs and other pieces of quality furniture littered the room, including a qualmwood desk blanketed with parchments, optipicts, data-slates and hololithic maps. There were several tapestries and a nicra mural, depicting one of the Emperor's early conquests in the Anoarch systems, dominated one wall. The fittings took the cold edge off the otherwise functional cabin and provided a contrast to the hyperbaric oxygen tent in the middle of the room.

Two of the commissar's attendants busied themselves over by the desk, momentarily flicking their eyes up at him before returning to their work. Pushing through the small forest of plastic sheeting, Krieg made his way inside the oxygen tent. Through the last sheet, the cadet-commissar could make out a bed and the wet hackle of laboured breathing.

'It's there to protect me from you, not the other way around, you fool,' came a bitter voice. It was brittle with age but still possessed the mettle of a man used to giving orders.

Parting the curtain, Krieg stepped through to the chamber beyond. He blinked and rubbed his nostrils in the oxygen-rich atmosphere. The bed was empty, with only a striking young attendant changing some kind of catheter arrangement on the far side. Upon seeing Krieg, the attendant's face creased with sudden churlishness, losing none of its winsome quality, before he became lost in the folds of the plastic sheeting. Having only spent a number of hours as an Imperial commissar, Krieg had already grown used to such a reaction and thought nothing more of the insolence. 'So, you're Krieg, are you?' came the same voice.

Krieg turned to greet his superior, expecting some steely-eyed Imperial hero to be sitting there with a boltgun wound and a glass of amasec. Words from the *Infantryman's Uplifting Primer* suddenly came to him: 'The Emperor looks down on the man who expects nothing with benefaction, for he shall never be disappointed.' As a young Legionnaire, Krieg had found these words to be at best cryptic and at worst completely unhelpful. Staring at the desiccated little basket case sitting in a wheeled-chair by the bed, the commissar couldn't help but feel cheated. This was Udeskee? Regimental Commissar Udeskee – his sponsor and mentor?

'Like staring into a crystal ball, eh?' the commissar laughed nastily through a device that looked like a water pipe inserted into his neck. His eyes were cloudy and his skin scaly and stretched over his sharp bones. His immaculate greatcoat hung by the bed, but he still wore his eagle-emblazoned cap.

'Sir?' Krieg still couldn't get his head around it.

'Accelerated decrepitude,' the man explained, each breath an agony. 'Symptom of Mortlock's Disease.

Caught it on Pariah V. Don't worry, it's past the contagious phase. One sneeze from you could kill me though, so keep your distance.'

Krieg took an obligatory step back. 'You sent for me, sir.'

'I've been through your records,' Udeskee cackled. 'Well, there's no fault in proficiency. But, you lack experience and you've probably already got a rod up your backside about the state of this regiment and both of those things are going to get you killed around here.'

'If I'm responsible for the welfare of these men, how can I let them indulge in practice that is detrimental to their physical and spiritual safety?' Krieg entreated. 'I had to walk past thirty Tactica citations just to get up here.'

The attendant suddenly reappeared between them and straightened the plastek of the curtain, resonating hostility towards Krieg that was clearly lost on the commissar. He busied himself with the valves and various pipes running into Udeskee's enfeebled body.

'Patience. The Imperium wasn't built in one day,' Udeskee assured him. 'You think it can be: so did your predecessor and see where that got him. Not a bad thing you're assigned to the storm-troopers. But make no mistakes, Mortensen is not a man to be trifled with. He expects a member of the Commissariat to be a pain, an inconvenience – but start stuffing the Imperial Creed down his throat and waving your pistol around and you're not likely to make it down the corridor.'

'Has the galaxy gone mad?' Krieg exploded. 'It is the Commissariat that should be feared…'

'Now you're sounding like an inquisitor,' the commissar told him grimly. Krieg swallowed and found himself staring at the floor. 'A dead one. The major won't need to do anything. His men will do it for him, without orders. They are fiercely loyal and won't need much excuse to dispose of one of our kind. And as for the Volscians: most of them would gut you soon as look at you.'

'What am I even doing here?' Krieg put to the commissar, knowing deep down that there was more than one answer to that question.

'The Emperor's work… Slowly. Change, at a pace. The Volscians are by and large hive gangers, and savage ones at that. Go back far enough and each them has a common ancestor who fought in an affiliated confederation of clans. For most of these people, ancient grudges have been put to rest and a common cause embraced.'

'The Emperor's cause,' Krieg reminded him.

Udeskee gibbered to himself. 'Wring the starch from your shirt, lad,' the commissar finally scolded.

'Or the blood, if I don't play dice.'

'You said it.'

The two men stared at one another for a while.

'What am I to do?'

'Your job,' the commissar spat. 'The Imperial Guard is our lord's bastion among the stars. Each regiment, each troop, is unique and has something different to offer the Imperial cause. A commissar's role is more than just citation and the sensationalism of battlefield executions. Lead by example, from the front. Let them see the doctrines you prize so highly in your words and actions. Inspire these men and bring them back to the one true path. In turn, it is your responsibility to understand these people, their history, culture, their way of life and the tragedies that have befallen them. Familiarise yourself with their equipment and tactics: "When in Terra" et cetera. You must be their voice out there: where, despite their gallantry and servitude, they'll be most misunderstood. Do what any commissar must, but try and bury these men wholesale and they'll send you back to the Pontificals with your balls in a sling. You won't be attached to them, of course.'

'Charming,' said Krieg.

Udeskee began to pull at the swollen knuckles of one crooked hand, the pain obvious on his face. The belligerent aide swooped in to help the aged commissar, the smooth olive skin of his own digits the very antithesis of Udeskee's spotted, wrinkled claws. With some gentle persuasion, the aide managed to slip the commissar's seal ring from his crippled finger and placed it on the bed in front of Krieg. He picked it up and inspected the winged-skull signet of the Imperial Commissariat it bore.

'Put it on,' Udeskee instructed. Krieg slipped it dauntlessly on his finger. 'Do your duty. And mine. A load of good it's going to do on the finger of a ship-bound cripple. You carry the full authority of an Imperial commissar in your right hand. Use it wisely. I'll sign off on your determinations, if you're around long enough to make any.'

Krieg looked up from the ring. Then it struck him. The young attendant was still holding the commissar's lame hand. Udeskee appeared to be holding it back. The commissar attempted a bleak smile. 'Try not to get yourself killed on your first day,' he cackled. 'Might want to insert a few more flak plates in that coat of yours eh? Might I suggest a few in the back as well?'

Krieg saluted and left Udeskee to his sick humour. As he pushed his way back through the oxygen tent's plastic sheeting, he could feel the bile slowly creeping up the back of his throat: a sensation of disgust, though not in the way he might have expected. It seemed Udeskee was infected with more than just Mortlock's Disease. He was infected with complacency; the lack of vigilance that allows other scourges to take hold of men's souls.

As he left Udeskee's quarters, the signet heavy on his finger, Krieg couldn't help but feel conflicted, his own soul swiftly becoming a battleground between the poison in his ears and the steel in his heart.

And then she shot him.

*Mortensen had half-expected to lose consciousness
again but the oblivion never came. The battle-sisters were
summoned and pulled his lifeless arms over their broad,
armoured shoulders. Between them they dragged the
major around the other side of the table and dumped his
rag doll body in the remaining chair, pinning him against
it with the side of the table to keep him upright. The
battle-sister sat opposite, boring her interrogator's eyes
into him. Her henchwomen stood at ease either side of
him.*

'What did you stick me with, bi–'

*'Name and rank,' the battle-sister cut in with imperious
authority.*

*'It might disappoint you to learn that this isn't the first
time I've been tortured,' the major informed her, his words
dripping with scorn.*

*'You can relax,' the battle-sister told him, amused at her
own little joke. 'I don't intend laying a finger on you.'*

'More's the pity.' Mortensen coughed a laugh and gave her a dirty grin. Then he coughed again. The grin faded; the sister waited. It suddenly felt as though his throat was bone dry and tightening.

'Come on,' the battle-sister taunted, 'it's easy. My name is Diamanta Santhonax, Canoness Regular of the Order of the Immaculate Flame. Now, trooper, your name and your rank.'

Mortensen screwed up his eyes and gagged. It felt like he was being strangled with glass wire. No air was getting to his brain and the veins in his temples pulsed horribly. Networks of blood vessels bulged across his neck and face.

'M-M-Mortensen!' he blurted painfully. Something gave and air surged down his throat, rejuvenating his lungs and making him feel dizzy and warm inside. 'Troop Major Zane Mortensen, Redemption Corps.' It was out before he knew he had said it.

Pulling back the longslide on the needler, the canoness deposited a second empty crystal canister on the table. Picking it up between finger and thumb she held it in the dim light. 'The first was the enhanced venom of the Catachan lugwasp. Actually quite harmless, but you won't have control of your lower body for some time.'

'You'd better get a mop then,' the major scoffed.

'This, however, is synthesised. A veracity compellent. I don't know what they make that from. Classified. I do know that it's very powerful: I've tried it myself. The Sisters of the Immaculate Flame prize truth over all things, so if you want to keep breathing, you'll give me the truth and nothing but. I wouldn't want you to choke on your own lies.'

'Are you out of your vrekkin' mind? Is that your problem?' Maybe one of those pins went in a bit too far, eh?'

'Major, please. I could kill you with my insistence alone.'

Mortensen felt an invisible choke-hold cut across his windpipe. Beads of trembling sweat clung to the storm-trooper's grimace as he fought the compellent's irresistible compulsion. Truth gushed forth with a lungful of spent air.

'You come from Gomorrah, yes?'

Mortensen wanted nothing more than to have the canoness wait, but with the compellent coursing through his veins, he found his responses came thick and fast.

'Yes.'

'Orphan?'

'Yes.'

'Schola progenium?'

Mortensen choked back his truth but the words painfully erupted from him: 'It didn't have a name. They called it The Claw, Hephaestus Hive East.'

'Tell me about the end of Gomorrah. Some say you saw it,' the canoness pushed.

The major's first few words were stilted, resistant, but soon they began to flow as the compellent cut through his reserve and into his honesty.

'I've seen my share of galactic battlefields; witnessed the taking of life on scales such that numbers become mean-ingless,' Mortensen declared with rough pride, 'but I'll never forget the day the comet hit Gomorrah.'

'I dare say I would have found it memorable also,' San-thonax hissed. 'It's not every day that you get to see a billion faithless heretics burn in the fires of their own blasphemy.'

'That's my hivekin you're talking about...'

'Let's stop insulting each other. Gomorrah was a galactic byword for sin and villainy. From the undersump to the palaces, Gomorrah's hives were corrupt to the core: factories of moral decay whose dark light was an irresistible beacon to the xenos and the pirate. Such a place is an affront to the

God-Emperor's very being and it was by His will that your precious home world was cleansed by the flame.'

'Usually, killing is just an unfortunate by-product of my trade,' Mortensen assured her, *'but I can see that I'm really going to enjoy bleeding you.'*

'Regale me further with particulars of your den of iniquity's decimation.' Mortensen swore that he saw something like delight in the battle-sister's eyes as she forced him to entertain her. *'The truth.'*

The major trembled in furious exertion, but the words continued to slip through his clenched teeth. *'Corpse mountains… hives ablaze… unbreathable air… the world… tearing itself inside out.'* Fat droplets of sweat rolled down the sides of his face, hanging, quaking and then spattering on the tabletop. At last, he had to breathe. With oxygen, came further honesties. *'Half of all life ended… in an instant,'* the major admitted slowly. *'It's humbling to be in the presence of such power. This,'* – Mortensen flicked his eyes towards his scorch smeared flesh – *'testifies to my dalliance. The cities fell and the toxic oceans rushed in to claim the rest.'*

'Catastrophes are often romanticised thus; after the fact. I see no justification for your outrageous abuses in such sentimentality.'

'Gomorrah was due to deliver its tithe, but the Munitorum didn't list us overdue for over a decade,' the major continued. *'The comet impact had blackened the skies with dust. My people had suffered global devastation; their world had been plunged into volcanic hyperdrive and then forsaken in an impact winter. When the tithe ships arrived with a hive-world's demand of a billion Guardsmen, all they found was a dead planet.'*

'Oh, but you're wrong,' Santhonax chided, *'they found you.'*

'When the Enceladus Crusade was forfeit their expected one billion reinforcements, what remained of Gomorrah was searched. I was the only survivor discovered.'

'A planet-wide search and you were the only living Gomorrian?' the canoness played, enjoying the obligation of Mortensen's responses.

'What the comet hadn't destroyed the lava swallowed: it covered everything. But still, tiny pockets of Gomorrians held on – living like animals, waiting for help to arrive. Those that had cared for me, helped me through,' Mortensen indicated the livid pattern over his skin again, 'this. They survived the six-hundred degree days, the quakes, the starvation and thirst. It was the cold.'

'The cold,' Santhonax repeated. 'Go on.'

'The sky was a blanket of ash. The temperature plummeted. The human body can only function within a particular range: below a certain point muscles don't work, behaviour becomes irrational, minds shut down. I watched it happen, to all of them: one after another. The shock kills you: your lungs can't breathe and your heart can't beat.

'But you beat it.'

'Because I couldn't feel it,' the major growled. 'Like they could,' he added. 'The mind-numbing cold couldn't numb my mind: while all they wanted to do was curl up and die. I could run a marathon in a snow drift and not feel a damn thing. It's easy to keep your body warm, your muscles on fire if you can bypass the inconvenience of agony.'

Mortensen went quiet. The canoness narrowed those bolthole eyes.

'You were transferred to schola cursus?'

'Yes,' Mortensen told her.

'And the tattoo…' the canoness pushed. She was, of course, talking about the numerals emblazoned across his skull.

C
C M
M X L I
X
C
I
X

'...999. M41?'

'The death of my world,' Mortensen admitted solemnly. 'Had it done at Cursus. Thought it should be marked – I should be marked – in some way.' A fierceness suddenly returned to the Gomorrian's eyes: 'There's a record of all of this. Somewhere. Why don't you go find it and while you are at it, why don't you go get me an antidote or something?'

The black gauntlet flashed before his eyes with sudden violence, smacking his face to one side and sending him to the floor like some kind of invalid. There was blood in his mouth. He spat. He'd forgotten how quick she was. Moving back around the table, she sank her sharpened fingertips into the sinew of his neck and hauled him upright. Leaning down she brought her head level with his.

'You will tell me everything I wish to know.'

'Don't flatter yourself, pinhead,' Mortensen shot back.

Santhonax's face darkened with a sudden fury. The major steeled himself for further abuse. He soon realised that her anger had little to do with him – after all, she must have grown used to his insults. As he was impervious to her torturer's techniques, she seemed unfazed by his cocky jibes and unvictimly behaviour.

The canoness put a finger to her mini-vox earpiece. 'I don't care if the world is ending, you tell the captain to hold his position until I state otherwise. No more interruptions. This is the Emperor's work: I won't have it sullied with trivial concerns. You understand?'

She returned her attention to the major, still rooted to the chair.

'Trouble with your people?' Mortensen sneered.

'My people are loyal,' Santhonax confirmed smugly, 'much like yours, and do what has to be done when called upon.'

'Oh, we're onto the "look at what we share, rather than what divides us" line of enquiry,' Mortensen mocked her. 'While you play personality disorder down here with me: the good sister, bad sister routine – the end of the world is literally coming to pass right over our heads. Listen to your captain, he knows what he's talking about.'

'There's plenty of time for all that,' Santhonax countered. 'We have to get off this planet…'

'From what I've seen of this world, it's not above a little calamity, survival of the most fit and all; most fit to serve the Emperor, that is.'

'You really get off on all the carnage, don't you?' the major sneered.

'You would defend those that, in the eyes of the Emperor, do not deserve to live?' the canoness remonstrated, leaning in closer to give him the pure spite of her eyes. 'You would defend heretics and anarchists, xenos lovers and those who would bargain with the hellspawn and warp entities of this universe?'

'No,' Mortensen answered, the veracity compellent forcing him to deliver absolute truths. 'But, I wouldn't defend apocalyptic zealots and puritans like you either.'

The canoness smirked: something about the insult clearly amused her.

'Now it's my turn to be truthful: what do I care if the xenos take this world or Ruinous Powers scourge the next? What do I care if the void vomits forth a colossal hulk and pounds your world to oblivion?'

'My world was struck by a comet…' Mortensen growled. His mind whirled. He saw the berg of rock and ice in his mind. Or could it be, as the battle-sister claimed, a colossal space hulk – irregular and impossible - sheathed in the cold of deep space?

'How do you know that?' Santhonax put to him with seductive reason. 'I mean: how do you really know that?'

'You lie,' the major accused.

Diamanta Santhonax licked her thin, sexless lips and leaned in closer. Her voice became low and conspiratorial: 'What if I told you that I was amongst those who stood and watched? One of a privileged few, spectators to the end of a world? A disaster allowed to unfold.'

Mortensen swallowed. That's why there had been no evacuation. No warning. He sat there, in his useless body; struggling with what he was being told, wondering what he wasn't.

'What if these privileged few stood by,' Santhonax continued painfully, 'and watched as your hive-kin perished in the flames of their own unworthiness, so that the truly worthy could rise, phoenix-like from the ashes of armageddon, better, stronger, more able to serve the Imperial cause and bring battle to the God-Emperor's deadliest enemies? Whatever fails to destroy us makes us stronger, is that not what they say? You are living proof of such a supposition.'

'I'm going to kill you,' Mortensen promised her.

'You might. But if you did, would that not prove my little supposition correct? Like humanity, you are at your strongest when you are tested to your limitations. Did not the Horus Heresy purge the untold billions that were disloyal to the Emperor? Did not the Age of Apostasy herald the coming of Sebastian Thor and the much needed reformation of our Ecclesiarchy? Did not the insurmountable odds stacked against truly great men like Macharius, forge legends that give hope to generations in dark times past, present and future?'

'You're insane.'

'One woman's insanity is another man's truth. Perhaps sooner than you think you will recognise the truth in my insanity. Until then, tell me yours.'

CHAPTER FOUR
Indifference Engine

I

ROSENKRANTZ HAD BEEN told to expect heavy resistance on her first storm-trooper sortie and thought it prudent to exchange *Vertigo's* long range auxiliary fuel tanks for rocket pods. She left it to Chief Nauls to oversee the refit and light a fire under the cogboys and servitors, Rosenkrantz being in no doubt that the Redemption Corps' dispersal would be swift and impulsive. The mechanics of the operation were already proving a real culture shock for the flight lieutenant.

Gone were the endless deliberations and slow preparations she'd been used to with the Volscian High Command, the Shadow Brigade being masters of strategic planning and clockwork execution. The common hiver was a rabid hound in the slips, but his spire-born superior was a methodical tactician. The Redemption Corps way of working was much more fluid: organic even. There were no sergeants barking threats of raw encouragement to their men; no squads double-timing it around the hangar with armour and weapons. Since the mutiny the corpsmen always had their armour and weapons and they were always primed and loaded. They sat around, smoking and joking, each man knew his part and he didn't feel the need to shout about it. There would be enough of that down in the field.

The mission briefing wasn't much different. The request for Rosenkrantz's presence alone had been a surprise. Mortensen's flag had been attached to an old Ryza-pattern Valkyrie, but the mission necessitated the transport of vehicles as well as troops and Rosenkrantz was the most senior Spectre commander.

The major had given Rosenkrantz and her bird the once over, only really showing any interest in her crew's impressive number of confirmed kills and the fact that they were Jopall Indentured. This seemed to reassure him and he in turn assured Rosenkrantz that she'd get plenty of opportunity to work off her debts flying with Mortensen and his men. The only other thing that seemed to catch his attention was Rosenkrantz's call-sign, stencilled across her flight helmet: 'Boltmagnet'. The irony seemed to amuse the major and Rosenkrantz didn't have the heart to tell him that her number of emergency landings almost rivalled her confirmed kill ratio, and that the *Vertigo* wasn't actually the *Vertigo* but the *Vertigo VII*. If he'd asked her she would simply have told him what she told everyone else: that she crashed better than anyone else she knew. At any rate, the major transferred his flag to the assault carrier and summoned Rosenkrantz to the mission briefing.

The pilot had expected to go to one of *Deliverance's* tactical suites. Instead the briefing took place on the flight deck in a small amphitheatre built out of ammo crates and fuel drums. One entire side of it was a Salamander Scout vehicle decorated with soldiers. It was kind of cosy and informal and Rosenkrantz imagined that this was the way all Redemption Corps business was carried out.

The hub of activity was focused on a makeshift table in the centre, awash with pictograms and data-slates. A young, intense-looking adjutant was trying his best to get a battered hololithic display operational, much to the chagrin of a master sergeant and a hideous medical officer. Corpsmen lay sprawled across the crates, cleaning weapons, exchanging jokes and insults, waiting for the briefing to begin.

In contrast, Magister Militum Eugene Trepkos of the skitarii tech-guard stood tall and rigidly to attention like some kind of statue, although it looked to Rosenkrantz like it would be difficult for him to do anything else. His bulbous head, which was knotted with muscular concentration, sat amid a slender metallic torso and two intricate mechanical arms. Like the mechanised mandibles of some robotic crustacean, the specialised tips of his fingers twitched across the torso, feverishly at work on some incessant programme of maintenance and repair. A vermillion hood and cloak swathed his oddly impressive body, revealing little of the bottom half, bar the toes of his officer's boots.

The ever-cheerful Captain Rask was introducing Cadet-Commissar Krieg to the major. The meeting was a cool, distrustful affair, each man's eyes unfriendly and deep with civil hostility. As hands were offered, Rosenkrantz clocked Mortensen twist the commissar's palm slightly in his own to get a better look at the heavy ring Krieg was wearing. In turn the cadet took in the ragged stitching of fresh gashes across the major's arms and shoulders. As the major flicked his eyes back up at Krieg, Rosenkrantz detected the slightest nod from the young commissar. Mortensen's lip curled into a dangerous smile and he slowly returned the gesture. The flight lieutenant felt like she'd just witnessed something significant pass between the two men, but couldn't bring herself to believe that it was anything good. Captain Rask hobbled past, smiling, of course, and settled himself on a crate next to Rosenkrantz, working circulation into his busted knee with his tough fingertips.

A ragged cheer swept the pit as Mortensen's harassed adjutant brought the hololith to life and decorated the space above the table with a three-dimensional representation of the fabricator moon of Illium. The small planet was one of the shepherd moons keeping Spetzghast's pole-to pole-ring system of dust, rock and ice in good order. Jagged holographic asteroids span across the display and past the Adeptus Mechanicus world, casting ugly shadows across the sickly factoryscape that plastered every available metre of space on the moon's surface.

'Right, lads. This swillhole is Illium,' Mortensen addressed the crowd of malingering officers and storm-troopers. He caught himself, bobbing his head contritely at Magister Militum Trepkos. 'Of course, no offence intended to you, sir.'

Trepkos nodded, his face a paralytic mask. It was well known that the skitarii underwent all manner of psychosurgical procedures to remove even the smallest traces of emotion and personality. Mortensen went back to work.

'Adeptus Mechanicus fabricator moon: culture mills and cybernetic workshops in the main, specialising in biological technologies. So that means built up areas and close quarters; limited fields of view and high concentrations of non-combatants crowding an already tight extraction zone. It isn't pretty – but then it rarely is. Sass.'

The adjutant recalibrated the hololith, zooming in on the black, baroque nightmare of the planet's capital. The Gothic metropolis sprawled across the fabricator moon's equatorial bulge and thrust skyward above the endless sea of greasestacks and cooling towers.

'Corpora Mons is the religious district and the moon's administrative capital,' Sass continued, relating the sum total of the gathered reports and intelligence from his freakishly photographic memory. 'There is open rebellion across many of the districts, major areas of civil unrest being centred on military and municipal targets. Mechanicus shrines have been desecrated and a significant section of the menial workforce has taken to the streets. The workers have used their knowledge of the infrastructure to sabotage communications and transport networks. Fires are widespread and large mobs of seditionists have converged on the capital.'

'What do these mungers actually want?' Minghella slipped in casually, as though he were actually interested.

'It's a straightforward rebellion, in all probability,' the adjutant said honestly. 'Although no figurehead or rebel organisation has been identified and no actual demands have been made.'

'Then how can you know that?' Krieg challenged.

'Sass knows a lot of things,' Mortensen intercepted.

Krieg fixed the adjutant with a withering stare and continued unfazed: 'What if you're wrong? What if it's some kind of cult influence, Chaotics or wychbreeds simply intent on mass destruction?'

'I don't know,' Sass retracted with new-found caution. He wasn't used to people questioning his strategic diagnosis. 'But I do know that they have taken out key tactical targets: the kind of targets that unchecked would make any kind of successful coup untenable.' Sass stabbed his finger into the holographic image of the city. 'A quarto-legio of Imperial Titans on loan from the Legio Invictus were being housed in a massive complex to the east of Corpora Mons. The Adeptus Biologus on Illium are famed for their refinement of Titan crew mind link technologies. These technologies have been sabotaged on all but two of the god-machines. They knew exactly where to hit them. They knew that the Mechanicus Titans would crush this rebellion. This isn't bloodlust or corruption. It's too cold, too audacious.'

'Cultists, freedom fighters, mechheads...' Conklin blustered, 'what does it matter? They all die the same way.'

'He's right,' Mortensen confirmed, hating to agree with the sergeant. He indicated his intention to move on. 'It doesn't matter.'

'It matters if you're waging war on an unknown enemy,' Krieg protested, his voice carrying. 'You have no idea of their capabilities. How can you prepare to counter them? Your approach is informed by everything you know, or more importantly, don't know about the enemy.'

Mortensen gave the cadet-commissar the slits of his eyes. 'We're not waging war on them: we'll leave that to the 364th Volscian Shadow Brigade. We're going to be in and out before the "enemy" knows we were even there. Anything else, quite frankly, doesn't concern us. All I really need to know is if one of these scummers puts themselves between me and an exit, are they going to drop when I put a bolt through them?'

'And you don't even know that…'

'The Shadow Brigade started landing troops yesterday,' Sass offered helpfully, 'and are making predictably slow and steady progress up through the slum sectors, taking it hab by hab. Everything by the book: but not fast enough to recover the assets.'

'We get on the ground and if it turns into a grox heap, we'll improvise: it's the Redemption Corps way,' Mortensen told Krieg. 'Live with it.'

Rosenkrantz watched the cadet-commissar's lip wrinkle before he got a hold over himself. Perhaps it was Krieg's inexperience, the recent events of the mutiny or something else entirely but the flight lieutenant had seen commissars have Guardsmen shot for less.

'What's the mission?' Krieg asked, his eyes burrowing into the back of the major's shaven skull.

'And where?' Rosenkrantz ventured, the mission location being of most relevance to her and the *Vertigo*'s crew.

Magister Militum Trepkos stepped forward with a stiff swish of scarlet. A series of ghostly lights flickered across the chrome of his trunk, activating the focal controls on the hololith and bringing the crackling image to full resolution on a gargantuan structure at the heart of Corpora Mons. His voice – a hollow mechanical echo – was everywhere at once and didn't come from his mouth, which remained tightly shut.

'This is the Artellus Cathedra: the centre of worship for the Cult Mechanicus on Illium. It contains the largest shrine to the glorious Omnissiah on the planet, in addition to a quad of orbital defence lasers, one housed in each steeple. The tactical as well as spiritual significance of Artellus necessitates an honour guard of two hundred skitarii troops and the Warlord Titan *Mortis Maximus*, outside the giant adamantium doors of the cathedra.

'As of sixteen hours ago, all contact with both cathedra and Titan has been lost. The skitarii garrison has orders to hold the cathedra for as long as possible under such circumstances. Final communications confirmed that the *Mortis Maximus* has no motive power or weapons control. Understandably the Fabricator General is concerned about the *Maximus's* current status, but the crew in themselves are a valuable resource and could be transferred to another god-machine if the circumstances allowed. He wants the assets back: in one piece.'

'How the hell do a bunch of trigger-happy menials take out a Titan?' Krieg shot across the pit with unmasked disbelief.

'Lucky shot?' the major asked with mock sincerity.

'Have you even read the reconnaissance files?'

'There are reconnaissance files?' Mortensen blurted back, his voice thick with meaty derision.

'Perhaps the war machine was critically damaged at the installation, with the other Titans,' Sass offered, hoping his hypothesis would throw a little cold water on the increasingly incensed Mortensen and Krieg.

'Or perhaps we've got some Alpha-level psyker running around down there,' the commissar hissed through clenched teeth. 'Or worse.'

'You're clearly new to this, so I'm going to make it real easy for you,' Mortensen rumbled caustically. 'If there was any evidence of corruption or the influence of the Ruinous Powers, the Volscians would have reported it by now. Believe me. These guys don't wipe their backsides without filing a reconnaissance report.'

'Better than wiping your backside on the recon report, which seems to be Redemption Corps standard practice.'

'Look, cadet-commissar,' Mortensen seethed, 'if you feel this mission is beyond your particular talents, whatever they are, please feel free to stand aside and let us do our duty.'

'I'd hardly be doing my duty if I did that,' the commissar shot back.

'Well, this is what we do Krieg, so you'd better get used to it. Your alarmist threat assessments aren't wanted or needed.'

The cadet-commissar's voice became cold and certain. 'Don't do that,' Krieg warned him with brutal sincerely. 'Don't question my courage. Your own infamous variety of bravado isn't worth spit if it does nothing to serve the Emperor's cause. You won't find me sending your men into the embrace of thoughtless slaughter. Mind that you do the same, major.'

Rosenkrantz had watched these two men publicly goad one another for the past few minutes, but when the flashpoint came, even she was taken off guard. The major's men were barely out of their seats and only a handful of corpsmen had managed to bring the greased barrels of their weapons to bear. Trepkos, of course, did nothing, despite having the only reflexes in the hanger swift enough to intercede. By then the two men had clashed in the centre of the amphitheatre. A dazzled Sass had been rammed aside and the hololith toppled, crashing to the metal floor. The gathered soldiers froze and Rosenkrantz with them.

The razor edge of the major's storm blade trembled against the flesh of the commissar's throat, each minute tremor nicking tiny slices across his oesophagus; the muzzle of Krieg's hellpistol hovered between the major's eyes, humming its supercharged intention to spread his brains across the flight deck. Each man had got a free hand to the other's wrist in a messy, makeshift hold and the two soldiers snarled at one another across the hate-charged space that separated their contorted faces.

Rosenkrantz flicked her eyes around the amphitheatre. No storm-trooper would move to stop them now. This wasn't shock or surprise anymore: shoulders and weapons had since sagged. It was respect. Honour. No corpsman would deny his commanding officer the opportunity to kill the commissar himself. The pilot could almost feel the soldiers willing it on.

Either way, Rosenkrantz sensed that she was about to witness a murder. Something gave inside her. She felt herself take a step forward, but became suddenly aware of Rask's bony fingers closing on her arm like a vice. She turned. He gave her an almost imperceptible shake of the head. She gave him an almost imperceptible shake of her own before breaking from his grip and striding across to the wrangling spectacle of the two men in the centre of the amphitheatre. They barely seemed aware of her presence.

'There is a saying on Jopall: "To Evil everything when good men do nothing",' the flight lieutenant cited softly. She slipped her slender hands slowly between the men, resting her fingers on the safety stud of the hellpistol and the clipped tip of Mortensen's survival knife. Pushing gently at both, the blade came away from Krieg's raw neck and the stud slid finally to safe. 'My bird is prepped and ready to fly. What'll she be carrying? Corpsmen or corpses?' she put to them.

The grip relaxed and the major and commissar untangled themselves. Krieg took a measured look around the amphitheatre to make sure the barrels were down before holstering his hellpistol. Mortensen turned and buried the storm blade in the table before helping Sass to his feet and righting the toppled hololith. Krieg straightened the lapels of his greatcoat. Mortensen stretched his brawny neck and faced the Redemption Corpsmen once more.

'Okay, just like Abraxus V. The extraction zone is too tight for a landing,' Mortensen continued stolidly. 'I will take the Redemption Corps and make an airborne deployment above the zone: a high altitude insertion directly onto the top of the Titan. Magister Militum Trepkos has agreed to accompany the insertion. He has the Mechanicus runecodes for the bridge top hatch. That should save some time.

'Second Platoon from the 364th Volscian Shadow Brigade will rappel to the surrounding roofs from the Valkyries – establish and hold a four-point ground extraction zone around the Titan's feet. Captain Rask will coordinate the deployment from the air.'

'What about the Reapers? Airstrikes prior to insertion would certainly soften things up a bit on the ground,' Minghella advocated.

Rosenkrantz nodded. She was all for Wing Commander Wharmby's Reaper Wing to blaze them a path up to the extraction. A fly-by from *Deliverance's* Tactical Reconaissance Group had already given Brigadier

Rob Sanders

Voskov valuable information on the situation at ground level. Why not have Wharmby's fighter squadron do a preliminary run? His strike fighters, Bolts and Marauders would only be sitting on the flight deck.

'Absolutely out of the question,' Trepkos cut in, the stainless steel timbre of his voice echoing around the amphitheatre. 'The Fabricator General would never sanction a bomber attack by the Aeronautica. The collateral damage to the faith district would be incalculable. What if Artellus or the *Mortis Maximus* were hit? It's one thing for the enemy to indulge in wanton destruction. You'll have to do what you can with your gunships and transports.'

A ripple of discontent and profanity swept the audience but Mortensen silenced the disgruntled corpsmen with a hand. 'A convoy of fire support Centaurs carrying Fourth Platoon in small groups under Lieutenant Deleval will deploy from a secure landing zone nearby and make their way to the extraction point.'

'How do you know the landing zone is secure?' Krieg threw in.

'The *Legio's* only other operational Titan – a Warhound Scout called *Ferrus Lupus* – is handling that for us, as we speak,' Sass declared with confidence.

'Cadet-Commissar Krieg will accompany the convoy,' Mortensen continued. 'Just in case they run into something they can't handle. By the time they arrive I should have the assets out, on the ground and ready for evacuation. All squads will then collapse back to the convoy. The column will punch its way back to the secured landing zone. The Spectres will then lift us back to *Deliverance*. Mission time, deployment to extraction – three hours. Like the lady said, let's make good on this. To your stations.'

Corpsmen around the amphitheatre evaporated. Mortensen's strident form cut a swathe through the exiting troopers, flanked by Minghella and the bruiser master sergeant. Rask hobbled to catch up, with Sass clutching the battered hololith and bringing up the rear. Before she knew it, Rosenkrantz was alone with Krieg.

'I want to thank you,' he said plainly, breaking the blanket of silence that had descended on the amphitheatre. 'A light touch was needed there.' She nodded slowly. 'But please, I must warn you. Don't interfere with Commissariat business again.'

With that, the cadet-commissar left.

'You're welcome,' the pilot called after him before setting off also, for a place that made marginally more sense to her: the cockpit of the *Vertigo*.

■

LIKE SOME COSMIC gliding behemoth, Sigma Scorpii extended tendrils of rusty light across Illium's asteroid-dominated sky. As the shadows began to recede across the fabricator moon, Flight Lieutenant Dekita Rosenkrantz rolled the *Vertigo* to port to avoid yet another belching smoke stack. Swooping in like angels of the armageddon, the procession of Spectre Valkyrie-variants had dropped out of the sky above the sea of Adeptus Mechanicus surgical sweatshops and cyber-netics mills, flanked by a cortege of Valkyries and lean Vulture gunships.

Lieutenant Commander Waldemar had been more daring than Rosenkrantz would have imagined, bringing his precious *Deliverance* down below the thin upper cloud layers and shaving precious minutes off their descent. As soon as Waldemar had delivered his payload, the Navy carrier vanished though, probably not too comfortable above Mechanicus defence lasers and missile silos.

Ordinarily, Illium's immigrant workforce would just be stirring in their bunks by now, but today was not an ordinary day. The citizens of the fabricator moon were already out in force and had been most of the night, lighting up the streets and dusty plazas with the flash of lasguns and pipe bombs.

As *Vertigo* led the formation across the skies of the greasy industriascape, Rosenkrantz's keen eyes were drawn to an irregular arrangement of fat, rusted chimneys and smog stacks. The cluster of mill vents belched thick, black smoke, but none of it was coming from the chimneys.

'No, no, no, no, no,' the pilot muttered to herself as the Spectre closed on the area. The configuration of chimneys was irregular because of their angle: it was the feature that had attracted her attention in the first place. The vast majority of the vents struck for the sky, vertically upwards; but these seemed at all angles, criss-crossing one another like fallen trees in a forest battered by a storm. Some were leaning or prone but largely intact; others had been demolished and smashed and lay broken-backed and shattered across the devastated district.

Rosenkrantz hit the vox-stud for the troop bay.

'Major, you're going to want to see this – forward portside.'

The pilot heard the storm-trooper grunt and direct one of his men to roll aside one of the Spectre's side doors. The gushing wind howled down the vox, drowning out a stream of the major's bitter oaths and curses as he saw what she saw.

Back at the vox Mortensen barked at the flight lieutenant: 'Have our formation hold and circle at this altitude. Inform them we are going in.'

'Benedict – handle that, please,' Rosenkrantz instructed, before dive-rolling the Spectre down towards the spectacle. As their angle of approach changed, more of the destruction was revealed. Instead of the stack tops the black smoke was pouring from the base of the chimneys where a coordinated set of explosions had levelled the district. At the centre of the fallen giants lay another giant: the *Ferrus Lupus*. The Mars-Pattern Warhound must have been making its behemothic approach to secure the landing zone when it stomped into the only trap bigger than itself.

The synchronised demolitions had to be the work of Mechanicus insurgents and their execution held a sad beauty. Gargantuan chimneys and smoke stacks had toppled and smashed against the Titan's mighty body, knocking it off-balance and over onto its armoured back. There the grand Titan struggled to right itself, its Vulcan mega bolter and plasma blastgun pointing uselessly at the sky as chimney after chimney tumbled over it, pinning it down and dashing its gleaming hull with brick and girder.

Out of the rat warren of wreckage the tech heretics crawled, shooting at the clouds in pride and jubilation with several groups firing on the Titan's impervious superstructure with cheap, single-shot rocket tubes. The Warhound's huge, leering muzzle flashed with optimistic blasts as the rockets flashed off the war machine's cockpit.

'Flight lieutenant.' It was Mortensen on the vox again. 'We're going to make an unscheduled stop. Prepare for disembarkation.'

She'd been afraid of that; but in reality, Magister Militum Trepkos was probably giving the major little in the way of choice. Their mission parameters had just been expanded.

'Affirmative.' Dropping the Spectre in over the Warhound's fallen form, Rosenkrantz span the aircraft down into a fast-moving descent. This was as much to give the Chief and his door gunners a free-rolling arc of fire as not to offer the Mechanicus rebels an easy target.

The four side doors of the carrier must have been thrown open because Rosenkrantz could hear the pneumatic thunder of *Vertigo's* heavy bolters cutting up the Titan's tormenters and driving them back under the rubble from beneath which they'd crawled. Holding the carrier still above the *Ferrus Lupus's* brazen chest the flight lieutenant waited with her heart in her mouth as *Vertigo* hovered like a bombastic dare to the rocket-armed seditionists.

Below, Mortensen and his storm-troopers would be no less vulnerable to small arms fire as they rappelled the distance between the Spectre and the Titan's chest.

'They're on the ground,' Captain Rask voxed up what seemed like an age later and Rosenkrantz banked the aircraft into a turn, once again opening up the arc of cover fire for her gunners and rolling gently into standard evasive manoeuvres around the drop zone.

This gave the pilot a better view of Mortensen and his recovery team. The major had selected only three other corpsmen, besides himself, who were advancing rapidly up the Titan's chest and collar plates in full carapace and packs. The storm-troopers advanced one after another in sequence, ducking under the barrels of each other's chunky hellguns, securing the path with conservative blasts of supercharged repression fire.

Las-fire lanced back, enthusiastic but undisciplined, as the tech heretics attempted to secure their prize from the safety of the shadows, hidden in caves of rubble and broken chimneys where the hammering of *Vertigo*'s heavy bolters failed to acquire them.

The Redemption Corps major strode across the Warhound's hull with supreme confidence. Helmetless and with hellgun slung, he pounded across the metal between his killers, feral and unreasoning. The Titan was his now and, like a jealous carnivore happening upon a fresh kill, he was intent upon running off the scavengers.

Trepkos followed his proud skitarii, hood and cloak flowing after like a vermillion advertisement. His movements were no less determined but mimicked more the stomp of one of his Titan war machines than the stalking, animal gait of the major.

Bounding up the cliff-face of the Warhound's throat, Mortensen attacked the climb with fervour, pulling himself up, arm over arm through the hydraulics and ricochets. As Trepkos went to work on mechanisms under the chin of the *Ferrus Lupus*'s great armoured muzzle and the prayers required to operate them, the major and his men positioned themselves about the cockpit section, weapons ready.

Rosenkrantz circled as the Mechanicus revolutionaries were drawn from their hiding places. *Vertigo* itself was now being repeatedly targeted, with several hopeful rockets streaming wide and a multitude of luckier las-blasts scuffing the hull and canopy. The storm-trooper's surgical insertion and bold advance had initially taken the rebels by surprise but now their territorial desperation was showing with individuals and small groups rapidly closing on the Titan cockpit from across the wrecked landscape.

With a deep, reverberating thud and a flash the cockpit awning mechanism fired and rolled, carried back by gravity and its great armoured weight. As the smoke cleared, the cramped conditions inside the Warhound were revealed with two stunned moderati and the stricken Titan princeps strapped into the confined space.

The Redemption Corps major had little time for ceremony and grabbed one of the moderati by his hard-wire lines and cables, traumatically tearing him from both his link with the downed Titan and his seat. A rocket from an advancing heretic, kneeling in a ladder cage that ran up the side of a nearby tumbled smoke stack, flashed before Mortensen's face. Before the projectile had time to strike the side of the opposing factory wall, the storm-trooper had his chunky autopistol clear of its holster. With a roar the major unleashed the weapon on his attacker, raining a light show of deflections off the bars and rungs of the ladder cage before finding his mark and riddling the trapped tech-heretic with explosive fire.

Hoisting the protesting moderati onto the shoulder of a nearby corpsman, Mortensen repeated the procedure with the princeps and his other crewman and sent them off towards the leaning smoke stack. Offering Trepkos a meaty hand, the major pulled the skitarii officer up the forward cockpit and directed him after the storm-troopers.

Mortensen's men had reached the fallen chimney, which lay at a forty-five degree angle across the Titan's plasma blastgun and several other demolished towers. With their recovered targets bundled over shoulder and pack, the storm-troopers stomped up the outside of the ladder cage, towards the chimney's punishing summit. With furious las-fire following them up the incline from pursuing seditionists, Trepkos and Mortensen followed.

Gliding up behind the escaping corpsmen, Rosenkrantz directed her door gunners to drive the Mechanicus menials back from the base of the smoke stack with a storm of concentrated fire, allowing Mortensen and his men time to get a little bit of distance on their pursuers. Proceeding on up the length of the stack, the flight lieutenant held *Vertigo* at the relative safety of the chimney top as the storm-troopers endurance-climbed their way towards them.

Las-blasts struck wildly at the chimney, several glancing off the Redemption Corps' thick, armaplas carapace and one burning into the back of the *Ferrus Lupus's* howling princeps. A rocket was more fortunate, launched from a factory window and burying itself in the base of the smoke stack. The entire structure bucked and a visible shiver ran up the metalwork, almost shaking the storm-troopers loose. Dropping to the mesh of the ladder cage and grabbing on, the corpsmen held and waited as the superstructure groaned and twisted inside.

Suddenly Mortensen was very animated, waving his arms and pushing his troopers on. Picking up the pace, as well as the extra weight, the armoured figures darted up the remaining length of the chimney and passed their loads in through *Vertigo's* side doors. The vox chirped.

'They're in,' Captain Rask reported.

Throwing back the stick Rosenkrantz blasted skyward, away from the toppled Titan and the industrial forest of fallen smog stacks that buried it. Back at the head of the waiting formation of Navy aircraft, the pilot banked towards the hub districts of Corpora Mons. Soon the sulphur towers, ventscrapers and the endless landscape of wretched slave mills gave way to the baroque lines and Gothic majesty of the faith district's tabernacles and cathedrals.

'Approaching first drop zone, flight lieutenant,' Benedict notified her.

'Is he always like this?' the major called, chomping down on a fat, stubby cigar. Rosenkrantz flashed him her eyes before returning her attention to the business of flying the aircraft through the narrower chasms of the new district.

The major pulled himself up the companionway ladder and slapped the servitor co-pilot on his cold, pallid shoulders. 'Lighten up, Navy boy. It's the start of a brand new, action-packed day.'

It was obvious that the storm-trooper was in his element from the cocksure grin and the veritable stink of adrenaline and testosterone in the cockpit. He came in beside Rosenkrantz to get a better look at the ground and snatched a headset from a canopy rack.

'Drop zone is hot,' reported Benedict as they banked into the space above an open plaza, 'I repeat, the dropzone is hot.'

Mortensen leaned in closer. 'Not for long,' he grumbled with concentration.

Rosenkrantz peered over the nose cone at their designated landing zone, the one Mortensen had boldly claimed could be made secure. On every other day of the year it was a large ornamental esplanade and cactus flower garden preceding the entrance to an Omnissiah mechshrine. Today it was the sight of unprecedented slaughter. Black smoke was pouring from the shrine and the garden's bloated ornamental cacti had been riddled with las-fire. Seditionists pelted the hallowed building with debris and bolts from their rifles. Ragged, beaten tech-priests were running for their lives down the length of the esplanade, pursued by posses of rebels wielding blood-splattered wrenches and lengths of noose fashioned from power cable. With the invaluable assistance of the *Ferrus Lupus*, this would have been nothing more than a plasma-bathed ghost town. There was little point in dwelling on that now, however, any more than worrying how Deleval's convoy would make it through to the cathedra without the firepower of the Warhound to clear the way.

'*Blazer One*, this is...' Mortensen stalled. 'What the hell is this bird called?'

'*Vertigo*,' Rosenkrantz enlightened him.

'*Blazer One*, this is *Vertigo*. We have some hostiles crowding the dropzone. Would you be so good as to strafe those malingering sons-of-bitches and clear the way, so to speak?'

Rosenkrantz watched as six Vulture gunships broke off from the main pack and streaked off in search of slaughter. Taking turns on rotational passes, the gunships tore through the esplanade peppering the murderous mobs with their multilasers.

'Yeah, get that maggot in the hood,' Mortensen buzzed. Rosenkrantz marvelled at the man. It was like he was watching a game of razorball. 'No, the other one. And watch the cloisters; I thought I saw some mechhead with a rocket...'

The sudden crack of a missile fire was instantly followed by a thunderous flash as *Blazer Two* took a rocket in the tail. Spewing smoke, the Vulture descended in a heavy spin, throwing its shattered tail section all around the plaza.

'We have a confirmed hit on *Blazer Two*,' Benedict reported helpfully.

'Yeah,' the major growled, his good mood evaporating fast. 'Thanks for the update.'

Rosenkrantz watched *Blazer Two* slam into the ground at the foot of the mechshrine steps. Her wings were alight and her hull shattered, but as far as the pilot could tell, her cockpit section was intact.

'*Blazer Two*, this is *Vertigo*,' Rosenkrantz announced. 'Report casualties and status. Please respond.' The vox gave a deathly crackle for a moment, before *Blazer Two*'s pilot called in.

'Rig's totalled. I think we might be on fire. I'm okay. Jesperson's taken some flak in the back.'

Pushing the microphone of his vox-set to his lips, Mortensen spat, '*Vector One* and *Two*, move in and offer cover fire. And don't get clipped. *Blazer One*, would it be too much to ask to bag that munger?'

The *Vectors*, the detachment's four Valkyrie assault carriers, plunged into the maelstrom below, the heavy bolter door gunners giving a good account of themselves.

The major proceeded to grumble orders down the vox as *Blazer One* and *Three* continued their strafing runs on the cloisters, their multilasers reducing the esplanade's architecture to a pit-cratered mess. Despite the joint efforts of the Valkyrie gunners, a small horde of ragged seditionists closed on the downed Vulture, hacking at the cracked canopy with lump hammers and track irons.

'Nash, get out of there!' Rosenkrantz bellowed down the vox. The pilot had his Navy issue pistol out and was trying to scatter the mob, but it was thankfully just as difficult blasting out of the canopy as smashing in.

'Can't… move… Jesperson.'

Vector One's shadow suddenly passed over the gang and a hail of bolter fire tore several of the rebels off the aircraft and deposited them in a bloody heap on the plaza floor. Not before a scrawny runt of a seditionist slotted a grenade through the small opening the lump hammer had caved in the canopy armaplas, however. There were assorted wails of desperation from the vox before the inside of the cockpit lit up with the momentary blast of a frag firestorm.

'Vrekkin' animals!' Mortensen roared, ripping the vox-set from his shaven skull. 'Put this beast down on the deck, now,' he ordered, shimmying down the companionway ladder.

Throwing the Spectre into a nose-dive, Rosenkrantz was determined to come in high and fast, giving the rocket launcher little time to acquire the *Vertigo* as a target.

'Benedict, prepare countermeasures.'

'Affirmative, flight lieutenant.'

Rosenkrantz altered the channel on her vox: 'Chief, we're going in. We'll need plenty of cover fire, the zone is still hot.' Nauls grunted affirmation back down the vox. As crew chief he would already have his hands full. Besides managing the *Vertigo's* four door gunners, he also had the cramped conditions created by the presence of two fully loaded Imperial Centaur fire support vehicles stowed in the hold to contend with; this with the extra headache of the major's storm-troopers, strapped into their bulky grav-chutes, sitting up forward. And now, with the Spectre packed to bursting point, he also had the morose Mortensen bouncing around down there to make his life even more miserable.

With a screech of air brakes, Rosenkrantz pulled the Spectre up, just in time to avoid burying the aircraft under the esplanade. The assault carrier's superstructure creaked in protest, but with Rosenkrantz at the stick it was used to such cavalier handling.

'Lowering landing gear,' the co-pilot droned.

It wasn't long before Rosenkrantz had given the crew something to do. All four heavy bolters sang an ode to death from the top of their barrels, sweeping the plaza of carefully advancing seditionists, intent on murder and mayhem. The Spectre came to rest gently on the esplanade.

Benedict saw it first, his usual demeanour abandoned in favour of something more direct. 'Starboard side!'

Rosenkrantz picked out their bushwhacker, resting his rocket tube against a bolt-mangled pillar, aiming straight at the *Vertigo*.

'Holy Throne. Brace for impact!' she screamed down the vox. One of the Vultures unexpectedly swept side-on between them, a constant rain of multilaser fire driving their assailant further along the cloisters.

If that wasn't enough, Mortensen was out on the plaza, striding across the killing ground between streams of heavy bolter fire and ducking under *Blazer One*'s swooping hull. Rosenkrantz watched as the gunship rose out of the plaza for another run and the seditionist stepped out from behind a cloister pillar, ready once again to fire on the *Vertigo* with his rocket tube.

Instead he came face to face with the Redemption Corps major, who was casually injecting a fresh magazine into the grip of his chunky autopistol. The two men looked at one another, the rocket launcher useless

at that range and limp in the rebel's hands. Mortensen
flicked up the pistol, blasting the rebel almost point-
blank. The first round lifted the seditionist's flailing
body from the ground and flung him back against the
cloister wall. Closing on the rebel, the major
unleashed further fury with the weapon as he blasted
away with each sure-footed step, three, four, five times,
before flicking to auto and riddling the mechhead's
body with the remainder of his clip. Kneeling by the
tattered corpse Mortensen emptied his weapon in the
seditionist's lap before slapping another magazine
home. Holstering the weapon, he scooped up the
abandoned rocket tube, with its single rocket.

A hammer-wielding maniac came at Mortensen
from the left on his return to the aircraft, but one of
the door gunners plucked him out of reach with a
short burst of explosive firepower. Rosenkrantz heard
him slap the side of the cockpit harshly.

'Lower ramp,' she instructed Benedict.

The Spectre gave another creak as a Centaur fire support vehicle rolled out from under the aircraft's beak
and came to a standstill by the downed Vulture's
blasted remains. A begoggled Volscian popped out of
the central hatch and got to grips with the pintle-
mounted assault cannon.

The Spectres and Centaurs combined gave the
Redemption Corps and their Shadow Brigade compatriots just the speed and flexibility they needed for fast
deployment in crowded battlezones. Chimera carriers
were not only too large to be transported in the
swollen hulls of the Spectre-class Valkyries, they were
too wide and slow for the chaos of Illium's narrow
streets. Fire support Centaurs were super-charged for
swift transportation under fire; they were also fully

armour-encased, unlike their tow-tractor brethren and packed the punch of a small infantry support vehicle.

Another slap and a wave from Mortensen. 'Benedict, close ramp. *White Thunder*, you are cleared to begin your descent,' Rosenkrantz assured one of the sister Spectres.

'He's in,' the chief told her curtly down the vox. Feathering the stick, Rosenkrantz took the aircraft off the deck and cleared the drop zone. It wasn't long before Mortensen was back in the cockpit.

'As soon as the last Spectre's cleared, have them go straight to the airstrip. Despatch the *Vectors* to establish hold points. *Blazer One* and *Three* to provide cover for the fire support vehicles; all remaining Vultures to escort the carriers and secure the evacuation. Clear?'

'As the skies, sir.'

'It'd better be,' Mortensen warned, 'I'm not losing any more birds to menials who get lucky with rocket launchers.' He tossed Benedict the rocket tube. Picking the blood-bathed weapon up with his thumb and fingertips, Benedict deposited the launcher on the ledge above his hullside codifier panel. 'Souvenir,' the major told him, before stepping back on the companion ladder.

'If you have any trouble I'll be in the hold, suiting up,' he called to Rosenkrantz, his good mood returning within moments, the prospect of diving head first out of a perfectly good aircraft appealing to the major's sensibilities.

The pilot pursed her lips, allowing the casual slur to hang in the air. She'd been wrong about carrying Mortensen, she mused. There would be a lot less trouble for her and her crew once the major was off her bird. And that moment couldn't come soon enough.

* * *

III

As VERTIGO'S RAMP rolled open and the full glory of the Illium warzone was revealed to Mortensen, Krieg's warnings came back to haunt him.

Corpora Mons and other periphery districts were overrun by heretics, defectors and infectious mayhem. The small-scale firefights and rioting mobs had found their way into every part of the city. The capital was turning itself inside out. The landing zone had been hotter than he'd expected, but he'd put that down to Sass and plain bad luck. Mostly Sass. From here the whole planet seemed ablaze with rebellion. Anything bearing the caducal helix of the Mechanicus or the Imperial aquila had been blown to pieces or razed to the ground. Thick smoke spewed from the urban nightmare below, the rough black lines carving up the sky like an insane tessellation. *Vertigo* cut through the pattern, her slipstream dispersing the stack so it appeared like the aircraft had snapped the threads of a giant spider's web.

For once Mortensen had to sympathise with the Shadow Brigade. Even with the 364th, it could take the best part of six months to retake the moon, street by street. Each district was a labyrinthine hell of gauntlets, sniper killzones and booby traps. This maelstrom had already swallowed the Adeptus Mechanicus skitarii forces that provided security for the installations and two companies of Spetzghast Mercantile Militia, scrambled from the subsector capital. Now it was going to swallow the Redemption Corps. More accurately, Mortensen and his fellow storm-troopers had volunteered to dive head first down the monstrous rebellion's throat.

Strapped into carapace and the chest-hugging grav chute, the major made preparations for the drop.

Rob Sanders

Pulling his helmet on and slapping down the visor, he walked towards the opening ramp. The Spectre was high above the Cita-Cathedra of Artellus-Magna, the most magnificent of Illium's many places of worship, glorifying the art and mystery of the Omnissiah and housing the Episcopal throne of the Imperator Fabricate. The cita-cathedra signified the heart of the capital, with Corpora districts segmentally radiating out from the centre: the spiritual quarters, administrative sectors, conurbation strips of Imperial tenement hab-blocks and, of course, the vast manufactorium zones of the city.

A swift rap on the side of Mortensen's helmet brought him back to the here and now. It was Rask, pointing up towards the cockpit and donning a headset. Sass was behind him but swiftly disappeared up the companionway ladder. The intense adjutant never did drops, having little liking for heights in general, despite being attached to an air-mobile storm troop. He usually helped coordinate operations with Rask, where his keen mind could wrangle with the big picture and weigh up alternative strategies, should the situation on the ground go tits up: which it usually did.

'Try and draw some of their fire from us,' Mortensen hollered, compensating for the helmet and turbulence in the bay. Rask nodded and smiled his crooked smile. 'You know,' the major added, 'without actually drawing fire on yourselves.'

The captain took an awkward step towards the companionway. 'Watch your back!' he called from the steps.

'That's why I brought you,' the major yelled back. Mortensen peered down at the roofs and towers of the

cita-cathedra. Standing astride the massive adamantium doors of the building was the mighty Imperial
Warlord Titan *Mortis Maximus*. The cathedra plaza was
a rippling carpet of revolutionaries. Mobs swarmed
around the Titan's gigantic feet and hung from suicidal
heights as they attempted to scale the sides of the god-
machine, desperately searching for some kind of an
entrance.

As the *Vertigo* rolled to port the major breathed in
the full, awesome lethality of the metal mountain
below. He wasn't the first to stare in marvel at the
destructive capabilities of the war machine; to wonder
what it would be like to command such incredible
power.

If he hadn't been so stunned by the spectacle,
Mortensen might have noticed that something was
seriously wrong.

As it was, it was Rosenkrantz that clocked it first and
broke in across the vox-channel in sickening realisation: 'Those plasma silos are open.'

Mortensen growled.

The Spectre's cargo bay suddenly crackled with a
blinding, searing light. A momentary shockwave of
heat rolled through the aircraft as a fat beam of plasma
energy blasted skyward past the *Vertigo*.

The aircraft took a stomach-churning tumble, throwing Mortensen into the wall of the belly compartment.
Rask missed his footing on the companionway and
fell. He skimmed across the slick floor of the carrier,
snatching wildly for a handhold. Several of the aircraft's door gunners and the storm-troopers struck out
their arms for him but their safety lines and harnesses
tore them back. The major dropped and sunk his fist
into the webbing of Rask's passing flak jacket, just

managing to grab the flailing captain before he slipped
out of the bay door. Rask's legs dangled off the ramp,
kicking at the spinning nothing below, desperate for a
foothold that wasn't there. Clawing his way up
Mortensen's carapace dropsuit, the officer hauled himself back inside the bay door. The major brought him
up to his helmet faceplate.

'You okay?' Mortensen bawled.

'Vrekkin' great: next stupid question,' Rask howled
back.

'Status!' the storm-trooper called into his helmet
vox-link.

'We just lost *White Thunder*,' Rosenkrantz shot back.
In macabre illustration *Vertigo's* rolling spin revealed
the Spectre as she fell past. Her belly, cockpit and tail
section were intact but her starboard wing was completely gone, burned out of existence by the column of
plasma firepower the cathedra had just unleashed at
some target in the upper atmosphere. As *Vertigo's* own
tail came around again Mortensen caught another
glimpse of *White Thunder's* spiralling form.

'Is *Deliverance* hit?'

Mortensen and Rask exchanged a grim glance as the
vox crackled with static suspense.

'Negative,' Benedict finally cut in. '*Deliverance* is
clear. Looks to Commander Waldemar like a ranging
shot. He thinks that it might be prudent to–'

'Yeah, yeah,' Mortensen barged in.

'You've got to go,' Rask called – still clutching the
ramp struts as the Illian industriascape whirled by
behind him. The major nodded.

'Get all aircraft down on the deck,' the major
ordered.

'We're not going to last very long at street level.'

'Longer than against those silos,' Mortensen answered with harsh logic. Rask nodded. 'Locate the Spectre and reroute the convoy to pick up them up. The whole city will be coming down on them.'

'Major,' Benedict piped up. '*Deliverance* reports the cathedra's plasma batteries are charging for another orbital assault.'

'We can't be here,' Rosenkrantz added, her words laced with alarm.

'Okay, keep your flight suit on,' Mortensen barked, signalling Magister Militum Trepkos and the Redemption Corps to come forward on their snaglines. Corporal Vedette presented herself, slipping a helmet down over her platinum blonde hair. Her limp was all but gone, but even if her thigh wound had been giving her hell, Vedette knew better than to show it on an operation. 'Ready?'

'Born ready, sir,' she beamed back.

A Mordian by birth, Zola Vedette had long been distinguishing herself in the storm-trooper ranks, when she met Major Mortensen. She'd been part of a rearguard force left to cover the withdrawal of the Noctan Strikes from the night world of Nebrus IX. Disease had swept across the tiny planet and the cities had been overrun by plague zombies. The Redemption Corps had been brought in at the eleventh hour with the clock already running on an Ordo Sepulturum sanctioned cyclonic orbital cleansing. Mortensen's men had snatched the Noctans and Vedette's stalwart rearguard from the planet surface mere moments before torpedo impact. The major had Rask pull some strings the next day.

'As you were.'

The drop troops were already filing down the ramp in their carapace armour and helmets. Like Mortensen, the storm-troopers carried their hellguns and weapons slung on their packs, in order to avoid distorting the aerodynamics of the Redemption Corps' trademark high altitude thunderbolt descent. The hope was that the troopers would move faster than the anti-aircraft guns could track. A distinct bonus when freefalling into a shooting gallery, where a street urchin with a flintlock could cut you in half with a stray shot.

Vedette proceeded to count the storm-troopers out, barking their names in quick succession as each in turn pitched off the Spectre's ramp with the certainty of newborn Tallarn thundervultures.

The last of the squad gave Vedette a nod of their helmets before vaulting into the maelstrom outside: Minghella, who'd been checking everyone's oxygen; Pryce, his carapace jangling with cheap icons and relics, and then the replacements: Greco – infamous spire-breaker and Progenium runaway; Teague, the Elysian young blood; Kynt, the one-eyed comms-officer and Quant, Gorskii's demolitions stand-in. The Valhallan storm-trooper had barely survived the 1001st's bloody rebellion and unfortunately had lost the battle, as so many had, on the operating table. As always, Rask had been ready with suitable substitutes: troopers the major could already trust or those that Rask believed he would get to.

They were followed by Vedette, who gave an obligatory salute that was more habit than requirement before peeling off into oblivion. The major watched them tumble away from the aircraft, taking a few steps of his own before launching off the ramp.

Holding his hands behind his back, Mortensen plunged helmet first through the thermals, rapidly falling into the slipstream created by the other drop troops. Like a small meteor shower, the Redemption Corps streaked for the planet's surface with the heavens howling around them.

Mortensen ate it up: heart racing with the desire to be part of the whole wanton abandon of it. He didn't hunger for blood – he was no savage or berserker. He merely thrived on the cutting edge of possibility. Nobody held Zane Mortensen's fate in their hand: what he did, his very next action, and the one after that, would determine his destiny for good or for ill. That was where he felt most at peace. Crossing the terminator of exigency, on the event horizon of the unforeseen, where he was at that very moment.

The entire city suddenly vanished as explosions tore the air to shreds around him. An oil slick of black smog swiftly blanketed the area in the wake of hundreds of enemy shells splatter-bombing the sky. Mortensen swung this way and that, making his trajectory more difficult to predict, but it was largely futile. Some insane genius inside the cathedra hadn't been satisfied with hurling shafts of boiling plasma into the heavens and had ordered the gargoyle encrusted macro-cannons manned and armed.

As he punctured the bottom of the inkblot cloud, the major caught sight of the *Vertigo*, corkscrewing around their descent pattern, attempting to draw the artillery fire. The Spectre was rewarded with an alarmingly obliging spree of thunder blasts across the nose of the aircraft, forcing Rosenkrantz to roll the Navy bird sharply to starboard.

Focusing once again on the fast approaching cityscape, Mortensen noticed that one of his stormtroopers had broken formation. Certainly, each corpsman would have had to negotiate the dangers of the blanket barrage, but Pryce was careering all over, arms loose and legs flailing in the backwash. Bringing his own arms in tighter and helmet down, Mortensen surged forwards for the trooper. As he crossed to Pryce's other side, he could see what had happened. The trooper must have caught the blast wave of one of the detonations: his left leg and arm were a ragged mess of blood and bone and the side of his helmet and visor were shattered. Unconscious or dead, he wouldn't be able to fire his own grav-chute.

Pushing his body to the limit, Mortensen willed himself onwards, drawing closer and closer to the injured soldier, desperate to reach the vectorpull and activate his chute. At least that way, *Vertigo* could swing in and collect him.

As his fingertips brushed the pack's repulsion vents, Pryce was ripped from his grasp. The air was quaking with a fresh shower of artillery explosions. Taking the full force of one of the sporadic shells, the unfortunate trooper was blasted skyward in a drizzle of gore and religious iconography, catapulting the major into a freefall spin. Little good the seals and relics had done him in the end.

For a small eternity, Illium became a vertiginous assault on Mortensen's senses: a vomit-inducing kaleidoscope of reversals with g-forces fighting inside his body for possession of his centre of gravity. Perhaps following some previous pattern of thought, Mortensen's fingers found the vectorpull of his own chute and he yanked it furiously. The pack bucked, trying to right itself in the middle of the major's rolling rotation. Simultaneously the chute cut the descent velocity and mastered the spin, sending a jolt through Mortensen that he could feel in his eyeballs.

Now his eyes had stopped swimming with motion, Mortensen got a grip on his position. The grav-chute had slowed his descent to a mere glide about two hundred metres above the cathedra concourse. Immediately below him the god-machine *Mortis Maximus* stood astride the mighty adamantium doors of Artellus-Magna. The Warlord Titan was silent and still, immobilised as Trepkos had told them. The concourse was flooded with insurgent mobs mounting a futile assault on the colossal war machine with small arms and grenades, although this seemed more of a display than a genuine attempt to breach the Warlord's impenetrable armour. Even the lowliest Mechanicus factory hand would know that the more optimistic options for forced entry lay with the war machine's bridge and the weapon system's maintenance bulkheads. And this was where a few hundred of the renegade Imperials were headed, surging up gangways and grapnels with little care for safety or sanity.

Below, Mortensen watched his storm-troopers establish a two-team perimeter on the metallic expanse of the Warlord's armoured hood. He could make out Conklin giving the enemy troops a headache with the constant chatter of his bolter. Leaning into a course correction the major drifted above them. Firing the clips on his harness Mortensen dropped the remaining metres from his grav-chute to the chilled hull of the monstrous god-machine. He rolled into a crouch, his pack activated and his hellgun humming

Suddenly Kynt was behind him, humping the extra weight of the troop master-vox. Helmet off and blinking with his good eye through the blasts hammering the metal about them, the copper-headed comms-officer extended him the vox-hailer.

'Major.' Rask said.

'Go ahead.'

'*Vector Four* has a visual on the Spectre crash site, couple of clicks south of your position. The pilots confirm movement within and large numbers of enemy targets moving in on their position.'

'How close is the convoy?'

'Not close enough. I've re-routed the column but Deleval's run into heavy resistance.'

'Can the assault carriers reach them?' Mortensen asked. It was the simplest choice.

'Negative. Too dangerous. They've tried and already taken several hits. I've had them move onto the pick-up.'

'Other options, captain?'

Rask swallowed.

'We could head in. *Vertigo* could rappel our snipers down near to the crash site, while it's still relatively quiet, and have them work their way over to the bird. Buy a bit of time until the convoy arrives.'

Mortensen grumbled to himself. The Spectres did carry marksmen for extra air cover on the dispersal. Still, he didn't like it. The Spectre; the convoy; the snipers. Things were getting messy down on the ground.

'Who is it?'

'Opech and Sarakota.'

He knew about Sarakota. He'd assigned him to *Vertigo*. Opech was Rask's choice: both of the snipers hailed from the feral world of Khongkotan, a bleak dust hole of canyons, cavern systems and backstabbing tribesmen. Whereas Sarakota spoke little, the Imperial Creed hadn't quite imprinted itself on Opech: he was still full of tribal belligerence and was known to brawl with his brother Khongkotans. As a people, however, they had the senses of a raptor and made excellent scouts and marksmen.

The major nodded silently to himself. 'Do it.'

'Rask, out.'

The metal around Mortensen flashed with the ricochet of las-fire. The Titan was crawling with Mechanicus defectors, some of whom had taken up position on and around the war machine's hulking shoulders, pinning the Redemption Corpsmen down and pushing them back. Apart from their own abandoned grav-chutes, the hood offered little in the way of cover and already Vedette's skirmish line was retreating.

The renegades couldn't shoot for dust – that much was clear from the wild pattern of fire – but the intensity of the assault was growing, with each new climber adding his muzzle to the collection aimed at the storm-troopers.

Suppression fire was all the corporal and her men had to offer the rebels in return, the hellguns hurling bursts of short range, power-conserving fire at the mobs. Such tactics were a necessary evil for the storm-troopers. They travelled light and moved fast: their missions dependent upon surgical execution rather than collateral damage. As Mortensen had assured Krieg, the 364th Volscian Shadow Brigade would mop up these degenerates – eventually.

Vedette clicked her hellgun briefly to automatic and bounced backward on the tips of her boots, splitting rounds between different clusters of closing insurgents. Mortensen met her at the lip of the Titan's hood where Greco and Specialist Elek Quant were lashing lines and descenders to a sensor array.

Squatting by the virtually non-existent cover offered by the small forest of aerials, Mortensen and Vedette crouched shoulder to shoulder.

'We lost Pryce,' the major informed her stoically.

Vedette reached into her carapace and pulled out a piece of shattered chrome shell, trailing leads, valves and gore. 'Trepkos.'

'Great,' he snarled back. 'Plan B.'

The Mordian was way ahead of him and turned to present Quant and TFC Greco.

'Run a bypass on the bridge main-hatch runelock,' Mortensen barked at Greco, who gave him the kind of furtive, guilty look he always gave him before breaking a security system.

'Mechs trust us to snatch the crew but they don't trust us with the codes?' the arch-larcenist sniffed. He'd dumped his helmet, his suit sweat-band and five o'clock shadow making his crab-face look even more horribly splayed than usual.

'Politics,' said the major, rolling his eyes theatrically and slipping into a harness.

'What if I can't... this is a Titan, after all,' Greco put to him.

'Just get us past the shell. Uncle can work his magic on the bulkhead mechanism.'

That's what the Redemption Corps called Quant. He was one of the squad's old hands. An adamantium nerve and a lifetime's working knowledge of explosive devices had made him an easy choice for demolitions specialist, and Gorskii had learned a great deal under his tutelage. 'Okay, Uncle?'

'We're Redemption Corps,' the old specialist murmured sagely under his moustache. 'We'll improvise.'

Snapped into his descender, Mortensen and the two corpsmen kicked off the edge of the hood and rappelled the distance between the hood and the command deck, leaving Vedette to bark orders and hold the skirmish line.

As soon as Greco's boots hit the dome roof he slid down across the convex armour plating and onto his stomach where he went to work on the bridge top-hatch. Uncle started to assemble the demolition charge he was intending to use on the pressurised hatch bulkhead, leaving Mortensen to watch over them with his droning hellgun.

Greco was surprisingly fast. The trooper simply lay back, resting his head on one arm as though he were reclining in an obscura den. The hull shell sighed and parted, leaving a circular opening gaping to the sky. 'Progenium installations have better security than that,' the spire-breaker told them. 'You know, there was this one time–'

'Greco.'

'Yes, sir?'

'Shut up.'

'All yours, old man,' the TFC told Quant, shifting back up the metal dome. The specialist moved in with his charge, trailing detonator cable and tools.

His charge assembled, Uncle began to back up the hull himself, a palm grip detonator in one fist. The three men backed in under the hood and put their backs against the cool hull.

'Ready?'

Uncle nodded.

'Should we really be standing on the command deck?' Greco put to them at the last moment. 'You know, if we're gonna like, well, blow it up?'

'It's a directional charge,' the demolitions man informed him icily.

'Oh,' Greco muttered. 'Good safety tip.'

Uncle clasped the detonator and the hatch vomited forth skull-splitting sound and light. A peal of thunder rolled through the command deck superstructure and the armour plating immediately around the opening creaked and buckled. A cloud of blistering white smoke pumped from the hatch. Donning his gloves and hellgun, Uncle skirted down the slippery hull and vanished, making a corpsman-shaped hole in the smoke.

A few moments later Mortensen's vox-bead crackled.

'I'm in.'

The major grinned, adjusting the troop channel: 'Sergeant Conklin, Corporal Vedette. Fall back by teams to the Titan command deck.'

'Affirmative, major.'

IV

'SEND US DOWN another dead-end and I'm going to come up there and rip you one, you hear me, flyboy?' That was Deleval: Lieutenant, Fourth Platoon. It didn't really matter to Krieg, although he was ashamed to admit that the Volscians all looked the same to him. There was little to pick between the officers and the men when it came to uniform and physical appearance; a complete lack of respect for Tactica formulations was equally evident in either.

Deleval was a charmer though. He was one of those tough hive bastards – the swill of corruption running in his veins. He had a hard face and unforgiving eyes that wouldn't have been out of place on a bounty hunter. Lieutenant's stripes or not, Deleval's word was law amongst the men of his platoon. Anything else was simply an invitation to wake up the next morning with your throat slit: if you were unlucky enough to wake up at all. Snyder, Turkle and Goinz, the three hive-world hyenas that sat behind him would have seen to that all right.

Krieg had heard Captain Rask call Fourth Platoon the 'Zombie Squad', primarily because it was largely made up of the worst kind of Volscians the 364th had to offer – brutal gangers and psychotics, unable to live without the blood and carnage of the underhive and who found new expressions of their old lives in the merciless way in which they interpreted their orders. Deleval himself was rumoured to hail from the notorious Jericho Hive, the site of a spook war that had raged across several generations for nearly a century.

This was, of course, the other reason Deleval and his men had earned their moniker – regimental supplies of spook, mankweed, gladstones, PNP, hulk dust and various unlicensed combat stimulants chiefly came from the Zombie Squad and their illicit contacts and suppliers.

Deleval's henchmen were typical Zombie Squad scum. They'd spent most of the run eyeballing Krieg and exchanging hazy slurs about the commissar. Without the reassuring presence of Golliant, barely squeezed into the seat next to him, Krieg was certain the Volscians would have riddled him with scatter shot from their combat shotguns and rolled his body out the back of the moving Centaur and under the tracks of the next. Snyder – a savage little scavver with a receding shock of wiry, ginger hair – and the loud-mouth Turkle had to content themselves with goading the commissar and filling the compartment with nefarious laughter. Goinz didn't say much – clearly out of his eyeballs on combat stimulants – but would simply chuckle nastily to himself, seemingly out of sync with the rest of the hilarity.

Blazer One had been less than helpful with directions, sending Deleval's convoy down more than one improvised cul-de-sac, where revolutionaries had toppled structures, erected barricades and stacked burnt-out cargo-10's and dozerloaders in an attempt to frustrate any kind of advance on the cathedra. It had worked.

Golliant had told Krieg that the convoy drivers were all handpicked Volscian ash buggy drivers, used to racing piles of scrap across the hellish and ever changing chemical wasteland that was their garrison home world. They were spoiled with the Centaur fire support variant: their pace and manoeuvrability put the universally admired Chimera chassis to shame. What the light carrier gained in handling, it lost in armour and armament, however, boasting only the snub barrels of a single, pintle-mounted assault cannon and heavy stubber up front for infantry support. The supercharged Centaurs did afford the hive drivers the vehicular verve they needed to put an armoured personnel carrier in positions conventional wisdom would otherwise state impossible. Compact enough to be slapped on the deck by a Navy aircraft, but able to hold its own in a firefight, the Centaur variant was a perfect fire support vehicle.

Unfortunately the labyrinthine freightways of Corpora Mons did not play to the Centaur's strengths. The convoy's initial run had been impressive, the cadet-commissar had to admit, the column maintaining high speeds across deserted plazas and clear thoroughfares.

It was only when the major re-directed Deleval's column to secure the *White Thunder* crash site that the convoy ran into any serious resistance. The crash site wasn't far off their route: the massive *Mortis Maximus* still stood sentinel above the convoy's armoured roofs, but the Spectre had gone down in a depository complex just south of the cathedra, at the heart of a rockcrete jungle of warehouse structures and semi-permanent giga-storage crate containers. The narrow accessways in between, like cholesterol-choked arteries, were strewn with debris and abandoned freight, creating a nightmare landscape of gauntlets and bottlenecks. There wasn't even room amongst the mayhem for a Centaur to about face and turn around.

It was here that the rebels had hit them time and again, waiting each time for obstacles to slow the convoy to a near standstill before unleashing hell from above with lasguns, rockets and grenades. With Deleval busy upfront, relaying directions from the passenger seat and manning the belt-fed heavy-stubber, Krieg had patched through to *Blazer Three*, their only other air support bird, instructing the Vulture to make strafing runs on the insurgent-crowded crate container rooftops. The pilot complied but was less than enthusiastic, claiming that the mobs were sending just as many rockets their way.

The Centaur rocked violently to an unexpected halt. The manoeuvre drew a furious scowl from Deleval, but Cruz, the Shadow Brigade driver, simply pointed and began manhandling the vehicle's chunky nest of levers into reverse. The lieutenant squinted through his cracked, blood-spattered viewport before lividly snatching the mouthpiece of his headset.

'Convoy, all stop!'

'What?' Krieg snapped, leaning forward over the Cruz's shoulder to get a better view of the road ahead.

'*Blazer One*, this is *Ironfire*. If I'm not mistaken there is a vrekkin' train across our route,' the lieutenant said dangerously.

Deleval wasn't wrong. Krieg found himself staring at a bulk freight repulsomotive, alight and clearly off its magrail. The automated hovertrain probably ran to a thousand cars or more, and would cut off routes across the line, possibly for kilometres in either direction. That wasn't the worst of it. With the convoy at a stand-still and a slow meandering reverse the only way back, rebel fire hit the Centaurs with renewed confidence and clout. The cadet-commissar found himself drop-ping his head, despite the fire support vehicle's reinforced armour plating. The crew compartment filled with the cacophony of las-blast impacts and thought-shattering ricochets.

Deleval's gunner fell back through the hatch like a sack of grain, his face and uniform a las-dappled mess of smouldering flesh and scorched webbing.

'Get on the cannon!' Krieg called, but his order was met with glares of venomous defiance from Deleval's men.

'Are you out of your vrekkin' mind?' Snyder asked, leaning over the dead Guardsman. He slipped his hand into the furious light show outside and snatched the hatch shut. Turkle proceeded to strip the unfortu-nate gunner of spare ammunition and in all probability, valuables.

Deleval was still spitting oaths and threats down the vox-link when a shadow flashed across his viewport, causing him to jerk back and let rip with the heavy-stubber. The weapon chugged a fierce blast of lead up the street, but uncertain as to whether he'd hit anything, Deleval yelled at the driver, 'You got anything?'

Cruz darted his pinched face around the viewport: 'Nothing.'

'Crenna?' Deleval yelled.

'Dead,' Snyder shot back, his eyes not leaving Krieg's own angry slits.

Everyone heard the clunk from up front and even Krieg was forced to break his livid stare. Its location was obvious from the way Cruz began clawing feverishly at his chair harness.

'Del…' he managed with white-knuckle panic, but the lieutenant had nothing but four words for him.

'Fire in the hole!'

The detonation was sharp, deafening and somehow worse inside the confines of the small vehicle. When Krieg brought up his head he found to his heart-striking dismay that he couldn't, leading him instantly to the sickening conclusion that he was trapped or worse – paralysed. What he found was that Golliant had leaned over to shield him and it was the weight of the monstrous aide that was actually pinning him.

Turkle, Snyder and Goinz had somehow managed to crawl out the back door and the extra ventilation cleared the acrid smog that filled the compartment. As the smoke disappeared Krieg found himself glaring at Deleval, who looked exactly the same as he had done a few seconds before. He was fiddling with the fire support's fried comms and playing with the limp and useless levers of the driver's station.

Cruz hadn't been so lucky. The magtube had been small but enough to disable the near side track and crack open the Centaur's armour plating. The vehicle's controls and steerage had been completely mauled and the unlucky driver had had his backside blown through the top of his head.

The grizzled lieutenant was back to his helmet vox-link and climbing into the crew compartment. 'Time to go,' he told the commissar simply. Then into his vox-link, 'This is Deleval. *Ironfire* is combat ineffective. Falling back to *Baptism*.'

To their surprise the three men met Snyder, Turkle and Goinz clambering back in the back of the Centaur. Turkle screamed something but it was lost in the split-second rumble and blast of *Baptism* behind. The detonation smacked *Ironfire's* back door closed, but Deleval viciously kicked it back open. The second Centaur was no longer behind them – just a flame-swathed wreck.

Krieg jumped down with Deleval, his hellpistol out and humming furiously by his side. Golliant followed with the bodies of Cruz and the Centaur's gunner over each broad shoulder and laid them against a nearby wall.

As with *Ironfire*, the rebels had been attempting to disable the second carrier's tracks, this time with a rocket from above. The lieutenant sent his men off with a bark, to extricate the survivors, before switching back to his vox-link. 'Staff Sergeant Bronstead, give me a perimeter and some suppression fire. We're going to have to load bodies.'

Las-fire chugged up the dirt road around them, forcing Krieg and the lieutenant to trot alongside the convoy with Golliant bounding calmly behind. They passed a glass-eyed Goinz who was crouched with his back to one of the massive crate containers, occasionally blasting his pump action skyward in an attempt to keep the insurgents away from the roof edge immediately above them. Turkle and Snyder were rolling one of *Baptism's* crew in the dust and grit nearby, his flak jacket and uniform alight. The rest of the Volscians were pouring out of the carrier's rear, seemingly unscathed. Once again it was one of carrier drivers that had paid the price.

'Gator' Bronstead trudged up the freightway with thick-set indolence. His helmet was crooked and he leaned his stocky shotgun across one shoulder as though he hadn't got the slightest intention of using it. A bulbous nose ring and belly added further colour and a scaly patch of skin running down the side of his sweaty neck – the remnant of some underhive pestilence and origin of his nickname – completed the picture. Bronstead and Krieg hadn't met and the sergeant, like the rest of his hive-kin, didn't fail to give the cadet-commissar a stabbing glare.

Dwarfing Bronstead for girth and even Golliant for height, a colossal mountain of flesh appeared behind the sergeant. This was Pontiff Preed, Krieg suspected. Dressed in acres of simple white robes and trailing holy relics, tomes and trinkets of faith from his thick, leather belt the priest seemed preoccupied with hiding his gargantuan bulk behind the Shadow Brigade vehicles. He was the breathing definition of an easy target.

The officers formed a circle in the shadow of *Steel Sanctuary* while Volscians dropped down from the vehicles and formed a hasty perimeter along the outside of the convoy. The air sang with las-fire but the Guardsmen seemed unconcerned. Only Krieg and the Pontiff appeared aware of their vulnerability: the cadet-commissar from a tactical viewpoint and Preed by virtue of pure self-preservation.

'Right, I'm going to make this fast,' Deleval began with authority, 'Recover the bodies and scuttle the forward Centaurs. I don't want insurgent scavengers using our own weapons and equipment against us. Fall back to the main avenue and continue as planned to the rendezvous.'

'What about the Spectre crew?' Krieg threw in above the din of the ambush.

'They're on their own. We tried.'

'That's not acceptable, lieutenant,' Krieg informed him.

'I don't know if you've noticed,' Deleval hissed, clearly riled, 'but there is a train across our path. What the hell do you want me to do about that? Look, we were ordered to swing by, which we've tried to do. Chances are if those Navy boys weren't killed in the crash they're gonna wish they had been – the way these mungers are coming down on us.'

'If it were the other way round, Navy aircraft would be directed to search for us, would they not?' Preed insisted.

Krieg found himself nodding in surprise. He shouldn't have been. The corpulent Preed was like some massive herbivore that had no natural predators. He'd outgrown the danger of his circumstances and had little to fear from the average hiver; besides, everyone knew that he had Captain Rask's ear. He could afford to disagree.

'And we'll probably have to if we remain here for much longer,' Bronstead said gruffly.

'We're out of time here,' Deleval told the group. 'If we don't move, and I mean now, we won't make the Titan on time. How happy do you think the major will be then? He grabs the targets but has no convoy to transport them. With all due respect, Holy Father, you and Krieg here are on your first outing. This is what we do. We're going after the targets. The Navy boys are on their own.'

The lieutenant went to walk away – a clear signal that the impromptu meeting was over. Bronstead began to peel away also.

'Give me a couple of your men,' Krieg called after him. His voice was thick with grit and it was difficult to tell whether he'd made a request or given an order. 'We can make our way on foot and work up to the crash site. If we can get the survivors back to your original route on the other side of the track, so be it. You've got to negotiate the train anyway. If not, you can go on, as planned, and make the pick-up.'

The platoon leader turned on his heel, a savage stream of las-fire cutting in between them. The mighty Preed shrugged affirmation. The lieutenant's face was screwed up with hate and annoyance, but the deep lines gradually faded as he took in the young commissar from boot to cap. Something seemed to suddenly amuse him.

'Done. I'll go one better. You can have three men,' Deleval told him, before yelling across his shoulder at the Guardsmen behind. 'Turkle, Snyder, Goinz, front and centre! You're going with the commissar.'

Krieg had expected a stream of complaints and oaths or even a downright refusal from the hivers. What he got was sly looks, through slitted eyes and a maniacal snigger from Goinz.

'Thanks,' Krieg mumbled, a little off guard.

'See you on the other side,' Deleval taunted and walked off with Bronstead at his side. Preed nodded slowly at Krieg, readjusted his monocle and then turned to follow.

The three Volscians slid their backs against the wall of a nearby cargo container for cover and had begun feverishly slotting fat cartridges into the breeches of their shotguns. Golliant was back after a brief absence. He'd deposited the *Ironfire's* casualties in the back of one of the other Centaurs and had liberated Deleval's heavy stubber from its forward mounting inside the blasted fire support vehicle. The weapon was a real monster, boasting a pistol grip and carry handle on the top of its belt-fed body and a long, fat, air-cooled barrel to deliver the bad news to its unfortunate targets. Krieg's aide had also stripped the vehicle of available ammunition, draping spare belts of bullets across each shoulder.

'Goll, you don't have to come. Go with the convoy...'

Steel Sanctuary and the column were already rolling backwards, out from under the thunderstorm of rocket-propelled grenades and las-beams the seditionists were pelting at them.

'How am I supposed to protect you from in there?' the hulking aide hissed with simple logic, his voice straining above the gunfire. He swung the elongated barrel of the stubber over the cadet-commissar's head and joined the three corpsmen against the corrugated wall of the container. Snatching his hellpistol from where it sat snugly in its holster, Krieg darted after him.

V

VERTIGO CAME IN hard, low and fast.

'Benedict, cleared to fire?'

'Affirmative.'

'Let's do our worst.'

Like some vision of angelic vengeance the Spectre tore across the industriascape. Holding the stick loose but firm in one hand Rosenkrantz cycled the ammunition drums on her wing-mounted autocannons and primed both weapons with the other. Her thumb did the rest, stabbing at the fire stud and releasing two blazing streams of certain death and tracer fire across the depot roof.

The depot itself was a marksman's dream: a rectangle of terrace roofs, catwalks and flat storage compounds. All with great cover – from the ground at least. Mobs of Mechanicus insurgents had swamped these spaces and rained firepower down on the *White Thunder*, which lay smashed and broken-backed on the rockcrete of the quad below. Nothing could save them from *Vertigo's* own variety of explosive vengeance, though. The incessant thunder of the cannons cut furrows of charred, twisted metal into the rooftops and turned throngs of insurgents into steaming smears of bloody chum.

This was the last of the terraces and it was just as well: the cannons were almost spent. In the meantime, fearless hordes of revolutionaries had weaved their way towards the disabled aircraft, using every gutted vehicle, every stack of abandoned cargo and piece of debris they could find to use as cover. Rosenkrantz herself had contributed to this. It was the nature of war – every action had an entire host of reactions – some anticipated and some not. The first of the compound rooftops she'd hit had been absolutely crawling with enemy targets and the flight lieutenant had seen little harm in slamming a couple of rockets into the side of the building. The strategy had the desired effect, burying an entire swarm of defectors in tonnes of metal and ceramite. It had also, with the collapse of the unstable compound and several towers, spread huge

pieces of cover-friendly debris across the south end of
the quad and allowed large numbers of individual
insurgents to close on the downed Spectre.

At least Rosenkrantz had the comfort of knowing
that her efforts were not in vain. There were definitely
survivors down there. On the wingless starboard side
someone had got one of the door weapons operational and was dong a good job of keeping heads
down with scenery-shredding bursts of heavy bolter
fire. The portside had taken the brunt of the crash and
rents and fractures adorning the aircraft's hull were
allowing for an intermittent, if steady, pattern of small
arms fire to present a front on the other side.

Rask and Sass were behind her: the major's adjutant
his usual serious self, the captain unusually so. 'Okay,'
Rask said, 'these boys are ready to do this.'

Rosenkrantz understood. It had been Rask's suggestion and now that they were here, the full scale and
overwhelming futility of the situation had dawned on
him. Rask clearly felt that he was sending the snipers
to their deaths but believed that it was necessary if the
Navy crew were to have any chance at all.

The pilot brought her assault carrier to a suicidal
standstill high above her sister Spectre.

'Chief,' Rosenkrantz called across the vox and was
rewarded with the chatter of fierce cover fire from her
own door gunners. Bolt rounds sprayed the rockcrete
around *White Thunder*, mangling cover and the occasional Mechanicus heretic, but more importantly the
weapons' higher elevation forced the hordes of kill-
frenzied Illians further back.

Slick cords tumbled from the bay door and the
insanely daring snipers bailed out and rappelled their
way to the roof of the smashed Spectre, molested by

snaps of las-fire that shot past the lines and the descending soldiers. The strategy was not without cost and Rosenkrantz's 'Boltmagnet' callsign became suddenly and uncomfortably appropriate.

Vertigo rolled slightly under the weight of pure firepower being directed at an aircraft that had been all but a blur of undercarriage moments before and now presented an irresistibly stationary target. Runescreens and augurs screamed warnings from a hundred different systems. The canopy flashed and sparked as a hail of fire washed over the reinforced armaplas. Rosenkrantz blinked involuntarily.

'Flight Lieutenant!' Benedict called out with an unusually high level of emotion for one of his kind. Rosenkrantz had expected this. He felt what *Vertigo* felt. He was more part of the aircraft than the crew: the information coursing through cables and conduits wired straight into his spine from the bird's various archaic systems was registering simply as pain.

'Rask?'

It was hard to tell when the captain was genuinely nervous – his face was usually taut with some kind of agony from his knee. He seemed nervous now though, white fingers pressing the vox-link to pursed lips. He hesitated for a moment, unsure.

'They're on the ground,' Sass finally confirmed. Rask nodded at her.

'Well it was going to be them or us,' Rosenkrantz sneered as she threw the vector thrust into direct ascension and blasted skyward away from the shooting gallery bellow. The cockpit auspex streamed a small saga of data at the pilot. 'Benedict, take over,' she called after the first hundred metres, tearing off her harness and slipping out of confines of her seat.

Sass couldn't help feasting on the detail sweeping across the console.

'The port tail boom's registering a gearbox fire,' he informed her. When she didn't respond he added, 'That doesn't sound good.'

'You think?' she asked before pushing past Rask who gave her a feeble smile.

'Good work,' he told her and probably meant it.

'I'm going down below. See how badly we've been hit,' she answered coolly and pulled away. Something wasn't right. *Vertigo* was hurting and she didn't need to be Benedict to feel it.

VI

MERCILESS AND QUIET, Krieg and the Volscians slipped through the smoke-spuming wreckage of the south compound and up through the warren of debris that had redecorated the quad floor.

A deafening cascade of fire flew overhead from the depot roofs and terraces – all directed at the blast-ridden Spectre. The aircraft was a sorry sight, but gave the Imperials the distraction they needed to work up through the enemy line undetected. The din of gunfire bouncing off the walls of the compound hid the cold-blooded blasts of the Zombie Squad Corpsmen as they trotted up behind Illian rebels, hiding behind girders and smashed slabs of rockcrete. Snyder and his cronies had no problem with shooting the boilersuited figures in the back, slickly working the pumps on their combat shotguns before riddling another unsuspecting heretic with shot and moving on. It was a brutal but effective procedure, leaving Golliant's heavy stubber to deal with any unwanted attention moving in from their flanks and Krieg to handle the rear.

They were moving at quite a pace, the shotgun crew ahead seemingly drawn on less by a desire to reach the Spectre than a dead-eyed thirst to spread blood across the esplanade. This gave Krieg little to contend with, very few of the insurgents moving in on *White Thunder* were faster than they were.

A begoggled lab-tech, making a dash between two warped girders, nearly ran straight into Krieg. The shock of finding an Imperial commissar in his path was a little more than disconcerting and the lasgun he was carrying came up a moment too late. Krieg blew a furious beam of supercharged laser fire through his chest, stopping the Mechanicus menial dead in his tracks.

In the no-man's-land between the crash site and the nearest cover, matters were less simple. Small pockets of insurgents who had successfully worked their way up to the downed assault carrier gathered in tight groups. With little in the way of communication, Snyder, Turkle and Goinz switched tactics from wholesale slaughter to a more cautious approach. Getting in position to make the run across to the aircraft they only gunned down those rebels that became aware of their position and intentions. This in turn stirred up a hornets' nest for Krieg and his aide, who were coming up from behind.

One particularly determined group rushed the two men from the servo-carriage of a toppled crane. The crisp crack of las-bolts surrounded them as the gang, still wearing their tight-fitting, rubber filter-hoods, came at them with furious firepower.

The ear-splitting chatter of the heavy stubber cut the group in two as well as several individual revolutionaries. Krieg stood his ground – storm-trooper style – his back and arm straight and his hellpistol moving smoothly and surely from one target to the next, lancing them with hotshot. The gang was completely pumped and wild, most of their bolts veering and going wide. Several got lucky and plucked at his greatcoat and it was perhaps this that made Krieg miss his own target.

They were running at him thick and fast and it had been a miracle he'd created the small mound of bodies that he had. His last shot had been intercepted by one of the crane's crumpled, plasteel cross-beams and several heretics slipped through Golliant's withering arc of fire and pressed their advantage in the face of Krieg's first mistake.

The leader of the group fired, missed and then proceeded to throw his hooded head and shoulder into Krieg's midriff. Krieg went down in an untidy heap, splitting his efforts between smashing the grip of his hellpistol across his assailant's blank, rubber face and blasting spasmodically at the shapes of the remaining defectors, who were skidding to the ground beside him, intent on holding down his arms.

The Mechanicus menial on top of him sat upright, his legs astride the commissar's prone form – the barrel of the lasgun gripped in two hands – the weapon's ugly stock wavering above Krieg's snarling face. In the muffled confusion the cadet-commissar noticed that the heavy stubber wasn't firing anymore. At first he thought that it had run dry, but an awkward glimpse under the arm of his attacker revealed the weapon lying abandoned in the dust and Golliant, impossibly set upon by six or seven hooded individuals, smacking his foes into the ground with his close combat weapons of choice – the two flight deck club hammers that usually sat snug in his belt.

Everything was still for a moment. Krieg's arms had been pinned to the ground and his pistol knocked from his grip. Ghoulish breath sounds filled the air as the hooded heretics, gasping with exertion, held him still.

It wasn't a great swing and nowhere near enough to take his head away from his shoulders, but it felt like it. The stock had flashed in front of his eyes, making contact with his cheekbone and dashing his skull into the esplanade. Numb with shock, Krieg found himself keeping it there. A dribble of warm blood rolled across his face from the gash on his cheek and pooled in his eyes. Blinking red ooze, the commissar found himself staring across the quad, the ground-level angle odd and disorientating. He saw Turkle and Goinz bolt across the open ground towards the shattered fuselage of the downed aircraft. Snyder was standing looking back at him, a sinister smugness hanging from a curled lip. He shouldered the squat combat shotgun he was carrying, turned and bolted likewise, leaving Golliant and the cadet-commissar to get on with the business of dying.

The backswing had taken an eternity but finally it came. The same reverberating deadness in his head; the same flush of blood: this time across the other side of his face. With the world running at slow motion around him, Krieg had time to consider how scars running across both cheeks would make him look like some kind of duellist.

He couldn't tell which came first, the sound or the sensation, but suddenly he could move his left arm. The flood of movement and relief was accompanied by a crashing thud and fresh blood on his face – this time not his own. Two more shadows disappeared and as he came back to his senses he saw the revolutionary sitting astride his chest, torn from his seat and his head come apart. With splatter still falling around him, the cadet-commissar managed to roll onto his stomach.

From the darkness of one of the Spectre's side doors Krieg could make out the shape of a bipod, the glint of a scope and the long, thick barrel of an anti-materiel sniper rifle. Their closest relative was the ubiquitous long-las, favoured by many a Guard sniper. Redemption Corps marksmen often needed something a little harder hitting for knocking out equipment and suppressing light vehicles, as well as blowing superfluously large holes in enemy combatants. Essentially a large calibre rifle, the fearsome weapon took the same ammunition as an autocannon and hit just as hard.

Scooping up his hellpistol, sitting in the grit just centimetres out of reach, Krieg turned the weapon on the swarm of bodies all over Golliant's massive frame. Somehow the aide had just kept swinging his hammers, to devastating effect, even with several rebels hanging off each arm. The numbers had easily doubled since the last time the commissar had glimpsed him and the wrestler was going down under the pure weight of his assailants. Aiming cock-eyed from the ground, Krieg sent a string of sizzling fire into the backs of the hooded workers. Alarmed, some made the mistake of turning their backs on Golliant to face Krieg but got a hammer in the back of the skull for their trouble. Caught in the crossfire of the commissar's pistol and the Volscian's brawny reach the rebels rapidly became a carpet of bodies at the brute corpsman's feet.

Snatching the heavy stubber in one hand and dragging a dazed Krieg to his feet with the other, Golliant marched them across the open ground, the reassuring crash of sniper fire all around them.

INSIDE THE TROOP bay of *White Thunder* the darkness was startling. It was a shock after the glare of the open quad and it took Krieg's eyes a moment to adjust. Beams of dust speckled sunlight crisscrossed the bay from holes and rents in the fuselage caused by the crash and some of the heavier weapons carried by the mobs outside. The only functioning heavy bolter kicked out an unrelenting roar from the starboard side and the Spectre crew fired warning shots from their laspistols through holes and doorways on the opposite side. Only just arriving themselves, Snyder, Turkle and Goinz crouched in the middle of the shattered troop bay, catching their breath. They eyed the commissar moodily, reloading their shotguns and taking swigs from their canteens.

Down on the ground by Krieg's feet lay one of Mortensen's storm-troopers wrapped around the brutal angularity of an anti-materiel sniper rifle. He wasn't even looking through the scope but was firing with complete confidence and in a steady rhythm.

'Thank you,' the commissar told the sniper. He didn't answer – just angled his almond face and nodded slowly, continuing to fire and from the screams outside, hit his targets.

'How–' the commissar began.

'The respirators in their hoods, mostly,' the Khongkotan trooper told him solemnly, 'and the hum of your pistol.' Obviously the sniper was used to questions from new blood in the squad. From a commissar he probably took the question as an order. 'Also, the mechheads: they smell different.'

Krieg looked down at the hellpistol in his holster, the cable running between the handgrip and the power pack on his belt. Turning his nose to his shoulder he took an experimental sniff.

'And your coat,' came a bitter voice from the far end of the bay, 'sounds like foil through a vox-hailer – even from across the damn quad.'

Another feral worlder sat upright against the Spectre's worm-holed hull. He clutched his rifle awkwardly to his chest as though afraid to let it go. As Krieg's eyes adjusted to the deeper darkness he saw why: the marksman was a mess, riddled through with holes, not unlike the aircraft, his flak jacket smouldering.

Krieg marvelled: he'd heard of feral world tribes whose senses had attuned to their environments, not unlike the savage, predatory mega-fauna they shared their world with, but the snipers' talents were something to behold. Krieg imagined what he could hit, if he could hear and smell as well as he could see.

The Spectre's co-pilot, still wearing a scuffed flight helmet, was manhandling a crate of bolter ammunition from beside the wounded sniper over to the door gun. His face lit up at the sight of the commissar's cap and greatcoat. It was not a reaction Krieg was used to. He thrust out a keen hand.

'Boy, are we glad to see you,' he blurted honestly. 'Hoyt.'

Krieg didn't bother to introduce himself. 'Pilot?'

'Dead.'

The commissar nodded. 'I've got good news and bad. The good news is that you're being rescued. The bad news is that we're it.'

Hoyt's face dropped. 'No airlift?'

'Too dangerous.'

'What about the convoy?' the injured sniper shot across the inky interior of the aircraft.

'Can't get through. We're it. The convoy will pass a few kilometres to the north of here in about twenty minutes, which means if we want to be on it we've got to haul some.'

'But,' Hoyt stammered. Several Navy crewmen had stopped firing and were staring at the commissar in disbelief. 'We're surrounded.'

'We got in,' Golliant rumbled, trying to be helpful. Deleval's men just looked at the ground, kicking empty bolter cartridges between their feet and lighting lho-sticks.

Krieg's eyes travelled across the bay, meeting each member of the crew in turn. It was an intoxicating moment. Krieg understood the nature of leadership – he'd been an officer – but with the flight crew staring at him as though their lives depended upon it – which they did – he began to empathise with Mortensen's predicament. Krieg could not be honest with these men. He couldn't talk odds and harsh truths. He needed fire in their bellies. He needed them to believe in themselves and in him. Like the major, he had to make them believe that he could get them out alive. He didn't know if that was cultish practice – as the canoness had seen it – but of all the evils it could be, at that moment in the Spectre's troop bay, it seemed a necessary one.

'How much bolter ammo have you got left?' Krieg asked.

'Plenty,' Hoyt told him. 'We've got enough for four guns, but only one is operational.'

'Golliant, help me.'

Between them Krieg and the aide took the crate the co-pilot had been carrying and dumped the contents in a pile in the centre of the bay. Then to the baffled crewmen: 'In order to make it out of the complex we're going to need a diversion. Pile every piece of ammunition you can find and stop firing that gun.'

'Stop firing?' an injured crew chief started incredulously, his arm bound with a hasty a sling.

'They'll think the gun's dry and that'll draw them in on the starboard side.'

'Excuse me, sir, but why would we want to do that?' Hoyt asked politely.

'Because we want as many of them as close to the bird as possible when we blow it up,' Krieg stated simply.

'We have no detonators, what do you think you're going to use as a charge?' Snyder sneered.

Krieg shrugged off the insolence and looked over at the Redemption Corps sniper who had saved his life.

'Think you could hit a fuel tank with that thing?'

VII

MORTENSEN HAD NEVER been inside a god before. It wasn't at all like he'd imagined. For a thing that looked so impressively gargantuan on the outside, it was a testament to claustrophobia inside the thick armour plating. A perpendicular tour puzzle of crawlspaces, gantries, bulkheads and laddershafts, the *Mortis Maximus* had swallowed the Redemption Corps whole.

Power was out the length of the Titan and the command deck had been dead and eerily empty. Snapping muzzle lamps to their hellguns, the stormtroopers descended, their swift but wary cover formation cutting patterns through the pitch darkness with the beams of their torches.

The major had had Greco seal the command deck sky hatch he'd originally hacked in order to avoid any unwelcome visitors coming in from the rear and through Uncle's ragged opening. He then had the troop split into three small groups under Conklin, Vedette and himself. While the master sergeant pushed on into the thorax network of modules and engineering vestibules below, Vedette and Mortensen took their sweeps in opposite directions, exploring the maintenance ducts and ordnance vaults above the mighty super-heavy weapons mounted on each colossal arm.

Vedette's team had drawn the Volcano Cannon protruding from the left arm of the massive Titan, meaning that her sweep consisted of a tour of the very heart of the god-machine: the dormant plasma reactor, that ordinarily powered not only the devastating Volcano cannon but the Titan's very automotive functions.

Mortensen on the other hand was landed with the nightmare of the gigantic gatling blaster. His men moved swiftly and silently through the darkness of room after room packed to the gills with mega bore bolt rounds, ready to fall upon instruction through the autoloader vents below and directly into the open breech of each titanic, revolving barrel.

'Major,' a voice came softly across the micro-bead. 'Best get up here.'

Mortensen worked his way up through a series of pokey, valve encrusted cubicles and padded along a narrow corridor. Trooper Teague had been leading the way but was currently waiting for him against a pressure hatch.

The major had taken an instant liking to Teague. Elysians spent their lives in the air and so the young trooper was a natural drop-soldier, despite his tender years.

The two men crouched in the companionway for a moment.

'And...' Mortensen prompted. Teague thought he could see it. He casually waved his hellgun in a wide arc in front of them. The lamp beam struggled with the black depths but revealed enough to prompt the major to add his own.

It was incredible. Smack bang in front of them the claustrophobic confines of the god-machine gave way to a small oasis of open space. It wasn't a conduit or chamber; it wasn't even square. A perfect sphere of freedom had been cut out of the restrictions of the thoracic decks. Metal decking, support struts, cabling and instrumentation all ended in polite, clean lines around the open space. Teague ran a finger over one curved edge, seemingly cut from a bulkhead.

'Smooth,' Teague told the major. 'Never seem anything like it. What kind of a tool can do that?' Mortensen nodded with hesitation. The Elysian was right of course: even a plasma torch, which was what someone would need to do something like this, left rough edges. This also left the question of why anyone would want to create a spherical hole of emptiness in the middle of a Titan. Mortensen's stomach tightened.

The major's micro-bead chirped. It was Conklin.

'Crew located, boss.'

That was something. 'Where?'

'Engineering – Thorax East, deck six, Void Shield Generator Room. Or at least that's what it says on the blast doors,' the sergeant came back.

'Status?'

'No idea. Something's got 'em spooked because we've identified ourselves and they ain't raising these doors for anything.'

'Stand by. We're coming down.' Mortensen switched channels. 'Vedette, you getting this?'

'Receiving, major.' As usual the Mordian officer was ever ready, monitoring the vox-traffic.

'Time to regroup. How's your sweep?'

'You might want to take a look at the plasma reactors. Someone's ripped the hell out of them.'

Mortensen mulled it over: Vedette wasn't given to exaggeration.

'No time. Meet me downstairs.'

'Affirmative,' she returned without question.

'Vedette,' Mortensen cut in before she signed off. 'Detonators or small arms?' There was a pause.

'By hand, sir.'

The major turned slowly towards the black emptiness and shone his barrel lamp up at a maintenance opening about six metres above them on the other side.

'Can you make that?' he put to Teague. The storm-trooper took it as a friendly insult: Mortensen had asked him to scale, crawl down and hang off worse things than that before. The major nodded. 'Push on and sweep the operational ordnance compartments. Anything out of the ordinary, I want to know about it. Otherwise, make your way down to ground level and the pick-up. Understood?'

By way of a reply, the nimble Elysian snapped his hellgun to his pack and vaulted the first gap. Without fear he took a succession of near gymnastic steps before launching himself up into an exposed set of coolant lines.

'Major,' he called, hanging by one hand and turning slightly. 'I'll beat you down there.'

Mortensen left the young soldier to his acrobatics and began his own descent.

It didn't take long for the major to reacquire his squad. As the bullet flew Conklin wasn't far below them, despite taking a spinal column ladderwell directly into the Engineering sub-levels. The major met Conklin cradling his bolter by the secured blast doors.

'How do you know they're in there?'

'Took a shot at us, didn't they,' Greco croaked from behind. He was sitting on a barrel of lubricant behind the open bulkhead. Minghella was with him, his back to the major and his head bobbing up and down as he went to work on a field dressing.

'You took one?' Mortensen asked.

'In the foot.' Uncle smirked, which was something he rarely did.

'Laugh it up,' Greco shot moodily, his usual good humour gone.

'They secured the blast doors and locked them off,' Quant continued, smiling. 'Emperor knows where they're getting the power. Engineers probably rigged something temporary.'

Mortensen suppressed the involuntary curl of his own lips. 'Will he pull through, sergeant?' he put to Minghella sarcastically. He didn't wait for an answer. 'Good. TFC Greco, hobble that bony ass of yours over here and hack those blast doors.'

Kicking off the barrel and sporting an exaggerated limp the storm-trooper made his way across, using the cool passage wall for support. He snatched his satchel of tools from an amused Uncle and trailed a ribbon of bandage where Minghella had not had time to secure the dressing. As Greco hacked into the hydraulic rune mechanism with his equipment he muttered guttural hive oaths to himself.

'How many?' Mortensen asked.

'I saw the flash of five barrels, at least,' Conklin informed him.

The door mechanism made an unhealthy sounding clearance before juddering open. Greco shambled back before snatching up his weapon, as well he might. As the robust door rolled open the Redemption Corps were met with the glare of bioluminarc lamps and a thicket of las barrels – primed and pointed.

After a dumbfounded second, storm-troopers' barrels followed suit; accompanied by the flash of open palms from both sides. Some screaming and bawling ensued with Mortensen's harsh roar coming out on top.

'Get those vrekkin' rifles on the ground!'

A crate-chested chief engineer waved an improvised flamer in his face and a spindly tactical officer, his cranial lines and plugs gathered together in a ragged pony tail, slid the long barrel of a lasgun over the engineer's shoulder. 'We're Redemption Corps, you slut-mongerers. This is asset recovery: someone wants you plugging in somewhere else, so unless you want to be walking out of here with a serious physical impediment – like death – you'll lay your weapons on the deck.'

A pistol came down and a woman in a black uniform and cap stepped forward, running her slender fingers along the trembling barrels and pushing them to the floor. She had rich, unsmiling lips and an eye-patch to match her dour uniform.

'Princeps Hess,' she enlightened him as her crew placed their weapons on the generator room floor. 'The *Mortis Maximus* is mine.'

'Not for much longer,' Mortensen informed her with casual hive-world smarm. 'My men are going to walk you out of here. A convoy of carriers will then take you out of the hotzone and you'll be airlifted to safety. That's the plan, but don't quote me on it.'

'No.'

'No?' Mortensen wasn't used to people refusing his offer of rescue. 'You're the second person today who was under the misapprehension that they can give me orders. I must be losing my powers of persuasion. But you see that's why I've got this.' He brought up his hell-gun and shone the lamp into her remaining eye. 'It speaks a variety of different languages but even that doesn't matter because actions – I'm reliably informed – are louder than words.' He primed the rifle savagely.

'The god-machine has been infiltrated and somehow sabotaged from the inside. That's why we are immobilised; that's why we're hiding in the generator room. This hallowed Titan cannot be left in the hands of the enemy.'

'It can,' Mortensen assured her, 'and it will. That's not within my mission parameters. Some idiot determined that your bony backsides were worth recovering and my men have in turn risked their own lives to achieve that end. We're not here to save your damn machine, princeps. That's someone else's headache, thankfully. We came for you. So if you'd be so kind, my men can only hold a perimeter for so long.'

'Our weapons…'

'My men can handle your security. I don't trust your trigger finger, anyways. You might be able to sunder worlds in this thing, but you shoot like cripples. You had a clean shot and the element of surprise and you pranged one of my men in the foot for Throne's sake.

Don't worry though; he had it coming.' Mortensen span, looking for Conklin.

'Sergeant, take the men and get the bridge crew and engineering staff here down to ground level as soon as possible. Double-time it. Be on your guard – we have unfriendlies in here.' Mortensen cast a disparaging eye over Hess and her crew as they began filing out.

'Affirmative.'

'Kynt: raise Deleval. Make sure that convoy is in position for our exit. Don't take any crap from that Volscian piece of trash. If he gives you any trouble, tell him it'll be my boot up his backside.' The young comms-officer nodded his freckled face and went to work on his equipment.

Mortensen started drifting towards the opposite exit.

'What about you?' Vedette put to him.

'I think I know how the infiltrators got in. Teague's up there.'

'I'll go,' the Mordian insisted, heading for the companionway.

'I sent him, I'll get him,' Mortensen growled, stopping her in her tracks. 'You make sure the Titan crew get to the ground alive.' The major streaked off in the opposite direction, leaving Vedette to protect the rear of the escort, his voice the only clear thing in the swirl of shadow. 'That might be harder than you think.'

It wasn't difficult to find his way back up the autoloaders, but Mortensen made considerably harder work of negotiating the sphere of open emptiness beyond than Trooper Teague had.

In Fire Control the major found signs of life, or more accurately: impending death. Scores of servitors, charged with the smooth operation and maintenance of the colossal gatling blaster, had been ripped from their stations and butchered. Heads littered the deck with the kind of sickly, flesh-drawn grins servitors were given to. Blood and the black arterial oil that ran through the drones' bodies ran down the walls and pooled around the dismembered corpses.

This didn't feel like renegade Mechanicus menials. This was something else. Mortensen moved through the carnage with cautious urgency, swinging his hell-gun around corners and up through vents and hatches.

A ripple in the darkness. Mortensen came to terms with the reality that he wasn't alone. The sting of vulnerability brought up the hairs on the back of his neck; the scrape of a footstep on the deck up ahead; the vanishing glint of an eye in his roving lamp. He was so preoccupied with these distractions that he almost missed Teague.

With all the gore and butchery already on show in the murky fire control station, the young Elysian's battered, blood-drenched body hardly seemed to merit a second glance. He was hanging in the chains of a block and tackle, his arms and head drooped through loops of an ammunition hoist. He'd been completely run through with some kind of wicked blade and his body was criss-crossed with deep gouges that were still leaking his lifeblood all over the mounds of ammunition below. He was dead though – that much was certain.

Mortensen suddenly had the feeling that someone was walking over his grave; if his grave had been the deck floor directly behind him then he would have almost certainly been right. Gripping his rifle tightly in both hands he span around, ready to unleash fully-automatic hell on his stalker. Whoever it was he was big, powerful and had reflexes the major hadn't accounted for. A fist came smashing down on the barrel, sending the weapon clattering to the floor. The powerful foot stamped down into the rifle's breech, impossibly crushing the converter underfoot, before scraping it backwards across the deck, tearing its power cable from Mortensen's pack.

The compartment descended into complete darkness as the weapon's muzzle smacked into the wall and smashed the lamp. Something like a hand slipped around his neck from behind and enveloped his throat in a vice-like grip. Mortensen's first instinct was to tear at the fingers with his own. His boots were off the ground now and the air in his lungs disappearing fast. The digits weren't moving, however, kept there by an incredible force of will and bulging tendons. If Mortensen hadn't been so preoccupied with the fading oxygen in his lungs, more of his panic-stricken thoughts might have been devoted to the strange, ribbed and leathery fingers grasping for him. It was probably some Mechanicus maniac in a pressure suit, the major reasoned, but he couldn't help considering the possibility that Krieg was in fact correct and he was in the presence of some malformed, chaotic mob devoted to some unholy cult. As he relived the moments of the attack through his blurring consciousness he could swear that he'd seen multiple limbs and claws.

His flailing boots had caught several limbs and bodies in the blackness and Mortensen suspected that he was surrounded. This was confirmed when some kind of blade slashed across his midriff, slicing through his carapace and into his stomach. He couldn't feel the pain of course, just the ugly tugging of flesh as it gave and tore in a ragged gash. His hands instinctively clutched his belly and were almost immediately slippery with blood.

His thumb brushed his belt and following it with his fingers he found his way to his holster and side arm. Snatching the autopistol in a fast-fading grip he brought the heavy pistol up, rested the top of the snub, quivering barrel on his shoulder and pulled the trigger.

Something died behind him. Mortensen's limp body tumbled to the floor. He couldn't quite describe the inhuman screech his assailant had made, but he'd heard more death-cries than most people and he knew that they were all sickeningly individual. A fully-automatic blast of autofire in the face couldn't be good news for anyone.

On his knees he bent over and kept pressure on the gaping wound across his stomach. In the dark it was impossible to tell how deep it was but he was pretty sure that his guts were still where they should be. With his forehead resting on the cold metal of the deck he could feel the tremor of heavy footfalls all around him and fearing another attack, let loose blindly with the remaining rounds in the pistol.

The savage roar of the weapon seemed to drive them back; he might even have clipped one or two of them. He fumbled in the darkness for a second clip but the magazine slipped through his blood-sticky fingers and onto the floor. It was a horrible feeling. With the sensitivity of his skin reduced to a cool numbness he relied heavily on sight for dexterity. Long gone were the days he could strip down an autopistol blindfolded. In the darkness his eyes could tell him nothing and he couldn't tell whether or not he was touching the magazine or the floor. He could hear at least and had to listen to heavy footfalls approach. The horde was back. In a rage of frustration Mortensen abandoned the clip and went for his last magazine.

Slamming it home he scrambled messily across the floor, hand scrabbling around in his own gore.

As gnarled and knotty appendages caressed the back of his armour he swung the autopistol behind him as both club and firearm, the short barrel sweeping the compartment, trailing the bright arc of a muzzle flash. It was a strange couple of seconds. It was a relief to have his fingers around something reassuringly unwieldy.

In the momentary illumination provided by the hot gases escaping the autopistol's barrel, Mortensen picked out the bulkhead by which he'd entered. The ghostly forms of his assailants were also fleetingly visible, moving with inhuman speed and receding with the shadows. The overwhelming impression, in the dull environment of the Titan interior, was one of colour: puce green flesh.

There was the swiftest notion of filthy fangs and claws, and his stalkers' bulbous bulk was decorated with corrugated flak and tattered robes. Greenskins. Greenskins on board the Titan. Greenskins here on Illium: just not like any greenskins Mortensen had seen before. Or half seen – Mortensen had only been privy to the barest glimmer in the lightless confines of the fire control station.

Crawling arm over arm for the bulkhead, the major kept the monsters at bay with short, sporadic blasts behind and around him as he dragged himself across the smooth floor. Lugging his torso across the bulkhead threshold, Mortensen pulled his legs through before slamming the heavy hatch closed. He could feel the rumble of a final desperate charge as the bulkhead swung shut, but he was already spinning the wheellock on the other side. With the hatch locked-off and pressure sealed, Mortensen rested the back of his head against the bulkhead but found himself rapidly kicking away from the door as a thunderstorm of blows rained down on the reinforced metal from beyond. Where successive impacts found purchase the hatch had begun to warp and buckle.

Mortensen couldn't believe it. He and Krieg had been wrong. A cult undoubtedly existed here, but not one devoted to forbidden gods as the commissar had speculated. Instead an alien sect had infected the fabricator moon, celebrating the potent brutality of their Kaligari Cradle neighbours – greenskin invaders out of the Gargasso Deeps. He shouldn't have been so surprised: Bellona, Scythia and Calydon Prime had all been hit and the stars of a number of greenskin warlords were certainly on the rise. It wasn't entirely unprecedented either: heretical human and greenskin alliances were not unknown, especially during extended campaigns where local populations of besieged worlds felt that their Emperor had abandoned them. The Burdock Worlds could hardly be considered major strategic targets, despite the speed with which they were sundered. Illium wasn't some backwater agri-world and the Lazareth System was a major strategic target. Too big for a single warlord, with little more than a few crop balls of momentum under his belt. Savage greenskins simply did not operate like this. Something was deeply wrong here.

These thoughts and more haunted Mortensen in the thick darkness of the passage, with the hammer of blows ringing in his ears. He had more pressing concerns, however, like getting down to ground level, through the Titan's labyrinthine interior, without spilling every drop of his precious blood. Pushing himself up against the wall he stumbled forward into the blackness, occasional blasts from the side arm lighting his way.

VIII

THE ESCAPE HAD run as much to plan as Krieg had any right to expect. A toppled security tower had provided the group with some much needed cover as they exited the Spectre on the least lethal side of the quad. The commissar's insistence that the silent heavy bolter would draw the enemy in had proved accurate with huge mobs of insurrectionists able to work their way up to within a stone's throw from the fuselage.

Krieg was the last out, allowing Snyder, Turkle and Goinz to provide a wall of scatter shot to shield the Navy crew's flight. Golliant had not only the weight of the heavy stubber harnessed to his wrestler's frame, but also hauled one of the aircraft's stretchers over the masonry-strewn court behind him. The wounded Khongkotan sniper was strapped into the bouncing gurney, crying out with every bump and feeling especially vulnerable on the occasions the aide had to drop him, reach around and awkwardly gun down approaching insurgents with his stubber.

Sprinting for the cover of the collapsed tower, Krieg kept his head low to allow the storm-trooper sniper he'd met inside room to line up his shot. Krieg had learned his name was Sarakota and that his injured compatriot was Opech: both tribesmen. There was little love lost between the two soldiers, however, Sarakota being the cold, commonsensical type and his brother-savage the militant loudmouth. Their marksmanship was the only thing the pair truly shared, as evidenced by the explosively precise cover fire provided by Sarakota's anti-materiel rifle as the group abandoned the aircraft.

As Krieg skidded to a halt in the gravel and dust around the tower he gave the order and the sniper popped a round in the Spectre's portside fuel tank. A chain reaction of faltering explosions tore *White Thunder* apart, vaporising the bloodthirsty crowds that had breached the aircraft and flooded her troop bay intent on discovering survivors. A backwash of flame and fury sanitised the surrounding area, leaving hundreds of closing revolutionaries scalded and aflame. With a small mushroom cloud of raging black smoke rising in the centre of the quad, fire from the compound roofs stuttered to a full stop. There were some isolated pockets of celebration and cheering but largely the rebel mobs were given to confused silence. Many stood up from behind cover and walked slowly towards the aircraft inferno.

Remaining concealed, the soldiers loped out of the complex with the bedraggled remains of the Navy crew in tow. This would have been a flawless escape, but for a Spetzghastian immigrant worker and his son waiting behind the ruined foundations of the tower. The smoke-stained face of the father swung out from behind a crumbling wall as he blasted the injured crew chief full in the face with a scavenged skitarii lasrifle. Simultaneously his street-urchin son took Hoyt in the shoulder with a similarly liberated pistol. The co-pilot fell back into Krieg's arms and immediately fired back, cutting the boy in two with a beam from his own laspistol. Sarakota ran up beside, his weighty anti-materiel rifle shouldered during the run, and plugged the father several times in the chest with assured semi-automatic rounds from his autopistol side arm.

Hoyt stood stunned at what he'd done. Slaughter must have appeared different from the cockpit. The child's screaming was already drawing unwelcome attention. Krieg handed the unsteady co-pilot to one of the Spectre door gunners and stepped forward, drawing his hellpistol.

'Move,' he ordered, prompting the crew on: Snyder and his cronies certainly wouldn't wait for them. Sarakota and Golliant nodded grimly and pushed on, motioning the Navy crewmen onwards.

The commissar stood over the broken body of the child. The boy's squeals had an odd quality to them. His eyes seemed impassive and blank. His were not cries of pain or fear. They were intended as a warning, despite their result. What had happened to this planet? Krieg could hardly imagine. 'Because you had not the courage to be loyal…' he informed the young rebel coldly and levelled his humming pistol.

At that moment the warning went home and scores of surrounding insurgents turned their weapons on Krieg and the fleeing line of Navy crewmen. After the lull, the firepower was explosive and harsh on the ears. Poorly aimed las-bolts cut the tower foundations to pieces, forcing Krieg to slip behind a puncture-riddled wall. He made one further attempt to implement Imperial justice but had to pull back further at the whine of a rocket winding its way down on their position. The frag-blast blew Krieg back off his feet and took apart what remained of the tower foundations and anyone else inside. Brushing grit from his eyes, the commissar stumbled to his feet, whacking his left ear with his palm until the hearing came back.

Another barrage of laser fire descended on his position and he bolted after the others with hundreds of armed Illians climbing down from the compounds and flying across the quad after him.

As he burst out of the other side of the derelict compound he found himself in a wide, dusty alleyway. Alone. His heart leapt as he saw Volscian colours flash past the far end of the freightway. Centaur after Centaur rocketed past, chewing up the sandy avenue: the convoy was here. He took a step forward but the air in front of his eyes suddenly spat with light and energy. Rifle barrels cleared broken plas from storm windows on the far side of the alley and lanced the freightway with a gauntlet of las-fire.

'Krieg!' came a voice from above, accompanied by the raucous bombast of shotgun fire. Scatter shot blasted out the remaining plas of the storm windows, forcing the barrels to retract. Staring up the commissar saw Snyder, Turkle and Goinz on the roof of the opposite building – a huge depository warehouse adjoining the compound complex – feverishly working their slide actions to keep up a sufficient onslaught of fire.

Further along the roof of the gargantuan warehouse Krieg could make out the Navy crewmen with Golliant and Sarakota, on each end of the stretcher, making for the convoy at a sprint. The freightway was clearly a suicide run and the hivers had directed them up an escarpment of rubble and wreckage left behind from *Vertigo*'s earlier rocket run. With shouting and gunfire already on his coat-tails the commissar had little option but to do likewise and threw himself up the mound, clawing his way skyward.

Turkle's sweaty palm was waiting for him at the bolt-bathed summit and Krieg allowed the Volscian to heave him over the lip of the depository roof. Breathless and exhausted Krieg pushed himself to his feet and began the scramble for the convoy. For the second time in as many minutes the cadet-commissar found himself alone.

Turning, he found the Zombie Squad standing behind him, their combat shotguns held at the hip, the gaping muzzles pointed squarely at him. Krieg twitched for his pistol, but Snyder shook his head darkly.

'Ah-ah. Lose the piece. Slowly.'

'The convoy is just down there,' Krieg told them, taking his hellpistol from its holster by the tips of his fingers and unclipping his belt power pack.

'Vox, too.'

The cadet-commissar unplugged his earpiece and wound it up with the side-arm. He tossed it to Turkle who snatched it out of the air with admiration. Krieg remained silent, flicking his eyes all around the roof for anything that might tip the odds in his favour. The roof was bare, however, bar the ragged holes the Spectres had blasted into it earlier and it was onto the edge of one of these the hivers had backed him.

'It's nothing personal,' Turkle told him. 'Eckhardt was an effete pig. But he's a Volscian pig. Clan code, you see?'

'One day, they're gonna stop sending you scholaswine,' Snyder blurted with venom, 'but until they do, there's a saying of Volscia – You got the shot, you better take it.'

Krieg's mind whirled: at first he thought this was Mortensen's doing. He'd only ever heard of Eckhardt from literature on the 1001st's revolt.

Turkle gave him a cruel grin and brought his weapon up.

'Wait…' Krieg managed, but Goinz had already fired.

The impact alone was nauseating, beyond the untold damage wrought by the deadly weapon. The air was knocked clean out of Krieg's lungs and the shot threw him backwards. Successive blasts caught his side and shoulder, spinning him around and towards the hole in the warehouse roof. A crippling shot square in the small of his back, flung the desperate commissar through the dark opening. As he fell, twisting and turning like an abandoned corpse, he caught brief, woozy glimpses of his three assassins – now standing around the hole, spewing gouts of optimistic shot after him.

Eventually his assassins faded – as did the boom of their target practice as the range became untenable. The darkness of the enormous warehouse swallowed him and Krieg waited the flailing eternity it took to reach solid ground and the end of his life.

His landing came sooner than he could have anticipated and to his utter astonishment, he bounced.

The depository housed a small mountain of some kind of green crop – a fleshy pod, no doubt some kind of off-world foodstuff harvested on a distant agri-world, imported to feed the army of immigrant workers that kept Illium a productive powerhouse. Krieg's bounce soon turned into a floundering tumble that picked up speed as he rolled down the side of the pod mega-mound. Many of the vegetative cases split and cracked under the commissar's rough treatment and by the time Krieg actually hit the dirt of the warehouse floor, he was thoroughly splattered with the pods' thick, jaundiced discharge.

He lay there for a moment in an unceremonious heap, pain coursing through his very being. Sitting slowly upright in the dust, surrounded by smashed pod cases, the cadet-commissar unbuckled his great-coat and allowed the heavy leather to fall to the ground – heavier than usual due to the extra flak plates Krieg had instructed Golliant to sew into the garment. Udeskee's advice had been warranted after all. He still felt like four ogryns had gone to work on him with iron bars and his uniform was torn and bloody where pellets had actually found their mark.

Probing his clothing at the shoulder, where the worst of the damage seemed to have been done, Krieg's eye caught movement on the floor beside him. Something was moving inside one of the pods. Curious and appalled, the commissar slipped a slim blade from out of a sheath in his boot. He'd had the blade since basic training on Galtinore: it was his Legionnaire's bayonet and it went everywhere with him. Poking the knife inside the split and twisting the blade, Krieg cracked open the pod. A small creature rolled out, enveloped in a stringy juice. Krieg retracted his hand immediately. The thing was clearly alien in origin and must have violated a thousand different quarantine and importa-tion by-laws just by lying there. It was roughly bipedal and had beady red eyes and a tough, leathery green hide. Its strange body was largely dominated by its man-trap maw, however, and as the docile horror yawned, it showed off its immature dagger-like fangs.

Krieg had seen these things before. Any soldier that fought orks and their foetid kind had. They had an equally repulsive name that the commissar could not recall, even staring at the nasty thing. To his knowledge the horrors went everywhere with the monstrous green degenerates. In turn it was widely believed that greenskin reproduction had a hierarchical biology relying heavily on spores and the pods that grew from them. Life in the 123rd Pontificals had been rarely dull: inquisitors had unhealthy interests. At that moment, Krieg reasoned, he was sitting amongst a giga-warehouse of greenskin pods, harvested and stored in an Adeptus Mechanicus facility at the heart of the Illian capital for some nefarious purpose.

Getting stiffly to his knees and then with even more care and forethought, his feet, Krieg pulled his flak-reinforced coat back on and fished around in the webbing for an arc lamp. Clutching the bayonet in one hand – his only remaining weapon – and snapping the torch to life he pierced the vast darkness of the depository searching for an exit. He found something else entirely.

Krieg gave a violent start as the arc beam cut through several dark figures in the dusty twilight. His bayonet came up, but the figures failed to respond. Every bone in his body wanted to turn back but with the warehouse wall to wall with the pods that had saved his life in the other direction, there was little choice but to creep forward.

Hugging the deeper shadow of the depository wall, the commissar sidled along, both knife and torch extended towards the statuesque figures. They could almost be sculptures but for the rise and fall of their barrel-chests and the epileptic flutter of their armoured eyelids. Hundreds and hundreds of ork savages: adorned with scraps of salvaged flak mail, spikes, and dripping with all manner of brute weaponry. They stood as if on parade – although Krieg realised that the comparison was ridiculous, second only to the fact that he was actually witnessing such antithetical behaviour – swaying slightly, a few metres equidistant from one another in the cavernous space of the depository.

The cadet dared not intentionally interact with the small army of hulking, sadistic man-eaters, but his lamplight and the scrape of his footfalls did little to disturb them. The tightness in his chest begged him to bolt for it but Krieg could not bring himself to do so – feeling as though one does in the presence of a rabid dog. He wanted to run but knew that he shouldn't. His calm, measured steps took all the longer to take, however and gave him further opportunity to make observations as he shuffled along the warehouse wall. The further he got the stranger circumstances became.

Some of the creatures drooled from their snaggle-tusked jaws as they stood in their trance-like stupor. Instead of glooping to the ground, though, the slobber dribbled upwards, finally dashing the depository roof above.

Orks on Illium was one thing; the same orks entranced in a warehouse was already one step beyond, but now with the laws of physics failing to apply, Krieg was ready to start questioning his own sanity. Had one of those shotgun blasts taken his head off: was he dead?

That wasn't all. Strange orbs of light proceeded to glide above and around the stationary monsters and the air crackled between them, resulting in the occasional blue spark leaping from one alien to another.

No one could pretend to know very much about the minds of orks, but Krieg had been told that greenskins generated a psychic field that individually accounted for their technological mastery and under communal circumstances could create unnatural social and physical effects. Krieg couldn't tell whether or not he was witnessing some of this bizarre phenomenon at that moment, but he did know that he'd never seen orks act this way before and he'd met them on the field of battle both as a Legionnaire and a Pontifical.

The worst moments were in fact those closest to the door. He could imagine reaching the postern gate and the barbaric horde coming back to their brutal senses. Forcing the lock quietly with the flat of his blade, Krieg stepped out into the deserted avenue and closed the door steadily behind him. Resting his back against it he slid to the dirt, the nervous tension evaporating from his body with such collective force that the relief made him feel light-headed and weak. Sitting in the road he didn't know what scared him more: the fact that the convoy had left him behind in enemy-held territory or the possibility that each of the gargantuan storehouses that surrounded him and the mighty cathedra beyond held a sizeable warband of battle-seasoned greenskins.

Getting to his feet Krieg started to jog in the direction of the *Mortis Maximus*. Deleval's fast moving column would have to rendezvous with Mortensen's Redemption Corps in order to move out the Titan crew and if he could move fast enough, that was Krieg's best bet. Either way, the commissar had to reach a vox-link: the 364th Volscian Shadow Brigade were being drawn into an insidious trap of monumental proportions and that warehouse was a target begging for an Imperial air strike. He could only hope that he'd make it in time.

IX

VERTIGO SOARED ABOVE the street-level maelstrom. For the past half an hour Rosenkrantz had been doing her best to keep the Spectre firmly in the air, where it belonged, rather than down in the Illian melting pot where the aircraft seemed to want to take her. Chief

Nauls had reported smoke trailing from the tail and the pilot herself had detected vibration in the pedals. *Vertigo* seemed to be holding her own, however, and while the Spectre seemed content to remain airborne, Rosenkrantz was obliged to remain on station above the rendezvous.

The evacuation point was actually a small landing strip west of Artellus. It had presumably been used for important personages and senior adepts, visiting the great cathedra. Burnt-out wrecks of lighters, shuttles and the occasional Aquila lander littered the runway but there was enough room to put down the Spectres, their bay doors gaping open and ready to take on board the returning convoy vehicles. *Blazer Four, Five* and *Six* buzzed around the evacuation point, occasionally ripping into surrounding buildings with their multi-lasers as pockets of encroaching insurgents were identified. By and large the reconnaissance data had been good and the rendezvous was secure.

Nauls broke through on the vox: he had more news for her.

'Chief?'

'Skip, we're seeing some unusual enemy movement to the south-east. Might want to check it out.'

'What do you mean, unusual?' Captain Rask broke in.

'Doesn't look like mob activity,' the crew chief drawled. 'They, well, sir, they look like troops and manoeuvres to me.'

Rosenkrantz leaned the Spectre into a half-turn. Rask checked his strategic data-slates while Sass pushed in past Benedict to get a better look through the canopy.

'He's right: they're in formations,' the adjutant confirmed.

'It's probably the Volscians,' Rask countered, but his data-slates weren't providing much in the way of evidence for that.

'There's no way they made progress like that.'

'Maybe there was less resistance than anticipated,' the captain hypothesised.

'What, with the flak we've been catching?' Sass put to him. 'No way.'

Rask tried to get a better view for himself.

'Give me a fly-by,' the captain finally directed.

'Are you out of your mind?' was the only response the pilot could conjure.

'If those are enemy troops down there, the major will need to know.'

Sass nodded. 'They could cut off the convoy; crush the hold points.'

Rosenkrantz shook her helmet from side to side. 'Benedict, I'm going to need more starboard thrust to offset the deviation.'

'Affirmative,' Benedict complied, 'Recalibrating for a high speed pass.'

Plunging nose first towards the urban anarchy she'd been so eager to avoid, Rosenkrantz pushed *Vertigo* as much as she dared. The distant jigsaw puzzle of alleys and freightways came up fast and she levelled the Spectre out at a rooftop streak, rocking to starboard and port to avoid various antennae and watchtowers. Ground to air small arms fire followed in their superheated wake, too sluggish to acquire the aircraft at such thunderbolt speeds.

Banking slightly to give the best view of the industrial metropolis below, Rosenkrantz and the corpsman watched as empty avenues turned to rivers of green. Heavily-armed ork warriors, all muscle, spikes and jumbo weaponry, were bounding down the streets. Bikes and buggies belching oily smoke and noise weaved in and out of the charging throng, tearing up the sand freightways with spiked tyres and suicidal acceleration. Capillary columns of troops stomped out of surrounding warehouses and stores, bolstering the already thick channels of alien ferocity converging on the cathedra.

Rosenkrantz brought the Spectre up off the deck and back into the open sky. She turned to face Rask.

'Take us back,' he told her simply. 'Benedict, patch me through the major. *Now*.'

X

As a LEGIONNAIRE Krieg had done plenty of running; the physical standards required to join an Inquisitorial storm-trooper detachment were tougher still. As a young officer he'd increasingly gotten used to giving orders, rather than the physical reality of actually carrying them out. As an Imperial commissar he'd expected to do even less. It should have been unsurprising, therefore, that his body took to the rude awakening of a long distance slog with less enthusiasm than expected.

Unarmed and abandoned, all the cadet-commissar had was his legs: two lifeless appendages sending constant and insistent updates to his brain amounting to little more than biological begging. The numb burn of each thigh and calf was unbearable and sent shockwaves of pain with each stumbling footfall through his already bruised and blasted torso. His lungs felt shallow and his reinforced greatcoat, now more in demand than ever amongst the chasing las-fire pitched at his racing form, felt like he was dragging a Chimera behind him.

The cathedra grew and the booming roar of the Valkyries hovering somewhere overhead became clearer. The pulse-snap of laser bolts sang in the air as Krieg stomp-jogged his exhausted carcass under the sights of Second Platoon manning the southern rooftop hold point. They weren't firing, which occurred to Krieg's adrenaline-addled brain as a good thing. It would simply be embarrassing to have been shot by his own troops twice in one day.

The convoy formed a ragged line in front of the colossal feet of the mighty *Mortis Maximus*, the combination of Warlord Titan and the Adeptus Mechanicus cathedra blotting out the sun. The deep shadow stung the blistering, sweaty skin of his face with sudden coolness. A mixture of storm-troopers and Fourth Platoon crouched in between the vehicles, weapons ready for any rebels that slipped through the Shadow Brigade's elevated hold points. Gunners swung their assault cannons round over the heads of a cluster of soldiers in discussion half way down the column.

Krieg's staggering attempt at a run collapsed into an unsteady walk as he leaned against the open back door of the rearguard Centaur, trying to find his breath. A storm-trooper in a headband with a bootless, bandaged foot gave him a curious look. A stretcher was loaded into the back alongside him bearing a more composed-looking Opech. The sniper had clearly received some much needed morphia and he gave Krieg a warm glance. The cadet-commissar patted the sniper's leg lightly, but didn't have the air for any kind of further conversation and stumbled on down the column. His bedraggled appearance drew further surprised looks from the convoy sentries and the huddle of Guardsmen simply fell silent upon his arrival: some with surprise, some with suspicion.

Corporal Vedette managed one of her crisp Mordian salutes, whilst the man-mountain Preed simply nodded to himself grimly. The three sergeants, Bronstead, Minghella and the dagger-faced Conklin began to break away: most notably the master sergeant and the bull-necked Bronstead, who were drifting towards *Steel Sanctuary*. By coincidence this was exactly where the ragged commissar was going.

Krieg tore the rear door open, revealing a small congregation of Guardsmen inside. Deleval was seated next to the driver, his face fast becoming a nest of infuriated creases. Snyder and Goinz rested up front, passing a canteen between themselves and the lieutenant and lighting up lho-sticks. Turkle sat with his back to the door and the barrel of his pump action aimed lazily across one knee at Golliant and Sarakota, who had been disarmed, and were seated on the other side of the Centaur.

The commissar yanked his hellpistol from where it sat snugly in Turkle's holster, the power pack still attached to the henchman's belt. Krieg put the muzzle straight to the back of the hiver's skull, just behind the ear.

'When you've got the shot, you better take it,' Krieg hissed and squeezed the trigger. The superheated blast filled the troop compartment and sent brains and fragments of skull across the stupefied Snyder and a still grinning Goinz. 'Good advice,' the commissar told them and leaned in across Turkle's headless corpse for his next shot.

Deleval leaned away, despite the fact that the pistol had clearly moved to Snyder and Goinz.

'Don't do it,' Bronstead growled, his hand hovering over his own laspistol, but Vedette reached out for his wrist.

'He's an Imperial commissar,' she reminded the Volscian sergeant.

'A commissar's word is law,' Preed agreed unhappily.

'He ain't no commissar, yet,' Bronstead reminded them, shrugging the Mordian off, and put his hand on the holstered laspistol.

Krieg swapped hands and extended his right fist towards the bridling hive sergeant: Udeskee's signet ring glittered in the dull light. 'These men have been found wanting,' he announced darkly.

'It's a lot worse than that,' a voice cut across the tense air. Major Mortensen stood behind them. One hand covered three ugly gashes that had opened up his carapace body armour at the belly and made the front of his fatigues sodden and slick with blood. 'Commissar Krieg here holds the life of every man committed to this operation, wanting or not, in that righteous fist.'

Vedette ran to the major's side, swiftly followed by Minghella. The commissar's pistol wavered.

'You were right, Krieg,' Mortensen continued. 'I was wrong. It's a cult. The rebels have alien allies. We've stirred up a stingwings' nest here and sprung a trap that was waiting for the main body pacification force. If we don't go now, we're all dead. So make up your mind. Shoot them. Don't shoot them. Either way, I have to get my men off this dirtball.'

Precious seconds came and went.

Krieg finally let the fatigue take him and lowered the hellpistol.

Mortensen immediately began to bark orders: 'Kynt, get back to Captain Rask. Have the *Vectors* come down to street level and have Second Platoon extracted from the rooftops. It's risky, but we don't have the time or space for anything else. As soon as they're loaded, send them across to the evacuation point with *Blazer One* and *Three*. We can't afford another bird to come down in this mess.' He turned to find a bitter Bronstead standing nearby. 'Likewise, sergeant,' Mortensen added with an edge and the fuming Volscian stomped away.

'Titan crew loaded on the convoy. No losses,' Vedette informed him crisply as Minghella tried to examine the major's wound. 'Teague?'

Mortensen shook his head.

Lieutenant Deleval had climbed out of his vehicle and approached the pair. Turkle's blood still dripped from his flak jacket. He flicked his head at Krieg.

'You gonna let that slide?' Deleval challenged: soldier to soldier, eyes aflame.

Mortensen cast a glance over the bedraggled, scatter-shot ridden cadet. He ignored Deleval and directed his orders at Vedette.

'Have the troopers climb into the Centaurs with Fourth Platoon.'

'They're already carrying the Titan crew and *Thunder's* boys,' the Shadow Brigade officer snarled.

'Our men could walk out and provide security for the vehicles,' Vedette offered. Again, the major shook his head. He had a soft spot for Vedette, probably more than he cared to admit: Conklin's replacement-in-waiting.

'Throne's balls, I don't care how cramped it is – get them in. Any man left behind is a dead man. Trust me.'

The Mordian shot off without further question to organise the sentries, followed by Preed and finally Deleval, who glowered at Mortensen and then pushed past Krieg's battered shoulder. The commissar didn't

have the energy to push back and simply let the hiver
bulldoze his way through.

'You can do that in transit,' the major told Minghella
irritably. The medic was already pulling counterseptic
spray from his medicae satchel and fussing with the
shredded carapace. Uncle helped Mortensen to the rear
of the forward Centaur, with Krieg reattaching the hellpistol's power pack to his belt and coming up behind.

'Zane, who the hell are we running from?' Minghella
asked, ignoring Mortensen's request and attempting to
stifle the major's bleeding.

'You wouldn't believe me if I told you,' Mortensen
answered with clear confidence.

'I believe I would,' Krieg muttered moodily to himself.

XI

IT WAS BREATHTAKING to watch from the sky.
Rosenkrantz couldn't imagine the pure unadulterated
madness it would be on the ground. Back on station,
high above the airstrip, *Vertigo* had the best seats in the
house. Rask and Sass sat at the rear of the cockpit, their
hearts in their throats as they all watched the Redemption Corps convoy hurtle up the winding freightways,
throwing up thick plumes of fine sand and dust
behind them.

Every few moments the captain would give another
solemn navigational instruction, taking the vehicles
one block further out of reach. Like a slippery eel narrowly escaping the closing jaws of some waterborne
super predator, the column weaved left and right
before accelerating explosively up the straights and
away from adjoining streets and alleyways already
engulfed by the closing swarm of green carnage.

Closer to the airstrip, the narrow lanes fed into a long stretch of broad freightway, allowing the Shadow Brigade drivers to prove their worth. The open road allowed the super-charged Centaurs the space to make some ground on the storming hordes, the degenerate savages hailing a blizzard of hot lead after them. The ork buggies were less easy to outrun, sharing as they did the same advantages as the fire support vehicles and their drivers on the long stretch up to the airstrip.

The Volscian drivers did their best: ramming scrapheap buggies into the walls of surrounding storage facilities and pulverising dare-devil riders and their bikes under track. The gunners, conversely, did their worst – spraying the gaining greenskin wagons with a torrent of unrelenting fire from their pintle-mounted assault cannons. The patchwork trucks would often simply erupt into flames and roll, causing other fast moving vehicles to smash into them and join the inferno. Looted Mechanicus tractors and carriers were more resilient, however, soaking up the damage with their superior armour, and it was these and a few of the nimbler speed-freak bikers that stayed with the convoy all the way to the airstrip.

Rask had a surprise for them.

Hugging the deck, *Blazer Five* and *Six* skirted the dirt track freightway on a collision course for the convoy, with rocket pods armed.

'Take us down,' the captain ordered. 'And open the bay door. This is going to be a touchdown pick-up.' Below, the other Spectres waited in similar configuration, their engines idling them a few metres off the rockcrete of the airstrip and their doors open and ready to swallow one of the approaching Centaurs.

Rask turned to *Vertigo*'s co-pilot: 'Benedict, contact Lieutenant Commander Waldemar and transmit our coordinates. Extend our compliments and inform him we'll be with him shortly. Give the order for the *Vectors* and remaining *Blazers* to scramble and begin making their approach.'

'Affirmative, captain.'

Rosenkrantz grunted. She could hardly have expected Mortensen to have been so cordial.

Like a flock of spooked birds the Valkyries and Vultures took off from the airstrip as the *Vertigo* descended. Only *Blazer Five* and *Six* remained, their rocket run on the convoy almost complete. Lifting a further few metres above the ground, the sleek gunships allowed the Centaur carriers to surge beneath them before propelling rocket after rocket into the oncoming ork vehicles. Some of the greenskin drivers had the common sense to brake but many simply blasted on, sure that they could clear the raging ball of pure annihilation the road ahead had become. As the *Blazers* vanished in the haze bank of dust and swarthy smoke, intent on turning for another run from the rear, the convoy fragmented, each vehicle rocketing across the airstrip for their designated Spectre carrier.

Hitting the ramps at perilous speeds, the Centaurs rolled inside, reversing their tracks and skidding to a full stop. With ramps closing and their freight intact the Spectres blasted skyward, intent on catching the comparatively sprightly *Vectors*.

Rosenkrantz felt the quake of extra weight in *Vertigo*'s swollen belly as Mortensen's Centaur mounted the ramp.

'They're in, skipper. Ramp closing,' Chief Nauls came over the vox.

'Let's get the hell out of here,' Rosenkrantz said and pulled back on the stick.

Vertigo gave a violent shudder before lurching and dropping back to the deck. Rosenkrantz was thrown forward in her seat before being suddenly wrenched back. The cockpit went wild again with klaxons and runescreens mounting an assault on the senses.

'What is it?' Rask yelled above the clamour. 'Are we hit?'

'Is it the damage from earlier?' Sass joined in.

Rosenkrantz was finding it difficult enough finding the internal vox-switch in all the cacophony.

'Chief? Chief! I need a damage report.' Nobody answered. Running her fingers across a series of glyph studs the pilot brought the instrumentation back under control.

'Captain, this may not be the time,' Benedict piped up, 'but I've lost vox contact with *Blazer Five* and *Six*.'

Rask turned from Benedict to Rosenkrantz and then back to Benedict.

'Do you still have them on the scope?' the flight lieutenant asked, before trying the bay vox once again.

'Negative,' said Benedict.

'I think I might know why,' Sass announced to the cockpit, snatching a pair of magnoculars from the rack and pointing a finger over his captain's shoulder. A dirty, menacing shadow flashed up against the dust and smoke screen churned up by the convoy. Rosenkrantz took the shape for one of the Vultures at first, but as it got simultaneously closer and larger it became apparent that they were not looking at an Imperial aircraft. The smoke bank began to drift, increasingly whipped up by the force of the emerging craft, and the shape assumed the definite outline of a silhouette before puncturing the cloud with lance-like antennae and telescopic barrels.

'We got problems,' Rosenkrantz said flatly.

Mortensen suddenly appeared bare-chested on the cockpit companionway, his belly freshly bandaged and dressed. 'Are we hit?' he called imperiously as he threw on a khaki vest.

'We're about to be,' his adjutant informed him. Mortensen took in the monster-copter erupting from the dust cloud. The bastardised aircraft had a hugely fat hull, from the underside of which sprouted the multitude of different sized tyres, tracks and landing gears required to get the beast up off the ground. Two great dragonfly-style wings extended from each side, supported by a network of mismatched cables. The wings formed a cross from the front and bowed under the weight of various bombs, missiles and rockets mounted on their underside.

The monster bristled with heavy guns and large-bore cannon and was crawling with greenskin gunners. Worst of all, along the colossal span of the Deffkopta's four rotor blades ran high speed, serrated, chain blades: as well as keeping the monster in the air the blades could be used to shear an inferior aircraft in two. And *Vertigo* was an inferior aircraft.

'We got problems,' Rosenkrantz repeated to herself, stunned by the brute spectacle of the ork super-gunship. 'Chief, talk to me!' she bellowed once more.

'Tail's on fire!' the chief suddenly bawled back. 'So we're kind of busy down here. Ramp opening.'

'Sass, why'd we lose thrust?' Rosenkrantz was all out and didn't have time to confer with the cognition banks. She figured she could lose little by consulting the adjutant's notoriously encyclopaedic brain.

'Depending on where it's spreading – an internal fire could short all kind of systems,' the adjutant replied.

Rosenkrantz's eyes widened as the huge deffkopta skimmed the depository rooftops, running down on them. As its killer rotor blades cleared the surrounding dust and smoke the green tsunami of ork ground troops reappeared. They washed through the streets underneath the nightmare aircraft and flooded the freightway, scudding towards the airfield with blades and bastardised weaponry drawn.

Rosenkrantz made her decision: 'Chief, get inside and close the ramp. I don't have time to explain.'

'What about the fire?' Sass interjected.

'Benedict, fire the thrusters.'

'The fire?' Sass reiterated, allowing moderate alarm to creep into his voice.

The co-pilot did as he was ordered. The fuselage bucked: the quad of engines choked.

'Again.'

'What if the thrusters short on us in flight?' the major's adjutant put to her with increasing hysteria.

'We crash and die?' Mortensen hazarded from the companionway.

Rask looked to the major for orders. 'We really gonna do this?'

'It's her bird,' Mortensen replied, holding on to both sides of the cockpit egress. 'She knows what she's doing.'

Geysers of dirt and rockcrete sprang up before the Spectre as the deffkopta unleashed its motley arsenal of forward firing cannons and chain guns. *Vertigo's* thrusters choked once more before indulging in an unanticipated last moment rally. The quad of engines cycled for a split second before reassuming its customary high-pitched roar.

Fighting the instinct to pull straight up with her rein-
stated power, Rosenkrantz rolled the bird starboard
out of the path of destruction that cut through her
landing zone like an angry elemental force. It was just
as well, as the Spectre would have almost certainly
climbed into the umbrella-like reach of the deffkopta's
buzzsaw rotors. Automatic fire danced across the
canopy and hull as greenskin blister nests along the
length of the enemy aircraft's armoured flanks let rip
with their own assortment of pintle-mounted
weaponry. Sparks flew in the cockpit and something
died in the instrumentation.

'Just lost comms and scanners,' Benedict informed
her helpfully.

The doom-laden shadow of the beast passed overhead, giving the flight lieutenant time to retract
landing gears that were fast becoming tangled in the
blasted shell of an Arvus lighter.

'Can we return fire?' the major enquired as he took
in the full horror of the bloated, greenskin gunship.

'Ordnance spent,' Rosenkrantz managed, trying to
shrug off the twisted wreck. 'We have the four heavy
bolters on the side doors and a cannon on the nose,
neither of which is going to put the slightest dent in
that thing.'

Putting everything she had into forward thrust, the
Jopallian pilot took *Vertigo* off the deck and blasted
back towards Corpora Mons, a ripple of ground small-
arms fire following in her wake.

Rask put his cheek to the canopy armaplas in an
attempt to spot the deffkopta. 'It's back on our tail,' he
told the pilot. The graceless piece of scrap had had to
waste time on a lumbering, ungainly turn, but now it
was back – the unbelievable span of those deadly

rotors equipping the helicopter with blistering acceleration.

A distribution complex below the *Vertigo* vaporised as a ragged stream of rockets and missiles seared past the Spectre and indiscriminately carpet-bombed the stretch of vat labs and slave mills rolling swiftly beneath their hull. Rosenkrantz fitfully nudged her stick this way and that, evading the shower of greenskin ordnance. The fact was that there was only a limited amount that she could do. *Vertigo* wasn't built for manoeuvrability like her waspish gunship cousins. Heavily-laden with a personnel carrier secured in her belly, she wasn't exactly going to be doing three hundred and sixty degree rolls either.

For a heart-stopping moment every soul in the cockpit thought that the thrusters had died. This was largely because they had, but this time it was the flight lieutenant's doing. The airbrakes cut deeply into *Vertigo's* vaulting run and the Spectre slowed, allowing a wire-guided death dealer to pass over their heads. It touched down on the ornate roof of a Genetor parliament building, vaulting a curtain of broiling flame skyward. Rosenkrantz had little choice but to punch through and re-engaged the thruster quad, hammering into the explosive backwash.

As the Spectre came through the other side, Rosenkrantz mused, 'Well, if we weren't on fire before – we are now.'

'Shouldn't we be heading for *Deliverance*?' Sass asked fearfully, his bleached knuckles wrapped around his flight harness. Rosenkrantz was growing weary of the corporal's questions, which she increasingly found difficult to ignore.

'We'd never make it,' Mortensen answered for her. 'The taller buildings around the cathedra and the narrower avenues will work to our advantage.'

Of course he was right. Rosenkrantz rolled the aircraft over as much as she dared to allow clearance before diving down between the Gothic splendour of high-rise bethels and tabernacular archways. The deffkopta was forced to decrease speed and rise: its murderous rotor blades no match for the constricted airspace and busy architecture of the Mechanicus religious district.

'Do you see it?' Rask called, his eyeballs once again at the reinforced plas. She didn't, but kept up the scorching speed along the monument-strewn boulevards, banking left and right high above the twinkling carpet of gunfire and green bodies until she found herself alongside the chasmal, gargoyle-encrusted walls of the Artellus Cathedra itself. She allowed the velocity to fall off until the Spectre found itself hovering alongside the grandiose detail of a vast, circular stained-glass window. The window depicted a hololithic representation of the Sixteen Universal Laws of Adeptus Mechanicus endeavour at work.

'Perfect,' Sass grumbled. 'Right back where we started.'

As the aircraft gently twirled in the greater space of the plaza avenue, all eyes were on the two open ends of the canyon boulevard where they terminated at the far reaches of the cathedra super-structure. These were conceivably large enough to accommodate the monster aircraft and Rosenkrantz's finger rested against the trigger-thrust.

'Maybe we lost them?' the major said, his usually grating tone unnecessarily hushed.

As the nose cone rolled round once more to the spectacular window, a niggling doubt appeared like a half-glimpsed phantom in the background of Rosenkrantz's already preoccupied thoughts. She felt her eyes climb skyward. She peered directly up through the Spectre canopy.

There it was.

The deep, black outline of the junker behemoth was holding still about a hundred metres above the surrounding Corpora rooftops. It was partially obscured by the fast growing shadow of a fat, cigar-shaped object falling rapidly towards the Spectre.

The words, 'No, no, no, no,' passed the pilot's clenched teeth, drawing further faces skyward.

'Shoot it out!' Mortensen yelled.

Rosenkrantz jerked back on the stick, unleashing the autocannon on the immaculate stained glass. The window imploded, the priceless relic blasted apart, leaving a gale-tormented hole. Dipping the nose and lifting the tail, Rosenkrantz glided the carrier in carefully through the improvised aperture. It was close: she felt the slipstream of the bombshell tug on the back of the Spectre as it fell past the shattered window.

There was a stomach-churning rumble, then a blast wave of furious energy; the wall of mighty Artellus visibly quivered. The gloom of the cathedra evaporated as a deluge of raging flame poured inside and washed up the walls of the building from the armageddon outside. A gust of pure explosive force pushed *Vertigo* up further towards the vaulted roof as a rainbow of shards cascaded down around them from other giant stained-glass windows put in by the blast.

The Spectre idled at minimum thrust in the confined roofspace of the cathedra, amongst the cord pulls hanging from the vertiginous heights of the cathedra bell tower like vines in a jungle treetop. The cockpit was deathly silent. Rosenkrantz clutched her stick, flicking her nail back and forth over the nose cannon's safety stud in a futile act of mock aggression.

The pilot and the storm-troopers watched as a descending shadow spiralled around the cathedra exterior, blacking out the holes left by the stained-glass. Fortunately the openings were not large enough to admit the deffkopta, but they would suffice for the almost solid stream of greenskin lead pouring in from the aircraft's heavy weaponry.

It was only a matter of time before they acquired the *Vertigo*.

'What I wouldn't give for a Hunter-Killer right now…' Rosenkrantz spat.

XII

AND THAT GAVE the major an idea.

Leaning over the stolid Benedict, Mortensen reclaimed his gift to the co-pilot earlier that day: the souvenir rocket launcher he'd taken from the mech-head that had dropped *Blazer Two* in the plaza.

It was the kind of cheap military hardware mass-produced on a hundred different forge worlds for use by PDF and conscript Guard troops. The single shot tube was dented and smeared with dry blood and while hardly a veteran's choice, it might be the kind of equaliser Mortensen was looking for.

'Lower the ramp,' he snarled, throwing the weapon's sling strap over his head and across one shoulder. His request was met by with a flurry of objections but by that time the major was already at the bottom of the companionway. It was their only real chance, anyhow.

The troop bay was hushed. The battle-scarred Centaur rocked in its restraints; the Navy gun crew harnessed themselves, fearing the worst, hoping for a miracle. It was out of their hands and in the bloody, sweaty palms of the major.

Commissar Krieg was lowering the ramp, his ragged greatcoat molested further by the breeze. He pulled down his cap and gave the Gomorrian major snake eyes.

'Who are you today, Mortensen: storm-trooper or saviour?' the cadet-commissar put to him as the ramp juddered down.

'I don't follow you,' the major called back across the turbulence.

'Do you believe you can save this ship? Save us?' Krieg asked, handing the storm-trooper his black leather gloves.

'Does it matter?' he returned, pulling them on.

'To me it does.'

'Well, Commissar Krieg,' the grizzled major said as he mounted the ramp. 'I guess you'll never know, will you?'

Mortensen looked out across the vast depth of open space below the Spectre; the eternity of distance he would plummet before hitting the mosaic, marble floor at the very bottom of the cathedra where a garrison of Trepkos's tech-guard had already lost their lives in the defence of the cathedra. He turned back to the intense young officer: 'But I suppose you'd better hope I can and that I will.'

With that he tore off the ramp and sailed across the emptiness. Snatching at the bell cords, the slick gloves slid at first, burning through the leather and taking the skin from his palms, until the major's pulverising grip brought him to a dangling swing. The boom of the Mechanicus bells reverberated around the roofspace with deafening power. The air trembled around him as each movement on the cord brought new jarring combinations of chimes.

Then began the agony of the rapid hand over hand climb which even Mortensen felt: the rancid burn of raw muscle deep within his arms. At one moment he was sure he was going to fall. The greenskin war machine routinely blasted a storm of shot and shell through the open windows, which inevitably plucked at the bell pulls, shredding cord and severing random strands above him. A bolt round yanked on his line cutting the material in half, but somehow the cord continued to hold his weight.

With little or nothing left in his arms the major pulled himself up past the titanic bell and in through the bell tower balustrade. The breathtaking view of an industrial metropolis in rebellion and smoke-streaming ruin would be enough to convince most men that they had reached the summit of the cathedra. The manned but silent plasma silos that had claimed *White Thunder* still towered above the major, however. That didn't matter to Mortensen.

Carefully climbing down the extravagant Gothic architecture of the cathedra, Mortensen slipped the rocket launcher off his back and primed the weapon. Below he could hear the shearing blades of the deffkopta's rotor as the hulking aircraft came round for another pass on the remaining machina opus-emblazoned window. As it came into view, the Gomorrian storm-trooper could see orks and their runts swarming over the thing, reloading spent, swollen cannons and cocking gatling-style heavy weaponry. *Vertigo* could only have mere seconds left.

Mortensen trained the tube's simple sights on the grotesque mechanism at the heart of the deffkopta's killer rotor blades. He aimed and he fired.

With a whoosh and a kick the krak missile was away, streaking for the enemy aircraft. Moments later the rotor blades were in disarray, chopping into the air with jolting irregularity as the warhead split the mechanism asunder. There was a brief flash and a shower of warped frag.

The monster began to lose altitude almost immediately, gravity dragging its heavy metal bulk towards the planet's surface. A rotor blade – still buzzing away with serrated lethality – struck the cathedra wall and smashed, throwing wicked shards of razor-sharp metal in all directions. It was all over for the deffkopta from that point on as the behemoth bounced between the walls of Artellus and the surrounding buildings, descending like some fallen meteorite, tail over canopy in chaotic confusion, explosive disintegration and carnage.

Mortensen hawked and spat a gob of stringy, blood-threaded saliva after the doomed machine. Tossing the rocket tube too, his hand wandered down to his vest, where new blood had broken through Minghella's field stitches with the exertion of the climb. He climbed down on the precipice of the cathedra roof and plucked the blood-soaked stub of a cigar from his fatigues' pocket.

Lighting it, the major sat and watched the topless towers of Illium burn.

Being an incarcetorium, Krieg thought he might have to put his pistol in a few faces in order to get past security. To his surprise and confusion he found the gates wide open and the sentry posts unmanned. Occasionally prison personnel in drab uniforms and riot gear-adorned guards would dash past him from the opposite direction, but they barely gave him a second glance. The cadet-commissar couldn't tell whether it was his cap and coat or the meaty bolt pistol he clutched in his good hand or perhaps simply that they had more important things on their mind. People were leaving in a hurry and they weren't waiting to politely close the doors behind them.

Krieg slumped his way along the corridor, the powerful opiates swimming around in his brain making his steps uncertain and clumsy. Using the back of his good hand for stability along the cool metal walls the cadet-commissar followed the glyph signatures for the Panopticon security tower, the symbol of a single unblinking eye taking him to twenty seconds precious respite in a juddering elevator.

243

As the doors parted Krieg led with the barrel of the bolt
pistol, sweeping the breadth of the circular observation deck.
The staff were long gone, however, and only a few servitors
remained, hardwired into their console seats, waiting
patiently for directions with their dead eyes and sickly grins.
Three hundred and sixty degrees of wallspace were decorated with continuous banks of porthole security pict-casters
with a canopy of ear horns dangling from the ceiling on
wires and swaying in the gust from the elevator doors. Here
the incarcetorium warden and his security force had kept a
close ear and eye on the prison population.

At the hub of the chamber was a stairwell that offered to
take him down to the warden's personal quarters but Krieg
found himself hobbling up the steps, drawn by the dull natural light flooding in from above. At the summit of the
Panopticon security tower was a small terrace commanding
a view of the incarcetorium complex and beyond. Pulling
himself up to the terrace, Krieg made his way to the rail.

The incarcetorium was a sunburnt sprawl of corrugated
metal blocks, partially built into the dusty, red rock of a
mountainous outcrop that thrust defiantly out of the coarse
sand of Spetzghast's equatorial desert. The mountains had
a craggy, angular quality making them look more like badly
sculpted columns or primitive monuments but they formed
a natural barrier on three sides of the complex, leaving the
security arrangements of the fourth to a tall, electrified wall
of rust encrusted metal that routinely fried leathery-winged
scavengers unlucky enough to land on the thing. A similarly
electrified portcullis had been left open and unattended and
anything with tracks or wheels and an engine had been
commandeered and gunned across the terracotta desert. It
wouldn't do them any good, Krieg reasoned, the bronze
light of day perceptively fading around him moment by
moment. An unnatural darkening: Sigma Scorpii wasn't

due to fall below the horizon for another month. The thin cobalt sky was a sea of shadows that were growing by the second.

Peering over one of the heavy stubbers, Krieg spotted an all but empty landing pad situated on the roof of one of the complex buildings below. Any atmospheric-capable craft had long left the incarcetorium behind. The only transportation remaining was Rosenkrantz's indomitable Spectre and two Valkyrie carriers – bearing the sinister insignia of the Ecclesiarchy – that squatted on the pad flanked by bolter-clutching battle-sisters standing sentinel on the strip.

Ducking back below, Krieg slipped into one of the console bucket chairs and began scanning the porthole pict-casters. Many showed empty corridors and abandoned compounds. The rest revealed the dire living conditions of the inmates' cells. Prisoners stomped back and forth – like caged animals – which of course, they were. Others hammered on the cell doors with simple bowls and spoons indicating that the present crisis had superseded mealtime in the incarcetorium. Others still were simply trashing the sparse furniture of their cells and throttling their cell mates.

It didn't take long to locate the Redemption Corps storm-troopers: a set of pict-casters two banks down were hard to ignore, flashing sporadically with every burst of fire from the Adepta Sororitas's bolters. He shouldn't have been surprised that the storm-troopers were out of their cells: Krieg himself had secured his liberty at the earliest opportunity and the corpsmen were used to busting targets out of places like the incarcetorium. The corpsmen had managed to lay their hands on a number of laspistols and the odd rifle, snatched from sentry posts and fleeing security personnel, but they were no match for the thunder of bolters and the clean, cold tactics of the battle-sisters. Gouts of plasma and streams of flame wouldn't be argued with and the troopers had been corralled in an access corridor with a security bulkhead at their backs, blocking their only escape route.

Fortunately for them Krieg could do something about that. Laying the bolt pistol on the console and rubbing the stupor from his eyes he scanned the forest of switches and toggles controlling the bulkheads and security accessways, trying to match the code on the porthole pict-casters to their designated controls. Flicking a succession of heavy buttons and not altogether sure if they were correct, Krieg swooped back in on the pict-caster to observe the fruits of his labours. In the grainy capture the cadet-commissar watched the bulkhead shudder and roll slowly towards the ceiling. The storm-troopers didn't wait and after the briefest of checks began shimmying backwards under the heavy metal door, their weapons still giving the Sisters of the Immaculate Flame something to think about.

On an adjacent capture Krieg spotted Rosenkrantz a little further up the passage. She was pulling on Pontiff Preed's priestly robes, trying to get him back to the yawning bulkhead. It was hard to believe that Krieg had initially missed the hulking ecclesiarch: he almost filled the entire pict-caster with his corpulent bulk. The commissar felt sorry for the priest. Like himself, Preed had been caught in the middle of this unholy mess. He was a member of the Ecclesiarchy and the battle-sisters were the priesthood's militant arm. His loyalties should have been with the Sisters of the Immaculate Flame. They clearly weren't, however, as evidenced in his brutal treatment of any of their number that came within his reach.

He might have been huge but his reflexes were excellent. Hiding at a junction, with his back flat to the dun metal wall – not easy for a man of his dimensions – he was waiting for the smoking nozzle of a flamer to creep around the corner. Krieg could see the Aphonac-Stack Probist coming, of course, but the pontiff's timing was perfect.

Snatching the stubby barrel of the flamer he yanked the gaunt zealot attached to it around the corner of the junction, using his irresistible centre of gravity to propel the figure into the opposite wall with uncompromising, brute force. The militiaman's bare skull smacked into the harsh metal; he half-bounced, half-staggered backwards before falling against the opposite wall.

Turning the flamer back down the opposite corridor, Preed unleashed an inferno at the oncoming sisters and their troops. Grabbing a fat stub gun stuck in the belt of the Frater's filthy robes, Rosenkrantz tore at the monstrous ecclesiarch's arm, finally getting him to back towards the open bulkhead, the remaining corpsmen shouting them on.

With the priest and the pilot through Krieg activated the bulkhead once again. As a security gate, it came down much faster than it had opened – a lethal velocity created by the slackening of gears and the intervention of gravity. As well it might, Preed's promethium bath had done little to slow the battle-sisters' advance. The remaining Probists stumbled about the flaming corridor, bumping into the walls and each other before succumbing to the inferno. Krieg watched the sisters simply march through the firestorm in their menacing black body armour and prepare a melta bomb for the bulkhead. The bulkheads weren't going to be enough.

Scanning the controls for something else he could use, the cadet-commissar's eyes fell across the porthole pict-casters with their motley array of murderers and madmen baying for their freedom. The prisoners.

Watching the corpsmen running for their lives along the accessway on the next capture along, Krieg dropped another bulkhead behind them. Not a moment too soon: the melta bomb had done its job and had turned the first into a ragged hole of molten slag. Sisters were pouring through,

their bolter rounds peppering the reinforced bulkhead clos-
ing before them.

One after another, Krieg stabbed at a sequence of chunky
buttons, opening the cell doors on the corridor in which the
battle-sisters were trapped. The doors rolled aside in unison
on ancient hydraulics and the cells disgorged a deluge of
human detritus into the corridor. A mob of emaciated
insanity and evil packed the passageway, each man intent
on securing his freedom at all costs. For some that cost was
fairly immediate, the battle-sisters cutting through the
swathe of filth-faced villainy with their bolters. Soon
enough, however it was wall to wall convicts in there and
the battle-sisters had to contend with an unstoppable rabble
of desperate men crawling over their bodies and clawing at
their weaponry.

Running his finger across a dimly lit schematic of the
incarcetorium complex on the observation deck wall, Krieg
went about clearing a route for the storm-troopers all the
way up to the roof-top landing pad. All other areas of the
prison he flooded with freshly liberated convicts intent on
creating their own brand of mayhem and setting upon anyone else with a furious onslaught of frustration and anger.
With just about everyone else evacuated, that meant almost
exclusively the Sisters of the Immaculate Flame.

This got Krieg thinking. *Cell-block Gamma,* Medical
Officer Crayne had said. The pict-casters didn't cover the
solitary confinement oubliettes. There would be no point –
most of the time the cells were kept in complete darkness.
Krieg didn't need to see Zane Mortensen to know where he
was being held. A solitary Celestian stood on guard beside
one of the oubliettes' pressure sealed trapdoors: it seemed
that denying their inmates oxygen as well as light and company was part of the regime in solitary confinement. It was
the canoness's personal bodyguard. Krieg had seen her

many times before: she had an odd face, her big bright eyes too wide apart. She never smiled, nor spoke and despite looking to all intents and purposes like a fourteen-year-old girl, wore a suit of the most ancient, priceless armour of her order. She clutched a massive adamantium crusader shield – some kind of ancient relic – and was never far from her mistress.

He would have to find a way to deal with her. Smashing the general alarm with his fist, Krieg filled the entire complex with klaxons, alarm bells and screaming sirens. Then leaving one route through the incarcetorium clear of the full-scale riot that had engulfed the rest of the complex, he snatched up the bolt pistol and limped for Cell-block Gamma.

CHAPTER FIVE
The Devil's Boondocks

I

LIKE A GHOST ship *Dread Sovereign* rode the swells and troughs of the Spetzghastian stratosphere, tossed this way and that in the turbulence of low orbit. Almost spectral in the powerful stealth fields that bathed her streamlined hull, the corvette haunted the skies above the massive mercantile world.

Krieg formed a silhouette against the cloister deck's stained glass observation port, legs apart and hands behind his back. The thin, azure brilliance of Spetzghast flooded in through the clear glass forming St. Valeria the Younger's crusader shield and threatened to swallow him whole. Beyond, Spetzghast's mighty ring system dominated: the planet's system of multitudinous shepherd moons keeping the miasma of tumbling rock and ice in check. Here, the jaundiced smear that was Algernon sat suspended like a bad omen, with the battle-scarred surface of Illium passing nearby – crossing the terminator into a brief Spetzghastian night. Below the corvette was the object of his fascination: the naval carrier *Deliverance*, hanging like a bird of prey over one of the mercantile world's polar mega-sprawls.

After several hours of gum-spittle castigation and tongue-lashing from an unusually animated Udeskee about almost getting himself killed on his first day, the regimental commissar had given Krieg an administrative errand to run on the *Purgatorio*. Leaving his superior to vent further wrath on Guardsmen Snyder and Goinz, who had been summoned to the commissar's quarters after him, Krieg made for his transport. Undoubtedly Udeskee would finish what Krieg himself had started on the fabricator moon and devise suitable punishments for the men. Dead or alive, they were to be made an example of.

Instead of the flagship, however, the humpshuttle he was supposed to be piggy-backing set out worryingly for the blank carpet of deep space in between two of Spetzghast's main rings – the so called Quirini Division. Here under its stealth shielding, *Dread Sovereign* was waiting for him.

He was escorted straight to the colossal cloister decks of the Adepta Sororitas – somewhere he'd never been before – and told to wait outside Canoness Santhonax's personal chambers.

The great bronze doors rolled aside on dampeners and Krieg turned to find himself being approached by a solitary figure leaving the chambers. She wore a tight-fitting body glove of obsidian sheen that jealously clung to every curve, leaving next to nothing to the imagination, and sable robes of some lighter-than-air material that streamed behind her like a trail of smoke. When light from the cloister lamps finally invaded her elegant hood the cadet-commissar was finally privy to the ebony lustre of the stranger's face. It wasn't the joy the rest of her body had been: half had the bewitching Imperial dignity of discipline and importance; the rest was a collapsed mess of sunken bone, knotted muscle and the rumpled flesh that covered it.

She in turn displayed absolutely no interest in the cadet-commissar: her eyes never deviating from their intended course along the cloister deck and within moments she was gone, her strident steps taking her out of sight.

'Enter,' came that burnished voice: its lightest touch commanding immediate obedience. Santhonax.

The canoness's personal chambers were a vaulted realm of devotion and shadow. Ancient artefacts adorned the walls, relics of priceless Imperial history balanced on isolated plinths, tapestries dangled from the dizzying ceiling illustrating the order's innumerable wars of faith. Krieg's boots clicked across flagstones of jet that shattered into a mosaic in the centre of the chamber depicting St. Valeria the Younger and the Nine Virgins of the Apocalyse.

'My personal collection,' Santhonax told the commissar as she joined him from the shadows. Krieg surveyed the canoness's collection of arch-heretics and iconoclasts. 'I'm sure that you've heard of the infamous Cardinal Krabbé,' Santhonax said as she passed an aged cleric in shredded, blood-soaked robes. He was hanging from the ceiling on a set of wicked hooks and chains that were embedded in his back-flesh from his scalp to his shins. His encrusted beard dangled towards a gently gathering pool of literal blood, sweat and tears.

The canoness pushed him gently as she passed, eliciting a desperate moan from the heretic as he gently rocked and the hooks went to work on fresh flesh.

Next was a tubular plas tank full of a thin, liquid murk – a sloshing filth of blood-threaded puce. An oxygen pump beat rhythmically on one side of the tank, feeding something inside air through a corroded metal pipe. 'Xenobi Quordaiyn – the Butcheress of Banzai,' Santhonax informed Krieg. 'The end of my predecessor: I promised that I would never be the end of her…'

The cadet-commissar leaned in to get a better view through the effluence. A single palm thrashed out against the plas causing Krieg to jump back. The hand was skinless and raw: ligaments, veins and in some places bone were all on show. It retracted as fast as it had appeared. 'Molecular acid,' Santhonax told him. 'The weakest I could find. She'll be slowly dissolved over a thousand years – less than she deserves.'

The final abomination in the canoness's personal collection was simply a portrait. A mercury daguerreotype of the kind popular at the Guethenoc Gate: a funereal image of an angelic infant, a newborn, at rest in a tiny wicker coffin. Some kind of mystic Mechanicus apparatus was fixed to the rear of the frame, emanating a headache-inducing hum and causing the antique capture to impossibly flick and shimmer.

The canoness leaned in close. 'And him: his name hasn't been spoken in a millennium and I'll be damned before I'm the first to let it pass my lips. I'll spare you a similar curse.' The nalwood frame creaked ominously. 'Oh, do be quiet,' Santhonax spat at the haunting image.

Krieg waited respectfully before a simple throne at the top of the chamber as the canoness took to her seat. Her strange bodyguard, the young girl with the unsettling eyes, sat on the step at the canoness's foot, beneath an iron tripod, her tender years at complete odds with the antique armour she wore. Under an equally archaic crusader shield on display in the tripod's ornate arms the girl played a delicate game of cat's cradle with the prepubescent fingers of a stone cold killer.

'Ma'am,' Krieg began, 'may I ask if you received my report regarding the situation on Illium?'

The canoness seemed preoccupied with her own thoughts momentarily and stared at the cadet-commissar blankly.

'Your ladyship, the fabricator moon has been completely overrun,' Krieg informed her, intent on communicating the serious nature of the situation. 'This is no longer a case of subjugating a rebellion. Orks in those numbers so far in-system, without an invasion fleet: it's unheard of. And these greenskins behave like no brutes I've ever fought: organisation, discipline, strategy. Like I said: the cult killings; the 'Doomsday Brethren'; Spurrlok's agricultural freight charters; the rebellion on Illium – all connected. Now, full-scale alien invasion.'

'Calm yourself, cadet,' Santhonax soothed. 'Inquisitor Herrenvolk has these intrigues in hand. The 364th Volscian Shadow Brigade can handle the slog work.'

'But ma'am, in my report–'

'I read your report: it was a pleasant work of fiction,' the canoness suddenly turned on him. Gone was the warmth that had lit up her pin-decorated face whilst perusing her heretical collection. Krieg felt like the sun had just disappeared behind a cloud. 'All that should concern you are the actions of that heretic major of yours. According to your measured narrative, Major Mortensen ignored your threat assessment of the situation on Illium, he put a blade to an Imperial commissar's throat and then proceeded to blunder his way through a mission that cost unnecessary lives and Guard resources...'

'It's complicated,' Krieg admitted, a rush of mixed feelings and confusion flushing his chest.

'The man is clearly a criminal incompetent and you should have administered justice when you had the opportunity,' Santhonax shrieked. 'I should have you bathed in acid for your own incompetence.'

Krieg swallowed hard. This wasn't one of Kowalski's tedious remonstrations or Mortensen's bullish threats: she meant it.

'He then did what you seemed unable to do and made a Guard-orchestrated attempt on your life...'

'I have no evidence that...'

'...and went on to accomplish further deeds of remarkable courage and endurance, adding further fuel to a dangerous myth and recruiting ever more willing rank and file acolytes to a fallacious hero cult.'

'He was asked to pull assets out of enemy held territory against insurmountable odds and an incalculable, unforeseen alien threat,' Krieg stated with forced calm. 'What can I tell you? He got the job done. As yet I have witnessed no actions of direct cowardice, incompetence or cult activity. From a Redemption Corps point of view, the mission was a success.'

'A Redemption Corps point of view?' the canoness burst incredulously.

'Look, with the right example...'

'Your example, Cadet-Commissar Krieg? It seems your example isn't particularly trustworthy,' Santhonax told him, her words a chilled indictment. 'You've just spent the past few moments lending credence to heretical suggestions of this man's indestructibility.'

'Indestructibility? I can only report what I saw.'

'You were on that aircraft, weren't you, commissar?' the battle-sister asked.

Krieg could see where this was going.

'Mortensen saved your life, didn't he? How does that make you feel – are you too now beholden to him? Have you become an acolyte?'

'I would eat the barrel of my own pistol if I thought such a suggestion could be entertained,' the cadet-commissar shot back.

'But you won't make the major swallow his for his own heresies?'

'Look, I hate the bastard,' Krieg informed her honestly. 'When he slips up, I'll be there waiting for him. I'll bring him in and you'll have the justice you crave.' The leather of the commissar's gloves creaked as Krieg tensed his fists by his sides. 'But we do this by the book. Any thug can kill. If we give in to temptation and take avoidable shortcuts then it makes us no better than the scum we're after.'

Santhonax stared at him through narrowed slits. They'd traded insults, accusations and warnings. Krieg couldn't tell what she was going to do next. Probably order another tank of acid. As it was, her eyes flicked over his shoulder. The tension in Krieg's fists instantly spread to the rest of his body as his fingers brushed the holster of his hellpistol. There was someone coming up behind him. He turned. It was his cheerless friend from the Narthex, her silver bob twinkling in the half-light and skull helmet tucked under one helmet.

The canoness was smirking; something about Krieg's uncertainty clearly amused her. 'Well, this is all about to be rendered moot. Major Mortensen is, as we speak, on board *Purgatorio* receiving orders for his next mission.'

The battle-sister handed Santhonax a data scroll, which the canoness unravelled and studied.

'Ma'am?'

'Where?' Santhonax barked at the Celestian.

'The shepherd moon of Ishtar, madam.'

'Perfect,' the canoness said, half to herself. Then to the Celestian: 'My compliments to the captain. Please inform him that *Dread Sovereign* will need to be in low orbit around Ishtar within the hour.'

'Should I return to *Deliverance*?' Krieg put to the canoness. Santhonax ignored him.

'Have Cadet-Commissar Krieg briefed, equipped and transported to the coordinates you have on the moon's surface,' Santhonax told the silver-haired battle-sister, handing her back the scroll.

The Celestian clicked her armoured heels.

'You want me waiting for him?' Krieg asked cautiously.

'Perhaps even Zane Mortensen isn't stupid enough to practise his heretical ideals directly under the nose of an Imperial commissar. Monitor the mission covertly: you will have the details, and when you observe the major act in accordance with his dark beliefs you can administer the Emperor's justice,' she confirmed with relish.

Krieg settled for a neutral, 'As you wish, your ladyship,' and lowered his head.

Escorted by the Celestian the commissar made his way from the elegantly gruesome chamber.

'Krieg,' the canoness called wistfully just before he reached the bronze egress. He turned obediently. 'Major Mortensen is not to return from that moon alive: you understand me? The Emperor has never expected as much of you.'

Krieg simply nodded and left the room.

As THEY STOOD waiting at the mighty doors of a baroque elevator Krieg, who'd been silent the entire length of the cloister deck, turned to the battle-sister and asked, 'What did she mean, "Perfect"?'

'Excuse me?' the Celestian replied.

'She said, "Perfect" after you told her the mission was on Ishtar.'

'Ishtar's a deathworld,' the battle-sister replied. 'With any luck the major will be dead before you even reach him.'

'Great,' Krieg mumbled, not exactly thrilled at the prospect of a jaunt down to a deathworld himself. 'What the hell are the Redemption Corps doing down there?'

With unmasked tedium the Celestian consulted the scroll once more.

'Well,' she told him, 'apart from a variety of different forms of certain death to be found on the surface, Ishtar boasts only one registered settlement: a sparse collection of stilt burgs in the supercontinent interior.'

'Stilt burgs?'

'Homo Sapiens Gigantus.'

'Ogryns,' Krieg grunted. He'd worked alongside these abhuman brutes before. Storm-trooper squads were sometimes coupled with ogryn shock troops in order to spearhead assaults. The barbarian creatures soaked up a tremendous amount of firepower and at full charge were virtually unstoppable. They were the hammer, excessive and unwieldy, to the storm-troop's chisel, skilful and precise. A stampede of ogryns could carry a storm-trooper unit a long way into the enemy lines, where the tactics and surgical execution of the specialists could do their worst. They were also clumsy and dangerous, taking orders like barely-tamed dumb animals; but with Illium drowning in a greenskin deluge and reinforcements a distant dream, the Guard was pulling on every in-system resource.

The grandiloquent doors parted revealing another visitor to the cloister deck. The entire space was dominated by a hulking form; begowned from head to toe in a ribbed, leather capote. Not a scrap of flesh or clothing was visible beneath. The voluminous hood dropped down to its belly, without so much as an eyeslit to allow its wearer to see where it was stomping. The mantle's baggy sleeves met at the belly also, with one of the giant's hands clearly clasped in the other beneath the material.

The goliath had ducked beneath the frame of the elevator doors, allowing a small throne – set between the monster's shoulder blades – to pass beneath. The diminutive throne was fashioned similarly from ribbed leather and secured to the gross bulk using a thick leather harness. It carried the tiny, atrophied body of a wasted ancient, whose obscene little form in turn was swathed in a leather cloak that was part of the throne. Only his head was completely visible, the bloated cranium hovering serenely above his enfeebled body.

Krieg was not a little taken aback at finding the hulk and its charge in the elevator but when he finally turned around he found that the Celestian had fallen down on one knee, with her head angled at the floor. As the visitor's bulk sailed past, Krieg noticed for the first time the Inquisitorial rosette dangling from a robust cord around the behemoth's neck. Swinging this way and that, the badge of office was almost hypnotic. Realisation dawned. This was Herrenvolk.

The commissar could hardly be blamed for not recognising the inquisitor: very few people had actually seen him. Santhonax and her battle-sisters worked in collaboration with the man and as such had more access to him than virtually anyone else. Beyond the Pontificals, he worked almost exclusively through a network of henchmen and spies that he kept on his payroll. Many claimed that he had a telepathic or telekinetic link with his closest operatives and Krieg had certainly witnessed Interrogator Angelescu, the Inquisitorial storm-troopers' point of contact with the inquisitor, act strangely from time to time: almost as though his body and mind were on occasions not his own.

The Celestian grabbed the back of his neck with her gauntleted hand and pushed his head down into an obedient bow. Krieg instinctively allowed his eyes to travel upwards and caught a final glimpse of the inquisitor, sitting astride his humanoid steed, as he passed. One of Herrenvolk's own oily black eyes were fixed on the commissar, peering over the back of his throne, set in a gaze as unsettling as it was unreadable.

+Koulick Krieg…+

The words rattled around inside the core of his very being. His soul seemed to expand to accommodate them. They were everywhere and he was nowhere.

+Koulick, son of Illarian, son of Spartak, son of Nestorr…+ The thoughtspeak faded and simultaneously returned a moment's eternity later. +…Hear me…+

'Cadet!'

The backhanded slap took him across the face like a basin of cold water. He was back – slumped in the corner of the ornate elevator with the battle-sister crouched over him, the fleeting traces of pleasure falling from her features: she'd enjoyed that.

'What happened?' Krieg managed, pushing with his knees and sliding his shoulders back up the car wall.

'You're male and you're weak,' the Celestian replied flatly, as one might recall an obvious fact. Then after a second's pause to establish she meant it: 'You fell unconscious: it's the inquisitor. He has that effect on a lot of people – he's, how can I put it… potent.'

'You seem fine.'

'I'm not you,' the Celestian answered making the sign of the aquila. 'Emperor be thanked.'

The elevator doors parted to reveal *Dread Sovereign's* crowded flight deck. Sleek strikefighters shared the hanger with landers and Adeptus Ministorum Valkyries.

Krieg attempted to stand without the assistance of a wall. It came… slowly. The equivalent of mental indigestion still reverberated around his skull.

'Suit up. That's your ride,' the battle-sister told him indicating the nearest Valkyrie. Krieg took a few unsteady steps closer, out onto the hangar. A sombre nameplate identified the aircraft as *Purity Control*. What the callsign lacked in finesse it compensated for in unequivocability: a book you could definitely judge by its cover. The Celestian hit the elevator floor stud.

'Not coming to enjoy the sights?' the commissar asked.

'You're going to the one place where the sights enjoy you,' she replied matter-of-factly. 'I'm going to the Pontifical's armoury; you're going to need something considerably harder-hitting than that a hellpistol to go hunting down there.'

The cadet-commissar's hand went down protectively over the holster of his hellpistol and gave her a parting look of mock hurt. The doors closed. Krieg turned, alone on the flight deck, and mused thoughtfully on whether the battle-sister meant the deathworld fauna and flora or the Redemption Corps' major.

II

ROSENKRANTZ HAD FLOWN all manner of skies and put down on all kinds of dirt, but Ishtar had almost immediately topped the Jopallian pilot's top-ten table of singularly weird crash landings.

It started with the drop. With *Deliverance* rapidly falling away above them and the Spectre plummeting for the velvet, malachite gloom of Ishtar's thick atmosphere, the *Vertigo's* velocity died and a shudder rang through the aircraft's superstructure. It was almost as though the bird had put down, beak-first, in the ocean; Rosenkrantz knew this because she'd done just that on more than one occasion. This realisation was reinforced by the backwash of glutinous slime that cascaded up the canopy. The pilot's initial fear was restricted visibility but the atmospheric spawn was largely transparent. Not that it mattered that much, the deeper they fell through the cloud layer the darker it got.

The engines soon began to struggle in the gaseous gloop and, one by one, the quad proceeded to short and cut out. This brought to mind a second concern: falling clean out of the sky. Despite the fact that the upper atmosphere should have had the drag-inducing qualities of a thick paste, they were still freefalling like a lead brick. A brief vox-transmission to the *Urdesh Ecliptic* confirmed that their partner Spectre was experiencing much the same problem.

Dark, voluminous shapes began to fill an already darkening sky. All about the aircraft, great organic balloons filled the air. Ochre bladders, packed with lighter-than-air gases and threaded through with fat, pulsating capillaries, drifted around the Spectre. Rosenkrantz guided the plummeting aircraft as best she could, through the school of drifting behemoths and down past their gargantuan filter feeding maws. To all intents and purposes they looked like giant, bloated squid, with webbed tentacles drooping for the planet surface. A sea of larvae sat suspended in the migratory spawn and the alien creatures were clearly descending on the congregated bounty. The appendages rippled gently, drawing the migrating sky-spawn up into the gossamer nets between each tentacle and then on into the gargantuan creatures' mouths. *Vertigo* had been unfortunate enough to come down through the middle of the spawn-slick.

It wasn't long until the inevitable happened – *Vertigo*'s wing tip tore through one of the bloated balloon sacks, dragging the peaceful monstrosity through the skies beside them until alien and aircraft parted, sending the Spectre spinning for the surface.

The Spectre's controls suddenly slackened as the aircraft punctured another cloud layer. The slime was gone, but was immediately replaced by a thin drizzle that foamed as soon as the tiny droplets hit the canopy plas. From unusually slack the stick became increasingly rigid and Rosenkrantz could hear the now familiar sound of an engine dying.

Benedict told her that the flaps had frozen, which seemed incredible since as far as the pilot could make out they were gliding through the downpour towards what looked like primeval jungle below. There was nothing else she could do: voxing that the crew should brace for impact, Rosenkrantz fought to keep the nose up and slapped the Spectre's swollen belly down in the heart of the alien rainforest.

Which was where they now found themselves.

Rosenkrantz unclipped the harness and massaged her bruised shoulders. It could have been worse. On Arborsia IV she'd had to put down amongst the titan-woods of Shadebarrens: the trunks had simply torn the wings out of the aircraft and a branch had cleaved in the reinforced plas of the cockpit canopy, impaling her newly assigned co-pilot.

An incoming vox-transmission confirmed that the *Ecliptic* had put down mercifully close by but had failed to level out and had lost a wing to the impact, rendering them combat inoperative. The crew were injured but alive, and its fire support Centaur payload was intact. The second bird was a wreck, however, rapidly sinking into the chemical mire beyond and was in the process of being evacuated and abandoned.

Leaving Benedict to a more detailed assessment of their own aircraft's status, the Jopallian pilot slid down the companionway ladder and into the hold. It was chaos. The fire support Centaur that had been strapped down in the Spectre's belly had unsurprisingly broken loose in the crash. Nauls was busy with the armoured vehicle, the moody chief cutting it free

of the mesh racks at the rear of the bay with a pair of
heavy-duty bolt cutters. Before it had buried itself in
the webbing it had smashed into the compartment
wall killing one of Rask's Shadow Brigade Guardsmen
outright – an officer by the look of him. The Redemption Corps had fared a little better in the crash:
Sarakota had some broken ribs and a suspected punctured lung, meaning he was now declared
mission-inactive and required constant mask-bagging
from one of *Vertigo's* gunners. This had been a temporary arrangement set up by the Second Platoon's
medic until the sniper could reach a medical bay.
Sergeant Minghella would have seen to the storm-
trooper's needs himself had it not been for the fact
that he was a crash casualty also, knocked senseless
by the bouncing fire support vehicle as it smashed
around the compartment. He'd been unconscious
ever since – breathing but unresponsive – and had
been strapped into his own stretcher on the Spectre
bay floor.

A small group of gangers huddled around their
fallen Shadow Brigade officer. They were as motley as
any of the 364th Rosenkrantz had come across when it
came to field dress and equipment. All of the hivers
wore the cerise sashes of their calling but the group in
the hold shared three distinctive features: drab khaki
trench coats, clean-shaven heads and glares of open
hostility directed at the pilot as she passed.

Her own remaining gunners sat hunched against
their heavy bolters, establishing a killzone around the
crashed aircraft: with Rosenkrantz at the helm, this
had become almost routine. She touched Spreckels on
the shoulder.

'The major?'

He nodded to starboard and Rosenkrantz made her way down the bay ramp. A thoroughly alien environment was waiting for her.

Mangrove was the only word she could find to describe it, but it wasn't like any she'd seen before. She'd landed in all kinds of forests and swamps on a myriad of worlds and no matter how different, they all had one thing in common: the unmistakable abundance of organic life. The fresh bouquet of new growth; the stench of decay. There was none of that here. Just a potent, chemical sterility.

There were trees everywhere, but no wood and no chlorophyll. Everything on Ishtar had a lucent, heliotropic glaze. The trunks were the equivalent of frosted glass and the leaves and foliage choking the spaces in between were like crystalline flint. *Vertigo* itself had actually come to rest upon a pyre of the shattered material. Not that it was easy to see: thick cloud cover doused the forest in a twilight haze and airbrushed the canopy with a coral corona.

Pontiff Preed stood on the edge of the ramp, peering out across this strange, new world through his single lens.

'They blame me,' she said as she joined him in the doorway.

'You did what you could. We all give the Emperor thanks for that. No one is exempt from dying, sister,' the Pontiff rumbled gently.

'Not everyone around here seems to share that sentiment.'

'You talk of Mortensen. That's just superstitious claptrap.' With some difficulty he moved his robust bulk in closer and in a conspiratorial hush told her, 'I believe in the Creed and I believe in the good major. You

268 - Rob Sanders

know that, but there are those who twist both to their own fervent ends.'

He nodded back at the group of hivers gathered around their fallen officer. They were Volscian – their tattoos and red sashes confirmed that – but their distinct trench coats and shaven heads marked them out as different. Their demeanour was stoic and solemn and lacked the underhive twitchiness and up-front bravado that characterised the other Volscians. One stood among them, giving quiet orders and instructing the others in how best to extricate the dead Guardsman's body from his mangled harness. Sergeant's stripes adorned one stout shoulder and fat wrinkles gathered at the back of his bald neck. His dark flesh glistened in the Ishtarian twilight.

'Lijah Meeks,' Preed informed her softly.

Meeks turned his head eerily to one side, as though he'd heard his name. Thick-rimmed glasses sat on a fleshy nose, beneath which his pink lips curled.

'What's with the heads and coats?' Rosenkrantz asked warily. Most of the Volscians resisted the concept of uniformity.

'Second Platoon has a fundamentalist streak,' Preed told her. 'Ardentites, as far as I can tell. Some kind of Thorian incarnationist faction.'

'Religious freaks?' she put to him. His nose wrinkled. 'No offence,' she added.

'None taken, sister. They are not of my flock. Ardentites look for evidence of the divine in those around them. They believe that when the God-Emperor fell He disseminated His gift. He believed the best way to protect humanity in His absence was to hide His power – His talents – among chosen individuals across the galaxy, so that they may individually serve

His interests and, as a collective phenomenon, hold back the darkness that threatens to engulf mankind.' The Pontiff sighed. 'The coats are gang throwbacks. House Zlaw: threw in their lot with the Redemptionists for a time, then kind of outgrew them. The heads are merely an emulation: a mark of respect to the major himself.'

'And what does the major make of Meeks and his boys?'

'He thinks they're psych-jobs who probably have a little too much time on their hands. But they're useful. Rask knows the 364th: he probably figures that troops that idolise the major are marginally less of a mission-risk than those out to frag him. After the debacle on Illium with the new commissar, you could hardly blame him.

'But if you're asking me if Mortensen "believes", I have no facts to give you. He's an extremely capable soldier with some extraordinary talents, but it's not for me to say if they are "divinely ordained". What I can tell you is that these ideas are not politely entertained in the higher echelons of the Ecclesiarchy and many might consider them heresy.'

A shiver worked its way across the pilot's shoulders as she recalled their encounter with the Inquisitorial corvette above Spetzghast.

Suddenly Meeks was among them, the hiver's silent steps carrying him across the troop bay in the space of a moment's inattention.

'Pontiff,' the sergeant uttered with a respectful bow of his head. To Rosenkrantz he merely gave a savage flash of the eyes through his thick lenses, before stepping out into the smashed landscape, disappearing under the starboard wing.

'Thanks,' Rosenkrantz said to the priest before stepping out herself. Her first footfall slipped as her flight boot splintered a piece of crystalline bark and slid towards the continuously foaming waters that lapped up against the shattered shore. Preed's stubby fist was suddenly there on her arm, holding her up and her foot just clear of the supercooled, chemical brume.

'Take care, lieutenant,' he said, setting her right on the glassy bank. 'This is a deathworld, after all.'

She nodded further gratitude.

It was only a few steps to the wing but it was enough to sample her new environment. The smashed trees crunched underfoot and sinister waters spumed up between the cracks. Some of the crystal canopy remained intact above the aircraft and drizzle collected amongst the jewellery on the branches and fell in fat droplets from above, spattering her flight jacket and chilling her to the bone. The ambient temperature was actually reasonably mild but the droplets frosted instantly on the leather. She jumped slightly as a blue-white beam of energy arced between the trunks of two nearby trees, forcing Rosenkrantz to put her back against *Vertigo* and sidle along the fuselage and under the wing. Every time a beam sizzled between two of the outlandish trees, it set in motion a chain reaction of electrical arcs, passing from one plant to another, lighting up the gloom of the glass jungle. After reaching a light show crescendo the forest would fade to darkness again, waiting for another trunk to gather enough charge to begin the phenomenon again.

'I could have done with more reconnaissance data on this deathworld,' she announced to the group of Guardsmen gathered under the wing. 'That kind of information comes in useful.' Conversation died in their throats. Flanked by Conklin and Vedette, Mortensen was peering intently through a pair of magnoculars up and out of the crystal canopy and along the surrounding relief.

Captain Rask stood nearby, leaning against the shattered trunk of a tree. Sass and the captain were studying a data-slate, angling it this way and that to make sense of the carto-pict they were studying. Meeks stood by looking on intensely.

'What difference would it have made?' Mortensen hypothesised from behind the magnoculars.

'Well, we could have expected...'

'The unexpected? You're not shipping out with the Volscian 1001st now, flight lieutenant,' the major returned. 'We're Redemption Corps: we move fast and with purpose. We get to it.'

'Krieg was right,' Rosenkrantz informed him with mock realisation. She let the insult go home before continuing: 'You hit Illium unprepared. You were lucky to get your men out alive, let alone the targets. You're making the same mistakes here.'

'No,' the Gomorrian told her, unfazed. He came out from behind the glasses. 'Just a few new ones. What's the bird's status?'

Rosenkrantz glared at him. Then, finally: 'The intakes are completely flooded with whatever we came down through and if that's not bad enough for you, the quad appears to be frozen solid. The only engine with any signs of life whatsoever is this one...' She kicked at the thruster behind Mortensen, 'and that's not going to be enough to get us off the ground.'

The major nodded gravely. 'Now, would someone return the favour,' Rosenkrantz put to them, 'and tell me what we're even doing here. This need-to-know crap is wearing thin.'

Rask looked up from his slate: 'Forty-eight hours ago, upon my recommendation, Field Marshall Rygotsk despatched Commander Qvist, a Departmento Munitorum officer, to the planet surface with a small recruitment force, seconded from the Spetzghastian Mercantile Militia. Qvist's orders were to swiftly establish contact with the indigenous primitive inhabitants and begin processing populations for immediate extraction and Imperial indoctrination.'

'They didn't come back...' the pilot interrupted, filling in the blanks.

'Nothing has been heard from the mission since its departure. Of course, I feel responsible for Qvist: he's relatively inexperienced and he was despatched upon my recommendation; but the brigadier needs these ogryns to augment our forces on Illium. Something's gone wrong here.'

'Something's gone wrong... here,' Rosenkrantz informed him, yanking a thumb at her downed bird. The officer shook his head.

'This is the Spetzghastian back yard: that's why I sent Qvist down with Mercantile Militia. The platoon guide was a Sergeant Lompock, Mercantile ogryn auxilia. They know the rudimentaries about Ishtar, its dangers. This is something else.' Rask turned grimly. 'Sergeant?' he announced.

Meeks cleared his throat. 'Lieutenant Gomez is dead, sir.'

'Poor wretch,' Conklin announced. An epitaph it wasn't. Mortensen raised an eyebrow, letting the magnoculars fall on their strap.

'Israel Gomez was a good Guardsman and a devoted Imperial servant,' Rask told Meeks. The Volscian nodded slowly. 'Lijah, I'm giving you Second Platoon. We're in a bit of a spot here and I need you to keep the men focused. You get my meaning?'

'Loud and clear, captain.' The sergeant's voice lacked enthusiasm but was thick with honesty. 'We're right behind you and the major, here.'

Mortensen gave Rask an uneasy look, clearly uncomfortable with the Volscian hero-worship. He was ready to move on. 'Sass, where are we?'

The adjutant stared back at the slate he was carrying.

'We can't be too far off the landing zone,' Rosenkrantz offered, staring around the alien jungle as the rain intensified. 'We were virtually on top of the coordinates you gave me when we left *Deliverance*.'

'Thing is,' Sass began, 'the map doesn't exactly reflect what I'm seeing here.' Mortensen stuck out one hand and Sass went to pass the pict on.

'Let me see that,' Rosenkrantz said, snatching the topographic slate from Sass's grubby paws. He frowned but she had, after all, a great deal more experience reading contours and orbital data than any of the corpsmen.

As she attempted to make out the confusing imagery on the slate a dark figure appeared in the clearing the fallen aircraft had created and padded its way carefully across the smashed crystal and gushing chemical potholes.

His colours identified him as a storm-trooper but his forehead studs marked him out as an Autegan. The Autegan Tactical Rangers were a deathworld regiment and the major had clearly understood that an Autegan's experience would be invaluable on a world like

Ishtar. On Autega, the Rangers' main duties were scouting the least perilous paths across the planet's lethal environs and providing mounted escorts to the pilgrim trains that continually moved between the cities and the shrines. As he approached, a double-barrelled grenade launcher rested across one carapace shoulder.

'What have you got for us, Eszcobar?' Mortensen put to him as the deathworlder leaned against the underside of the *Vertigo*'s wing.

'Beautiful,' the Autegan began, although with his thick accent it was difficult to tell whether he was complimenting his surroundings, cursing them, or both. 'Silicon rainforest: it's like walking through broken glass.' He angled his armour to reveal bloody gashes in his jacket, thighs and calves. 'I found the *Ecliptic*. She's due west. I told the crew to remain with the Centaur.' The deathworlder sniffed and spat. 'I only got about fifty metres in, but it wasn't just the foliage that stopped me. This whole area is just one big flood plain. Most of it's submerged, which wouldn't be a problem except that it's not water.'

'What is it?'

'Some kind of supercooled chemical soup seeping up through the planet crust.' He pointed up into the drizzle. 'Which accounts for the frost on the fuselage. This and the fact that the trees themselves seem involved in some kind of electrical defence mechanism of their own, and you basically have an environment pretty inimical to human life.'

'You're telling us that we can't traverse this terrain,' Conklin confirmed.

'Frozen alive, cut to pieces or electrocuted: you decide,' Eszcobar replied, impressed. He regarded

Mortensen. 'I'm not saying it can't be done, major. But the losses would be astronomical.'

'What about the Centaurs?' the master sergeant suggested.

'They'd offer protection from the foliage and the cryogenic drizzle, but wouldn't get past the trees.'

'But this stuff is as brittle as anything,' Conklin said, stamping his boot down on a piece of crystalline bark that obligingly shattered to prove his point. He gestured around. 'Look at what the bird did.'

'I wouldn't want to be inside a Centaur when one of these discharges hits the hull exterior,' Meeks mused.

'So what are you saying? We pull out?' Conklin cried incredulously.

'Bad intelligence,' Rosenkrantz said, flipping Sass back the nonsensical slate, 'and no possible way to reach the targets – if they're alive which, now that we're here, I very much doubt. Damn right we should pull out. Vox *Deliverance* and request an evacuation.'

The pilot's assessment was met with a hail of testosterone-fuelled objections. Only Vedette and the major remained silent throughout, the Gomorrian back to peering through his magnoculars.

'She's not wrong,' he mumbled, drawing a gaze of disbelief from his master sergeant. The major turned on the pilot. 'But he's right. Redemption Corps don't run. There's more at stake here than Rask's young commander and a few Merc Militiamen. We're going to need those ogryns on Illium. For the ogryns, we need to make contact with the recruitment party.'

The major's calm logic went some way to soothe the tension crackling between the pilot and the gathered Guardsmen. Nearby a loud snap of piezoelectric power vaulted between a splintered trunk and the tree line beyond, bathing them in a powerful – if brief – wave of sterile heat. All eyes were on the searing arc as it set in motion another blazing lightshow.

'Besides, we'll have more to worry about if we stay put.' He passed the magnoculars to Vedette and pointed up at the silhouetted highlands above. 'What does that look like to you?'

The Mordian took the glasses and aimed them up at the distant horizon. The magnoculars steadied with sudden realisation.

'Gun emplacement,' Vedette confirmed with satisfaction.

'We're not alone on this moon.'

'Ogryns?'

'Certainly looks makeshift,' Conklin replied, now staring through the glasses.

Mortensen put them out of their misery. 'Greenskins.'

'Here?' Rosenkrantz asked, wondering why even orks would choose to visit such a hostile corner of the galaxy.

'Which is why we can't fix our position on the charts,' Sass put forward, a sense of relief evident in his voice. 'These,' the storm-trooper pointed up through the canopy at the irregular highlands beyond, 'are not natural features. That is probably an ork rok.'

If Rosenkrantz had felt vulnerable before, the possibility of being surrounded on all sides by greenskin megafortresses, bristling with large-bore artillery and shot through with subterranean airbases, did not put her at ease.

'Guess we know what happened to Commander Qvist,' Conklin muttered at Rask.

'If they're here,' the pilot began, 'well, that means the entire system has to be infiltrated.'

Mortensen gave her one cocked eye. 'You think so?'

'They probably saw us come down,' Eszcobar insisted.

The major looked up at the sky, unconvinced. 'In this? Perhaps. But I don't think any of us want to be here, should our greenskinned friends decide to dump a ton of ordnance on our position. How's the *Ecliptic*?'

'Totalled,' Rosenkrantz confirmed. 'The crew are fine – no fatalities. They've recovered *Gundozer* but the bird is slipping rapidly into the flood plain.'

'How long to get this beast off the ground?'

Rosenkrantz shrugged. 'We could use flame units on the thrusters, but clearing the filters; that could take hours.'

'Okay,' the major nodded. 'Then you've got your work cut out. We'll get out from under your boots. I need this bird in the sky as soon as is humanly possible.'

'Think I want to remain here one moment longer than that?' Rosenkrantz replied.

'Sass, Eszcobar: ignore the surrounding relief and plot me a route to those coordinates.'

'You want us to use the waterways?'

'Yeah,' Mortensen affirmed. Rosenkrantz saw a flash of inspiration cross the major's features. 'I got an idea.'

As a rule Navy pilots didn't tend to have a fear of heights; when you're soaring hundreds of metres above the ground, distances and their associated fears become meaningless. Hanging off the corrugated compound walls and dangling above the ceramite quad, falling to her death felt like it had more meaning for Dekita Rosenkrantz.

She wasn't in fact clutching to a wall at all, but Preed's fleshy back. On the ground the priest's mass was cumbersome and somewhat of a handicap. Above the ground, carried up and across the improvised ledges and clawholds of the compound wall, the ecclesiarch's body assumed a surprising grace. Sandalless feet took lighter steps than Rosenkrantz would have thought possible, pushing him up wall to crennelated wall. Stubby arms and those big, hairy hands felt for holds from which to haul his three hundred kilos of devout bulk. It revealed to the pilot just how much of the ecclesiarch's massive girth was in fact pure muscle.

As Preed pulled his huge form up on the roof edge, Rosenkrantz could hear the fury of a firefight beyond.

Someone had been smiling on them: the route through the incarcetorium to the landing strip was all but clear. The battle-sisters would almost certainly have posted sentries on their own aircraft and the storm-troopers had been forced to formulate a brief but brutally simple plan to take the pad under such circumstances. The corpsmen would rush the sentries from the security bulkhead with whatever ammunition and weapons they had remaining, while Preed volunteered to scale the wall and get their most valuable commodity – their only pilot – safely to one of the aircraft.

Two Adeptus Ministorum Valkyries squatted on the landing strip, one behind the other, their fuselages parallel to the compound wall. Like a prisoner, the sorry-looking Vertigo *sat between them. Rosenkrantz could just make out the short, power-conserving flashes of las-fire coming from the security gate and the stacks of prison supplies palleted nearby. The storm-troopers had done their best to rush the battle-sisters and their Fraternis Militia brothers, but simply didn't have the coverage to work their way up to the Inquisitorial carriers. She could see the bodies of the dead and dying on the rockcrete; those who had paid the price for such desperate tactics.*

Leather masked zealots, draped in chains and brandishing stubbers and shotguns held their ground on the strip. Heavily armoured battle-sisters had fanned out across the landing pad, laying down suppressive firepower from their boltguns and tossing the occasional grenade into the carnage – careful not to damage the precious aircraft. The Spectre *and the Valkyries had the worst role to play in repelling the bungled attack, however. The side doors facing the security bulkhead had rolled aside to reveal primed heavy bolters that proceeded to chew up the corpsmen and their fast disappearing cover.*

No one could have possibly anticipated an attack on the landing pad from such a position, but the Sisters of the Immaculate Flame were thorough if nothing else. So confident in their ability to ward off such a pitiful attack, they hadn't even committed all of their troops.

A black-armoured figure watched the slaughter from behind the protective wall of blazing gunfire provided by the assault carriers, holding her sentry point on the wallside flank of the aircraft. Rosenkrantz suddenly became aware that they'd been peering at the firefight from between her legs. The sister unexpectedly turned, her tight, raven curls flowing with the light breeze.

Preed lowered them both on his trembling fingertips as the figure swept the roofline with her bolter and then took several strident steps towards the edge. There, the mighty ecclesiarch's fist grabbed her booted ankle in a vice-like grip and tore her from her footing. Slamming into the rockcrete roof the armoured figure almost bounced and then slipped into the terrifying emptiness of the quad below after her plummeting weapon.

Gravity latched onto the heavily armoured figure with all its irresistible might. Several wild bolts went skyward as the falling sister's pistol finally cleared its holster, but by then Rosenkrantz and Preed had already scrambled onto the roof.

There wasn't a second to waste. With every moment that passed, men were dying on the roof. Thumping up the rear Valkyrie's wing with heavy strides, Preed bounded for the cockpit exterior with Rosenkrantz struggling to keep up behind. By the time she breathlessly clambered alongside the priest he'd already got a grip on the canopy's hydraulic slide. Fired by the climb and their close brush with death just heartbeats before, the ecclesiarch's righteous rage broke its banks. With an appalling roar he tore at the canopy release.

Inside, Rosenkrantz could see an ordo pilot reaching, wide-eyed, for his Navy pistol. Preed grunted. The canopy gave and squealed along on its hydraulic runners. The muzzle of the Navy pistol shot out of the cockpit and at the priest's leering face. Rosenkrantz slipped her arm inside the open cockpit and yanked the firing mechanism control handle for the pilot's emergency ejection seat. She shielded her eyes and ears as the rocket-propelled seat shot for the skies. When the ecclesiarch came out from under his ample sleeve he was wearing a monstrous smile.

Rosenkrantz dropped down into the empty cockpit space and slid down one section further to the co-pilot's bucket-seat.

'Preed!' she called. The priest nodded and slid the cockpit canopy back along its runners and into place. With that the priest set off to create more havoc in the troop section with the Aphonac-Stack Probists manning the heavy bolters.

Rosenkrantz had two initial priorities. First, prevent her newly-acquired Valkyrie firing on the storm-troopers. Second, prevent Vertigo and the forward Valkyrie firing on her.

It felt good to be back in the confines of a Navy cockpit and her fingers slid automatically across the glyphs and runes of the instrumentation. She'd been born to fly Spectres, but had trained in a Valkyrie and the operations and orientations instantly came back to her.

Almost immediately the rancid chatter of the port gun was silenced as she remotely closed the accessway and locked it off. Of course, she didn't have control of the side doors on Vertigo or the sister ship. Her finger hovered over the button. She couldn't believe that she was going to destroy her own bird. The Jopallian pilot sighed. A moment later it was over. She sent a hellstrike straight up the open troop compartment of the battered Spectre.

The Spectre just vanished. One moment the aircraft was sitting on the landing pad and then nothing. Light. Sound. The clang of distant debris, spinning across the compound roof. But as Rosenkrantz well knew, what went up, must come down. The firestorm wreckage of the Spectre flew back to earth, the raging fuselage landing upside down on top of the Adepta Sororitas Valkyrie.

Firing the thrusters Rosenkrantz took the carrier off the deck and turned the aircraft slowly at an effortless hover. The Valkyrie, whose callsign was Purity Control, *according to the side of the co-pilot's helmet, was unsurprisingly sprightlier than a Spectre and gave her an instant view of the burning, debris-strewn roof. Armoured bodies littered the landing pad and those few battle-sisters using* Purity Control *for cover had been swiftly denied by the Jopallian's impromptu take off.*

The situation on the compound roof rapidly reversed. Spurred on by Rosenkrantz's and Preed's decisive taking of the aircraft, the Redemption Corpsmen had swept in on the remaining zealots, scooping up abandoned bolters and pinning the armoured figures of battle-sisters down behind a blazing section of wing that had settled not far from the roof edge. Rosenkrantz's fingers strayed across the multilaser stud but decided to leave the bruised and battered stormtroopers to their own victory.

The pilot suddenly became aware of weapons fire from the troop compartment: the dull crack of a Navy pistol. She flicked the internal vox-switch and listened in on the gruesome sound of bodies being flung into the hull wall of the assault carrier.

When the sound of skull cracking and neck breaking had ended Rosenkrantz called: 'Still with us, Father?'

'Alive and kicking, my child,' came the ecclesiarch's reply. 'Although regrettably several of our brothers in the back here *had to take their leave.' Rosenkrantz heard the manhandling of bodies in the bay. 'Ramp closing,' Preed informed her as soon as the militiamen had been disposed of.*

'Preed, I've been thinking.' It had never really occurred to Rosenkrantz until now because she hadn't really thought they'd get this far: 'What about Krieg and the major?'

The priest broke into a throaty chuckle. 'I can't speak for our cadet-commissar, but if I know Mortensen, he'll be having his own particular brand of fun.'

CHAPTER SIX
Skin Deep

I

CRAKE'S WORLD, LESSER NOX, UB-26, Autega, Endymion Prime, Byssta... Deathworlds every one, each a ball of unprecedented lethality and doom. And either as a Galtinore Legionnaire or as Pontifical, Koulick Krieg had visited and survived them all. It was, however, this unknown hintermoon, this perennially ignored, backwater planetoid that had finally done for him.

Rappelling in from *Purity Control* a few kilometres from the coordinates Santhonax had given him, Krieg's plan was to locate the storm-troopers and observe the mission. He would then wait for Mortensen to damn himself with anything that might be considered cultish practice – as the Canoness Regular would have it – and administer Imperial justice.

That was before Ishtar's glass forest had sliced him up good and proper. This might have been tolerable if it weren't for the colossal detours he had had to make to avoid the warren of steamy, frothing channels and flood basins that spread out across the crystal rainforest like a cryogenic delta. Throwing himself down flat on a sandy patch of earth, the cadet-commissar covered his head with his hands. Every few minutes the forest lit up in an electric power storm, with arc flashes jumping this way and that, striking and forking between the crystalline trunks and searing the surrounding air. Like synapse sparks between the cells in a brain, the chain reactions carried for kilometres across the deathworld forest and the thought was always the same: kill Koulick Krieg.

Suddenly everything went quiet and the furious display faded. Bringing his head out from his arms the commissar peered around the forest. There was no time for catching breath or congratulating himself on surviving electrocution yet again. It was only a matter of minutes before the charges building in the silicon shrubbery reached critical mass and unleashed their firestorm fury again. Pushing himself up and out of the fine sand, Krieg made a bolt for it.

Swinging his Ryza-pattern plasma gun about him like a machete, Krieg battered aside the flinty branches of the strange alien foliage that choked the space between the trees. The glass leaves shattered about him as he pushed himself from one translucent trunk to another to retain momentum. The sea of razor blade edges through which he was wading was taking its toll. Upon being informed that he was being dropped on a deathworld, Krieg had decided to abandon his heavy greatcoat in favour of a Pontifical flak jacket, goggles and commissar's cap. He'd had the coat shipped back to *Deliverance* with his hellpistol. The jacket was offering next to no protection from his hostile environment, however. With foliage routinely nicking and slicing open his flesh at every opportunity, his vest and undergarments felt sodden with sweat and blood.

Pain suddenly flashed up one leg as his boot unexpectedly plunged through a sinkhole. He screamed out instinctively and then threw himself down into a clumsy roll: this meant falling through more of the punishing silicon vegetation as stalks and leaves slashed clean through the flak on his back and cut open his flesh with the smoothness of a scalpel. All he could think about was his foot, however, that at first had flared with stabbing cold pain, but now felt like it was submerged in boiling oil. Slapping his belt for his Galtinore bayonet, Krieg slipped the blade down past the frosted buckles and laces of his boot and slashed them open. With his other foot he kicked off the steaming boot. It flew through the air and hit the trunk of a nearby tree, the reinforced leather of the toe and the sole shattering on impact.

Clutching his frostbitten foot, Krieg let out another unintentional roar of pain and frustration. Professional soldiery swiftly took over and, realising that his cries of pain might have been heard, attracting some as yet unseen deathworld predator, Krieg made the uncomfortable glass-crunch scramble required to lay his hands back on the plasma gun.

Nothing came, however, and all Krieg could hear was the hum of his weapon's cell-flask. Sitting there with his seething flesh, the cadet-commissar suddenly became aware of a change in his surroundings: colours and shapes that seemed unnatural, if such a thing were possible on this wholly alien world.

He was sitting underneath a makeshift walkway, set on stilts to provide significant ground clearance. It was constructed from rough planks of irregular crystal, seemingly smashed from the thick trunks of the surrounding trees. This made a surprisingly robust structure, considering the fragility of the materials.

Limping carefully underneath the crude trail and following its crookedly winding path, Krieg became aware of great, rough-hewn obelisks sunk into the ground at increasingly regular intervals. The concentration of trees and the swarm of cut-glass foliage became less dense the more of the monoliths he came across. As he encountered one situated close to the trail he took the opportunity to inspect it. The totems were covered in large simple runes and symbols – many jagged in appearance – and were made entirely of pure copper. The network of copper totems must ground the electrical dangers of the silicon jungle, Krieg reasoned, and prevent the crystal foliage spreading. A huge arc suddenly leapt before him, leading the cadet-commissar to the further conclusion that he was not yet close enough to the village to enjoy that privilege.

Krieg could now see the telltale rush of flecks surging up and down the surrounding trunks, heralding the advent of another deadly electrical blitz. He had to work fast. Ground-level was bad: the pattern of former arcs and bursts had already taught him that beyond the chemical floodplain, it was probably one of the reasons the trail was elevated on stilts. The commissar thumbed the heavy, archaic primer on the plasma gun and adjusted the emission setting. Aiming the sun gun at the base of the nearest set of stilts he released a blinding ball of superheated plasma at the structure.

As sizzling puddles of dissipating plasma scooted about on the surface of the foaming pool Krieg had just blown in the planet's surface, the walkway section beside him promptly collapsed. A hobble, skip and a jump later Krieg was belly down on the planked section that had tumbled to the ground. Throwing the shimmering barrel of the plasma gun over his shoulder on its strap he proceeded to heave himself up the incline and up to the next section of elevated walkway.

Kicking with his good foot he managed to haul himself halfway above the ground by the time the electrical storm hit. Every muscle in his body cramped and spasmed, causing him to lose his position on the walkway and slide back down the smooth crystal slats. Bolts of piezoelectric power coursed over the surface of his skin, paralysing both mind and body and lancing the nerve clusters with spears of excruciating agony. He was hit.

It was impossible to tell how long the torture lasted: seconds, moments, minutes... but it felt to Krieg like an infinity of light and affliction.

When the darkness returned, the commissar was a crumpled mess at the foot of the toppled walkway. His flesh felt on fire and, indeed, in one or two spots his uniform was aflame. His breathing had been reduced to strangled gasps as his chest muscles refused to contract and allow sorely needed oxygen into his lungs. His constricted fists trembled but he dared not move for fear that his heart, raw in his chest, might burst like a ripe fruit inside his wracked body.

As his roving pupils caught a further glint of light Krieg tried to push through the paralysis, but his body would not answer. He couldn't take another round of the torturous treatment and began to panic, his rasping breaths becoming further constricted. The light grew as it drew closer and his numb brain finally processed what he was seeing. He'd never been so glad to see the twisting, golden tongues of a simple flame in his life. It was a torch held by one of a group of dark shapes milling around him in the twilight. Large, powerful digits clasped one of his arms and turned him gently over onto his back. Bodies were still just a shadowy amalgam but the torchlight now illuminated several heavy-weight faces. Brute features and black wiry manes, plaited through with gems and crystals, decorated their scarred, colossal skulls.

Ogryns.

Krieg's heart lifted for a moment. Ogryns were typically obedient Imperial servants. With Ishtar's proximity to Spetzghast it wasn't unreasonable to expect that he wasn't the first of the Emperor's servants to visit this miserable little corner of the galaxy. The barbarians jabbered some kind of spitsnaggle vernacular at one another, apparently fascinated by the aquila emblazoned on his cap.

A sudden fracas erupted amongst the group: growling, mawling and snapping. Something squatter and more repugnant barged its way to the front of the congregation and thrust its rancorous features in Krieg's face. The foetid rank of that daggered maw washed over the commissar, giving him further reason to gag. Cracked, spinach-green flesh and two bloody beads for eyes sealed it for Krieg. Orks, here on Ishtar also. It too seemed interested in his cap.

A wet hackle of what Krieg could only interpret as laughter began deep inside the creature's barrel chest. The ogryns followed suit, as was their habit – imitation being the sincerest form of flattery – and filled the forest with their savage, booming laughter.

With each fading gasp, Koulick Krieg was forced to accept that this soulless mirth was likely to be the last sound he would ever hear.

II

THERE WERE TIMES when even Zane Mortensen thought he'd pushed his luck too far. This was one of them.

A tense silence filled the darkened interior of the Centaur, which was unusual for the Volscians, whose battle preparations usually involved hive banter and raw humour.

The major glowered in the half-light of the instrumentation panels as *Kataphract's* enclosed, armoured hull creaked ominously about him.

'This is madness,' Hauser muttered as Garbarsky did battle with the Centaur's controls. Hauser was one of Meeks's believers, as his shaved dome and hooded trench coat testified, but he had a rebellious streak that often found expression in his furtive features and loose mouth. Meeks thumped a meaty palm against the corpsman's chest that reverberated around the tiny confines of the vehicle. 'In a good way,' Hauser added sheepishly, dutifully chastised.

Mortensen smiled through his own anxiety and clasped the back of the Guardsman's bald head good naturedly. 'That's the genius of it,' the major assured him. 'Those greenskin whoresons won't see this coming.'

It was true. Nobody would have seen this coming. Nobody would have thought it possible to completely submerge an armour-enclosed Centaur fire support vehicle in corrosive, chemical slush and infiltrate enemy territory via the tributaries of a deathworld river basin. And in the eyes of the major this was what made the plan typically Redemption Corps; other storm-trooper regiments had their specialisms, but only the Redemption Corps were known for pulling off stunts like these. Only Mortensen and his men made the impossible happen. Balls and brains, the major mused. It would have been their motto if the Redemption Corps had use for anything as useless as a motto.

Mortensen snatched up the vox receiver. '*Gundozer*, still with us?'

Crunching through the silicon shale that made up the sterile riverbed, *Kataphract's* sister Centaur carried Conklin, Vedette and the rest of his troop. Mortensen had opted to go with Rask, Eszcobar and the Volscians, reasoning that the Shadow Brigade soldiers were much more likely to lose their nerve.

'How the hell did you talk us into this?' came back the master sergeant's dulcet tones. 'I don't know how much fight this crate's got left.'

'She'll hold,' the major told him. 'The seals are good. Remember Hesperidus?'

'Trying to forget it. Seawater doesn't exactly eat through the damn hull though, does it?'

'Conklin, you're scaring the women and children.'

'Check my pulse, for sumpsake.'

'You need to take a right up ahead here,' Eszcobar informed Garbarsky as he sat next to the Shadow Brigade driver, reading from one of the topographical slates. The driver furrowed his one furious eyebrow.

'How much?' Garbarsky put to him moodily.

'How the hell should I know?' the deathworlder carped back, shrugging. 'Hard right.'

The corpsman heaved sets of levers simultaneously forward and back, throwing the fire support vehicle into a turn. The Centaur gave a whining rattle of protest as frost-shattered gears struggled with the effort. Mortensen gave the Autegan the vox.

'Okay sarge, we have another turn up here. Right, this time.' Eszcobar listened intently to Conklin's reply before an involuntary shrug rippled once again across his shoulders. 'Er, hard right?' Once again Garbarsky's single eyebrow set in a cantankerous wrinkle.

The deathworlder turned to Mortensen with the slate.

'Major, once we've navigated this bend we'll be right on top of your coordinates.'

'Thank the Emperor,' Hauser muttered to himself.

Mortensen nodded to the rest of Meeks's Volscians, cramped in *Kataphract's* cramped hull – more so since it also housed the Centaur's stripped down exterior weaponry – setting in motion a burst of activity.

'Give Conklin the good news. Have his men prepare for heavy resistance.'

Eszcobar was about to comply when a splintered crack shot through the compartment. This was almost instantaneously accompanied by a stifled half-scream, mercilessly cut short. A shaft of streaming slush had fractured the driver's armaplas viewport and blasted its way in, splashing Garbarsky full in the face. His hands had instinctively reached for his ruined features and, caught in the stream, had frozen fast to his skull.

Mortensen and Meeks were the first to act, reaching for the unfortunate driver, one under each arm. They tore him out of the seat and into the rear compartment. The Shadow Brigade soldier was thrashing and squirming like a man who was being held under a pillow.

Chemical soup was gushing through the opening now, pressing its advantage and shattering the viewport. Garbarsky's seat warped and creaked as a growing pool of foaming death began sloshing around the compartment floorspace. Hauser and the thuggish Thule began to retreat, crawling their way up the compartment walls like cats.

'Sal!' Rask yelled across the foggy compartment, calling forth the Second Platoon's field medic, Salome DuBois. Dark-skinned and close-cropped like her sergeant, DuBois pushed forward with her kit.

Meeks and the major dumped the mutilated driver in her lap, where she already had a surgical kris at the ready. In one well-practiced manoeuvre she passed the blade across Garbarsky's throat, spraying Hauser with hot blood, opening a new mouth in his neck through which the driver took his first desperate, slurping breath. The emergency tracheotomy had given the Guardsman the vital oxygen he needed and DuBois went to work slotting a length of plastic tubing from her kit into the neat slit.

Meeks threw himself towards the gaping viewport but Mortensen grabbed him by the hood of his trench coat and wrenched him back.

'Sergeant,' he bawled, slipping out of his flak jacket. 'See to your man.' Using the back of his carapace as a shield, the major reversed on the breach, forcing back the stream. Finally he had the armour flush to the hull and slammed his back against the port to hold the blockage in place. Steaming liquid foamed about the edges of his carapace plates, cracking and hissing its way, feeling for a weakness, a way in.

'Drive!' he barked at an astounded Eszcobar, who did his best to straddle the compartment floor and manipulate the gears at arm's reach. *Kataphract* bucked and groaned. She was dying and she knew it. The tracks and transaxles had barely coped with the turn Garbarsky had imposed upon them to negotiate the river bend. A harsh angle compounded by the bank's incline had all but done for the fire support vehicle.

'Get us up on that bank, trooper,' the major rumbled.

The deathworlder grimaced, fighting for control of the Centaur: 'Trying, sir...' he snarled through clenched teeth.

Sergeant Meeks crossed to the other side of the crowded vehicle and reached for the swinging vox receiver. 'Mayday, mayday. *Gundozer* are you receiving?'

'I'm losing him!' Sal called across the chaos of the compartment as Garbarsky thrashed in her arms, shock finally setting in. Similarly the Centaur was giving its last, the damage now spreading to the engine column. Crippling cold had eventually found its way into the power plant and was playing havoc with the heat exchangers. The tracks pulverised the shale of the river bed, dragging the carrier towards the surface in starts and spasms.

'C'mon, you piece of junk,' Mortensen urged affectionately.

Eszcobar went after the final few metres of their watery grave with renewed vigour on the stick-throttle, but the steaming slosh rolling about the floorspace had done its worst. With a splintered snap the lever came away in his hand, prompting a moment of ghastly realisation that swept through the compartment.

'You've got to be...' Hauser blurted, not believing his eyes.

As if on cue the engine died, allowing the deep freeze precious seconds to take hold, in turn extinguishing the remnants of combustive life from the vehicle and hope in the compartment.

Nobody moved as minds wrestled with the reality that they were now seriously screwed. Even Garbarsky remained still, although it was unclear as to whether this was due to sedation or cessation. They sat there for what seemed like an age, wired and wary: looking anxiously at the major for some kind of miracle. All Mortensen could hear in his head was Rosenkrantz and her earlier accusations of rashness and irresponsibility.

The silence was finally smashed by a grunt of raw frustration that erupted from Thule, who slammed his fist at the compartment wall.

'No!' Rask roared, reaching for the brute's wrist, afraid that the hiver might put his knuckles straight through the frost-weakened hull.

Mortensen silenced them all with a single 'Wait!' before putting his ear carefully to the glistening rime on the frozen metal wall and tapping against the armour with the knuckle of his middle finger.

A grin of pure relief broke across the major's brassy features. Tearing his shoulders from frozen carapace, as well as the top layer of skin from his back flesh, Mortensen moved away from the shattered opening. A moment of alarm and caution filled the vehicle as he pulled away from the opening, but the cries were silenced by the whisper of warm air that coursed in through the breach instead of the expected gallons of chemical fleshstripper.

This was accompanied by the sound of a Guard boot on the hull outside. Peering through the opening Mortensen could make out the robust lines of *Gundozer* further up the bank and the silhouettes of his storm-troopers securing the shoreline.

Kataphract's viewport and a section of roof above the driver's seat had just made the glassy surface of the

deathworld river. Conklin was standing outside, straddling the deadly waters between the rooftops of the
two Centaurs; attaching a hastily adapted tow cable to
a suitable pinion.

'Hold onto something,' the master sergeant called in
through the port before hop, skip and jumping back
across his own vehicle to the shore. *Gundozer* grumbled up the bank, dragging her creaking sister Centaur
along behind.

When both carriers were clear of the channel, Thule
fired the lock seals on the back doors and kicked them
wide open, liberating the trapped liquid and clearing
the noxious air inside.

Mortensen was last to leave, walking along the
scarred and smoking shell of the fire support vehicle
and wondering just how close they had really come to
a truly awful death. Gone was the brash swagger and
cocky grin. As he stood on the shale, tree lined bank
surrounded by his corpsmen, the major's face assumed
a bleak sobriety.

'Report,' he charged them gravely, wandering casually around the group, turning to each of the
Guardsmen in turn.

'Both Centaurs are out of action, Boss,' Conklin
informed him. 'Salvaging equipment and ammunition
as we speak.' Behind them some of *Gundozer*'s men
were stripping the vehicles of anything remotely useful.

'Mostly burns and frostbite,' DuBois told him, strug-
gling to keep her voice free of accusation, 'but
Garbarsky needs nothing less than a surgical bay. Also,
I need to examine your back.'

'No time for that.'

'You probably have chemical burns...'

'Later,' Mortensen insisted.

Eszcobar padded up behind them, crunching softly across the silicon, his swift reconnaissance completed.

'Trooper?'

'Tree line thins up ahead,' the Autegan confirmed, gesturing to the huge shadows blacking out the sky beyond the crystalline canopy. 'Coordinates identify our target as an abhuman camp, designated "Fort Skagg" by the Spetzghastian Mercantile Militia recruitment parties: a settlement on stilts and elevated walkways with huts all made of local materials. The greenskin rok sits just beyond.'

'Great,' Hauser mumbled to himself.

'It's subsiding on the flood plain,' the deathworlder continued, 'which is why it looked so much like a natural feature. Looks like they recruited extra muscle from the ogryn villages to erect a scaffold of props and braces to prevent it from sinking further and flooding.' Mention of the supercooled flood plain only served to further unsettle the Volscians, who bridled visibly.

'Well, that's it then,' Hauser announced. 'The recruitment party must be dead: the ogryns are party to the enemy. Why not just hold up and evacuate when the bird is ready?'

'Qvist could be alive,' Rask inserted, his tone heavy with caution and guilt. 'Greenskins sometimes take prisoners and equipment.'

'Unlikely,' Mortensen replied slowly. He didn't like disagreeing with Rask, but his judgement was clouded with responsibility. 'But that's not our problem. Now we've got eyeball confirmation that it's a rok, we can't ignore the threat. That thing could open fire on *Deliverance* or one of the warships.'

'We're not equipped for that,' Hauser pointed out with increasing desperation.

'Hauser,' Meeks warned.

'Let's call in some backup,' the Volscian continued.

'No,' Sass put him straight. 'If the enemy has Qvist's men or their equipment they could be monitoring channels. Fearing an attack they would most likely hit first, before our ships had time to manoeuvre.'

Mortensen regarded the gathering evenly: his storm-troopers were used to vox-silence on such missions, but the Shadow Brigade soldiers and even Rask were having difficulty with the grim reality of the situation.

'All we've got is the element of surprise,' the major told them. 'I suggest we use it. Captain?'

'We can't mount a direct assault on an ork rok,' Rask confirmed finally. 'That would be plain suicide.'

'Looks like the blood and guts routine to me, sir,' Conklin suggested with relish. 'Spring any targets, sabotage the rok, quiet like.'

The major nodded. 'Agreed. And the fewer there are to go in, the fewer there are to get caught…'

'Finally something I can agree with,' said Hauser with resignation.

'Which means, I go in alone.'

Even Hauser's nodding head suddenly lost its enthusiasm.

'Alone, sir?' Meeks put to him. 'Take me and a couple of my boys: we'll make the workload a bit lighter.' Mortensen shook his head appreciatively.

'That wise, boss?' Conklin finally pitched in.

'Wise, no. Necessary, yes. As soon as we're rumbled, the entire mob will come down on us.'

'The major knows what he's doing,' Hauser blustered.

'Glad you feel that way, Guardsman,' Mortensen replied, once again cupping him behind his shaved skull, 'because in order to get into that rok, I'm going to need one hell of a diversion.'

Hauser's gusto evaporated.

'We're going to need Uncle,' Mortesen told Vedette, who peeled off to fetch him.

'What have you got in mind?' Eszcobar enquired.

Mortensen playfully unslipped the double-barrel grenade launcher from the deathworlder's shoulder and popped open the weapon at the breech. He grinned down the gaping barrels at the Autegan.

'Something big.'

III

'WORK FAST,' ROSENKRANTZ instructed as the three of them reached *Vertigo's* roof. Only seconds before one of the forest's furious electrical lightstorms had faded, opening their slim window of opportunity. Clambering off the hull ladder and over the starboard quad, the pilot slipped the flamer's fuel cylinder from her back. Chief Nauls and Osric, one of her door gunners, fell to work straight away on the intakes. While Rosenkrantz bathed the quad shell with flame, blasting away the rime and warming life into the frozen thrusters, the unsmiling crew chief thrust his arm deep into one of the vents, extracting fistfuls of ice-resistant slime. Meanwhile Osric fiddled with roof valves and calibrators Rosenkrantz hadn't even known existed.

The Jopallian was barely a boy, but Nauls had selected him because he originally hailed from indentured maintenance stock. His slender fingers moved with natural certainty across the unfamiliar machinery, his lips mumbling half-remembered incantations and blessings.

As Rosenkrantz moved to the second of the roof-mounted quad engines the aircraft became lost in deep shadow. Something wet and rubbery unexpectedly caressed the back of her neck and the pilot bolted round, sending a stream of promethium over the helmeted head of the chief.

Rosenkrantz brought the weapon under control and Nauls came out from behind the filter mount, his face furrowed with surprise and anger. The lines faded as he saw what the flight lieutenant was staring at. The shadow belonged to the bloated, ochre behemoth that *Vertigo* had torn through in the skies above. The collision had gashed an opening in the side of the beast's sky sack and the creature had spent the best part of an hour drifting slowly to the ground.

The tip of one webbed tentacle drifted past Rosenkrantz and slapped the hull of the aircraft before following the gently tumbling monster into its canopy-shattering crash-landing. The giant octopoid just lay there amongst the destruction, cut to pieces by the tree-top crystal foliage, one huge, sad ocular appendage flickering around the forest in uncomprehending confusion and fright. Rosenkrantz couldn't help but feel responsible for the alien creature's demise, but had her own survival in this terrible place to consider and went back to work with the flamer.

That was until Chief Nauls, finished with the first intake, stood up next to the Jopallian and nudged her with his elbow.

'Flight lieutenant,' he murmured, nodding into the silicon forest. Shutting off the flame and dropping the flamer next to its fuel canister she followed his gesture.

Hefty humanoid shapes were moving through the smashed tree line: huge, brawny savages who decorated their slabs of gross muscle with crystal trinkets and the thick blood that oozed from the myriad of nicks and slices that covered their scarred bodies. Wearing only simple skirts made of hundreds of thin copper rods hanging from their thick belts, they made eerie windchime-like chords as they crept through the crystal foliage.

'I've got targets!' an alarmed Speckels hissed across the helmet vox.

'Hold your fire,' Nauls growled back. Rosenkrantz found herself nodding silently as both she and the chief began to fall slowly into a rooftop crouch in an effort not to be seen: this was of course ludicrous, since they could hardly hide the aircraft also.

Ogryns. It made sense, Rosenkrantz considered. They were, after all, the only variety of human robust enough to exist on Ishtar. The ogryns fell upon the downed sky-squid with primitive bronze flensing blades and began stripping flesh from the beast as it breathed its final mighty breaths.

'No...' the leatherneck crew chief snarled beside her. Turning around she saw more of the abhuman primitives closing in slowly on the Spectre. Their progress was slow but steady across the treacherous forest floor and their intentions obvious. Rosenkrantz made up her mind.

'Let them have it,' she ordered across the vox. The flight lieutenant wanted to keep the brutes as far away from the aircraft as possible: if they actually got their hands on the Spectre they'd crush it like a tin can. Doors rolled aside and bolter fire chattered from both sides of the aircraft, reducing the tree line to a crystal frag storm. The ogryns were incredibly fast, however, tearing away at an explosive pace; their gargantuan strides clearing broiling rivulets of chemical ooze and blasting across the nightmare landscape, their black manes trailing after them.

Heavy bolt rounds plucked at their flesh, mashing up muscle and bone, but the ogryns soaked up the punishment like rockcrete, roaring through their discomfort. It was only when streams of fire crossed and doubled their stopping power did individual brutes finally succumb.

Osric was suddenly on his feet, charms and catechisms suddenly failing him among the vision of oncoming ogryns and gunfire. He'd left his side arm down in the troop bay but Rosenkrantz and Nauls both had their Navy pistols out of their holsters as a last resort.

Staring along the nose of the Spectre Rosenkrantz suddenly became aware of two monstrous savages surging across the open ground towards them. Aiming their pistols over the young gunner's shoulder the two Jopallians plugged round after round into the barbarians. The ogryns barely flinched as the gunfire washed over them.

'Benedict, a little assistance please,' Rosenkrantz called down the helmet vox as her pistol went dry. As Nauls reloaded *Vertigo*'s nose-mounted autocannon boomed from below. Impossibly the first ogryn ran up through the merciless firepower, each direct hit punching bloody holes in his reinforced ribcage. As the monster's head disappeared in a spray of blood and brains, his snaggle-toothed companion swung past, catching several blasts in the abdomen himself. Hauling himself up on the shoulder of his falling comrade, the ogryn bounded incredibly for the aircraft's nosecone, his huge steps carrying him up past the annoyance of the autocannon and thundering up the Spectre's canopy.

It was all sickeningly swift. Before Rosenkrantz knew it the ogryn was upon them, swinging his unwieldy flensing blade like a Shadebarren trunkcutter. Osric was simply cleaved in two. There was no scream or struggle: the unfortunate gunner's body just spun furiously off the roof in two different directions.

The chief managed to slam a fresh clip home and turned his pistol on the unstoppable creature. He'd buried four or five slugs in the ogryn's thick neck and barrel chest before the flat of the flensing blade came down brutally on Nauls's helmet. The flight helmet and everything inside it was instantly pulverised, disappearing inside the crew chief's trunk.

Rosenkrantz fell. She could have slipped but it was more likely some kind of primitive instinct: an unmistakable signal of her complete submission in the face of superior physical prowess. Her hand smacked the recently cleared filter and her Navy pistol bounced out of her smashed grip and skittered down the aircraft hull and out of reach.

The heels of her boots squealed on the slick roof as she attempted to get back to her feet, but this was cut short by an off-balance, opportunistic swing of the flensing blade. Arching her back and throwing her face skyward, the pilot felt the bronze blade sweep past, splashing her frantic wide eyes with the weapon's searing slipstream. There would be no second chances. She could feel that this unthinking brute wanted to kill her; wanted to chop her up and paint the fuselage with her thick, warm blood.

It was the only weapon left to hand. Scrambling for the flamer, her heart thumping in time with every moment the beast took to bring its heavy blade to bear, Rosenkrantz unleashed the full fury of the weapon on the creature's meaty legs. Flame roared around its knees and ankles, funnelling up the copper rod skirt and razing whatever hung beneath.

The ogryn released a baleful moan and let the mighty flense fly out of its fingers and into the forest. Its palms spread instinctively before the inferno in a futile attempt to deflect the stream before its snaggle-fanged jaw snapped forward with the intention of mangling the pilot's face. Her response was the same. A gout of explosive promethium flayed rough, knotty flesh from the ogryn's skull. Blaze-blasted knees finally gave and the monstrous abhuman buckled, falling down between the cockpit and the quad.

Charred, fat fingers locked around the ankle of her flight boot and lugged her across the cool metal, dragging her off the roof. New levels of nauseating fear and panic radiated through Rosencrantz as her body left the hull for the uncertainty of a plummet towards a sterile, broiling grave.

Suddenly there was a hand where Rosenkrantz had no right to expect one. Five fingers and a thumb bolstered by hydraulic ichor and the aircraft's power plant reserves. Through the open canopy the flight lieutenant could see Benedict's straining face, his thin lips curled back even further than usual and his face a whirlpool of rippling tendons and wasted muscle. Conduits and cables erupted from his back as the servitor extended his fixed torso and her reach to accommodate the extra pull inflicted upon the pilot's body from the flaming dead-weight below.

Rosenkrantz hung there for what seemed like forever, suspended between the abhuman's death-grip and Benedict's programmed desire to keep *Vertigo's* skipper alive. In the end it was the buckle that decided it. The metal rings of the flight boot were not designed to withstand such abuse and promptly bent, snapped and slipped free, liberating the pilot's bare foot and dropping with the burning body below.

Sliding in through the opening the Jopallian's response was swift and merciless. Slipping into the harness and settling the bare ball of her foot amongst the pedals, she fired the struggling engines and yanked the stick back between her thighs.

Vertigo answered, the sudden demand of the engines clearing the remnants of slime from the intakes and blasting the frosty thrusters back to life. The aircraft rocketed skyward, shattering the surrounding vegetation and throwing the pilot's head back into her seat. After a short burn the livid pilot slammed on the airbrakes, throwing everyone on board towards the ceiling. Sweeping determined digits across the runes of the ordnance panel, Rosenkrantz armed the hellfires before simply detaching the missiles from both wings. She didn't bother to fire them.

They fell silently towards the silicon forest before impacting on the planet surface and cleansing the vicinity directly below the aircraft in a superheated tsunami of destructive power.

As the rumble passed through *Vertigo's* superstructure the pilot flicked the vox and opened a channel to the troop bay.

'Status.'

'Where's the chief?' Speckels came back at her.

Rosenkrantz paused, momentarily reliving the horror of Nauls's death. 'Chief's gone. Status?'

'Osric?'

'Status?' Rosenkrantz commanded.

The vox crackled for a few empty seconds, then there came a resigned 'Bay secure' from the gunner.

Rosenkrantz looked back at her servitor co-pilot. Benedict was a lifeless husk, his chest barely rising from the interface seat into which he'd resettled. The cockpit floor was black with his lifeblood both organic and automatronic.

The lieutenant returned her attention to the aircraft's controls and the lethal deathworld beyond the armaplas of the Spectre's canopy.

'We're leaving,' she finally decided and blasted for the horizon.

IV

KRIEG COULD SWEAR the floor was moving.

A firm hand smacked his face, jarring him to consciousness. The blackness evaporated, leaving the indelible smudge of two dark shapes hovering in front of his aching eyes.

'Sir?' came a voice he didn't recognise. 'Commissar?'

Suddenly everything became painfully clear. They were battered and bloody – but they were Guardsmen. Dust cloaks and dungaree jackets marked them out as Spetzghastian Mercantile Militia, as well as their cheap, assembly-line equipment and perpetual understack squints. The figure speaking to him was a whelp of an officer, with green eyes and flaxen hair. Beside him squatted a hard-faced PDF sergeant with one milky-white eye, the Mercantile Militia's Libra-style insignia sat below his thick shoulder stripes and his name: Endo. Behind them both was a merciless row of bars – probably of a cage or cell.

'Sir?' the officer persisted.

'Where are we?' Krieg croaked. He tried to move under the filthy blanket: thought better of it. The officer graciously deferred to the sergeant's experience.

'Ork rok,' the Spetzghastian confirmed, his voice as hard as his face.

Krieg rolled with the information, his mind whirling with the dark possibilities it presented.

'The whole system's got to be swarming with greenskins.'

They both nodded gravely. As his eyes accustomed further to the gloom, Krieg could make out possibly ten or twelve other Guardsmen, sitting miserably around the walls of the crude cell. 'Mission?' the cadet-commissar managed.

'Recruiting party: abhuman auxilia,' the young officer added, almost suspiciously. He made a casual salute. 'Bastian Qvist. Commander, Departmento Munitorum.'

Krieg took in his grim surroundings. The chamber was an irregular space with walls, floor and ceiling of raw extraterrestrial rock, cut in half by a row of thick bars, probably ripped from the hull of some junker spacecraft. On the far side of the cell chamber, out of ear-shot, a greenskin sentry occasionally fixed them with two glazed, bloody red beads.

The cell rocked with sudden violence, knocking the sergeant from his crouch and forcing some of the Guardsmen to grab for the bars. The muffled thunder of explosions found their way through the labyrinth of rough-hewn rock passages and bounced around the chamber.

'What the…?'

'We were going to ask you,' the commander put to him.

'We're definitely going down,' a cut-lipped woman in a shabby Mercantile Militia uniform called from behind.

'You here alone?' Qvist asked with an unmistakable hint of incredulity. Krieg wouldn't have minded – had it not been the truth – but he could hardly tell them that. Krieg knew what the rock-smothered din outside meant.

'Storm troop: Redemption Corps,' he told them finally.

The reaction was instantaneous: a wave of relief and premature jubilation crashed through the group, with the whippersnapper commander slapping aside the sergeant's shoulder with warm aggression.

'I told you.'

The sergeant nodded coolly.

Another stomach-dropping jolt cut their bleak merriment short as the floor simply left them and came to a crashing halt a metre and a half below their feet. Krieg hit the uneven rock floor with a bone-aching smack and moaned gently in quiet torture.

Despite the initial shock of the plunge the Militiamen were swiftly back on their feet. Cries of alien alarm and thuggish panic filled the access corridor outside. The cantilever bulkhead leading into the cell chamber was ajar, clearing the floor by a bayonet's length and allowing the Guardsmen a view of the stampede of boots crashing past the doorway outside. The cell chamber suddenly became swathed in steam and this was enough to rouse even the attention of their half-fanged jailer. The warty, bottle-green man-eater had

been filing its remaining tusk to a cruel point and picking meat out of the gaps in its monstrous teeth with
grubby claws. The clamour outside the door had barely
raised one of his wiry eyebrows – orks given as they
were to regular brawls and slaying, even amongst their
own kind – but the sudden mist and foaming sheet of
chemical brume that washed in under the bulkhead
was enough to galvanise even it to action.

Sweeping up its rough-and-ready shooter from
where it hung on a gory strap of plaited human scalp,
the jailer loped past the alarmed calls of the Spetzghastians towards the door. It silenced the
Guardsmen with one stab of the bolter barrel, driving
them several steps away from the bars, before
approaching the bulkhead.

The steaming flood receded as quickly as it had
entered. It seemed the ork rok was succumbing to the
supercooled flood plain, sinking deeper into the silicon swamp and flooding as it did. Undoubtedly it was
being helped to its doom by the explosions outside.

The greenskin brute followed the retreating waters,
yanking up the cantilever door on its rollers and sticking its snaggle-toothed maw out into the corridor. As
the door seesawed a body dropped from the roof door
space and hit the cell chamber floor with practiced fluidity, rolling across one carapace shoulder and righting
in a combat stance. With one knee to the ground and
a hellgun up and aimed squarely at the door, the
storm-trooper waited for the greenskin warder to turn
and re-enter.

Krieg and his cellmates watched with eager antici-
pation as the storm-trooper blasted the monster with a
disciplined staccato of supercharged las-fire. The thuggish alien was flung back into the corridor, slamming

into the rough-hewn wall. Dropping its weapon it put up two meaty, green palms that soaked up the last few bolts. The storm-trooper clearly expected the beast to drop and halted his fire: it was standard practice for specialist troops – power had to be conserved and was reserved largely for precision kills and suppression.

The alien monster smouldered in the corridor before blasting away from the wall and out of the smoke at the lone storm-trooper. A green blitzkrieg of savagery, the ork charged like an enraged grox, surging across the cell chamber with shocking speed. The storm-trooper hammered the monster's barrel-body with another tidy stream of fire before the creature acquired him. Backhanding the hellgun aside with animal rage the ork sank its filthy claws into the storm-trooper's torso carapace. Lifting him off his boots, the greenskin ran the trooper into the opposite wall, drawing an audible, lung-emptying gasp from the soldier. Holding him there with one brute fist the jailer proceeded to beat the storm-trooper to death with the other.

Like a rag doll the monster beat him this way and that, one particularly savage blow finding its mark and knocking the helmet across the chamber. Slamming the storm-trooper's body back and forth between the craggy wall and the unforgiving bars of the cells the greenskin eventually settled on throttling the soldier against the crooked metal.

Krieg leaned forward. Even from the back, the shaven skull of the storm-trooper was easy to identify as Mortensen's, with its grim numerals and scarring. Incredibly, the cadet-commissar marvelled, the Gomorrian must have slipped into the rok, spilling blood only when he had to – and then as silently and surreptitiously as possible.

There was nothing surreptitious about the way Mortensen buried his storm blade into the back of the ork's bald, green head. The beast blinked and its sadistic features froze as the major's survival knife squirmed around in the monster's brain. Taking full advantage of the creature's bewilderment, Mortensen used the handle of the weapon to haul himself up on the green-skin's hunched shoulders and slam the serrated blade straight down into the sinew of its muscular neck.

The jailer's crushing grip on the storm-trooper suddenly intensified, its great brawny arms encircling the Gomorrian in a crushing bear hug. As the desperate melee continued, with Mortensen and the monster smashing each other against the cell, the grip of the major's side arm played a messy tune on the jagged bars. Up until this point, Krieg had kicked painfully back into one darkened corner, out of sight: he would have a hard time explaining to the major how he came to be incarcerated on board the ork rok. Qvist's slender hand slipped through the bars eagerly for the weapon, but Krieg managed to lay his frostbitten fingers on it first, yanking it free of the storm-trooper's belt holster.

'Not yet,' he told the officer solemnly. Krieg didn't exactly know why he'd gone for the weapon. Instinct, he supposed. The Departmento Munitorum officer would in all likelihood have emptied the clip at the ork brute, but the commissar realised that they could ill afford to attract any more attention to the cell-block. On the other hand, it was possible that Krieg had claimed the weapon merely to deny the major an easy rescue. It was tempting to consider Krieg's mission all but completed at the hands of some alien thug. At the very least the commissar needed Mortensen alive to open the cell door. If nothing else, the major would have spent himself in the battle with the greenskin and, if it came to it, made himself an easier target for the cadet, who wasn't exactly in the peak of fitness himself.

The Redemption Corps major had other things on his mind at that moment, tearing his knife back across the ork's throat and severing both its windpipe and jugular. Something like a survival instinct, embedded deep inside the creature's primitive brain, gave and the greenskin got to the weapon first. To the great relief of the storm-trooper the ork released its grip on the carapace and wrapped its meaty claws around the handle of the embedded storm blade. With his weapon torn free of its knotted neck, Mortensen was forced to cling onto the patchwork flak and ringmail adorning the greenskin's back as the ork clutched for him.

After several near misses, with Mortensen's head almost finding its way into the greenskin's vice-like grip, the major finally got a better hold on the wild beast. Krieg flinched as the major struck the bars with unforgiving force. Stripped of the kind of weapons likely to stop an ork in its tracks, Mortensen was using the only resource left to him: brute strength. Somehow he'd snaked his bulging arms around the greenskin's gushing throat and was squeezing for all he was worth.

The ork was clawing at the storm-trooper's arms and throwing itself into the rocky walls and the bars of the cell. Krieg could hear the major's ragged sighs as each impact increased in power and determination. It was gruesome to watch – Mortensen broken up against every hard edge and sharp corner in the chamber – but still the Gomorrian held on, denying his opponent vital oxygen. Finally, like some wounded beast of the plains, the ork staggered to its knees, clasping the bars with both hands – only to be lashed at and stamped upon by militia issue combat boots.

When the creature was still, and he was sure it was down, Mortensen unsaddled himself and reached for his storm blade, swiftly finishing what he had started and leaking the unconscious greenskin's life all over the rough-hewn floor. There was little in the way of Spetzghastian euphoria: freedom was close and the Mercantile Militiamen stood there in desperate expectation.

The key was a simple barrel turner and was shaped like a pronged tuning fork. With guidance from the militia sergeant, Mortensen found it hanging around the jailer's neck on a wire cord. Swinging the cell door open, the bruised and beaten Mortensen took in the rag tag band of Guardsmen.

'Commander Qvist?'

'Me, sir,' the recruitment officer said, stepping forward and offering his hand.

Mortensen didn't take it.

'Right, listen up,' the storm-trooper announced, addressing the entire cell. 'My name is Major Zane Mortensen: the Redemption Corps storm-troopers will be your rescuers today. Don't go losing your heads, though. We're not out of the woods here yet by a long shot.' The flint-faced sergeant nodded quietly. 'The escape route is simple: follow this corridor and turn left. Then just follow the bodies.' Mortensen entered the cell and began helping the wounded militiamen to their unsteady feet. 'My men have organised some preoccupations for our greenskin friends, so you shouldn't encounter much in the way of resistance. My corpsmen will be waiting outside with medical supplies, weapons and fresh ammunition. Be ready to give as good as you get. Go!'

The Spetzghastians responded immediately, stomping and hobbling for the cantilever bulkhead. As Mortensen helped the cut-lipped Spetzghastian to the cell door, Commander Qvist went to pick up the greenskin's abandoned shooter.

'Leave it,' the major commanded. The young officer hovered over the weapon. Krieg watched Mortensen approach and slunk into the farthest, darkest corner of the cell. He stopped, vaguely annoyed. 'You won't be able to aim the damn thing and most probably, it'll blow up in your hands. That junk only works for the greenskins.'

Still Krieg hadn't moved. 'What's with him?' Mortensen asked, surprised that the prospect of freedom hadn't put a spring in the figure's step.

Qvist stood with the major at the doorway, confused. 'I thought he was one of yours.'

The major squinted. Krieg came out from behind the filthy blanket. So did the autopistol.

'Krieg?' Mortensen hissed in disbelief. Qvist's young face creased in further perplexity.

The cadet-commissar levelled the weapon at the Gomorrian. Diamanta Santhonax's commands cutting through the confusion in his heart.

'Major Mortensen: you are charged with one hundred and five Tactica violations – edicts epsilon through alpha – sixteen counts of confederacy, martial treason and sedition of the creed and finally contravention of Stoltz Ultimatum.' Krieg let his words hang in the bleakness of the cell. 'Which is punishable by death.'

Mortensen just stood there, arms and neck pulsing with the tension of the situation. His eyes burned back into Krieg's own unflinching orbs.

'Best save a couple of slugs for yourself,' the major recommended coldly. 'Because once you're back in the world, your life won't be worth spit.'

'I'll take my chances,' Krieg assured him. The commissar suddenly felt the ghostly sensation of a weapon being pointed at him. Without taking the autopistol off the major, he gave the Militia commander austere eyes. And found himself staring up the short barrel of a laspistol. Endo had returned from the greenskin's grotto where the Spetzghastian rifles had been scavenged and stored. He clutched his own lasgun to his chest and looked on in horror as his commander committed career suicide with his own reclaimed side arm.

Krieg's lip curled. 'This doesn't concern you, commander. This is the Emperor's work. Don't be a fool.'

'Sir!' Sergeant Endo called. The Spetzghastian wanted nothing to do with what was happening between Krieg and Mortensen and urged his young officer to follow suit. Qvist flicked his eyes from Krieg to Mortensen to the sergeant and then back again. Words abandoned him.

'I appreciate the sentiment commander, but Commissar Krieg here is right about one thing – at least – this is my problem,' Mortensen told the Departmento Munitorum officer through gritted teeth. 'Let me deal with it.'

It happened so quickly.

Mortensen hovered, eager for an advantage. Qvist's finger slipped across the trigger of his laspistol, although it was anyone's guess as to whether or not he actually intended discharging the weapon. This was not a chance the commissar had been trained to take. Krieg's thumb snapped across the autopistol, priming the heavy-weight side arm. Suddenly the cell chamber was filled with excruciating noise. Commander Qvist had been thrown backwards across the room as Krieg put a round through the commander's gut. Sergeant Endo vaulted across the chamber, skidding down on his knees to the officer's side.

Mortensen went to move, but Krieg shook the autopistol at him, keeping the major pinned to the spot.

'Well?' Mortensen barked across the room. The sergeant rapidly fell to checking the young officer's vitals. His belly was already sodden with gore as the stomach wound steadily leaked the commander's lifeblood. The wound was clean, however, as Krieg had intended it.

'He's alive,' the sergeant confirmed stoically.

'What's the matter, Mortensen?' Krieg put to the major. 'Worried about your reputation?'

'Bloody idiot,' the Gomorrian erupted at the prone, glaze-eyed Qvist.

'Get him out of here,' Krieg ordered. 'Now!'

Endo took the softly groaning commander over one shoulder, then holding the major's gaze for a second, disappeared through the bulkhead in pursuit of his men.

Mortensen sagged and then stared down at his boots.

'Major Mortensen, you have been found wanting,' Krieg informed him. 'Prepare to receive the Emperor's judgement.'

Mortensen's eyes came up to meet Krieg's own. 'Do it…' he instructed with soft resignation. It wasn't a dare.

Krieg tensed his finger; the trigger was reassuringly heavy. The pistol willed itself to fire.

+Koulick Krieg…+

Krieg blinked. Something was inside his head: it felt like an arachnid nesting in his brain, giving birth to a thousand tiny but irresistible thoughts, crawling around his mind.

'Do it!' Mortensen snarled, almost indignant at the delay.

Krieg tried to comply. He thought of his backbreaking Legionnaire's servitude on a hundred different worlds, his years of pious service to the Ordo Hereticus – and Canoness Santhonax standing over him, her eyes alight with passion and her thin lips curled in righteous dissatisfaction. Every second of his service to the God-Emperor had led him to this moment – yet he struggled to act. He felt the trigger meet the resistance of the pistol's firing mechanism.

+Koulick Krieg…+

A stream of bright, thick blood fell from his nostril and splattered his arm. Krieg looked down for the briefest moment, moving his fingers from the splatter to his nose. He was going to be sick.

His stomach flipped, launching everything inside skyward. Vomit hit the wall and floor of the cell beside the cadet-commissar and just kept coming. His eyes were closed and his torso heaved but his arm was pumped like some tormented serpent, ready to strike at the slightest sensation that the major was advancing.

When he came back up for air, with some of the stringy gruel still clinging to his chin, Krieg found to his surprise that Mortensen hadn't moved.

'Krieg?' Mortensen asked, but the commissar stopped him by smacking the grip of the pistol repeatedly against his temple and roaring in aggravation and anguish. He turned the weapon on the major once again, but the desire simply wasn't there.

'I...' the cadet-commissar began.

'Save it,' Mortensen growled. Both men turned to find their charade had been played out in front of a small audience. Endo and Commander Qvist were being manhandled through the bulkhead and the chamber had become a gallery of green faces, beady eyes and gun barrels.

'You had your chance,' the Redemption Corps major told Krieg. 'You still want my blood, you're going to have to get in line.'

V

HE'D VISUALISED A hive of mayhem: a barbarian force in preparation for war. Mortensen was sorely disappointed. There was no fighting, no tusk baring, no shooting. As the major was dragged up through the rocky levels he was witness to the rank and file thug-soldiers of the rok going about their outlandishly orderly business. It went against the grain of every microbe of knowledge and experience the major had gathered over the many years he'd spent fighting the damn things.

Fully manned orbital gun emplacements swarmed with greenskins and runts and aircraft bays brimmed with squadrons of heavily armed patrol aircraft: if the major and his men hadn't risked their treacherous up-river infiltration, it was unlikely that they would ever have got near the ork rok. Between the deathworld swamps and the greenskin guests, Ishtar was turning out to be a pretty inimical place to be.

The four soldiers were taken to a cavernous chamber right at the top of the rok: Mortensen could tell this because there was a massive hole in the roof, allowing the dim, deathworld twilight to flood in. There was a similarly sized opening in the floor of the cave, leading back down into the heart of the riddled asteroid, illumination from which waxed and waned with the rhythmic roar of mighty machineries below. A ramshackle concentric structure of girders, pylons and suspension wires ran up out of the hole, up through the chamber and out of the top of the rok, reaching for the sky like some great antennae to the stars. The mysterious structure hummed unnaturally and crackled with a sallow energy.

Here the brute squad put them on their knees with savage blows to the calves and left them. Mortensen cast a look up around the rims of his eyelids, catching the impression of a walkway and sentry posts, each manned by a begoggled, gun-toting, greenskin thug. Something thundered up steadily behind them across the hollow grille flooring. Something big.

Mortensen went to turn his head but was dissuaded by a fat green hand that enveloped his head like a scrapyard claw-winch and snapped it back front and centre.

The floor suddenly jolted as a brutal clockwork mechanism went to work on one wall. The grille platform juddered upwards, bringing it in line with some kind of command centre carved into the cavern wall. It was crowded with levers, wheels and simple gauges and dripped with sparking cables and steam lines.

The barbaric instrumentation was crawling with greenskin runts: monitoring, adjusting and trying to keep out of the way of their larger brethren. At the heart of this chaos lay a battered captain's throne – Imperial in design – probably ripped out of some unfortunate vessel that became lost in the warp and fell foul of this rocky behemoth. Prowling around the throne on knotted chains were a pack of walking jaws – man-eating pets that greenskins traditionally kept close. Upon seeing the four of them rise before the throne on the rumbling gantry, the dagger-fangs went insane, tearing at their rusty leashes and yapping a horrible chorus of throaty gnarls. On the throne sat a mournful looking creature in thick, gaudily painted armour, a crocodilian cloak and a tooth-inlaid headdress – giving him the appearance of being swallowed by some horrific alien creature. The greenskin was clearly very old, its mauled face-flesh cracked and dark with age and its protracted skull and tusks sagging with overgrowth.

There was something eerie about the entire atmosphere, the major noted. Mortensen couldn't quite place it at first and then he realised, it was the sound. There wasn't any. Orks, by their nature, were loud and bombastic creatures, their huge barrel chests and cavernous mouths equipping them to terrify their enemies with a cacophony of savage blood hunger. The mock bridge of the ork rok was as silent as a cathedral, however, each monster communicating effortlessly with one another through what seemed to be the silence of passive fang-baring and narrowed eyes. With the slightest of gestures the enemy commander engaged the attention of a junior officer – an obscene individual in a parody uniform and cap, complete with trailing tassels and jumbo medals.

It wheeled an unfamiliar looking object across the bridge on a tracked trolley and positioned it in front of his warlord. It looked like one of those clunky, old-fashioned diving helmets Mortensen had seen some of

the more desperate archeohunters use in the submerged caves of the Haephastus undersump. Instead
of an air hose, the box trailed a pipe and rubber face-
mask that the officer affixed to his boss's long face. On
two sides of the device were crude speakers and upon
the front, a faceplate that the greenskin aide slid aside
with a fingerclaw.

Inside sloshed a sickly yellow liquid and in the suspension sat a large ragged head. The head was shot
through with fat, dirty needles and had clearly been
separated from its torso for a reasonable amount of
time: despite that, Mortensen could make out an
abhuman face and one that had seen service in the
ranks of the Imperial Guard, if the primitive forehead
tattoos were anything to go by. Then it clicked.
Mortensen shuffled on his knees. He was staring at
Sergeant Lompock – the ogryn bonehead that had
been guiding Qvist's Mercantile Militia platoon to the
villages.

The major felt a shiver run down his spine as the
contraption came appallingly to life. As the warboss
spat his guttural greenspeak down the pipe the ogryn's
eyeless head twitched and spoke, the bass gargle reverberating around the control centre.

'Have-fought-the-weak-bastard-spawn-of-the-Carcass-
Emperor-my-whole-life.   Your-rags-and-regalia-have-
meaning,' the boss accused, pointing a crooked,
gauntleted finger at Mortensen and Krieg. 'This-much-I-
know.   Tell-my-shootas-send-plenty-lead-the-way-of-
such-markings.' The ogryn coughed a kind of macabre
chuckle.

'Your shootas can't be very good then, can they?'
Mortensen spat smugly. 'I appear to still be here.'

'Not-for-long,' the long tusk told him. 'Your-little-assault. Inventive-or-suicidal-cannot-tell-which. Matters-not. Simply-sent-ten-thousand-of-my-battle-kindred-to-the-world-you-call-Tancred-day-ahead-of-schedule.'

'You're greenskin savages,' Krieg seethed. 'You don't keep schedules.'

'Schedules-yes-battleplans-yes. How-you-think-forces-coordinated?'

The major laughed. 'Didn't think they were.'

The ork warboss thrust his elongated jaw at the Gomorrian. 'Mine-are...' he assured them with conviction. 'And-I-have-the-Imperial-pig-citizens-of-Tancred's-World-under-my-knife-to-prove-it.'

'Impossible,' Mortensen shot back, his forced merriment evaporated. 'We'd know.'

'Like-knew-about-your-factory-world?'

'Cult spree killings preceded invasions on both worlds,' Krieg informed the major. 'Algernon, too.'

'Algernon-belong-my-masters-already.'

'What are you?' hissed Mortensen, shaking his head. He couldn't believe that he was talking to an ork. Mortensen had fought all kinds of greenskin filth on a score of different worlds. He'd never come across anything that spoke like this thing. Its words were laced with more than the usual animal cunning he'd come to expect from greenskin barbarians: and that was dangerous enough. There was something distinctly alien about this alien, if that were possible.

The ancient warlord seemed to consider his question seriously. 'Am-evolving. Am-enlightened.' The greenskin slumped – back to business. 'Like-I-know-things-you-know-things. Things-I-must-know. Quickly. System-reinforcement. Fleet-deployment,' the boss gestured at the open sky. 'Usually-get-my-sawbonez-to-sew-your-puny-flesh-as-one,' the ancient warlord told them, nodding at the monstrosity that stood behind them. Again, Mortensen attempted to snatch a glance at the greenskin surgeon, but the beast's mechanised, mantrap jaws snapped in cold and close, causing the storm-trooper to swallow, wrinkle his nose and turn back towards the warboss. 'Have-you-share-one-set-of-organs-till-one-spillz-gutz-at-my-feet,' the ork warlord continued. 'Sadly-no-time. Quick-demonstration-needed. Make-intention-clear.'

The surgery-happy hulk behind them stirred. He snatched Sergeant Endo from his knees and dragged him across the platform, towards the metal structure at the centre of the cavern.

The soldiers watched as the stoop-backed monstrosity effortlessly trailed the militiaman behind him. Its head was a metal nightmare: serrated, hydraulic maw, metal dome skull and two telescopic eyes that protruded like insect antennae. Despite its spine being buckled by years of supporting the overgrown cranial adaptations, the greenskin's back was still a head taller than any of the Imperials. Clomping boots, a butcher's belt and a blood-splashed leather apron completed the picture.

'What's it doing?' the major hissed.

'Teleporter,' Krieg informed him. 'Some tribes reputedly have a good grasp of the technology. Explains how they've infiltrated so successfully. There are probably roks like this dotted all over the Spet-zghastian system: waystations for transporting hardware and troops from one moon to the next. That's how an entire invasion force just seemed to appear on Illium.'

Mortensen recalled the strange empty hole burned out of existence below decks in the *Mortis Maximus*: how the greenskins must have gained entry with similar technologies, bypassing the god-machine's armour and shields.

The warboss left his throne, trailing its ghoulish translator, and crossed the cluttered bridge, throwing heavy levers, tapping gauges and spinning wheels as he did. As it yanked a handle on the wall something heavy was released from the ceiling and Mortensen, Krieg and even the dazed and bleeding Qvist all hit the deck in the belief that they were going to be flattened. Metres from the platform the object was snapped unceremoniously to a halt by the heavy-duty chains that supported it and swung to one side. As Mortensen dared to stare upwards he found himself looking at a burnished metal disc: something not unlike the magnetic attachments used on some derricks to unload vessels in cargo bays.

'Teleporter. Yes,' the warlord confirmed. It simply glanced at the barbaric surgeon who took the writhing sergeant in both crushing fists and pitched Endo off the rampart. The Spetzghastian, who had been so calm and sober up to this point, let rip a single scream before falling through the girders of the pylon and disappearing in the stream of imperceptible teleporter energy streaming up out of the rok.

Mortensen and Krieg turned back to the aged greenskin. They found it closer than ever – manipulating further control knobs and fat switches. As the greenskin casually span an important looking calibrator, Mortensen went to rise once again, his ill-restrained fury spilling over like stew in a cauldron. Krieg grabbed his shoulder and tore him back down. The disc above their heads suddenly washed them with an unnatural heat. A kind of charge built across the surface of the metal with sparks skittering around the outside and falling in towards a power vortex gathering in the centre.

The major closed his eyes as the air about them blanched. When he opened them again everything was blurred, but as the seconds followed and realisation dawned he found that everything was in fact very clear: it was Endo that was blurred.

The sergeant had been rematerialised in front of them, but the warboss had intentionally warped the insane genius of the device with his ham-fisted alterations. Endo quivered and steamed: the teleporter had shredded his body, molecule by molecule and then reassembled him as a botched and bloody flesh sculpture. With gut-punching horror Mortensen realised that some structures had achieved true replication. One barely comprehending, milky eyeball thrashed its pupil at them in agony and somewhere deep inside the pulp of mangled bone and organs a mouth squealed incessantly.

Mortensen broke free of the commissar's grip and surged for the ork warlord: he didn't get far. The brute surgeon was behind him, grabbing the storm-trooper by the skull and forcing him back down on the grille. The boss came closer still – confident in its experimenter's ability to restrain the puny human. Sergeant Lompock's drowning commentary echoed around the cavernous chamber.

'If-you-don't-wish-to-see-the-inside-of-your-own-body-tell-me-now-all-you-know. Promise-I-kill-you-quick. A-soldier's-death.'

Mortensen's eyes flashed from the spasming mess that was Endo to the uncompromising, alien orbs of the ork warboss. 'Don't-worry-about-your-friend. He-won't-suffer-long.' The greenskin turned his back on Mortensen and clicked his claws, signalling one of the gretchin runts attending his throne to unslip the warboss's dagger-fanged pets. The pack of monsters bounded across the control centre, their chains flashing after them, and set upon the malformed mound of human flesh, tearing the unfortunate Spetzghastian to shreds.

Mortensen took his chance. With the greenskins enjoying the wretched spectacle, the major threw back his head and pushed away from the floor with a powerful thrust. Putting his left hand on his right fist he threw his arm backwards with all the might he could manage. The elbow buried itself in the greenskin surgeon's midriff and would have broken an ordinary man in two. The alien monster simply gave a muffled grunt from beneath its trapjaw maw.

Then, something completely unexpected happened. Instead of reacquiring the major, who was now loose and backing away from the greenskin, the creature instead reached for its stomach. Mortensen fantasised that he'd actually hurt the brute: perhaps broken something inside its alien body. Suddenly something dropped to the floor from below the surgeon's blood-stained leather apron. A belt of sandbags had hit the deck, one splitting open and spilling deathworld sand through the grille. Human and alien stared on in shock and confusion. The moment was broken with sudden action – this time from the greenskin surgeon, who bounded forward like some prehistoric reptile, closing with its slowly comprehending superior.

A shape thudded across the grille floor between the soldiers and the feasting pack. It was green, bloody and fixed in a mask of shock and confusion. As it bounced to a full stop on the gore-splattered platform Mortensen realised that it was the ork warlord's head, snapped clean off by his surgeon-henchman's metallic jaws.

Tearing a clawful of stikkbombz from its belt the greenskin lobbed the grenades deep into the rok's crowded bridge. Runt operators and the warboss's vicious pets had the good sense to bolt for their lives but the bully-boy minders and the mock-uniformed officer couldn't extricate themselves fast enough from the cluttered command centre and went up with the bridge in a tempest of frag and fire.

The platform sang with the percussion of shots from above. Crouching low the major grabbed the injured Commander Qvist and pulled him to a sheltered spot in the now blasted bridge. Krieg tried to hobble to the girder-lined wall but was forced back by an unlucky confluence of fire. Crouching beside Mortensen the two men watched the ork torturer stand amongst the lead storm, his meaty shoulders hunched and his metal skull expressionless and steady.

During a break in the fire the greenskin slipped its bloodstained hands beneath its leather apron and pulled out two chunky, automatic pistols with drum magazines and snub barrels. Turning the weapons skyward the greenskin went to work on the clumsy marksmen. Rounds tore through the gantry with precision and economy, ripping up through the legs of each shooter before the chief torturer moved on to the next target. Mortensen had never seen such dexterity and aim in a greenskin before: the day was proving, however, that there was a great deal about this particular breed of ork he'd never seen before. Bodies were crashing to the platform like meteorites and as the greenskin turned its weapons on the last of the gunners with a final, murderous arc of fire, it let out a savage bellow of rage and triumph that bounced around the walls of the cavernous chamber.

Mortensen couldn't take his eyes off the creature: its brute potency was entrancing. Then, as the roar continued, it began to assume a more recognisable pitch. The major watched as the alien's brawny arms and legs rippled and spasmed – the puce-green flesh blotching ebony brown and then black. Sandbag after sandbag of disguised bulk rained from beneath the leather apron. Pieces of scavenged armour and barbaric tools of torture thumped to the ground as belts and harnesses slid off the new slender lines of the transforming torso. Bone stretched and splintered; sockets popped and dislocated limbs ripped through sickening undulating flesh and snapped back in place. The monster's clockwork cranium slipped down the figure's straightening back and smashed into the floor. The roar was now a scream and the pain was of a very human variety. She had a face of two halves: one side wore the distinction and solemnity of an Imperial servant; the other was a crater of hollow bone and wasted flesh.

Finally the scream came to a resonant close and the stranger stood in the middle of the blasted platform in only a black gossamer bodyglove that seemed to cling to her torso like ink. Only at the wrists did the garment seem to expand to accommodate forearm reinforcements, helping her to support the weight of the huge greenskin pistols she was carrying.

Mortensen turned to Krieg, who was just as mesmerised and, possibly for the first time aboard the ork rok, a little fearful.

'Could today get any vrekkin' weirder?' the major burst and went to present himself to their new ally. Krieg grabbed him and pushed him back against the ruined command centre wall.

'Are you out of your mind?' the commissar said. Qvist groaned and slumped at their feet, the shock of his injuries causing him to fall regularly in and out of consciousness. Mortensen frowned.

'Very possibly. She's an infiltrator – here for the boss. She infiltrated the infiltrators,' Mortensen told Krieg, not a little amused by his impromptu jest. 'We're ahead of the game, for once.'

'They can't be trusted,' Krieg insisted. He hesitated, before committing himself: 'Trust me.'

'Trust you?' the major guffawed. 'She's an Imperial assassin: the operative word here is "Imperial". I don't know if you've been keeping up on current events but she single-handedly vanquished our enemies. I trust her more than I trust you: she hasn't put a gun in my face.'

Mortensen shrugged the cadet off and stepped out from behind the corner. The assassin was walking calmly towards them.

Mortensen smiled. 'Throne, am I glad to–'

The assassin's arms came up and unleashed a stream of rapid fire at the major. Slipping down the rock and skidding back around the corner, Mortensen turned his head to one side, feeling the rounds pepper the wall behind him and whiz past his cheek. It had all happened so fast, he was still smiling. 'You were say-ing?' he put to the commissar.

Mortensen hated the idea of relying on the young cadet but it was increasingly evident that the man was becoming a necessary evil. Despite his turncoat sensibilities, in the face of such fast-moving events and a singularly terrifying opponent, Krieg wasn't looking half bad as an ally.

'I've seen this operative before. I think the boss was a bonus. You're the target.'

'Groxcrap,' the major hissed back.

'She would have killed you outright, but she would have had to blow her cover before she was ready. She waited until you were both together.'

'Look, I piss very important people off on a daily basis,' Mortensen admitted. 'Enough even – it seems – to justify a battlefield execution, but I've done nothing to warrant the attention of one of the Temples.'

'Apparently, they don't agree.'

'You knew about this?'

Krieg exchanged places with Mortensen, who was more than happy to place the commissar between him and the assassin.

'Think I'd waste my time being here if I did?' the cadet put to him. Krieg ventured one eye around the rocky corner and was rewarded with a fresh eruption of gunfire. The pair edged further around the rock, dragging Qvist with them.

'Doesn't seem too hot on you either,' Mortensen said with some satisfaction. At least while the assassin had her weaponry clearly levelled at the both of them it was unlikely the commissar would have time to follow his own interest in spilling Mortensen's blood. In order to have any chance at all against their attacker the major reasoned that Krieg would need him as much as Mortensen needed Krieg.

Krieg edged away from the corner. 'The Officio Assassinorum aren't known for their fondness for loose ends – she'll kill us all.'

Mortensen's top lip wrinkled. He threw glances around the chamber with its myriad of floors and mighty clockwork mechanisms. Looking down through the grille flooring he could see a thunderhead of freezing gas billowing its way out of rocky bulk-heads and up through the floors below. Greenskins were fleeing: stomping and scrambling their way to freedom, away from the certainty of a supercooled, watery grave.

A gloriously familiar sound greeted the major's ears. The simple click of a firing mechanism with nothing to fire. Mortensen wasn't going to hang around while the assassin reloaded her pistols. Grabbing a length of tita-nium piping from the abundant debris of the control centre, Mortensen pulled the commissar aside once again and sidled along the wall to the corner.

'This is an Imperial Assassin: she could kill you in her sleep,' Krieg stated flatly.

'You got any better ideas?' the Gomorrian growled dangerously.

Krieg pulled his Legionnaire's bayonet out from where he'd hidden it in the lining of his flak jacket.

'We take her together.'

Mortensen ground his teeth. He had no idea why he was being targeted – let alone Krieg. He made a promise to himself to find out if he made it off the deathworld alive. In order to do that he knew this was an alliance he could ill-afford to refuse.

Mortensen gave the commissar an unreadable look before nodding slowly at him and then to himself.

'On three, then…' the major mumbled.

Krieg flicked his eyes at the corner: the assassin was already standing there – her good eye burning into them with expectation.

'Damn,' Mortensen spat before launching himself at the dark figure. The pipe came down with all the power and precision the Gomorrian could muster, and would have cleaved an ordinary person into the ground. The assassin was a blaze of movement, however, shifting effortlessly to one side. As the pipe bounced off the grille floor, Mortensen followed through with another brutal pitch. This time the assassin weathered the blow, smoothly deflecting it off her reinforced forearms. Krieg came at her from the other side, holding his bayonet like a dagger and flashing it at the assassin with well-practiced flourishes. Time and again the pipe and blade came at the operative with increasingly desperate and inventive combinations, but to little avail. The assassin was merely toying with them.

Finally she began to counter with her own exotic and decisive combat manoeuvres, turning Krieg's knife aside and slamming the back of his skull into the wall with an inescapable flat-footed kick to the chin. It almost looked like the assassin had grown bored. Everything up to this point had been mere training or the frustrations that came with assuming a form that was not her own.

Krieg's bayonet clattered to the floor and the stunned commissar slid to the ground, his face bloody and his eyes blank. Another of the major's vicious swings cut through the air beside the evading Imperial agent. Twisting gracefully along the length of the pipe the assassin stabbed at nerve clusters in Mortensen's neck with the tips of her palms before acrobatically flipping and slamming the major back with the ball of one foot. She was about to conclude with an equally outlandish flykick and would have done so, if it hadn't have been for the sudden lurch experienced by the rok as the colossal craft continued its inevitable journey to the depths of the chemical flood plain.

Krieg tumbled along the wall and Mortensen fell backwards, the floor simply not being where it had been seconds before. Only the assassin managed any kind of a landing, launching herself back off the grille with her hands, somersaulting and dropping the new distance to the ground with assurance. Mortensen was waiting for her.

Hitting the floor first with his face and then rolling across one shoulder, the major was ready. Sweeping the bar parallel to the floor, Mortensen hamstrung the landing operative, sending her crashing to the platform. Scrambling across the floor the major buried the warped end of the pipe in the assassin's already mangled face. The agent was sufficiently dazzled to allow two more of the Gomorrian's sledgehammer blows to go home before formulating a counter-move.

Reaching out with both arms the assassin released spring-triggered armaments from the reinforced forearm plates adorning each wrist. A short blade of peculiar fluorescent metal exploded from one appendage, whilst a pistol of unusual alien design shot out from the other on a lightweight carriage.

Somehow the killer got the blade between Mortensen's bat and her face, shearing off the tip of the titanium pipe. Like a blacksmith working metal off an anvil the major pressed on with his attack, leaning into another powerhouse pounding. This time the blade sliced the pipe in half, before flicking elegantly around to take the last of the length down to Mortensen's feverish grip.

The major had little time to think: the advantage was fading fast and the assassin's otherworldly pistol was coming up. Dropping the titanium stub, Mortensen threw himself down on the assassin's arm and grabbed for the hand holding the pistol. The operative's arm turned and twisted like a muscular snake and it was all the Gomorrian could do to keep it straight and aim the pistol out of harm's way. In response the assassin's blade tore through the cool air of the cavern in a devastating curve, ready to impale the major through the head. Again Mortensen came for the assassin's face, gripping her wrist with one hand and slamming his unfeeling elbow with bone-cracking force into the killer's collapsed face.

The blade-arm went down – at first in skull-splintered shock – and then with the intention of pushing the assassin up off the grille floor. Mortensen heard the scrape of another blade and darted his eyes around the chaos of limbs and frantic movement, attempting to anticipate another attack. Fortunately the blade was the bayonet and its wielder was Krieg, fresh from his close encounter with the wall. Snatching the weapon up in both hands the commissar leapt at the pair of them, slamming the blade down through the back of the assassin's grasping palm and squeezing it inbetween the lattice of the mesh flooring.

A wheeze of agony escaped the assassin's lean lips. Mortensen lay still. Krieg stared at what he'd done. Suddenly the assassin bucked, sending a spasmic ripple through her shapely body, throwing Mortensen into a roll across the platform floor. The pistol was free. Krieg shuffled and kicked back towards the wall but the major wasn't as fortunate. He broke the roll by thumping his palms into the grille but found himself staring back up the weapon's odd length.

Mortensen snatched his storm blade from a sheath on his armoured thigh but a metallic shimmer had reached out for him from the end of the strange weapon's barrel, striking him in the chest before writhing across his body in divergent streams. Muscles spasmed and the storm blade clattered to the grille decking.

The strange, silver fire coursed through Mortensen's being, burning its way through his insensitive, deadened flesh to the live nerve-shot tissue beneath. That's when the suffering began. Everything else went black. Only the pain mattered. His brain became nothing more than a filter for the transmission of the hell he was experiencing. He thrashed like a faulty servitor, smacking his head, knees and elbows across the mesh flooring as the ethereal agony passed through the nerve-crammed muscles of his chest and thighs. It found a new expression of pain as it hit his solar plexus, throwing his abdomen off the platform and forcing his limbs to assume the tortured formation of a crab. The white-hot sensation felt like it was burrowing out of his wracked intestines like a bullet passing through his back and out through his cramping stomach.

Then it was gone. Mortensen collapsed, still clutching his abdomen. As he unscrewed his eyes he saw the assassin waving the pistol at the swiftly retreating commissar. It seemed the torturous side arm only had a short range and the assassin was still pinned to the deck. The pistol slid efficiently back along its carriage and disappeared as the operative fell to heaving at the bayonet, but the blade was stuck fast.

Krieg looked at the stranded assassin and then back at the major for instruction. He slid another length of shattered pipe from a pile of debris gathered against the wall. Mortensen shook his head as he got unsteadily to his feet. He didn't think he could experience anything like that again.

'Screw that,' he blurted, throwing a finger at the struggling killer. 'Get Qvist.'

Krieg yanked young Qvist to his feet and stumbled him across the platform to the pylon superstructure. The two of them went down as the floor dropped violently once again. The rok was really sinking now. Mortensen exchanged a venomous glance with the assassin before bounding for the structure himself.

They arrived together. Mortensen's first priority was to get Qvist back to his senses. Belly-shot or not he needed the boy to climb. Sloshing the commander across the face with the back of his hand, the major shook the Spetzghastian awake. The boy's head lolled to one side, his eyes rolling before falling back into unconsciousness.

'Plan?' the cadet-commissar put to him.

Mortensen grunted: 'Simple. Climb for your life.' Throwing the limp body of the Departmento Munitorum officer over one shoulder the major vaulted the distance between the platform floor and the girders. Krieg followed, after a tottering run up, hitting the pylon higher up, being slightly lighter of foot. The two men began their desperate scramble for the cavern ceiling.

Thirty metres into the gruelling ascent a dull howl caused both of the soldiers to halt, chests heaving. Looking down, they saw the assassin had given up her futile attempts to extricate the wedged bayonet. She had to. The rok was flooding badly – the steam from the raging deluge below was rising up through the grille flooring. Pulling the impaled palm to one side the assassin had slit the blade through one side of her hand – severing bone, tendon and gristle. What she was left with was a useless appendage that she bound quickly with a strip torn hastily from her body glove. Mortensen watched her assess the situation, her eyes moving around the cavern like a jungle cat's.

The mesh flooring frosted up as floodwaters bubbled up in between. There was no way she could make the pylon now. Instead the assassin made the short run to the chamber wall and bounded up the first few metres of the rock. Incredibly the professional killer intended to scale the cavern wall and ceiling, swinging across to the pylon structure at the rim of the colossal hole in the chamber roof. Impossible ordinarily – beyond the realms of all credible likelihood with only one hand.

As the assassin shot up the wall it seemed like nothing would stop her and with Mortensen tiring under the extra weight of the Departmento Munitorum officer, he began to wonder if she had a chance. Krieg had spotted the advancing assassin also and called down to the major, who'd now completely stopped.

'Wait there!' Mortensen yelled, throwing himself up the aching distance separating them. Just before he reached the cadet a new phenomenon presented itself. Chemicular slush was streaming in from the roof. The rok was all but submerged now, the gargantuan mass of the craft forcing the groundwaters up and over the summit of the asteroid. Only the teleporter array, reaching up and out of the rok, still cleared the rising cryogenic swamplands. Curtains of deathworld precipitation splashed in over the brim of the roof hole, creating a circular waterfall that sprayed and dashed the pylon with droplets of chemical superfreeze.

Mortensen sagged, screwing up his face. 'Come on!' he bawled at his rapidly deteriorating prospects. Krieg must have thought he was talking to him because he clambered the remaining metres down to him.

'Take the kid,' the major ordered, passing the rag-doll body up to the struggling commissar. Krieg wasn't squat and powerful in the way the major was and Qvist presented a serious impediment to his efforts. A frost-bitten foot hardly helped matters.

'I'm the target?' Mortensen confirmed, steely-eyed.

Krieg nodded gravely.

'Then she'll follow her target,' the major reasoned, slipping through between the girders and launching himself across the space between two adjoining sides of the pylon interior. He felt the phantasmal shock-wave sensation of the fat teleporter beam wash across his eyeballs as his vault carried him close by. It was hard to believe that the unstoppable greenskin machinery was still operating beneath tons of liquid: a testament to alien technology, indeed.

Hanging off struts on the other side, Mortensen shot Krieg a meaningful glance. The cadet was still staring at him: an understanding passed between the two men, culminating in a silent nod from the commissar. Mortensen then watched Krieg surge purposefully for the ceiling before disappearing up through the roof. The assassin had predictably changed her course, moving rapidly across the wall of the cavern like an insect, bringing herself parallel with the major before negotiating the craggy, concave ceiling of the chamber.

Mortensen put on a final spurt – his teeth gritted, arms on fire – bringing him in line with the assassin. At that moment she blasted through the sheet of chemical death cascading in from above. She'd swung from the roof, freefalling at the pylon. She passed Mortensen, slamming onto the side of the structure with two sure feet and a firm, if frostbitten, handhold.

The assassin was like some unstoppable machine. There would be no outclimbing her. Instead of scrabbling skyward, the major let go. Using his boots to guide him along the girder he was scaling, he slid down the pylon, crushing the frozen fingers on the assassin's remaining hand under his heel. The predatory killer fell backwards some distance before becoming tangled in a set of support struts further down.

This was his chance. Mortensen blasted up the network of bars and supports after Krieg, committing everything he had left to scaling the antenna array and putting as much distance as possible between himself and his executioner.

As he breached the roof opening Mortensen's heart sank as he realised just how far above the rok surface the telescopic transmitter extended. What was even more worrying was the fact that he could not see the silhouettes of Krieg and Qvist above him. He'd expected to be able to pick them out clinging to the structure overhead, against the twilight of the deathworld sky. He shouldn't have been surprised. The rok summit, and by extension the pylon, was shuddering metre by metre down into a broiling, white-water vortex of crashing deathworld brume. There wasn't a sandy bank or piece of silicon foliage in sight.

Without warning the tower moved. It wasn't the jolting plunge Mortensen had become used to. The pylon had never been pointing straight up, but it was generally aimed at the sky. Now the entire structure was careering wildly towards the furious chemicular riptide. Digging his fingers into the metal, the major rode out the inevitable bounce. The tower was collapsing and although the structure was holding on to its rigidity, the pinnacle was rolling violently around, picking up lethal momentum.

The assassin had returned. She was rocketing up one of the core beams, using the tips of both toes and working fingers. Her ruined hand was finding fresh usefulness with its deadly blade extended – the shimmering, otherworldly fluorescence agitated as she slashed through high tension wires and support cables.

Mortensen stopped climbing. There was nowhere left to go. The pylon was creaking uncomfortably and bouncing gently towards the foaming breakers below. The taller waves were crashing against the structure, causing both Mortensen and his executioner to keep moving back and forth along the length of the pinnacle in order to avoid instant petrification. The assassin was walking now, casually flicking the tip of her weapon at the struts and chains holding Mortensen's section of the pylon out of the maelstrom below.

'I don't suppose there's any chance we can work something out,' the major bawled sardonically over the intense noise. The assassin began to pick up speed, bounding up the girder towards him, blade held ready for some exotic and lethal manoeuvre.

'Had to ask,' the major explained softly to himself, steeling his body for the inevitable path of the alien

blade. Holding tight and closing his eyes, Mortensen
shut out the drama of his surroundings and prepared
for a swift and clean death. Surely he could trust an
assassin to deliver that.

The ear-searing roar of a familiar engine rolled overhead, causing Mortensen to blink open his eyes and let
the reality flood back in. Everything he needed to
know was carved into the assassin's snarling half-face.
Vertigo. Turning, the major streaked up the remaining
length of the pylon apex. As an angry breaker swept
past and doused the structure behind him the Spectre
was revealed, hovering over the chaos, turning gently.
The bay ramp was down and a collection of figures
were violently gesturing encouragement from inside.
Among them was Commissar Koulick Krieg.

Mortensen didn't dare look back. The aircraft's door
gunners were giving his assailant all kinds of hell with
streams from their heavy bolters – but Mortensen had
seen the daemonic character walk through worse than
that. Blasting off the end of the teleporter array, legs
kicking with wild effort, Mortensen sailed across the
chemical death raging below.

It wasn't pretty, but it was a landing. His chest had
struck the end of the ramp awkwardly and he could
swear that a couple of ribs had snapped inside his
molested torso. He kicked at the slick hull of the aircraft and his fingers slapped the ramp frantically for a
grip. A sea of gloved hands came at him, latching onto
his carapace and fistfuls of raw flesh before pulling
him unceremoniously inside.

'Ramp closing,' Eszcobar called across the bay, the
deathworlder being first to the activation stud. The
gaggle of corpsmen fell in a heap in the centre of the
troop bay, Mortensen held like some kind of prize

between them. The Navy gunners were still crashing at shadows outside and the aircraft swung uncomfortably above the whirlpool.

'Sir, are you alright?' Meeks asked urgently, suddenly beside him. When Mortensen didn't initially reply the sergeant shook his shoulder, attempting to bring the major out of his daze. 'Are you injured?' he asked. He didn't wait for an answer this time and simply yanked a harassed-looking DuBois and her medical kit away from Krieg and the unconscious Qvist. There were others too: Minghella was still unconscious and Sarakota incapacitated. Hauser was sitting in a pool of his own blood, growling in incessant pain at the far end of the compartment and a faceless Garbarsky trembled under a mask of bandages and pipes. Thule and two Guardsmen from the other squad cradled blasted limbs and head wounds. Even Rask had taken one in the gut.

'Is he in?' came Conklin's gravelly voice over the bay vox-com.

'In,' Eszcobar confirmed.

Mortensen staggered away from DuBois's healing hands and Meeks's remonstrations. He felt like he just wanted to collapse, but there was something they had to do before returning to *Deliverance*.

He snatched the vox from the Autegan scout: 'Rosenkrantz!' the major called, fighting for breath. 'Fly low. Give the bird's belly a taste of the canopy.'

'What the h–'

'Just do it.'

After a moment's hesitation the aircraft banked and accelerated, carrying them clear of the rising flood plain. Suddenly the Spectre bucked and everyone inside the compartment was thrown forward. Silicon shrubbery slammed the aircraft as Rosenkrantz guided

Vertigo's swollen belly down into the razor-sharp canopy. Leaves and branches shattered, immersing the hull in a relentless slipstream of crystal shards and glass splinters.

Everyone heard a body slam flush to the aircraft exterior and then the unearthly scream of a woman literally sliced to ribbons in an instant. Blood streamed in though through the gunner's ports and ran across the inside of the compartment wall.

Mortensen sank down the side of the compartment wall – job done. The Gomorrian hadn't underestimated the assassin and had been rewarded for his vigilance: he could hardly risk the deathstalker roaming the corridors of *Deliverance*.

The enormity of what had just happened was just beginning to sink in. Death was a constant companion on Redemption Corps missions but he'd almost been assassinated. Someone very powerful wanted him dead. His mind buzzed with a thousand possibilities.

As ROSENKRANTZ PULLED the assault carrier out of the treetops, silence reigned once again in the troop bay. The mood was wretched, however, with blood, pain and hangdog faces sapping any sense of victory or the jubilation of survival.

'Orders, boss?' said Conklin who'd just appeared on the companionway, breaching the hush that had fallen across the corpsmen. Mortensen was lost in thought.

'We need get back to *Deliverance* and alert the fleet to the situation,' Krieg insisted.

'Sir?' Conklin persevered intently as though the commissar had never spoken.

'The fate of this system may very well depend on what we decide to do right now,' Krieg put to Mortensen and the compartment.

Conklin took several dangerous steps towards the commissar.

'Do what he says,' Mortensen interceded.

'But boss, the ogryns, the mission was–'

'A trap,' Captain Rask answered for him. The officer looked empty and desolate.

'But one that might just serve to save this system from the clutches of an alien invader,' Mortensen assured the captain. He turned to Krieg. 'Yes?'

A moment of cool concord passed between the two men.

'Yes,' the cadet-commissar answered finally.

'Speak, damn you!' the canoness seethed, slamming her armoured palms into the table.

Mortensen's eyes were glazed, his face – like his body – lifeless. He hadn't spoken in what seemed an age, he just sat there watching Santhonax pace the oubliette, soaking up the battle-sister's fury. Once or twice he caught her checking her chronometer or fidgeting with her vox-piece. It was probably already too late to get off the planet's surface and she knew it.

Despite feeling emotionally drained and physically exhausted, Mortensen felt the irresistible pull of an utterance. He felt compelled to satisfy her demand to know his mind.

'All those people, died…'

'Yes,' the canoness confirmed with unusual feeling, quick to exploit the opening. 'But not for you or because of you. There are those amongst the fighting men of the Imperium who might trade in such untruths and poison your faith *with their own heretical needs and ideals. But in Gomorrah's death, men like you found new life. You wouldn't have become what you are, had not adversity been your making.'*

'What, a cursed cripple?' Mortensen lamented.

Santhonax turned his chair from the table and knelt down in her armour by his side: 'Can't you see? This isn't a curse, it's a gift.' She stroked his battle-scarred chest with the cruel tips of her gauntlet. 'It may not be divinely ordained, but whatever you lost in your world's calamity, you gained the ability to achieve the impossible. You succeed where others fail. You walk tall where others have fallen. You live when you should die. Adversity gave you that.'

'The assassin?'

Santhonax nodded slowly.

'Krieg?'

More confirmation from the battle-sister.

'That bounty hunter on Targretta Prime?'

'Not one of mine,' the canoness admitted, narrowing her eyes and coming in closer, 'but the same principle applies.'

'Why the pretence? Heresy? Why not just come for me?' the major goaded.

'There are those,' Santhonax admitted with regret, 'that do not share our vision.'

'Really?' the Gomorrian teased.

The Sister of the Immaculate Flame continued unfazed: 'They are without the steel in their soul to do what is necessary. They do not understand and consider our ideas dangerous. In turn, we ourselves stand accused of heretical ideals. Surely you can empathise with that, Major Mortensen?'

'Let me let you in on a little secret: I think your ideas are dangerous,' he told her straight, 'and since you included me in them, I've never been more than two decisions away from a horrible death.'

'It's easier to avoid your accusers if you appear to be one of them. See, adversity forced me to become stronger. My pretence was part of the adversity you are enduring right at this moment, but in time I have hopes that you will outgrow my protection.'

'Protection!' Mortensen guffawed angrily. 'You've done nothing but try to kill me or get me killed. You talk of adversity like it's some kind of necessary evil. You're wrong,' he told her sourly. 'The end of my world gave me nothing but pain. And when it finished giving me that, well, it just gave me nothing.'

'It gave you a role to play: a life useful to the Emperor.'

'You may revel in adversity,' the major went on. 'You may believe that the Imperium is all the stronger for the enemies at and within its borders, but there's an alien war host out there who says different; who are different – because from what I've seen and from what I know, I don't think they're going to stop.'

'Men like you will stop them,' the canoness assured him. 'And you will be all the stronger, sharper and more vigilant for your victory. But if there's no enemy, there can be no victory and no one able to stand against the future foes of mankind. Greater evils.'

Mortensen shook his head, which surprised him because formerly those muscles had been all but stupefied. He pushed on, eager that the battle-sister not detect his growing mobility.

'You talk like you can control this.'

'Control? No. Do not take me for a fool: I've fought the Imperium's enemies all my life,' she warned him. 'But if you study what you hate, you come to realise that mankind's enemies can be encouraged to be predictable. And of all the wretched alien detritus that pollute the galaxy, greenskins are amongst the most predictable.'

'You're out of your mind, did you know that?'

'Centuries reducing garrisons on the Burdock Worlds. Generations spent thinning fleet deployments along the Kintessa Gauntlet. Enceladus drew millions of able-bodied fighting men out of sector – an unnecessary crusade providing a hole in the fence, as it were. Don't misunderstand me, it had to be a very big hole, but orks can't resist an opening like that. Studies of greenskin invasions and unintentional strategic weaknesses long taught us that.'

'You…'

'And those before me,' Santhonax informed him. 'Gomorrah was bold – even by ork standards. We'd never seen tactics like that before. That hulk was colossal and more than enough to sunder a world – but we never expected it to actually strike the planet. Genius, really. As a hive-world, Gomorrah would have supplied the lion's share of recruits required to repel an invasion of the system. It was then we truly realised we'd chosen wisely. The warlords of the Gargasso Deeps proved on that day their suitability for this venture. We could trust their intention to unify and push coreward on a green tide of unthinking alien brutality: funnelled through the weakened inroad of worlds making up the Kintessa Gauntlet and spilling out upon an unsuspecting Segmentum Solar.'

'You–'

'Could have stopped it? Yes. But why should we? This will be the greatest alien incursion the galaxy has ever seen. It will galvanise generations to action, across hundreds of worlds, and make thousands more like you.'

'You don't know, do you?' Mortensen marvelled with sickening horror. Something about the quality of the major's accusation stopped the fanatic in her tracks.

'Explain,' she finally ordered.

'They're not greenskins,' the storm-trooper spat at her. He let his words sink in. 'You've damned not only yourself and me. You've damned us all. This alien host will sweep down on Terra and if you and your secret society have strategically crippled Kintessa as you say, then nothing is going to stop it.'

'You'll stop it,' Canoness Santhonax put to him, her words laced with the fire of the faithful.

'Why tell me this?' Mortensen asked with rising anger. 'I'll expose you – inform the authorities.'

'We are the only authority,' the battle-sister reasoned, flashing her insane eyes at him. 'You, as I've painted you, are a traitor and a heretic. But in any case, were that to come to pass, I expect I'd be long dead.'

'And your warped superiors and associates – what of them?'

'As I've tried to tell you: we're all here to be tested.'

Mortensen bored into her with cold, furious eyes and made his play. 'Well, my test is over. I'd rather be in someone's crosshairs than part of some raving scheme to feign galactic destruction – especially one that's gone as spectacularly awry as this one. I'll sit here and die before lending credence to your sick theories of delusion and, well, I never thought I'd be the one saying this but, heresy.'

The canoness came in close, her potent eyes fixing the major with a piercing glare. Mortensen met them with his own brand of cocky truculence. A minute must have passed like this: the canoness appraising both the major and the situation, the holochron clearly twitching on her wrist. She could see he meant it. Mortensen did all he could do. He waited. Waited to see if she would grant him his wish.

Then it happened.

Santhanax folded. Her finger moved to her vox-earpiece.

'Purity Control, this is the canoness…' Her face creased with annoyance and confusion as the seconds went by without a response. 'Purity Control,' she repeated before cycling through the open channels. As she hit the fourth the creases softened and her lips pursed. Even Mortensen could hear the unmistakable crash of gunfire across the vox-waves.

The major enjoyed her momentary uncertainty.

Santhonax clicked her fingers, bringing her battle-sisters out of the cell shadows, and tuned her vox into an alternative channel. 'We're leaving,' she simply notified the person on the other end. The pressure door in the ceiling gave a hydraulic wheeze and squirted gas from nozzles situated around the bulkhead rim. The trapdoor opened upwards and a robust wire ladder fell, unravelling itself to the floor.

The two sisters hauled Mortensen's body out of the chair, putting each arm across their sinewy shoulders and toned necks. The canoness put the sole of one boot on the first wire step. The sisters approached with Mortensen supported between them.

'When we get back to the ship, you can ask the other specimens in my personal collection: you die when I say you die,' Santhonax told the major evenly.

Mortensen gave her a conceited smile. 'Life's a bitch. Mind you, I'm told it takes one to know one.'

CHAPTER SEVEN
Cradle of Darkness

I

'MIGHTY GOOD TO see you, sir,' Golliant rasped, his boot steps echoing around the deck elevator as he helped a tender Commissar Krieg into a fresh great-coat. Krieg didn't hide his relief and slapped the aide on the shoulder.

'It's good to be back onboard,' he told the hulking Volscian. It also felt good to have the wrestler by his side after events down on the deathworld moon.

As the elevator doors parted, the major stepped confidently out onto the bridge. Krieg followed with more caution, realising that this was actually the first time that he'd been up there. Golliant hovered steadfastly by the elevator doors as the cadet limped across the deck.

The bridge was quiet and bathed in a harsh cerulean glow. Mortensen silently joined the silhouettes of the bandaged Rask and Sass as they stood before the great screen, below the captain's pulpit. Lieutenant Commander Waldemar climbed out of his throne and stood gripping the balustrade rail. He caught the cadet-commissar's eye as he entered, but Krieg's line of sight was swiftly drawn to what everyone else was gazing at on the screen.

Before him blazed the cold sheen of the Spetzghastian mesosphere, but something was impossibly wrong. The mercantile giant's spectacular ring system was in complete disarray. Instead of a neat dust belt of spinning rock and ice fragments, chaperoned by shepherd moons like the verdant Tancred's World and the pockmarked Wormwood, the girdle was fragmented: irregular asteroids were peeling off in different directions, many falling planetward with building velocity. Ishtar was fairly far out for one of the Spetzghastian moons and they could see everything. It was as though gravity had simply failed and the ring system was breaking up.

Krieg stepped forward, rubbing his tired eyes with forefinger and thumb, making sure that he wasn't hallucinating. A closer inspection revealed the reason for the unusual phenomenon: titanic engines and bulbous propellant tanks grew out of the natural rock of the jagged asteroids. Primitive boosters span the gargantuan bodies on their axis before the main stage engines rocketed them towards the planet surface, Spetzghast's potent gravitational pull doing the rest.

The bridge was shell-shocked; Krieg had never seen such a spectacle. An apocalyptic blitz of ready-made planet-smashers, plunging towards the heavily populated mercantile world, like thunderbolts from an angry god. Both the workmanship and tactics were greenskin by design: headlong suicide runs of crushing effectiveness. The system had clearly been infiltrated for a long time and the asteroids mined out and modified to create an armada of kamikaze roks and bouldered hulks. It was clear to everyone on the bridge that Spetzghast would be pounded to dust.

As they tumbled sickeningly towards the planet, the ork roks rolled to present previously hidden batteries of superguns and cannons, laying effortless waste to the anchored fluyts and bulk cruisers in high orbit. Swarms of luggers and freight barges impacted on the rocky surface, their pathetic detonations giving the impression of sparks and ricochets. A sleek sprint trader broke orbit, crashing through several sister vessels before soaring narrowly between the two converging behemoths. A rogue trader freighter attempted the same manoeuvre, only to end up a blazing wreck, tangled across the rockface.

Krieg watched as adamanticlads and monitors bore down bravely on a jagged giant as it flipped and span wildly through the spindly appendage docks of the Exchequer orbital tradestation. The rok left a field of spinning debris in its wake, sending a ripple of explosions up through the crippled station. The system ships were soon joined by one of the convoy escorts, the frigate *Orpheus*. Pooling their firepower, the Firestorm-class frigate met the ork craft head on, cutting deep into the rock with its raging prow lance. Incredibly one of the heavily-armed monitors made an impression on the rok's swollen engine column, a lucky shot setting off a chain reaction that blasted the greenskin vessel unexpectedly to starboard. The rok's craggy surface lightly brushed along the side of the *Orpheus*, tearing up the frigate's armour and exposing thousands of Navy crewmen to the searing cold of space.

Rob Sanders

The ancient and impressive garrison ship *Stang Draak* was smashed free in the ensuing chaos and perfectly placed to rake the length of the rok with its obsolete guns. The grand cruiser's much younger crew had only ever fired the weapons on exercise or to salute the arrival of dignitaries and touring port admirals. Their response was slow and sloppy, many of the shots wide and misranged, which was incredible bearing in mind the size of the target.

A jolt of shock and disbelief swept the bridge as the grand cruiser died before their eyes. Something beautiful was there one moment and then suddenly wasn't, replaced by a breathtaking display of power and destruction, which seconds later also vanished.

A promontory prow thrust forth, out of the nothing where the garrison ship had been. Behind it, incalculable tons of extraterrestrial rock and scavwelded salvage thundered through the silence of space. The space hulk was like a mountain range, imposing and impossible: an unstoppable monster, smashing roks and Imperial vessels aside with equal, crushing indifference. A grotesque flagship hewn from pure hate.

The *Vatividad*, the *Algonquin Royale*, the *Morningstar*, the *Countess of Scarbra*... The fat troopships careered and coursed full thrust for safety, but the behemoth overreached them, drawing parallel with its magnabore artillery, consuming all in a growing bank of flame and fury. Krieg stared on in disbelief as the lives aboard the transports were snuffed out like a row of candles in a sudden breeze. The commissar felt sick to the bottom of his stomach. Sicker, if that were possible.

His heart lifted for a moment, no doubt foolish pride in the futile gestures of his compatriots. The hulk's underside was suddenly bathed in flashes as a stream of torpedoes found their mark. The successive glare of the hits faded, however, to reveal the greenskin ship unscathed. The *Purgatorio* surged up, its baroque beakhead breaking free of the black depths like some rising leviathan. The Dictator-class blasted uselessly at the impervious giant, the passing salvo a disciplined and worthy pattern of fire for the flagship. The space hulk rocketed on through the barrage and slammed into the vessel's mid-section.

Krieg's fists tightened and his knuckles cracked. Like a tug tearing an uncooperative giga-tanker round in a system dock, the broken flagship tried to roll the hulk planetward. The cruiser's towers and flank arrays tangled with the hulk's own irregular structures, grappling with the beast and forcing it into a slight turn. The *Purgatorio's* dorsal finally snared the cosmic predator, a dying push from the plasma drives doing the rest. Like a featherweight throwing a much heavier opponent in a scud wrestling ring the Dictator played to what centre of gravity it had left and sent both the hulk and itself spinning towards the upper atmosphere of the besieged mercantile world.

It was Mortensen that broke the solemn silence that blanketed the bridge and paralysed all those who were witness to the murder of a world.

'How could we have not known… about this?' he managed.

Waldemar, his patrician accent a little softer and less grating than usual, told him, 'Communication blackout. We lost all feeds. I assumed it was a technical problem and had my engineers run the appropriate diagnostics and litanies.'

'What about astropathic lines of communication?' Rask offered. 'Surely Spetzghast or the other ships–'

'Total black-out,' the austere Waldemar assured him. 'My psykers received nothing and nothing they sent got through.'

'How is that possible?' the major asked grimly.

'The teleporters,' Krieg threw in. It was more of a flat statement than the victorious solution to a problem.

'That kind of greenskin technology would play havoc with our comms,' Sass confirmed.

'Especially if it was being engaged across many points in the ring system,' the commissar added. 'We have every reason to believe that the system is completely compromised. A large number of troops would have to be moved to prepare for as bold an advance as this.'

The major's adjutant shook his head – unhappy with the conclusion: 'The astropaths would still be able to get through.'

Krieg gave them the benefit of his Inquisitorial training. 'The greenskins generate a collective psychic field in such circumstances. Perhaps that was enough to block astropathic communication. Psychic static, if you will.'

'It's never been enough to disrupt communications before,' Waldemar informed him, unconvinced.

Mortensen nodded slowly: 'He's right,' the major growled. 'I've fought this scum on dozens of worlds and it's the first time I've come across that.'

Krieg juggled the concepts crackling inside his head. He thought of the rebels on Illium, the formerly loyalist abhuman populations of Ishtar and the cultists he'd hunted on Spetzghast. How the Sisters of the Immaculate Flame had failed to find a psyker among them, only a psychic blankness that seemed to link them all.

'Then it's something else,' Krieg insisted. He couldn't formulate a web of relationships that linked all the elements and explained all the factors. All he kept coming up with was half-digested hunches and ghostly, paranoid suggestions.

Mortensen turned back to the battle, feasting his eyes on the annihilation. An idea was eating away at his soul and he finally he found the words to express its brutal simplicity.

'How long to get us on the planet's surface?'

Waldmar called his amazement across the bridge: 'You can't be serious?'

'I'm always serious,' Mortensen updated the officer, turning away from the screen, catching Rask's unsettled expression as he did. 'Except when I'm not.'

'It's over,' the lieutenant commander told him. 'What do you think you can do: save the planet?'

'No,' Mortensen said, clearly lost in thoughts of his own home world's demise. 'I can't do that. But we can pull the flagship crash survivors offworld before those ork roks pulverise it. I can't stand those mungers: on any other day Brigadier Voskov and his tight-ass Shadow Brigade commanders can go to hell. Today, a greenskin battlefront is opening up right on top of us and we're going to need some of that Volscian methodology to formulate a response to this mess. It could be months before a tactical command structure is back in place otherwise, and think how far these greenskins could have rushed us by then.'

Waldemar was no coward, but he looked like one as his eyes moved from the major's stony glare to the destruction beyond and then around the bridge at his own officers. His eyes lingered for a moment on Krieg. It was common knowledge that he and the major were at each other's throats. Krieg returned his gaze. At heart Waldemar was a sound and inventive officer and had one final play to make before committing to a potentially disastrous course of action, one way or the other.

'Major, I think that you are overestimating the capabilities of this ship. *Deliverance* is a small carrier. She won't last ten seconds against that kind of firepower. You would have me risk every soul aboard, including every single one of your storm-troopers, in one foolishly bold and futile manoeuvre?'

Krieg watched the major mull it over.

'As one of the only combat operative vessels in the system,' the captain continued, 'isn't it protocol to make for Aurelius and warn other nearby systems, so that they might prepare for the eventuality of war?'

Mortensen glared around the silent bridge.

'You just don't get it, do you? Redemption Corps don't run. Aurelius? Warning the fleet? Leave that to some freighter,' Mortensen spat. 'This is a military vessel: I say we stay and we do what we can. And what we can do right now is get my men and the remaining 364th into any and every available sub-atmospheric craft you have, and get them down on the surface so they can do their job.'

Waldemar's eyes narrowed and the coin-shaped scar on his cheek flared. 'I'm sorry. I can't do that.'

'You think you can stop us?' the major seared. Both corpsmen and naval security both tensed, their side arms but the flick of a wrist away.

The commander's own trembling hand went down to his Patrician hanger: 'Try it, you mutinous dog...'

Krieg's hellpistol was already clear of its fresh holster. A burst of super-charged las-fire drummed into the deck, bringing the attention of all squarely to his feet. Both Waldemar, proud and uncertain, and the major, feral and fearsome, turned at the sound of automatic fire on the bridge. Only a newly-promoted security ensign in a spanking uniform and creaking, new boots was foolish enough to point his weapon at the Imperial commissar.

'Think that prudent do you, boy?' Krieg put to the ensign, without looking at him. The young officer stared at Krieg and then his pistol before slowly drifting the muzzle to the floor. The ensign suddenly became aware of a presence, turning to find the hulking Golliant immediately behind him. Wide-eyed, the ensign dropped the pistol on the deck and turned, backing to the cognition banks adorning the wall.

Krieg took in the bridge with one sweeping glance. Waldemar wasn't wrong. They were seconds from actual mutiny: storm-troopers exchanging fire with Navy grunts on the bridge of one of his Beneficient Majesty's hallowed warships. There was only one authority on the ship that superseded both the lieutenant commander and the Redemption Corps major and it sat snug on his finger. He presented the ring and his fist to both men, letting the hypnotic power of the winged-skull signet take effect.

With Regimental Commissar Udeskee below decks and out of reach and the ship's commissar, a firebreather called Locke – well, dead – Krieg was the only one who could legitimately act in this situation.

'Back to this, huh?' Mortensen shot sardonically across the bridge. It was a dare. As it was, on this particular occasion, Krieg didn't actually disagree with the major.

'Captain Waldemar, can you actually get through that?' the cadet-commissar asked, nodding his cap at the screen. 'Can you get us to Spetzghast?'

'This is madness,' the captain settled upon. 'And I should have you all thrown in the damned brig.'

'Can you do it, captain?' Krieg insisted.

The officer bridled, professional pride prevailing.

'Yes,' was the simple answer. 'But Commissar Krieg, that is not–'

'Oh, but unfortunately it is,' Krieg cut in with regret. 'At present velocity, I'd say we have three or four hours, at most, to get on and off the surface before those roks hit.'

'Three hours, forty-two minutes to first impact,' Sass interjected, soaking up data from the bridge picts and rune screens like a sponge.

'If we're not knee deep in Spetzghastian sand within two, captain, I'll have you escorted to the brig for cowardice, dereliction of duty and negligent conduct. I'm sure the ship's commissar would agree if he had the misfortune of still being with us.'

'You imperious cub,' Waldemar snapped back, 'You can't…'

'I speak for Udeskee; I speak for the Commissariat; I speak for the Emperor, in this matter,' Krieg told him with searing certainty.

A stunned bridge continued to hold a bated breath.

'And if I refuse?' Waldemar asked, his scar burning bright.

'Your actions will be judged by your superiors in light of your witnessed refusal to save Imperial lives, your refusal to at least attempt a rescue of Commodore van den Groot and the Volscian High Command and your seeming preference for conduct unbecoming an officer of one of his beneficient majesty's warships.'

Waldemar went to retort but Krieg hadn't finished.

'But that's irrelevant because long before that, Captain Waldemar, I'll have you shot,' the commissar informed him plainly, 'and empower Major Mortensen's men to take command of this vessel, by force if necessary. And we are all too ready to face the Emperor's judgement in that. Believe me, captain, we are martyrs all. There's a reason we're called Redemption Corps.' The commissar let his words sink in, and since it seemed that he had overplayed his hand regardless, added: 'Who is the executive officer of this crate, anyhow?'

A lieutenant with a shiny head and thoughtful brown eyes stepped forward hesitantly.

'Name?' Krieg requested. The first lieutenant went to speak, getting as far as opening his lips, but the voice that came across the bridge was not his.

'Mister Caviezel,' Waldemar supplied. 'Be so good as to plot an evasion course through the Quirini Division. Calculate the location of the *Purgatorio*'s crash site and establish a low entry orbit around Spetzghast. Best possible speed: there's a good fellow.'

Krieg nodded and reholstered his hellpistol. Walking for the elevator he was joined by Mortensen and his men at the doors. Golliant was already holding them open with his brawny arms, allowing the commissar and the storm-troopers to walk in underneath. As the doors closed and the car began its descent, an awkward silence prevailed.

'You realise this is suicide?' Krieg eventually piped up.

The major grunted.

'You know,' he told the cadet-commissar, 'I like to think that anything is possible.'

'Yes,' Krieg returned. 'I've heard that about you.'

▌▌

VERTIGO WAS A wreck.

The Spectre was smashed up and running like a junker after her deathworld encounter, but Rosenkrantz would be damned before being relegated to an Arvus or humpshuttle.

Clearly the major felt much the same way, stamping up the ramp with his men, all with hastily donned carapace and hellpacks. Mortensen had given Rask the unenviable duty of coordinating the mass ground retrieval from one of the available Valkyries. Other aircraft laden with naval security contingents and the 364th's Second Platoon were lifting off the deck. Despite Meeks's men being cut to shreds, the sergeant had no qualms about kitting up and heading straight back out on the coat tails of Mortensen and the Redemption Corps. Mortensen shouldn't have been surprised. *Vertigo* was to carry Mortensen and his storm-troopers, leaving the rest of the hold empty in expectation of the recovered flagship's senior officer corps.

Somehow Captain Waldemar had negotiated the swarm of roks and hulks closing in on the unsuspecting Spetzghast and held precarious station in a low orbit above the *Purgatorio*'s last known trajectory, but below the descending asteroid storm front. He'd met Commissar Krieg's well-advertised deadline of two hours but what worried Rosenkrantz more was the length of time he'd be able to hold that position.

With Sigma Scorpii throwing the bronze glow of a new half-day over the horizon, *Vertigo* plunged through the cobalt clouds. Gunships, carriers and shuttles plummeted before them like a flock of birds evading a predator, banking and swirling into a vortex that spiralled for the surface. A squadron of Marauders thundered overhead, ghosting the rescue operation. Mortensen had insisted on bringing along Wharmby's bomber group for extra muscle, despite Waldemar's objections, just in case the greenskin hulk still needed softening up from the ground.

The major came up behind the co-pilot's station expecting to see Benedict. Rosenkrantz had been sorry to see him go, especially after saving her life down on the deathworld, but the servitor had to be taken off to wherever such things were taken when damaged or injured. The Jopallian shuddered to think: medicae-hall or repair shop, Rosenkrantz couldn't tell. Instead an unusually grave Leland Hoyt sat in the chair, trans-ferred from *White Thunder*. Hoyt, normally a fount of bright optimism, had returned from Illium a changed man. Gone was that boyish smile and playful good humour. Now the co-pilot looked as if he had the weight of the world on his shoulders.

Rosenkrantz sighed. Perhaps it was the view. Staring up through the cockpit plas she could spot the sinister silhouettes of the first mighty ork roks to kiss upper atmosphere.

'Major,' Hoyt said quietly, offering Mortensen a headset. '*Crow Road* – Captain Rask.'

Mortensen slipped on the set. 'Well?'

Rosenkrantz could hear the captain's craggy voice across her own vox-set: 'Zane, it's a hell of a mess down here. Looks like both vessels went down grappling but the impact was shallow: the crash site must stretch a good ten or twelve kilometres. Equatorial desert, so little in the way of local casualties – thank the Emperor.'

A brief respite, Rosenkrantz pondered, considering the hailstorm of colossal asteroids heading their way. *Vertigo* cut through the lower cloud layers, getting a glimpse of dawn reaching across the red barren wastes for the first time.

'Major,' Rosenkrantz called, drawing Mortensen's attention to the canopy.

'Yes, I can see it,' Mortensen declared. The *Purgatorio's* plasma drive and the hulk's sheer mass had propelled the two vessels in a dance of death towards the planet much faster than the stately pace of the converging ork roks. The crash site itself was now clear but for kilometres around a tsunami of dust and sand obscured surface detail.

Angular outcrops of rock and toxic metals had torn up both vessels badly, smashing up the *Purgatorio* and leaving flaming sections of the Dictator-class the length of the crash landing. The space hulk, robust as it was, had also suffered, breaking up on planetary impact: individual pieces of rock and scavenged alien craft, tumbling and scoring a wide tract of depth and destruction into the Spetzghastian surface.

'The command decks and bridge separated from the main body of the vessel in the crash,' Rask told them. 'They came down with a section of the hulk just off the main landing site. Transmitting the coordinates, now.'

Hoyt scanned his rune screens for the new information.

'Point two-five. Roll thirty degrees port-yaw.'

Rosenkrantz responded.

'I had *Prayerstalker* do a fly-by,' the captain continued. 'Not much left. *St. Scimitar* picked up a small
group of survivors from the dunes nearby. Among
them is the *Purgatorio*'s third lieutenant. He says the
command decks were the site of an overwhelming
boarding action – even before the crash. Says he
couldn't see much because of the smoke, but what he
did witness was all hand-to-hand, with prisoners
snatched and taken back to the hulk section close by.'

'Taken back?' Rosenkrantz questioned. 'That's a lot
of self-control for orks.'

'Nothing about these green-skinned bastards sur-
prises me anymore,' Mortensen enlightened her.
'They're a breed apart.'

'Major, the bombers,' she reminded him, the thought
only just occurring to her.

'Tyberius, call off Wharmby's Marauder group. With
friendlies being transported across the open space
between sections we can't afford bombing runs. Send
them back to *Deliverance* immediately.'

'Confirmed.'

'Okay, listen and listen good,' Mortensen said, pushing the vox-receiver close to his strained lips. 'Commit
all aircraft to make one touchdown – as soon as is
humanly possible. Order them to fill their holds and
everywhere else for that matter, with as many crash
survivors as they can. Then, back to the carrier. One
trip only. Make sure they understand.'

'What about you?' Rask sent back.

'We'll raid the hulk section for the captured officer
corps.'

'There's no time for that,' the officer insisted tightly.

'Make sure they understand, captain,' the major
repeated, 'One trip and then back to the ship.

Commander Waldemar will then get his trip to Aurelius. *Vertigo* out.'

Rosenkrantz craned her flight helmet around to see the storm-trooper. He gave her his grim, determined eyes.

'Take us to hell.'

The pilot complied.

III

MORTENSEN HAD VERTIGO close with the shattered hulk section. Even as just a piece of detached wreckage its dimensions were impressive. Rosenkrantz had found a gargantuan rent where the cratered rock face met time-burnished alloy and the crash had done its worst. Dropping the Spectre expertly in through the opening she was descending as fast as she dared, searching for a landing zone somewhere in the alien darkness.

The major stood helmetless on the tip of the aircraft's lowered ramp, hellgun humming.

'Ready?' he called casually over his shoulder.

Corporal Vedette and a hangdog Conklin joined him on the ramp, a gaggle of corpsmen huddled behind, going through final weapons prep. The doom-laden gloom of their surroundings did little to dampen the Mordian's spirits.

'I'm surprised you still ask, sir.'

Vertigo's ghostly hull lamps slipped down the cavernous wall of the enormous chamber they were traversing, passing across spectacular mineral deposits in the dull and dusty rock before glinting off rust-eaten hull and finally something distinctly biological.

'By all the saints and their bastard children,' Preed cursed. 'Where the hell are we?'

Mortensen turned. The barrel-bellied priest stood beside Krieg and his Volscian shadow, dwarfing both the cadet-commissar and even his aide with his immense girth. Golliant had snatched a snub-nosed Volscian-pattern autocannon from *Deliverance's* armoury and cradled the monster protectively above his charge's gleaming cap.

'Expect anything...' Mortensen told them. He scowled as he realised the only weapon Krieg was packing was his trusty hellpistol.

'I see a platform,' Vedette announced, peering off the edge of the ramp into the pit below. She hooked the tip of her boot under a coil of rope and kicked it over the side. Greco limped up the other side and did the same with his good foot.

Mortensen thumbed the troop bay vox. '*Vertigo*, hold position. Squad disembarking.'

Shouldering his hellgun and snapping his harness and descender to the line, Mortensen kicked off the aircraft and rappelled the deep, dark, distance between the Spectre and the platform. The soles of the major's boots touched down on the unnatural metal of the platform, his steps echoing eerily around the chasmal chamber. These became a hammer of footfalls as the storm-troopers gathered, establishing a holdpoint around the dangling ropes of their escape route.

Sarakota and a second almond-faced sniper crossed in front of Mortensen. They moved either side of him before going down on one knee and sweeping the inky murk of the hulk with the long, chunky barrels of their anti-materiel rifles. The snipers had detached their scopes, which would be all but useless in the cavernous confines of the spacecraft, but retained their Hellshots, more out of sentimentality than practicality.

'Should we fan out, sir?' Vedette checked. Mortensen's nose wrinkled. He didn't like the idea of splitting his firepower in here, but time wasn't on his side. He needed to locate the Imperial officers fast.

'Best guess?' Mortensen asked after giving the snipers a few moments to orient themselves. The tribesmen had grown up in a maze of cavern-systems and had the most finely-tuned senses of the squad.

'Between all the crotch scratching and boot shuffling it's a wonder we can hear anything,' the hot-headed Opech complained. He was fresh out of the infirmary and the pain of his wounds had made him cranky enough even to gripe at the major.

'Just give me the short version, corpsman,' Mortensen bit back.

'Difficult,' Sarakota murmured, embarrassed at his kinsman's hasty words. The Khongkotan tribesman had also been in the infirmary, but Mortensen hadn't heard anything other than a rib-fractured wince out of the sniper in complaint. 'The different materials and custom structure of the vessel make the vibrations hard to read.'

'Kota,' the major hushed. 'Where are my targets?'

The sniper turned his head this way and that and then sighed, settling. Taking the weight of his heavy rifle he got up off his knee, turned and headed off behind them. Mortensen stared after the disappearing Sarakota and then back to the remaining sniper. 'You?'

Opech similarly lifted his weapon and nodded. 'The walls still throb with recent activity to the north-east. Large numbers, moving fast.'

Mortensen looked at Conklin, Vedette and then Krieg.

The commissar shrugged, 'What are we waiting for?'

The Redemption Corps swept through the black cavities and passages of the hulk, hugging the walls and throwing the barrels of their weapons around lopsided corners. Conduits, hangars, vents, gangways: all alien and ancient. And upside down. From what the major could make out, and he was no expert, craft after bizarre craft had been melded together into some kind of amorphous whole: some without care for orientation or natural gravity.

'Incredible,' Preed mumbled every so often, soaking up the foreign grandeur of the place. Greco was less enthused, hobbling up unnatural inclines and maintaining an almost constant stream of reasons why they should probably be heading back: the officers were probably dead, the hulk was so massive they could easily miss them, I think we're being watched. He began a cautionary tale about the time he broke into the Sultana Babooshka's tower villa, but Mortensen stopped him, telling him to stick to what he was actually good at, which was shutting the vrek up.

Every so often the progenium runaway and archlarcenist would be called upon to run a bypass on a security bulkhead or some other fused and ancient egress, and when that didn't work Uncle had to create an artificial opening with his cordite charges and melta bombs.

Sarakota and Opech pushed on ahead with their hefty anti-materiel Hellshots primed, swinging the heavy rifles crisply around dark corners like they had done this kind of thing before. Eszcobar fiddled with the regulator on his flame unit, the Autegan favouring the incinerator over his trusty grenade launcher in the confines of the hulk. Krieg was strangely quiet, hellpistol in one hand and a chunky arc lamp in the other, aiming both experimentally up a narrow, twisted stairwell: expecting trouble. In the tight corridors and labyrinthine shafts of the massive hulk, the commissar clearly favoured the side arm/lamp combo, more so that he didn't fall to his death down some hidden duct or pipe.

Mortensen merely stabbed at the shadows with the muzzle of his hellgun, ready to blast to oblivion anything stupid enough to stick its ugly face out of the darkness at him. He was getting impatient, their distance from the bird growing at the same time the minutes were ticking away in the back of his skull. Despite the immediate threat of his surroundings he couldn't quite get the vision of thousands of heavily-armed asteroids falling out of the Spetzghastian sky out of his mind. He wanted those officers, though. Organised Imperial resistance in the system might depend on them being alive and Mortensen sure as hell didn't want to end up as ranking officer on the precipice of an opening greenskin warzone.

Climbing through a warped, open bulkhead, the major was hit by the powerful stench of fumes from the chamber beyond. Flashing his rifle lamp around he found his boots smeared with a brown oily substance that had seemed to cover the entire floor of the chamber. Sass's occasional chant of 'Commodore van den Groot', 'Brigadier Voskov' or 'Lord Commissar Ver-hoeven' boomed in the new chamber. It seemed to stretch for hundreds of metres.

'Sir, I think you should look at this,' Sarakota called gently. Krieg and the adjutant had pushed on. Loping up behind them, the group gathered around. They had found the commodore. Greco jerked back, hand over his mouth like he had been physically struck. The others just looked blankly at the pile of entrails and the bloodied naval cloak that had once been the fleet commander. Vedette plucked the commodore's ridiculously flamboyant hat from the mess, shaking the gore from the feathers and wiping clean the leather around the emblazoned aquila. She handed it to the major. It was definitely van den Groot.

'Greenskins did this?' asked Preed.

'Maybe,' Mortensen replied.

'Come on,' Greco broke in, 'the fat bastard's been turned inside out.' The trooper was seriously starting to lose his cool. Mortensen grunted. He'd fought greenskins across the galaxy. They did not kill like this.

'Movement…' Sarakota called, strangely without a hint of panic. The effect on the others was instantaneous: weapons came up and lamp beams were thrown around the darkness. The sniper knelt down, sinking his knee into the oily brown residue and touching the deck with his fingertips.

It all happened fast. Kynt span around, simultaneously bringing up his hellgun. As the twitchy comms-officer fired, Mortensen kicked the barrel aside, sending the blasts thudding harmlessly into the blackness. In the illumination of Eszcobar's lamp, Brigadier Voskov of the Volscian Shadow Brigade stumbled forward holding a broken arm. He looked like a cadaver in the harsh light. His immaculate if dour uniform was gore splashed and torn and his gunmetal grey crew-cut matted with blood from a gash on his head. His craggy face was etched with more than just years and the expression of martial fanaticism that never usually left his face had gone. Only a blankness remained.

He fell against Krieg, who half caught him. Holstering his weapon, he cradled the spireborn to the deck. The brigadier looked like he had been to hell and back. He tried to say something but choked and descended into a coughing fit. Sergeant Minghella knelt in and gave him a sip of water from his canteen. Voskov's eyes rolled over and bulged. Once again he tried to say something.

'Easy,' the medic told him.

'Redemption Corps,' he managed to the major, through an agonised smile. Mortensen didn't think he'd ever seen the Volscian commander smile before.

'Don't try and talk, Gil. We'll get you and your officers out of here,' Mortensen pledged solemnly.

'Rescue…' the brigadier croaked, before seeming to relax for a moment. A throttled chuckle escaped his torn lips. His throat was swollen and his neck violently bruised. 'No…' he hissed.

'Rhen?' Mortensen prompted his medic.

'Head wound,' Minghella found in the Volscian's wiry hair. The sergeant would know: he sported a fresh one himself from their crash on Ishtar. 'Looks like he's been out for a while. Severe trauma to the neck and throat: beyond that superficial cuts and bruises, most likely from the crash. We need to get him out of here and on some oxygen.'

Voskov shook his head violently, froth bubbling up around the edges of his mouth. He said something but Mortensen couldn't make it out and leaned in closer.

'Sir, what is it?'

Again, a rasping emptiness.

'Gil?'

'Leave here!' the Volscian managed finally.

Suddenly the deck was lit up by a las blast. Voskov's head fell back and his hand clattered to the floor. In it Krieg found his own hellpistol, slipped out of his holster. While the storm-troopers had fussed over their commanding officer, he'd taken the weapon from Krieg's person and got the muzzle to his temple.

The Redemption Corps stared at each other in disbelief.

'I...' Krieg began, but there wasn't time for explanations or regrets. Mortensen shook his head at the commissar.

'Trap,' he said with conviction. He didn't have to wait long for confirmation of his suspicions.

'Footsteps. Large number this time: closing with caution,' Sarakota announced.

Mortensen span around, taking a fleeting three-hundred and sixty degree glance at the surrounding darkness. He re-primed the hellgun. 'Remember we're looking for friendlies in here.'

'I see 'em!' Greco cried out, demonstrating none of Sarakota's self control. The muzzle of his hellgun flashed as he let off a stream of fire into the empty gloom. Conklin, Kynt and several others joined in, the master sergeant's bolter in particular, puncturing holes in the darkness.

When nothing appeared Mortensen ordered, 'Stand fast!' The automatic fire died but Greco's hellgun was still dribbling short bursts at the shadows and Uncle had to thump him in the shoulder to get him to stop. 'What'd you see?' the major demanded as soon as the corpsman had finished.

'S-S-Skins, I think,' the spire breaker told him.

'You think?' Vedette marvelled.

'They were vrekkin' green. I don't know.'

'Kota?'

'Still closing.'

Krieg was still on the floor with the dead Volscian commander, flashing his lamp in the direction of the sighting. Mortensen snatched the fat arc lamp straight out of Krieg's outstretched hand and falling into a crouch himself, skimmed the lamp across the chamber. The light travelled far, carried along by the viscous brown tar coating the walls and floor. Suddenly it struck something and flipped, bathing the area in a moment of radiance.

Damn.

The chamber was full of creatures. Armoured and huge, they were all claws and tusks, arms outstretched like fast-moving crustaceans. And green.

Mortensen's mind shot back to his encounter in the darkness of the *Mortis Maximus*. What he'd glimpsed for merely a second on the artillery deck of the Titan was staring him in the face now, intent on ripping it off with tooth and claw. Long experience had prepared the major for first contact with many heinous alien races, but these creatures seemed neither one thing nor another. They were brawny and muscular like orks, but moved with an alien dexterity and grace that shot fear into the heart of every man and woman in the chamber.

'Flamer! Now!' Mortensen roared.

When the blast didn't come, the major turned, half expecting Eszcobar to have fled. He wouldn't have blamed him. The sketch the lamp had painted in the deep darkness of the chamber was enough to strike cold fear into the chests of all who had witnessed it.

As it was, he was still having difficulty priming the gas reservoir and setting the regulator. The deathworlder had been so preoccupied with the drama on the deck that he hadn't noticed the pilot flame flicker and die in the unimpeded draught of the chamber. As the storm-trooper fingered the flamer furiously, it let out an angry chugging sound, followed by a whining hiss.

Rounds ricocheted off green carapace as Vedette and her master sergeant attempted to lay down suppressing fire. The creatures came forth in a wave and seemed completely undeterred by the Redemption Corps assault.

'Get that weapon operational, trooper!' Krieg yelled at the stunned Eszcobar, but the weapon merely churned promethium. Mortensen hammered the advancing line of monsters with everything his hellgun had to offer before hastily adjusting the power setting and giving them some more.

Kynt shot past him, eyepatch askew, squinting with his good eye and peppering the green horde with auto-matic fire from his pistol. Mortensen grabbed the back of his master-vox and tore the comms-officer back, burying a salvo of fire in the encroaching left flank.

The cadet-commissar was suddenly beside him, the steaming barrel of his hellpistol resting across one shoulder and lancing the mob with bolts.

'We're not going to find anyone in this,' he managed between blasts, giving the major the moments he needed to re-orient his weapon. Mortensen nodded bitterly and went back to work with the angry hellgun.

'Fall back!' he bellowed. 'Back to the bulkhead.' Between them, Krieg, Mortensen and Conklin pushed the storm-troopers back. Vedette and Minghella were already supporting a gutted Uncle between them, one of the creatures having bounded impossibly at them, ripping into the demolitions man with its dagger-like claws. Golliant messed the beast up with a close-range hammering from the autocannon, leaving the blasted creature twitching on the deck as the hulking adjutant retreated.

The autocannon was singing over the storm-troopers now, keeping the worst of the swarm at bay with the two snipers adding to the mayhem with crashing fire from their Hellshots.

Sweeping the darkness with his rifle the major turned and pushed Sass and a pistol-reloading Kynt into the retreat, only for all three of them to come face to face with more monsters, who'd scuttled up behind them. 'Close quarters!' Mortensen bawled, but before he knew it one of the barbed bastards was among them, slicing through armour and slashing Sass across the face as the adjutant swung his rifle around to bear. It snapped wildly at Kynt as the comms-officer struggled to wedge in a new clip in his autopistol. Mortensen swung his rifle at the creature like a bat, but the stock simply bounced off the alien's plated skull. A ribbed hand found its way to the makeshift club and snatched it free of the major's grip. Before he could blink the green fiend had slashed it in half with the sabre claws on another limb, the one piece falling uselessly to the deck – the other sparking and trailing from his hellpack powerline.

The major kicked the heel of one booted foot at the beast but it merely retreated, sweeping its jaws past the still struggling Kynt, ripping out the trooper's throat. Mortensen's furious face was sprayed with warm blood from the fountaining wound.

Demonstrating a stone cold understanding that Kynt was finished, the armoured, puce-green thing was coming at him again, without the comms officer's body even having chance to reach the slick floor. Mortensen was ready for the beast also, having sloughed off his hellpack and pitching it at the monster with both hands.

The alien menace shrugged off the impact, talons flashing forward, but the pack had provided Mortensen with the opportunity to slip a storm blade from his thigh-sheath and he batted the wicked claw aside. Another came and Mortensen span into the creature's embrace, grabbing its outstretched wrist with his gauntleted hand and lopping its appendage off at the trunk.

Again the monster retracted, retreating behind its barbed grapplers. Light and brains suddenly erupted from its forehead, the green monstrosity shuddering and falling. Commissar Krieg was standing behind, the shimmering muzzle of his hellpistol aimed along the length of his tensed arm. Krieg seemed to notice something, squinting into the darkness, and shot off through the mayhem. There was little time for celebration.

Golliant's arc of explosive death swept by, driving back the closing gauntlet of alien bodies. Several determined slayers braved the shower of slugs and sparks, vaulting at the throng of storm-troopers, instinctively exploiting opportunities and holes in the fire pattern.

Uncle's high-pitched shrieks echoed around the ancient vastness of the chamber, the demolitions man dragged off into the darkness and run through with razor-sharp claws. Clutching his own gushing belly wound Eszcobar was now dragging Greco: one of the creatures had done something terrible to his back and the trooper could no longer walk unaided. Green carapace was suddenly all over them, monsters leaping above the autocannon's hailstorm and landing on top of the unfortunate corpsmen.

Vedette and Conklin had been carrying a mauled Sass but had been forced to lay both hands on their weapons during the unrelenting assault. The two of them beat the armoured forms with the protrusion mags and grips of their autopistols but as the malformed faces emerged from the armoured shell of torsos swamping Opech, it was clear the tribesman had been savaged and was dead.

'Back!' Vedette ordered.

'Yes, ma'am,' Greco agreed, grimacing at the agony lancing through his back. But there was nowhere to go. The aliens were all around them and around the aliens was cold, harsh darkness. The shadows just kept spawning wave upon concentric wave of monsters.

Mortensen buried his storm blade in the armoured skull of a passing alien, but the thing barely seemed fazed, shaking the survival knife free. Reaching for his autopistol Mortensen brought the fat side arm level with the creature's disturbing face. The weapon bucked as it disgorged its explosive package, taking the alien's head with it into the darkness. Feverishly plugging green bodies left and right, Mortensen blasted a path through to Pontiff Preed.

Unarmed, the gargantuan priest had been able to contribute little to the suppression fire that had so far kept the full weight of the mob from swamping them. Up close and personal the huge ecclesiarch came into his own. A red mist had descended on Preed's contorted features. Charging like a cannonball he blasted into a throng of the vicious creatures intent on overwhelming a withdrawing Minghella on a pistol reload.

The green tide parted, alien bodies and limbs flying this way and that. Several went down under the priest's pummelling fists as he thundered into the enemy line. Sarakota redirected his merciless fire to re-establish the distance and capitalise on Preed's insane assault. Golliant would have joined them but the steaming autocannon had feed-jammed and the aide was forced to use the ungainly weapon as a club, swinging it in a wide arc and keeping the monsters away from the open bulkhead they'd used to enter the fuel chamber. Krieg was already there, holding the exit with blinding fire from his hellpistol and directing blank and bloody corpsmen through the opening.

One savage beast sailed over Mortensen in one impressive bound, landing squarely on Preed's fleshy back. His white robes tore and streaked red as the monster dug in with its talons and brought its horrific maw in for the kill. The snaggle-toothed alien opened its jaws and shot an ovipositor at his face. The ecclesiarch strained, desperate that the muscular, eel-like appendage not reach his bloodied lips. Rage burned in his eyes and the priest finally opened his own mouth and chomped on the length of the alien thing with his own teeth. Snapping the horrible appendage free of the monstrous mouth from which it came, Preed spat out the ovipositor and wrenched the creature over one shoulder, bouncing its thick skull twice off the deck before flinging the thing up into the air.

Mortensen had been slamming a fresh magazine into the grip of his chunky pistol when the thing landed in an untidy heap in front of him. Snapping back the autoslide, he blew the thing off its feet as the monster tried to scramble up off the oily deck. Two further storms of shot peeled another pair of green gargoyles from the ecclesiarch's limbs.

'Pontiff!' the major yelled, slapping the priest on one sliced-up shoulder. The giant turned on him, his teeth clenched and his eyes unthinking. 'Preed!' Mortensen tried again, before breaking off to blow a hole through the shoulder plate of another monster attempting to scale the man-mountain before him. The alien went somersaulting back into the bloodthirsty crowd. The priest barely noticed. Mortensen leaned in close: 'Father, we have to leave. *Now!*'

Grabbing a fistful of bloody robes Mortensen tugged at the giant, leading him towards the bulkhead and the hands and gaunt faces picked out in the shadow of the opening, gesturing wildly at them to hurry. Sarakota had only just abandoned his post and was manhandling his long Hellshot through the doorway, leaving Krieg and Golliant either side of the heavy maintenance duct entrance, the commissar cutting into the hordes with supercharged las-bolts, his aide pounding into the deck anything that got past with the jammed autocannon.

Preed followed, gradually returning to his senses, and even picking up the pace a little to get there ahead of the major, providing enough time to cram his corpulent bulk through. Golliant and Krieg followed, leaving the major alone in the chamber with the bulbous hordes. Mortensen turned for the final few metres, emptying the pistol as fast as he could into the converging masses.

'Ready?' he called to the corpsmen waiting in the entrance.

'Ready,' Conklin bawled back and Golliant's tree trunk arms shot out of the bulkhead opening and latched onto the back of the major's carapace suit. Mortensen shot backwards through doorway and found himself in the cramped passage surrounded by shocked and shivering storm-troopers. Conklin had Greco on the door controls, the spire breaker somehow managing to re-route power and breathe new life into the door mechanism. The bulkhead shot across on its rail and sealed the encroaching army of savage creatures on the other side.

The entire squad went limp, the relief visible on every man and woman's face. Minghella quickly went to work on a quietly groaning Sass and Vedette secured the passage ahead with her blood-splattered hellgun.

Mortensen expected the hammer of blows on the maintenance bulkhead, but they never came. His eyes flickered around the dim compartment before resting his sweat-beaded brow on the cool metal of the door.

From behind came a strange whoosh and the sigh of lock clearance. Mortensen lifted his head slightly, straining to hear. Suddenly the metal in front of him rolled aside revealing the full horror of alien jaws. Panic swept the passage with Preed and Golliant lending their weight to the rapidly opening door.

'Greco…' Conklin began.

The spire breaker swore. 'They must have severed the hydraulics,' he blurted in amazement.

The creature's head vaulted out of the darkness and through the growing opening, snapping at the stunned major. Mortensen brought up his autopistol with a growl and yanked on the trigger. The unsatisfactory click of an empty firing mechanism filled the compartment. With sudden urgency the major re-worked the slide and tried again but the pistol was spent.

Claws and fingers from the chamber beyond filled the aperture, intent on forcing the door open. Mortensen pounded on the alien digits with the grip of his weapon but made little impression on the armoured knuckles. Conklin and Greco – who was fading fast and slumped against the wall – were arguing about the door mechanism, the corpsman professing that there was nothing he could do with it now. Meanwhile it took all of the strength of the huge pontiff and Krieg's aide combined just to hold the bulkhead where it was.

A sudden hiss at the back of the compartment grabbed the major's attention. As Krieg and Sarakota parted he saw Eszcobar with his back to the wall of the compartment, the pilot flame burning victoriously at the end of the deathworlder's flamer. Pushing Conklin back away from the door and shielding his face, Mortensen told him: 'Burn it.'

The Autegan came forward, sticking the barrel in through a space between the gnashing alien jaws and grasping claws and bathed the bodies beyond in a raging stream of thick flame.

The response was instantaneous. Claws and faces disappeared, as did the weight on the door. Pulling back the deathworlder allowed Preed and Golliant to slam the bulkhead shut once again. Beyond the inferno raged.

Heavy breathing and involuntary smiles filled the passage.

Greco put into words what everyone else was thinking: 'What the vrekkin' hell were they?'

'They're genestealers,' Krieg answered coldly.

It took a moment for the corpsmen to soak up the concept with their adrenaline-addled brains.

Mortensen nodded: 'Hybrids.'

'Ork-genestealer hybrids?' Greco echoed, racing to catch up. 'That's impossible.'

'Unfortunately not, my son,' Preed rumbled from the back, back to his old bookish self. 'Why, we've known for a long time that genestealer races use human hosts to pass on genetic material. Why not other races? Orks are amongst the most widespread races in the galaxy.'

'The genestealers could have already been on board the hulk, when it came out of warpspace in a greenskin system,' Krieg hypothesised. 'A greenskin salvage team were probably infected when they tried to get the ship operational again. It's not that hard to imagine.'

'It explains everything,' Mortensen admitted grimly. 'System infiltration. The cultists on Illium. The roks and teleporters… Greenskin tech is notoriously unreliable – but imagine the brute hordes guided by the cold logic and singular purpose of genestealers. You'd have the best – or very worst – of both voidspawn species.'

'And Spetzghast,' the cadet-commissar added. 'Cross-species infection. The psionic fields produced by the different races would play havoc with one another. Add humans to the mix and well, no wonder you've got spree murders and general mayhem across the system.' Krieg shook his head. 'The orks and their allies have been importing reproductive pods with common agricultural freight. Even without the orbital bombardment, this system's doomed.'

'Not just this system,' Preed interjected. 'This isn't a greenskin warlord on a roll here. The cold alien discipline of the 'stealers combined with greenskin resilience and numbers. Think of the systems that could already have been infiltrated.'

'Sir,' Vedette addressed the major; the Mordian, as always focused on the mission and less on the trivia. 'What about the targets?'

Mortensen bit at his bottom lip. He was thinking of Voskov and what they must have done to him and the mind-aching discipline it must have taken to do what he did.

Decided, Mortensen announced: 'We're leaving them.'

'Sir,' the Mordian continued with undying professionalism. 'The commodore wasn't far–'

'You can't help them,' Krieg told her.

'With all due respect–'

'They'll be infected, my child,' Preed assured her with paternal benevolence.

'Boss,' Conklin said with his ear to the compartment wall. Mortensen joined him at the door. More strange noises were emanating from beyond, this time something bigger than a clearing door mechanism. Eszcobar's flamer had driven the monsters back and hopefully had fried a couple in the process. What Mortensen was hearing, on the other hand, equated to hundreds of mournful alien shrieks swallowed in the boom of a full-scale inferno. There was also some thrashing.

Mortensen pulled away from the tarnished metal, hawked and spat on the bulkhead. Anxiously he rubbed at the spot with the bottom of his fist, revealing an ancient designation plaque: 'Maintenance Duct C – Reserve Fuel Tank.'

Mortensen could barely imagine what it must have been like in there: monsters having their shadows burnt into the walls and floor as the fuel vapour erupted around them. The Redemption Corps had more urgent problems. The bulkhead began to grow hot to the touch and tremble on its rails.

'Go, go, go, go!' the major urged, pushing the storm-troopers out of the compartment and away from the door. Moments later the bulkhead was blasted out of its seals, blue flame fanning out across the ceiling. The corpsmen hit the deck, shielding themselves from the intense heat. Only Mortensen could stand the unbearable temperature, feeling nothing as he did, and pulled the last of his men through a second bulkhead. Gritting his teeth, the soot-stained officer slammed his shoulder against the hatch and manually rolled it aside.

As the air in the corridor cooled, the troopers staggered tentatively to their feet cursing and complaining.

'Quiet!' Sarakota suddenly cried putting his hand up and twisting his head left and right.

'What can you hear?' Mortensen demanded.

The sniper was about to reply but the words died in his throat. He merely looked up in horror. A pair of grapnel-like claws shot out of a ceiling vent behind them, hooking themselves under Eszcobar's jaw and tearing him up off his feet. The hybrid had problems getting the death-worlder up through the opening at first, with the Autegan refusing to let go of his bulky flamer. The corpsmen were largely back on the floor but Preed and Sarakota were near enough to grab for the trooper's flailing boots. Eszcobar's spasming trigger finger caused his flamer to chug sporadic puffs of flame wildly around the room, forcing both men to duck.

Krieg was better placed from behind and leapt for the corpsman's rapidly disappearing legs. The creature wasn't going to release its prize that easily, however.

Eszcobar let out an awful roar of pain and frustration that echoed horribly around the vent system. There was a crack and a gush from above. It looked like Krieg had had a bucket of blood poured over him. The death-worlder's arms went limp and the ungainly flame unit fell to the floor. With this the Autegan's body was tugged upwards, taking Krieg's head and right arm up into the vent. Now Krieg's Commissariat trousers were flailing, his left hand patting furiously for his hellpistol.

This time it was Golliant who got to the vent, grabbing one of the commissar's leather boots, preventing Krieg ascending any further. Mortensen dived for the second, swinging from the commissar's calf, hoping the extra weight and momentum would drag him down. A similarly horrific roar was building in the cadet-commissar's chest as the two soldiers wrestled him down.

Something gave and all three men tumbled to the floor. As Mortensen pushed himself off the deck he was stunned to realise that Krieg had lost his right arm at the shoulder: the slashed leather greatcoat hid the worst of the gushing stump, torn flesh and sheared bone. Sarakota swooped under the vent, pushing the business end of his rifle up through the opening, plugging round after explosive round up at the creature. Finally the rifle ran dry and the hybrid's strange, alien screeching died away, the commissar's amputated limb falling back out of the vent with a light thud.

'Vrek that!' Greco declared shaking his head and hugging his hellgun to his chest. Keeping his injured back to the wall he sidled along the corridor away from the gaping vent. Ordinarily Mortensen would order him back but had to admit that the corpsman had the right idea. They had to get back to *Vertigo*.

'Sergeant, get 'em up,' Mortensen ordered, looking at Krieg's vacant and mangled face. 'Back to the bird, double time it.'

Minghella was already up to his elbows in the commissar's gore.

'Rhen, we've got to go,' Mortensen insisted firmly.

'Got to clamp this artery or he'll bleed out well before we reach the bird,' grumbled Minghella, half to himself.

'Better him than us, sergeant,' Mortensen barked.

'Got it!' Minghella announced, precious moments later.

Vedette and Sergeant Conklin started barking orders and encouragement, pulling the injured Sass and Greco to their feet. Minghella took the arm of the dazed and bleeding Necromundan over his shoulders. Conklin did the same with the spire-breaker.

'Vedette, we lost the master-vox. See if you can raise Rosenkrantz on the bead,' the major continued. 'Inform the flight lieutenant that we will be requiring an immediate evacuation.'

'Roger that, sir,' the Mordian returned with bleak enthusiasm.

Mortensen watched a stone-faced Golliant scoop Krieg's trembling body up from the blood-drenched floor and throw him carefully across one shoulder, the commissar's detached limb in his other hand. Nodding, Mortensen watched the solemn aide stride up the corridor before turning his attention back to Sarakota who was still pointing his rifle at the ceiling.

Mortensen snatched up Eszcobar's blood-drenched weapon and handed it to the sniper who abandoned his own spent rifle.

'Kota, get up front and find me a way back out of this deathtrap.' Holding the flame unit out in front of him with both hands the corpsman ran from the room. Casting his eyes up at the vent with a shudder, Mortensen did the same.

What was left of the troop hurtled along the foreign passages and oddly-orientated corridors of the alien hulk. The horrific denizens of the place were not the only reason for their hustle. A chain reaction of explosions was now wracking the warped vessel, undoubtedly initiated by their unintentional ignition of the reserve tank fuel vapour. Most of the time the dull detonations seemed to be tearing up the craft in the sections behind the escaping corpsmen, but occasionally they sounded like they were ahead of the fleeing column of soldiers, no doubt down to the vessel's insane design and construction. The second and even more pressing concern was the fact that a gathering horde of hybrids not far behind them, crawling literally out of the metalwork and flooding the passages with danger and death.

Mortensen had never been so glad to see the *Vertigo* – and she was always a welcome sight. Rosenkrantz had brought the bird down further into the cavernous chamber and hovered above the platform still trailing their ropes. Then the damnedest thing happened. *Vertigo* opened fire.

At first the major thought the pilot was offering cover fire as usual: he expected the vicious hybrids to be on their backs at any moment. The Spectre's autocannons were shredding the deck in front of their toecaps however, driving the corpsmen back across the platform and into the embrace of their pursuers.

'Vedette!' the major bellowed. She hadn't reached Rosenkrantz and now he was beginning to realise why.

Black-armoured shapes began to appear on the ramp and rappel down the dangling ropes. For the first time Mortensen noticed the damage in the troop bay: the shredded conduits hanging from the ceiling, the faint smoke still escaping from the crew compartment. It looked like the Spectre had been rushed: taken by force with grenades and merciless determination. As the autocannons fell silent it became apparent that Flight Lieutenant Rosenkrantz was no longer in command of the craft, forced down to the edge of the ramp as she was, hands bound behind her back and pushed down onto her knees. Her captor was a slender figure in obsidian armour and a ribbed cape, sporting a crown of twinkling metal pins that were inserted over her entire skull. She was holding a bolt pistol to the pilot's temple.

If that were not plain enough, two Inquisitorial Valkyries dropped down out of the roof, flanking the captured Spectre and fixing the storm-troopers in their sights. The first wave of battle-sisters down off the ropes were now advancing towards them, helmets on and bolters raised. A Celestian with a skull face-plate came boldly forward, the barrel of her bolt pistol never straying from the major's chest.

'Drop your weapons!' she ordered simply.

The corpsmen looked around at each other, the prospect of abandoning even an empty weapon daunting. Conklin hugged his beloved bolter and threw the gathering one of his replacement fingers. Mortensen pulled the master sergeant's arm down. Enough of his men had died today for what amounted now to little more than a half-baked idea.

The major wouldn't sacrifice any more just for him and it was clear from what Krieg had told him that was what they were here for.

'Do as she says,' the major told them unequivocally; slowly unbuckling his belt and letting it fall to the floor. Vedette hesitated and Mortensen could feel her eyes around the chamber, looking for an opportunity, a chink in the armour. 'While we still have time, corporal,' the major added softly.

Slipping out of her hellpack, the Mordian allowed the weapon system to topple to the platform. One by one the Redemption Corps emulated their officer, reluctantly abandoning their weapons and raising their palms, including Golliant, who had to dump Krieg's beloved hellpistol on the deck.

As one of the sisters came up behind the major and began to bind his wrists behind his back, the skull-faced Celestian drifted forward, resting the muzzle of her ivory inlaid bolt pistol on his chest.

'Your mistress is going to wish that she'd never met me,' Mortensen told the sister with menace.

'On the contrary,' the Celestian came back confidently. 'She's been looking forward to this for a very long time.'

IV

THE INCARCETORIUM WAS in chaos: fleeing security staff; escaping corpsmen; a full-scale prison riot and battle-sisters fighting for their lives.

The only route through the complex that Krieg's time locks had left secure was the maximum-security subway, leading between the oubliette sub-section that held the incarcetorium's most dangerous criminals and the compound landing strip.

Sidling along the subway wall, his right arm still strapped to his chest where Crayne had re-attached and bound it and the ivory-inlaid bolt pistol gripped firmly in his left, Krieg waited and listened behind a sharp corner. He was finally rewarded by the march of boots on the rockcrete and the sound of something being scraped along the floor.

Krieg waited. And waited.

+Koulick Krieg...+ Like a jackhammer inside his mind. The inquisitor was inside his head again. Not this again, the commissar thought. Not now.

+...Kriiiiieg+

Blood fell from his nose in a brief, thick stream, striking the rockcrete floor with a splat. The hand around the pistol began to shake, but not in the way he'd come to expect. His whole arm felt pumped for action: the adrenaline burning through his veins. Instead of the disorientation and sickness that overwhelmed him before, he felt completely in tune with his surroundings: like he was capable of anything, despite his pitiable physical condition. His heart flooded with the desire to kill. The pistol felt like it was going to explode in his hand if he didn't sate its desire to end lives with it. The commissar's eyes narrowed. This wasn't common bloodlust or battle fury. Only one life would do.

Finally two sisters rounded the corner, dragging something between them. The first couldn't have even seen him. His bolt pistol simply slid forward along the wall and spat several rounds of explosive-tip straight through her temple. The second had a millisecond to come to terms with the very definite fact that she was going to die. Instead she decided to go for something on her belt, dropping the load she was carrying with her compatriot. It didn't make any difference to Krieg. He still spread the contents of her devout little mind across the subway wall.

It was only then the commissar realised that they had in fact been carrying the major and that he'd come very close to blowing the Gomorrian's head off. At first he thought he had, Mortensen's body lying as it had fallen in a naked heap. He wasn't moving.

Stepping out fully from behind the corner, Krieg presented himself to the remaining battle-sisters. Diamanta Santhonax stood there, a vision in her obsidian armour and dramatic cloak, the pins adorning her shaven head glimmering in the dim light of the corridor. Her thin lips curled unreadably. Krieg brought up the bolt pistol. It was her life he needed.

The canoness's bodyguard stepped out from behind her. As usual the odd-looking fourteen year old was clutching the adamantium relic of their order – the crusader shield of St. Valeria the Younger. Her eyes, always seeming to Krieg just a little too far apart, flashed with a feline intelligence but the rest of her face was just a lifeless mask. She was nimble, even in her ancient armour, and broke into a run, darting up the subway at the commissar, her ermine-lined cloak flowing behind her.

Instead Krieg was forced to turn the wrath of his side arm on the henchwoman, but she had a well-practiced fashion of hiding her agile little form fully behind the shield as she rocketed up the passage towards him. Krieg hammered the relic time and again, hoping age had weakened the ancient shield, but the adamantium soaked up the punishment. Sparks flared off the metal, the bolts not even leaving the hint of a blemish on the gleaming surface.

In seconds the ammunition was spent and the Celestian leapt the final few metres, using the shield to batter Krieg into the wall. She was light, but the artefact wasn't and the impact made the cadet-commissar cry out as the shield pressed his strapped arm into his chest and his chest into the wall.

Krieg had no time to get over the burning throb rattling up and down the delicate, re-attached limb. The subway was echoing with the chugging bleat of the short chainsabre the henchwoman had drawn from behind the shield. The sister gunned the sabre and flew at Krieg, swinging the blur of wicked barbs in well-practiced manoeuvres. As Krieg ducked and weaved like a drunkard, the sister span and swung, carving up the wall in plumes of dust-shredded rockcrete. Krieg realised that he couldn't keep up with the furious assault when the chainblade came in low and wide and ripped across the flesh of his thigh. He clutched the deep wound with his good hand and staggered into a clumsy evasion.

The sabre came straight at him, the intended target his solar plexus. His awkward turn managed to grant him the precious centimetres he needed and the force intended to take the sword through his body actually put the sabre deep into the wall by his hip. Krieg knew he couldn't waste the opportunity and snatched at the sister's face with his bloodied hand. For his trouble the henchwoman brought the adamantium edge of her shield across his jaw, slamming the back of his skull into the wall. She brought it back and forth in this way, sloshing the commissar's head around like a toy until he released his grip and crumbled to the floor.

Putting one boot up against the wall she gunned the sabre handle once more and heaved the struggling chainblade out of its rockcrete scabbard. Krieg heard the blade slow to an idle chug as the sister held it over him. Looking up Krieg saw her glance at Santhonax for approval to kill him. Santhonax stepped over the still, naked body of Zane Mortensen and clapped her gauntlets together in cruel appreciation.

'Cadet-Commissar Krieg,' she grinned nastily. 'I gave you a simple task: I asked you to kill one man. I gave you the authority and opportunity and you failed miserably. Please forgive me if I don't seem a little more concerned.'

'Any thug can kill,' Krieg echoed from their earlier conversation.

'And yet you seem to have trouble doing it.'

'I'm happy to disappoint you,' the commissar croaked. 'But tell that to your battle-sisters and the pilots of your carriers. I didn't have too much trouble with them.'

The canoness's grin waned: 'If that's the truth then they're even more pathetic than you are and therefore don't deserve to live.' She nodded coldly at the hench-woman. 'End this fool's feeble existence.'

The chainsabre roared. The commissar steeled himself for the furious blade. He flashed his eyes once more at the prone major, surprised to find him not so prone anymore. Swinging his legs around for momentum and his lower back off the floor, Mortensen brutally ham-strung the canoness, sweeping her boots clean out from under her. He'd picked the moment perfectly. So unex-pected was the attack that Santhonax fell straight back, unable to break the fall with her gauntlets, and smacked the back of her head sickeningly against the rockcrete. The adamantium pins found their mark, hammering straight through the skull and into the brain.

The chainsabre died in the henchwoman's fingers as she watched her mistress fit and spasm on the floor, with blood frothing and dribbling out of the corner of her mouth. Mortensen squirmed around, holding his meaty elbow above her nose in an open threat. One move from the Celestian and the storm-trooper would drive his arm through the battle-sister's face and drive the pins in flush to the bone, killing Santhonax instantly.

'You have your orders,' Santhonax coughed with fanatical determination at the henchwoman.

Bolstered by the canoness's insane certainty, the battle-sister brought the hungry blade back to life above the cadet-commissar. Once again, Krieg prepared himself for the buzzing caress of weapon's serrated teeth. For the second time in as many moments, Mortensen saved his life.

Tearing the canoness's tapered pistol out of its belt holster, the major blasted at the henchwoman, the lasbolts slashing at the side of her face and forcing her to bring up the crusader shield. The final few impacted uselessly on the artefact, but as the shield lowered Krieg could see the major had caught her several times on the cheek and once in the eye. Instead of the usual cauterised holes the commissar had come to expect from a laspistol, the wounds were merely light burns, although the one in her eye had clearly ruptured something.

The chainsabre clattered to the floor and the heavy adamantium shield came down, dragging the svelte body of the henchwoman down with it like an anchor. Her one good panic-stricken eye jumped around the room, but her body lay awkward and motionless as though she were paralysed.

Mortensen turned back to the canoness, his elbow still hovering above her face. She gritted her perfect teeth and willed him on.

'You said you'd kill me.'

'What, and prove your sick fanatical fantasies true: whatever fails to destroy us makes us stronger?' The major hawked and spat at the wall. 'Well, I rather think to let you live.'

The major got up and walked unsteadily towards the henchwoman and ripped the ermine-lined cloak from her back and began to fashion an improvised sarong.

'I watched your world burn!' Santhonax screeched.

Mortensen nodded at the ceiling; at the tonnes of spinning rock freefalling towards the doomed Spetzghast.

'Don't worry,' the Gomorrian told her. 'You'll burn all right. But not by my hand.' He went to walk away.

Krieg picked up the chainsabre and limped over to the shaking body of the canoness, using the wall for support. He fired the blade mechanism and let the weapon kick over in his good hand. The desire to slay still ached inside him. He stood astride the battle-sister's heaving chest, her livid eyes boring into him.

'I, of course,' the cadet-commissar informed her, 'cannot offer any such reassurances.' And with one fluid flourish of the buzzing blade, her head came away from her shoulders and rolled across the floor. The intention was his: the canoness had betrayed him and was clearly a dangerous heretic. The action was not, however. He'd never swung a sword like that before. It was as if someone else had guided his movements – a puppeteer willing on his puppet. Clearly Aurek Herrenvolk concurred with Krieg's judgement and had deemed, in his own unsettling way and in his own disturbing fashion, that Diamanta Santhonax no longer deserved to live.

Even though he knew in his heart that the Emperor's work had been done, Krieg was horrified at the alien entity that had reached into the deepest recesses of his mind and had so easily influenced it. Something still did not feel quite right but there was little the commissar could do to ease his troubled mind and so he took refuge in the hot simplicity of casual revenge.

As the commissar closed on the paralysed henchwoman, the major called up the passage at him: 'She's just a child, Krieg.'

The commissar shrugged. 'I very much doubt that,' he told Mortensen, mulling it over, before finally bringing the savage chainsabre to a full stop. He tossed the blade at the Celestian's feet with the beloved shield of her order.

Dragging Krieg's good arm across his powerful shoulders Mortensen helped the commissar limp and lurch down to the elevator at the bottom. Throwing Krieg inside, Mortensen stabbed at the button with his finger.

'Think we can still get off this dustball?' the cadet-commissar asked.

'No,' Mortensen told him honestly. 'But it's never stopped me trying before.'

V

THE SKY WAS black and oppressive. Colossal ork roks were everywhere, breaching the cloud cover and sapping the air of light and possibility. A cataclysm was unfolding before their eyes: decimation of such magnitude that it was sure not to leave a soul alive on the planet surface.

Rosenkrantz had heard the thunder of distant impacts roll across the murderous horizon and watched the mushroom plumes of ash, dirt and incinerated humanity rocket back at the doom-laden heavens. *Purity Control* hovered above the incarcetorium landing strip, with what remained of the Redemption Corps safely strapped into the troop bay, waiting for the pilot's decision to surge skyward.

'Just give them a few more minutes,' Vedette urged across the vox. She was down on the open ramp with a bruised and beaten Conklin, watching for any signs of life on the strip.

'I don't even know if *Deliverance* will still be there,' Rosenkrantz returned. 'In all likelihood Captain Waldemar has broken orbit. Can you really see a carrier negotiating this?'

'We stay,' came the storm-trooper's unequivocal reply.

'I've held on this long haven't I?' the pilot insisted. Her mind was made up. 'But every moment we wait brings that gamble closer to a certainty. I appreciate your loyalty, but we can't risk everyone just for two men.' Rosenkrantz's finger moved across a nearby stud. 'Ramp closing.'

'I see them!' Vedette cut in, with more emotion in her voice than Rosenkrantz had ever heard from her.

The pilot looked down over the Valkyrie's nose and at the open elevator doors. Two figures stumbled out amongst the wreckage of the landing pad: Krieg looked like hell in his ragged greatcoat and Mortensen, naked as the day he was born, bar some makeshift loincloth that flapped around his thighs, stomped with grim determination towards the bird. She swooped in as close as she dared to allow both men to clamber on.

'They're on board,' Conklin confirmed across the vox, closing the ramp.

'Strap in,' Rosenkrantz warned them.

'Let me guess,' Mortensen crackled across the vox. It was surprisingly good to hear his voice. 'We'll be experiencing some turbulence.'

Rosenkrantz stared up through the canopy at the gathering gloom and nodded to herself. The pilot wrenched the stick towards her and vaulted for the boiling firmament.

The lively little Inquisitorial carrier answered well, rocketing away from the ill-fated planet. Like an iceberg emerging from a fog bank a gargantuan asteroid plummeted towards them. Clouds rolled away from the beast, electrostatic charges leaping between the ork rok and the churning atmosphere. It was like a mountain falling out of the sky, with its own geography and of more concern, its own heavy weapons batteries.

The airspace around the asteroid shook as a thousand exploding shells ripped the sky to pieces. Gentle course corrections became violent tugs on the stick, throwing *Purity Control* to port and then to starboard, diving and weaving around the artillery blastwaves.

Reasoning that it would only take a single hit to cripple them, if not blow them out of the heavens, Rosenkrantz turned the Valkyrie on its side and threw it at the ork rok. Closing the distance made it even harder for the guns on the plunging craft to acquire the carrier. As the pilot took the aircraft closer still, deeper into the natural canyons and craters of the asteroid, the passing cannons fell silent. The Jopallian allowed herself a little smirk. That was clever.

Suddenly the rock face fell away and the Valkyrie was in the darkness of the open sky. What the pilot hadn't allowed for was the exhaust vortex created by the rok's mainstage engine. *Purity Control* shook violently, sparks flying from the cockpit instrumentation. The engines choked and like an insect batted aside by a giant invisible hand, the aircraft span away. Fighting for breath and control of her senses, Rosenkrantz pulled the aircraft out of the sickening rotation. Allowing the Valkyrie to fall she swiftly shut down the cockpit's overloaded instrumentation and sat there for as long as she dared, listening to the atmospheric howl of the aircraft falling tail-first back through the tumultuous cloud.

Rapidly re-activating the systems, she heard the alarmed calls of the storm-troopers across the vox. As the engines screamed back online, so the panicked shouting subsided. As she blasted skyward two more behemoths hove into view. One of the ork roks was rolling across the firmament, coming in much shallower than its neighbour. Rosenkrantz banked but the inevitable happened and she didn't have the moments or manoeuvrability to do anything about it. The two asteroids crashed, setting in motion a series of explosions in and around the greenskin roks. Shafts and splinters of rock fell towards the Valkyrie in a deadly shower, the fragments gaining in velocity and lethality.

The pilot had to think fast. Flicking the safety off the stick weapons controls, Rosenkrantz feverishly fingered the firing stud, launching salvo after salvo of rockets from each wing. The barrage tore away from the Valkyrie, striking the first of the fragments and initiating a column of explosions through the cascade. Surging for the blasts, the pilot put the nose of the aircraft through the dissipating epicentre of the column, the flaming vapour washing over the canopy armaplas.

Things were no better on the other side. The two asteroids were in full collision now, the smaller irregular companion rolling across its larger compatriot, smashing the violent rocky landscape inbetween and threatening to steamroller *Purity Control* in the process. This, Rosenkrantz could not allow. Her response was simple. Weaponry and manoeuvres could not help her here. All she had left was the greasy, raw speed of the aircraft. Hammering the velocity controls she pushed the Valkyrie to its limits, streaking up the length of the colossal ork rok, with the craggy tidal wave of destruction cascading towards them.

'Come on, come on, come on...' she repeated therapeutically, squeezing every bit of power from the thundering engines. For a moment Rosenkrantz allowed herself the fantasy that they were going to make it, but her heart turned to stone as another dark shape appeared above, creating an artificial ceiling and a very definite end to the Valkyrie's dramatic run.

The cockpit suddenly lit up with blinding white light. Cannons were firing somewhere and fat beams of unbearable energy were cutting across *Purity Control*'s flight path.

A shaft of natural gloom struck the canopy as the two roks parted, the smaller trailing a smouldering path of wreckage, the victim of the intense attack. Rosenkrantz was about to hit the airbrakes and bank towards the opening chasm when something struck her about the silhouette above. The angular lines and wedge-like prow, the lance batteries and carrier decks. *Deliverance*. The tiny carrier was down there in all the cosmic turmoil of the upper atmosphere, a sitting duck: its feeble armament and propulsion systems working double time to keep the thousands of Guardsmen and Navy crew out of harm's way.

Something cool caressed her face and blotted her helmet visor. Overwhelmed by their excruciatingly narrow escape or simply glad to see the ship, the pilot couldn't tell, but she was crying: something she hadn't done since leaving Jopall. Transmitting their clearance codes and coasting the Valkyrie onto the flight deck approach vector, Rosenkrantz loosened her grip on the controls. She felt the circulation return to her fingers and hit the vox-stud. The troop bay was silent. Expectant.

'We're home,' she announced simply. And allowed the rest of the relief to roll down her cheeks.

VI

THE OBSERVATION DECK was empty.

At first it had been crammed with off-duty Navy crew and Patricians eager to get a morbid glimpse: to see a world die before their glassy, uncomprehending eyes. The Redemption Corps had had their fill of apocalyptic visions, however, and were not to be found on the observation deck. Most of them were restricted to the Orlop where Minghella fussed over their numerous wounds and incapacities, patching them up for the demands of their next mission – it was the Redemption Corps way. A virgin Guardsman might expect a mercifully swift death in the ranks of the Emperor's bastion, but the invaluable skills and experience of a veteran storm-trooper were always in demand.

Mortensen didn't spare himself the pain of the observation deck, though. In fact, he found himself indulging in long, lonely walks there, drinking it all in. Seeing Spetzghast but dreaming of Gomorrah: spinning through the frozen, empty void. In those long hours he relived the fate of his home world and the nightmare of what he now understood to be not some random cosmological accident, but a cold and calculating attack on the human race: an opening salvo in the war that was to come, with first blood going to the enemies of the Imperium.

Spetzghast was a broiling, black ball spinning around a dying star, with a thin girdle of equally doomed moons for company. The major could barely imagine the hell down there. The air, choking and heavy – a black smog of soot and dust; the geological chaos of earthquakes and flooding; blazing cities and rotting corpses, the plagues of scavenging coot imps, picking the flesh off the dead and the dying. And everywhere the alien intruder, infecting and enslaving.

He had survived, however. Again, he'd walked out of the apocalypse. Given men like Lijah Meeks more excuses to fan the fires of their faith. Lived to fight another day. He thought long on Santhonax and her insanity: her Istvaanian beliefs and her desire to do good by ill. He couldn't bring himself to think of her as part of the alien conspiracy – her own particular brand of lunacy had testified to that. She had undoubtedly been played by someone or something whose desire to test humanity to the limit surpassed even hers. To not just craft heroes from the raw stuff of adversity but to eradicate the very Imperium from the face of the galaxy.

Ultimately his survival and that of his men had rested little on his shoulders. Rosenkrantz and Krieg had facilitated their escape on the doomed world below and the good commissar had been wise enough to ensure their escape route had remained open for as long as possible.

Mortensen couldn't be sure that with so many of his men off the carrier that Commander Waldemar wouldn't try to press his advantage, up anchor and leave them there to die. In all the chaos and confusion of the greenskin assault, who would know? Krieg must have thought the same thing because before boarding *Vertigo* he had orderlies relocate Regimental Commissar Udeskee's oxygen tent to Waldemar's bridge. *Deliverance* was going nowhere. Try arguing the merits of mortal danger with a man accelerating towards decrepitude and death. Undoubtedly Waldemar would have tried.

The flotilla and the spindly Exchequer space station were gone, smashed into oblivion in the descending turmoil of the colossal greenskin bombardment. All that was left now made up the dismal numbers of their fleeing convoy. A ragged train of bleeding fluyts and crippled sprint traders were shepherded along by the bloated troopship *Argus* and the superheavy transport the *Demiarch Dante*. Without frigates and torpedo boats, the Guard transports – by virtue of the fact that they were armed – had been promoted from escortees to escorts. Their only true frigate, the remaining Firestorm-class Frigate *Cape Wrath*, led from the front under the command of Port Admiral Gordian Ferenc – who by a twist of fate had actually been on a citation hearing aboard the decrepit passenger liner the *Witch of Shandor* when the Exchequer and the *Stang Draak* had been destroyed. The *Witch* was now part of the pitiable procession, limping alongside a battle-scarred rogue trader. *Deliverance* brought up the rear, her lances watching over the convoy's sluggish exodus. The greenskins took little interest in them, however. They had wanted to decimate a world and they had done it.

As predicted, the Port Admiral had decided on Aurelius as their destination. There had been favour, especially among the Volscians, to make for Field Marshal Rygotzk at Scythia, but Aurelius was eventually deemed the better bet. The Viper Legion Space Marine Chapter was based there and the system had been the departure point for Enceladus. Now that the crusade was over it was possible that a fairly large contingent of troops and vessels were still hung over there, waiting for despatch orders and reassignment.

Thank the Emperor for Imperial bureaucracy, Mortensen had thought: he'd always been a fan. With the comms blackout still in play and the strange but potent web of psychic interference – undoubtedly an unforeseen boon of the stealer-greenskin interbreeding experiment – making astropathic communication impossible, all the convoy could do was trawl up the Kintessa Gauntlet, under the weight of their precious intelligence. Pushing on, hoping to reach beyond the limits of this strange effect and warn Aurelius in advance, as well as other systems in the Kaligari Cradle deemed at high strategic risk of similar treatment.

The only combat-effective vessel not to remain with the convoy on this long and lonely journey was Krieg's old ship, the Inquisitorial corvette *Dread Sovereign*. The vessel had some other dark purpose and with little warning had disappeared, leaving a stranded Krieg on board *Deliverance*. Port Admiral Ferenc was hardly going to disagree with a member of one of the Ordos and deemed it best to simply let the *Dread Sovereign* slip away with its much needed weaponry and troops.

The whisper of leather sauntered slowly up behind the major.

'Commissar,' Mortensen acknowledged.

Krieg stepped up to the thick plas in silence, his arm still strapped to his chest, lost in the spectacle of loss. 'Hard to believe we were just down there,' he murmured finally.

'Believe it,' the major told him. 'It's gone.' The storm-trooper sighed. 'What about you then? Aurelius, then back to the Pontificals?'

The cadet raised a singed eyebrow, clearly surprised that the major knew of his origins. Mortensen grunted. 'I read a file. Let's not make a big thing out of it.'

Krieg managed a bleak smile and put his hand against the plas, almost touching the void outside. 'Thought I'd stay. Complete my rotation.'

'Might take a long time, out here,' the major warned. 'If that battle-sister spoke even a word of truth, Gomorrah and Spetzghast are only the beginning. Bellona, Scythia and Calydon Prime are already hit. If the Kintessa Gauntlet is compromised, then the Segmentum floodgates won't have been opened, they'll have been blown off their hinges.'

'I'm in no hurry,' Krieg stated, pulling down the brim of his cap to his eyes. 'After all – the Emperor expects.'

'He does rather, doesn't he,' Mortensen echoed before leaving the observation deck and the young cadet-commissar, framed in the raging apocalypse beyond.

ABOUT THE AUTHOR

Head of English at a local secondary school, **Rob Sanders** is a freelance writer whose first fiction was published in *Inferno!* magazine. He lives off the beaten track in the small city of Lincoln, England.

WARHAMMER 40,000

MITCHEL SCANLON | STEVE LYONS | STEVE PARKER

IMPERIAL GUARD

OMNIBUS: VOLUME ONE

FIFTEEN HOURS | DEATH WORLD | REBEL WINTER

UK ISBN 978-1-84416-671-8   US ISBN 978-1-84416-611-4

WARHAMMER
40,000

Beneath the sands, something is stirring...

DESERT RAIDERS

Lucien Soulban

ISBN 978-1-84416-492-9

WARHAMMER
40,000

⚔ AN IMPERIAL GUARD NOVEL ⚔

ICE GUARD

Steve Lyons

UK ISBN 978-1-84416-672-5 US ISBN 978-1-84416-609-1

WARHAMMER
40,000

⚔ AN IMPERIAL GUARD NOVEL ⚔

GUNHEADS

Steve Parker

UK ISBN 978-1-84416-587-2 US ISBN 978-1-84416-698-5

WARHAMMER
40,000

⚔ AN IMPERIAL GUARD NOVEL ⚔

CADIAN BLOOD

Aaron Dembski-Bowden

UK ISBN 978-1-84416-770-8 US ISBN 978-1-84416-771-5

WARHAMMER
40,000

DAN ABNETT

'He makes war so real that you want to duck!' – Sci Fi.com

THE FOUNDING

A GAUNT'S GHOSTS OMNIBUS

ISBN 978-1-84416-369-4

WARHAMMER
40,000

DAN ABNETT

'So believable you can almost feel the gut-wrenching G forces.' – SciFi.com

THE SAINT

A GAUNT'S GHOSTS OMNIBUS

ISBN 978-1-84416-479-0

WARHAMMER
40,000

DAN ABNETT

'Dan Abnett is the
master of war.'
SFX

BLOOD PACT

A GAUNT'S GHOSTS NOVEL

UK ISBN 978-1-84416-825-5 US ISBN 978-1-84416-824-8

WARHAMMER
40,000

CIAPHAS CAIN
HERO OF THE IMPERIUM

Contains
For The Emperor,
Caves of Ice and
The Traitor's Hand

SANDY MITCHELL

SURVIVING THE 41ST MILLENNIUM, ONE BATTLE AT A TIME

ISBN 978-1-84416-466-0